Disaster Was My God

Bruce Duffy is the author of the critically acclaimed *The World As I Found It*, a fictional life of Ludwig Wittgenstein, and *Last Comes the Egg*. His first novel, *World*, was rereleased this year in the *New York Review of Books* Classics series. He has reported on such places as Haiti, Bosnia, and Taliban Afghanistan. In researching this book, he also traveled to Rimbaud's town Harar, and to the still lawless desert tribal lands near Somalia. He has three children, Lily, Kate, and Sam, and he lives in Bethesda, Maryland, with his wife, Susan Segal, a psychotheraj

Disaster Was My God

A novel of the outlaw life of *Arthur Rimbaud*

Bruce Duffy

THE CLERKENWELL PRESS

First published in Great Britain in 2011 by
THE CLERKENWELL PRESS
An imprint of Profile Books Ltd
3A Exmouth House
Pine Street
London EC1R 0JH
www.profilebooks.com

First published in the United States of America in 2011 by
Doubleday, a division of Random House, Inc., New York

10 9 8 7 6 5 4 3 2 1

Printed and bound in Great Britain by
Clays, Bungay, Suffolk

A CIP catalogue record for this book is available from the British Library.

ISBN 978 1 84668 527 9
eISBN 978 1 84765 001 4

The paper this book is printed on is certified by the © 1996 Forest Stewardship Council A.C. (FSC). It is ancient-forest friendly. The printer holds FSC chain of custody SGS-COC-2061

FSC
Mixed Sources
Product group from well-managed
forests and other controlled sources
Cert no. SGS-COC-2061
www.fsc.org
© 1996 Forest Stewardship Council

For Susan

Contents

Note to the Reader

Although this book seeks to be faithful to Rimbaud's character, artistic aims, and the general trajectory of his life, it is not, as fiction, captive to the facts or the strict flow of events. Quite the contrary.

In a life as enigmatic and contradictory as Rimbaud's, the more I considered the facts, and the many missing facts—and the more I studied his blazingly prescient writings and poems—the more I found it necessary to bend his life in order to see it, much as a prism bends light to release its hidden colors. To be, if you will, more allegorical than historical, as befits a legend. I do this cheerfully, respectfully, and without apology.

This book, then, is as represented—fiction.

Disaster Was My God

I called to my executioners to let me bite the ends of their guns, as I died. I called to all plagues to stifle me with sand and blood. Disaster was my god.

—ARTHUR RIMBAUD, *A Season in Hell*

Prologue

ROCHE, A FARM IN THE ARDENNES OF FRANCE,
AUGUST 1901, TEN YEARS AFTER RIMBAUD'S DEATH

♪ Raising the Dead

The gravedigger raises his pick, then drives it, with a cough, into the hard, rocky soil. And there in a black gig, not thirty feet away, sits the old woman draped in black veil, a pool of shadow watching the man's every move. Raise the dead.

For behind the gravedigger, laid to the side in the grass, are two now-to-be discarded grave markers, white, like upturned faces to the sun. Such was the gravedigger's hard task today, to rebury the old woman's two children, two of the four, a daughter gone for twenty-five years and the son, the famous poet Arthur Rimbaud, for almost ten. When *clang*. The gravedigger's pick strikes another large stone.

"*Careful*." The veil stirs, revealing a glimpse of craggy face and spud-like nose. "Monsieur Loupot, there is no hurry. *Obviously*."

"Madame—"

"*Veuve*. Widow," she retorts in an unhand-me voice. "Do you forget the conversation we had earlier? You will call me Veuve Rimbaud. And as for all these rocks, do you blame the shovel? Do you blame the pick? Who, then, Monsieur? God above?"

"Unavoidable," replies Loupot, a solid man, beefy, mustached, and sunburned. Beery-smelling, she thinks. And the insolence of him, holding out a rock as he adds, "There is a reason, Veuve Rimbaud, why your farm is named Roche."

"What?" she says, now aroused, raising the veil, like two black wings. "So we surrender to the rocks? To break the legs of our cows and horses?"

"But, Madame, please, as I have told you—repeatedly. I did not dig this grave or leave these stones. On this you have my word."

"Words," she sneers, dropping the veil. "For you, Monsieur, I have but one word—*dig*."

*D*ig, then. For once unearthed, away they will go, these two old coffins. Away from Roche they will go to the town *cimetière* of Charleville, lofty, sanctified ground at the summit of the rue de Mantoue, the main avenue, where a tall budded cross stands atop an old stone arch. There, with a groan, when the church bells toll eight, an ancient watchman slowly swings shut the iron gates, then padlocks them against thrill seekers and wandering lovers—against any who might disturb the peace of this *petit village*.

Stone chapels. Urns. Obelisks. Commandment-like stones. Beneath the cinder paths of this marble forest lie Charleville's finest families: Blairon, Corneau, Demangel, Tanton-Bechefer—folk bunched in their old-fashioned suits and cravats, wilted corsages and gowns of lace, their rosaries tied like mittens round their withered fingers.

As one might divine, however, the old woman's family does not flow from such exalted bloodlines. *Au contraire*. Her people are mere peasants, granted from high, as it were, conspicuous exemption into this exclusive club. And, loath as she is to admit it, only because her dead son wrote such deathless works as "Vowels," "The Drunken Boat," *A Season in Hell*, and his cycle *Illuminations*, virtually all completed by the age of twenty. Consider just one, his sonnet "Vowels," an early masterpiece written in 1871, at the age of sixteen, and this in a discipline in which, unlike music or mathematics, prodigy is almost unheard of, and all for the very evident reason that, at that age, most of us are as impulsive and unformed as we are lacking in life experience. Start there, then consider a work that in sensibility and diction is decades ahead of its time.

Revolutionary, in fact. And, unlike the work of virtually any prodigy in literature, is still read, passionately admired, and even now genuinely disruptive. Poetry that comes with a sword:

> Vowels
>
> A black, E white, I red, U green, O blue: vowels,
> One day I will tell you your latent birth:
> A, black hairy corset of shining flies
> Which buzz around cruel stench,
>
> Gulfs of darkness; E, whiteness of vapors and tents,
> Lances of proud glaciers, white kings, quivering of flowers;
> I, purples, spit blood, laughter of beautiful lips
> In anger or penitent drunkenness;
>
> U, cycles, divine vibrations of green seas,
> Peace of pastures scattered with animals, peace of the wrinkles
> Which alchemy prints on heavy studious brows;
>
> O, supreme Clarion full of strange stridor,
> Silence crossed by worlds and angels:
> —O, the Omega, violet beam from His Eyes!

But then just a few years beyond this time, at twenty or so—at the point when most careers have barely begun—Arthur Rimbaud stopped writing. Utterly stopped. Stopped forever, an act itself as rare as literary prodigy. Even more troubling, Rimbaud ended his career by denouncing—*in* writing, and indeed in one of his greatest works, the long prose poem *A Season in Hell*—the cheap sophistry of writing and the cheat of art itself:

> For a long time I had boasted of having every possible landscape, and found laughable the celebrated names of painting and modern poetry . . . I dreamed of crusades, of unrecorded voyages of discovery, of

republics with no history, of hushed-up religious wars, revolutions in cus-
toms, displacement of races and continents: I believed in every kind of
witchcraft.

His abandonment of art, poetry, style, vocation, belief—all of it—
fell like a curtain on his life, a total eclipse, deliberate and irrevocable. As
he had calculated so brilliantly, it was deeply disturbing to art's believ-
ers, the hero-rebel turned traitor. A self-defrocked priest. A willed disgrace, if not an artistic suicide. And worst of all, a man who, some time
later, after years of drifting, went on to sell guns in Africa, on the edges
of the slave trade. Most preferred to forget *this* Rimbaud, the cynical
gunrunner, in favor of the young genius, the bad boy Rimbaud. For
what on earth had happened to him? Had he turned yellow? Lost his
mind? Who could square the two images? After all, writers may stop
writing for a while or find themselves blocked, but where is the poet or
writer, or artist of any type, who renounces his or her craft as folly and
fakery—a lie? Who then refuses even to *read* poetry or novels? Who
wants none of it. Any of it, or France or Europe, either.

I grew accustomed to pure hallucination: I saw quite frankly a mosque
in place of a factory, a school of drummers made up by angels, carriages
on roads to the sky, a parlor at the bottom of the lake; monsters, myster-
ies. The title of a vaudeville conjured up horrors before me.

Then I explained my magic sophisms in the hallucination of words!

At the end I looked on the disorder of my mind as sacred. I was idle, a
prey to heavy fever. I envied the happiness of animals—caterpillars rep-
resenting the innocence of limbo, moles, the sleep of virginity!

No matter: now, in death, Rimbaud, in Charleville at least, is utterly
redeemed—arisen, in fact. Once the town pariah, he is now Charleville's

chief claim to fame. Why, soon to have his own statue! A monster made cherub. Actually *cute!*

Morons, thought the Widow. Needless to say, she wanted nothing to do with their little charade. And yet, note the site the Widow has picked to nest her small brood, the old social climber. Why, there it lies even before the graves of Charleville's former bigwigs, at the vertex of the cemetery's two diverging gravel paths—the first grave a visitor will see. Trip over, in fact. Here the brother and sister will rest under two baroquely ornate markers, even as the old mother lies almost prostrate before them, beneath a great icelike slab of Carrara, the marble of Michelangelo. Night! And stone! And at this one thought, of this bull of rock crushing her bones, the Widow Rimbaud will feel a shiver, then a fatal tingle. To think! That at the summit of this packed necropolis her son's idolators, the loose-tongued, the easily led, and the snoops, that they will see these seven letters beetling back at them in warning, evoking the dignity of the noble, the God-fearing and now never-to-be-forgotten name:

RIMBAUD

Stop, then. Look down upon this name, once so blighted. Feel lucky. Hug your life like a child and be of good cheer. For perhaps in this life you will be wiser or better or more fortunate than this man and his small troubled family. Or failing that, blessed with better children, or at least better *balanced* children. *Dominus vobiscum! Et cum spiritu tuo.*

*B*ack, then, to Roche, ancestral farm of the *famille* Rimbaud. Back to this disinterring, to this Pietà scene where the mother, Marie-Catherine-Vitalie Rimbaud, sits perched in the antique black gig with two dented, now cross-eyed brass lamps.

As for this cloaking veil draped over her, this is against the gnats—*gnats*, she will tell you—not an attempt to hide the face of some old shoe weeping on virtually the worst day in all her life. For what can you—any of you—know of the sufferings of an old woman who has been called by God? Spoken to in days of dark, silent, overflowing ecstasy, like those bald-pated saints you see in illuminated manuscripts, robed men with tiny flames over their heads, blessed by the Holy Spirit. Many, many times as a girl and young woman she, too, was so blessed, only to have God utterly and summarily ignore her. Suddenly deaf to her. Punishing her for what crime she does not know! As she would read in her missal, from the Psalms:

My God, my God, look upon me: why have you forsaken me? O my God, I cry out by day and You answer not; by night, and there is no relief . . .

But imagine: God was silent to her not for one year or two or even a string of years but for forty-five years, three months, and now thirteen days, a lifetime of darkness and privation. Why? she wondered, weeping as she prayed through this blear darkness. How could God be so cruel? *Why?* To test her faith? Was that it, as a priest told her once? But still, for *forty-five years?* To yearn but feel nothing of Your Holy Presence? To pray and hear nothing? To give—to give endlessly, like a fool—all to receive Your Holy Contempt? Paralyzed, then enraged, then despairing, Jean-Nicolas-Arthur Rimbaud's suffering old mother, she would think it was her, her unworthiness, her mothering, her ignorance, her two terrible sons. There was, there had to be, a reason.

When lo, two months before this time, early one morning, Mme. Rimbaud's forty-five-year drought finally broke. The old woman was just waking up, dawn breaking, golden still and cool, when suddenly she heard Him—*Him!*—a surging river of force so strong her jaws clenched in ecstatic ache:

LIFT THESE BONES. THEN BRING THEM TO ME. YOU, THEIR MOTHER.

You, their mother. She knew exactly what God meant by this utterance. She—she personally would have to shoulder their untombing, and not merely with hirelings, gravediggers, undertakers, and other such riffraff—no! And so against all argument she refused the services of an undertaker, without whom two gravediggers flatly refused to take her money. Never when the mother insisted on being present, and especially not with the daughter, also called Vitalie, in the ground for twenty-five years. Please, Madame, they reasoned, this was surgeon's work, carried out, often, with small spades and even teaspoons. But certainly not with the departed's mother present! Never! Unheard of! Madness!

In her stubbornness, the Widow likewise refused the offices of a priest, believing, in a kind of ecstasy, that God was moving through *her*, not through his various earthbound flunkies, these *priests*, sanctified know-nothings for whom, as men, she had no high regard. The blow, however, was when her other daughter, her forty-year-old daughter, Isabelle, the scatterbrain, refused to accompany her, willful girl—and never you mind about Rimbaud's brother, just one year older, banished years before as an idiot no-good and a bum. Much to her vexation, this is not the same Isabelle whom she had bullied and ordered around for years when the two worked the farm together. Now married, freed, Isabelle is no longer so pliant or scatterbrained. Now she is like a nun who has left the order, talking back to Mother Superior.

"Mother, why are you doing this? It's ghoulish. Ridiculous. Leave them be."

"Because God *told* me, daughter," insisted the old woman. "Have I ever told you that *God* told me to do anything? Well, then. Did Noah hear God's voice, then ask *hirelings* to build his Ark? Did Noah ever do such a thing?"

"The Ark, Mother, wasn't *morbid*."

"Morbid! When here you two"—meaning Isabelle and her husband and literary collaborator of five years, Paterne Berrichon—"when here you two are both writing Arthur's, what do you call it, biography? Stirring up gossip! To stir this pot of this stinking?"

"To *correct* his memory, Mother. To stop the gossip, the lies!"

"What—so your ridiculous brother becomes even *more* famous?"

Fame: for the old woman this was the true plague, his would-be acolytes and the curious now descending on her with their impertinent questions. Scruffy littérateurs and journalists. Threadbare poets. Pincenez professors and similar busybodies from Paris, Bordeaux, London, Brussels. All knocking on her door. Accosting her on her street. Shocked that *he*, their god, could have sprung from such as *her.* And all with the same idiotic questions:

But why did he stop writing?

Did he stop?

But how could he just . . . stop writing?

And why to Africa?

And did he not return with manuscripts?

And you are quite sure, Madame, there are no other manuscripts? Hmmm?

Add to this the many rumors heaped on her. That just before his death, when he returned from Africa, he brought back a great final outpouring of poems, indeed, the future of poetry, which she then burned like witches in a great bonfire upon a wintry hill. *Whoof.*

*T*he Widow, then, is the only Rimbaud present at the disinterring, and not merely to observe, for this is her land, beautiful rolling country, green pastures, oak and aspen and silvery river birches—hers, all hers.

There, to the east, peering out in four directions—vigilant like her— is the craggy, mansard-roofed farmhouse in which she raised her four children, then lived for years more, running the dairy farm with her daughter, Isabelle, the dizzy one, as she thought of her. That is, until four years ago, when, surely on the last train out of spinsterhood, Isabelle was married and the old woman was forced to give up the farm. Renting to a serflike tenant, the feckless Mercier, the Widow then took a small flat in town. Ah, but see it now, below, Roche, in all its sweep. Surrounded by trees and deep hedgerows, her whole world can be seen, the house and the two once-spotless barns that her tenant farmer, the aforementioned Mercier—*crétin*—has left to choke with manure.

And see down there, see that brown horse, the gelding, now staked to a chain, eating a circle in the grass, *c'est la vie* since he can do nothing else. And who staked him today after she drove out from Charleville? Who dragged, by her own shoulder, seventy-six years old, the heavy chain? And who then banged the stake with a great mallet, this as bald Mercier the tenant (hoping she would not raise his rent!) begged her:

"*Veuve Rimbaud*, please, in this heat! You should not be doing this!"

"Ce n'est rien." She whacked the stake harder, with steam.

"Madame—Veuve Rimbaud, please."

"Away—"

Whack and whack—*victoire*. Pleasure immense, to show these two males how an old woman can toil like the stallion, like a *fiend*, never helpless.

But then, once back in the gig, as suddenly, the fear returns. Clouds blot out the sun. She feels a shudder, then a mounting panic at this long-dreaded resurrection. When *clang*. Blessed distraction. The gravedigger—his back now a sopping tortoise shell of sweat—strikes another large stone.

"Monsieur Loupot!" she erupts. "Deny it no more. It was *you* who buried my son nine years ago."

The gravedigger stares at the sky.

"Veuve Rimbaud, please," he says, "look at my face. I am not yet forty. Ten years ago I was still in the army. As God is my witness. Back then I was not even *in* this miserable trade."

"Eh," she retorts, "so then it was your father, perhaps blinded by his great beard, who left these stones? Eh? Is that how you evade the truth? Blame your father?"

The black gig rocks as the old fury climbs down. Then, throwing back her black veil, she faces him, her glasses two fiery ovals as the sun bursts once more through the clouds. "It is all right," she soothes. "We know your story. You are of the people of troubles. A lost, gypsylike people thrown off their land, lost and wandering with their shovels." Her twisty eyebrows rise. "What? Do you deny this? That you are a *Jew*—is this not true?"

"We Loupots," he thunders, "we are *Catholics*. Dwelling here for generations!"

Hmmph. Does he think he frightens her, standing on his hind legs like a circus bear? Frightened? She who must unearth her two children today? With a shrug, she returns to her gig. Climbs up, spreads the black veil, loudly blows her nose, then resumes her lonely vigil. Crouched over herself, she is like a lone fisherman, sick, soul-sick and now trembling before the storm.

*B*ut was the Widow indeed a widow? Only God knew. Certain only was her husband's desertion, not his decease. Abandonment—this was her widowhood. A life's vocation, a profession in fact.

The deserter in question was Captain Frédéric Rimbaud, an army chasseur who in the winter of 1852 arrived in Charleville in a splendid blue uniform with golden epaulettes and splendid black boots. A handsome, compact man, the captain was blond and swarthy from the equatorial sun, with the regulation long mustache and goatee that drove to a point, like a spade. Expert in fencing and riflery. And, as befit an officer, expert in the equally vital skills of whoring, dueling, horse racing, and gambling. A veteran, too. As a captain in the artillery, he had served in the Crimea and before that had fought the bedouin in Algeria, one of the myrmidons of the imperial and resurgent France of Napoleon III, an empire then bent, as all the European powers were, on building colonies and spreading Christian civilization. That is, once they could put down the dark peoples, the Arabs and the *noirs*, fanatics, most of them.

Indeed, in the great cause of subjugating the Mussulmans and the *noirs*, Captain Rimbaud was particularly useful owing to his great love of languages: Latin, Greek, Spanish, German, Italian, Arabic, and Swahili. Bush dialects, too. The man was a sponge. Why, in a matter of weeks, Captain Rimbaud could pick up virtually any language. *Smart* was his problem, the young Mme. Rimbaud used to say, for at first she was in awe of him, an educated man. But then tapping her index finger against her temple, with sly conceit the new bride would add, "But, as you can see, God blesses the slow and the stupid."

After all, her family, the Cuifs, peasants, lard heads perhaps—well, they knew what they knew: money and timber, land and beasts. But what the Cuifs really knew was how to spit on nothing, rub it up into something, then sell it for a tidy profit to the next fool. And of all the Cuifs, the slickest by far was her father, Alphonse Cuif. Bald and broad, with wads of hair in his ears, Alphonse Cuif was the master when it came to selling the nearly dry cow or the kicking horse. If he could do that, he said, surely he could find a man for his then twenty-seven-year-old daughter, in those days a Methuselah age, connubially speaking.

Stuck—this was Vitalie Cuif's other great theme. Stuck she was, stuck since the age of five, when her mother died. And since her father never remarried, stuck with taking care of him and her two useless brothers. Cooking, cleaning, milking, chopping, emptying, then washing the chamber pots—all this and more Marie-Catherine-Vitalie Cuif did. Even as a girl, she was effectively a wife for her father, not only a demanding man but also a quite thirsty and, frankly, physical man. Every night at the tavern he drank too much ale, and so every night, once he had stumbled home, he always had a terrible thirst, calling out, *Daughter, I'm thirsty.*

Her brothers slept far downstairs, muffled. But to be ready, she slept upstairs, at hand, in the next room. Where in the middle of the night she would hear, *Vitalie, bring me water.* Cold, cold water brimming fresh from the pump, this was her father's wish. Good girl. There's a good girl. After all, it was water, just water, and it was dark and all so long ago. Her brothers, with their private boy language, they might as well have been deaf and blind—they heard and saw nothing. And why would they with a father who was merely thirsty and demanding, as was his paternal right, to be served quickly—and with no sass—by his women. *Woman,* rather.

It almost goes without saying that nobody ever saw anything or remembered anything because, of course, nothing had happened or could happen. Forget it. The girl had to forget it. Even in the confessional there was nothing to say about it, not when there was a male sitting on the other side. For after all, was not the father thirsty? Was the girl not his daughter and was he not her father to obey in all things? Girls needed to be quiet and kept busy, with their foolish wagging tongues, and so they were. There was church. There was needlework and crocheting, ironing, and chicken plucking—plenty for a girl to do. And for those spoiled girls that couldn't be happy, the malcontents and hysterics, there were options. There were nunneries. Asylums, too. And Alphonse Cuif's daughter, as he warned her repeatedly, was on the cusp, for she had a nasty disposition—*un sale caractère*—and, with almost no time to call her own, virtually no friends, save God, of course. Talking to herself, the girl was always talking to herself, desperately clutching herself as she wandered the fields, hair blowing, truly a peculiar and disagreeable girl, everybody said so. In short, even among the gossips there was nothing to think. It was blank; it was null; nobody in those days ever wondered, or would have wondered, why the girl was so. Weeping so. Upset so. Don't be foolish. Think what? There was nothing to think.

Well, finally, inevitably, the father kicked out her useless brothers, true, both drunks like him, but sissies with no heads for business, no instinct for the jugular. Alone with her father—this was what did it for Marie-Catherine-Vitalie Cuif. Alone, she felt completely trapped, exposed for the first time and shamed before God. And so for the first time she said no—no to what she couldn't remember, but *no*. No more water. No more nursely visits. *No.*

Vengeance was swift.

"*Petite salope*," cried her father, pounding on her door. "Find a man or I'll find you one—blind, or crippled, or crazy. Or even ninety years old. Be a nun for all I care, but get out! I want you *out.*"

It was hopeless. She was far too old. She knew no men and had no women friends to invent the clever pretexts and make the necessary introductions. But then in the tavern one night, deep in his cups, her

father looked up to see, through the swirling blue pipe smoke, an officer, a captain in the chasseurs.

"Captain," said Cuif *père*, red of face, raising his tankard of ale, "I
drink to our brave defenders! Sit, captain. Allow me to buy you a glass!"

Hooking his thumb on his upper teeth, or what remained of them,
the old sharp had sold his share of cows and horses, but never one that
came with a farm and a dowry of 15,000 francs. Why, the little bitch sold
herself.

And so, about every year, the captain would return on leave, just
long enough to force upon her the same old feelings of panic and suffo-
cation. Jammed himself in, bucked a while, shuddered, then promptly
rolled off. Wiped himself on the sheet, then fell to snoring. And so each
visit, Vitalie Cuif Rimbaud was stuck and bucked, then stuck again . . .
Frédéric in '53, Arthur in '54, Vitalie in '58. And finally, in '60,
Isabelle—the baby.

And of course, once the money was spent, adieu, the captain was
gone, too. Slamming the door, he narrowly missed being brained by the
heavy brass jug that she hurled at his head. It rang. Ricocheted. Spun like
a top on the floor. The two boys stood frozen. It was the size of a head,
his head. She picked it up, started smashing it on the table, weeping and
shrieking. Stuck again—stuck with three and, soon, four.

"Here," she said, showing the battered jug to the two small boys.
"See what your father leaves you?" She pointed to the two dents. "There,
do you see?" Two holes, like the Man in the Moon. "Do you not see his
face?"

And so atop the mantel stood the smashed jug with the two dents
for eyes and the jug handle for a nose. Warning from the queen that, in
her hive, men were drones, utterly expendable and easily banished.

*T*hen, down the road, the farm dogs are barking. It's the gravedigger's
boy, a blubbery, freckled, red-faced youth riding bareback a sideways-
trotting plough horse heaving his great neck and flapping his tail against
the flies.

"*Bonsoir*, Madame." Wondrous the lad's unsurprise at the old sphinx. Does she not realize she is pointing an open clasp knife at him?

"Whoa, boy," she says. She holds up the old clasp knife with which she is peeling an apple, white like a doll's head, trailing a spiraling ribbon of peel. How tiny she looks before the enormous plough horse. "First, boy, it's *Veuve* Rimbaud. Second, I know all about you young jackasses, flapping your jaws. And you did not blabber? You swear?"

"Nothing, Veuve Rimbaud." Placidly, he slaps a fly. "I do not swear."

"And you were not followed?"

The gravedigger pops up.

"Ah, Georges," he says with relief, "right on time." But then as quickly his tone changes. "Veuve Rimbaud, they are present now."

"Who?" She feels a chill.

"Your two children. Please, I say this to prepare you."

"I *am* prepared."

Then, to distract her, the gravedigger pays her—he thinks—a compliment.

"I hear they are giving Arthur his own statue. In the town square."

"Ridiculous. Give the money to the poor."

How she hates it when the townspeople call him *Arthur*, as if he were theirs, the friendly village ghost. One leg. Of course she has heard the awful joke. That, against his terrible mother, he had only one leg to stand on after they amputated his other in Marseille. It was an emergency operation, when he returned from Africa with his right knee swollen the size of a beehive with a carcinoma. Twelve hellish days being carried on a litter across the desert, followed by hostiles. Sixteen litter bearers, fifteen camels, six drivers and a dozen hired gunmen—all that and a family of four, two of them young children. Thirty-eight souls, they had crossed the Abyssinian desert, a capsized land of blue mountains, red mud, volcanic washes, and dried-up riverbeds that might have been ploughed by whales. For those twelve days, sunburned and thirsty and losing two men, the party pushed on to the Gulf of Aden, below the Red Sea. Even then Rimbaud's ordeal was not over. He was fifteen days more, steaming to France, half out of his mind, terrified he would lose the gold that it had taken him years to amass—a pittance, he thought, compared with what had been devoured by thievery and murder, extortion and fictitious taxes. From first to last, his was a life of antipodes, veering from visionary idealism to the guttering twilight of capitalism, the only constants being restlessness, grandiosity, and the sand-blind tyranny of dreams.

At his death Rimbaud was only thirty-seven but, after a decade in the desert, looked at least a decade older. His once blond hair was gray, and he had grown a small razor mustache. In his kepi, he looked, in fact, like a Muslim, and on his chest, in a special vest, he carried some four kilos of gold, a .32 pistol, and, in case of capture, a double-shot derringer: one shot under the chin. Better that than castration, the rule in the Danakil Desert, preferably while the victim was alive to watch. In this state, Rimbaud arrived. That is, before the ether-soaked gauze was laid over his face and night, blessed night, filled the globes of his eyes.

"Oh, of course," said his mother as she and Isabelle rode the train to the hospital in Marseille to see their prodigal. "Only when there is trouble—or he needs money—only then does he come home."

"Mother," corrected Isabelle, ever his apologist. "Whatever else, he needs no money from you. Not now."

"But he *needs*. He *needs* and he *feeds*, and here I am. What am I, a cow with four teats? And when does he return? But of course, when he is going to die."

"But why should he die?" yelped Isabelle. The amputation had been successful. In no way, then, was his death apparent—to her. Hatefully, however, her mother, with her sudden fears and premonitions, was rarely, if ever, wrong about such things, especially when it came to death.

*W*hen deep in the hole, a boom is heard: deep, wooden, *inhabited*.

"That's him," cries the undertaker. "Arthur's coffin. Perfect. Why, almost new."

Go, says the voice and her hands tremble as she pulls off the veil. But

no sooner has she climbed down from the gig than the gravedigger calls
to his Buddha-sized boy, locks arms with him, then up—out of the
hole—he flies. Arms upraised. To stop her.

"Madame"—blocking her—"Veuve Rimbaud, please. Please, no further. For your daughter, believe me, an undertaker is required."

"Nonsense. Stand aside."

And look, as Mme. Rimbaud peers down, below the lip of turf,
deep in the late sun, there it shines—hair. A shock of reddish blond hair.
Like yesterday. Exposed to air and life, in the late rays of the sun, as
if through some mighty, subterranean phosphorescence, even after
twenty-five years, the girl's red hair ignites, as her mother stands above,
clawing her elbows, then grasping her trembling knees.

Snow, it snowed that day twenty-five years ago, then turned bitterly cold—cold and dry, she remembers. Sitting with Vitalie in her
boatlike coffin, rocking and crying, she felt almost pregnant with grief,
her eyes swollen like two boiled eggs. The wood stove was pulsing hot
and the wintry air, it itched her nose it was so dry. So dry that, behold,
the dead girl's red hair—electrified by the mother's helpless stroking—it
rose, almost living . . . *right to her palm*. Only hair, she thought. Just
hair. The hair but not the girl.

And Arthur, that albatross, then twenty-one, once again he was
home, and again "around her neck," this after a two-year rampage
through Paris and London and Brussels with his lover, Paul Verlaine, a
poet ten years older. That it had been the most creative period of either
poet's life—much less that her son had written poems in a language
never before heard—naturally, of this the Widow Rimbaud knew nothing and cared even less. All she knew were the horrifying reports from
Verlaine's mother and Verlaine's teenage wife—of crimes so foul that her
son most certainly was damned. Nevertheless, she had come to his aid,
visiting him in London, where he and Verlaine were living, openly
cohabiting, when they came home drunk or high from the opium dens
by the wharves, foul rookeries in which cadaverous men lay on benches,
as long pipes—pipes stuffed with burbling black goo—were served up by
Chinamen with quill-like nails and longer beards. For the kid, by then,

pretty much everything had collapsed or was collapsing, dying like the dreams of childhood. His great boast, for example, that he knew all forms of magic and would revolutionize love. Or the still more ridiculous claim that he and Verlaine would live as children of the sun, baptized in the new faith, in new loves and new hopes, surging like the sea. Rot, thought Rimbaud, all rot. As he wrote then in his own dark night of the soul:

> *I had to travel, to dissipate the enchantments that crowded my brain. On the sea, which I loved as if it were to wash away my impurity, I watched the compassionate cross arise. I had been damned by the rainbow.*

His blindness! His arrogance! he thought. In his four years as a committed poet, had he changed anything or improved anyone, least of all a moral toad like Verlaine? Had he written a word that wasn't a lie and self-delusion? Had he, who said that charity was the key, had he not been a demon of pride and selfishness, perhaps even *the* devil, leading Verlaine to destroy his marriage, desert his infant son, and squander his inheritance? And even then he could profess, abracadabra-like, with no apparent hypocrisy, that he had absolutely no interest in money. He was the rain without the wet. The crime with no consequences. The rhyme that rhymed with everything.

All this was bad enough, but then the kid (and it was he who called the shots in their relationship), he told the older man that he was leaving for good, *really* leaving this time. It was for the best, he said, the good, the kind, the logical thing, a mercy, really. Sentimental as ever in such matters, uselessly burdened as adults are, the elder poet, Verlaine, was weeping. Uch, bawling, and at that moment Rimbaud, as clear and cold as a star, had the sensation of drowning him—of smothering the very love that he had sworn to reinvent. Outwardly, the kid was completely calm, explaining everything matter-of-factly as one can only from the unassailable and unknowing bluffs of youth. That accomplished, the kid went to buy a rail ticket, leaving Verlaine to sob himself to sleep. Two hours later, however, it was a different story. Returning, he found Verlaine swaying drunk and enraged, aiming at his chest a small-caliber pawnshop pistol that he had just purchased.

"Silly bitch! What is that?" demanded Rimbaud. He was almost insulted. "Asshole, do you seriously think you can threaten me with that peashooter? Do you?"

Rimbaud grabbed for it. He never heard the report, but look, he was shot, shot in the arm. The angels had fled and he was staring at his own dark, fast-dripping blood. Incredible. He was not God but flesh, human flesh, he realized, as he blacked out and hit the floor.

And so Verlaine was thrown in prison. As for Rimbaud, only mildly wounded and now fingered as an invert, he, along with sundry other undesirables, was put on a locked train car back to the French border, back to his mother and the now approaching death of young Vitalie. In the end, so violent were the girl's coughs that bright blood, lung blood, sprayed her white sheet. No poem to be had here. For Rimbaud, it was like watching a mouse held in the jaws of an enormous cat. Numb, never a tear.

"Uch," said his mother, "look at you, frozen like a snowman! Like a tailor's dummy!" Yet characteristically for him, his suffering assumed a different form. Really, a kind of stigmata: ice-pick migraines, red-blue blooms of pain radiating out from the center of his skull, engulfing his eyeballs in flame. And all because of my hair, he thought. The crushing weight of it.

And so on the day of Vitalie's burial, a bleak and snowy day, desperate, Arthur took off, resolved to find either a barber or a guillotine—anything to be freed of this horrid *hair*.

Three hours later, having crunched back across the ice, he slammed the front door. Nothing. As before, Mme. Rimbaud was in the parlor, seated by the open coffin, that death canoe, purring over her red-haired Vitalie. Carbolic. Heat. That sharp, singed-sweet smell like absinthe or almonds—sickly sweet, death sweet, to the point that he sneezed, as he did with strong peppermints.

"It's so hot in here." Twirling off his muffler, he removed his cap. Horrifying, he was shaved bald. *White.* She bounded up.

"*What* have you done to your head, you crazy cracked-in-the-head! What, so that all Charleville can see you shaved white! Like some lice-infested schoolboy! Like a *cranium.*"

He stopped dead. Dulled and death regressed as he was, he was actually shocked by her reaction; no one really understands another's grieving. "But Mother, I told you, it's my migraines. My hair was killing me."

"Out!" Her arm was a saber. "Out, you crazy cracked-in-the-skull— you *craaaaaa-nium!*"

*T*wenty-five years later, the old woman's laced black shoes are two wedges before the two open graves, long like keyholes in the setting sun. And the gravedigger's boy lied—for look, they are invaded. Look at these busybodies, these ghouls coming out of the *trees,* five, then ten, then twenty and more, crowding in to see the corpse of the great Rimbaud. Even Mercier's filthy children—urchins who run wild like the chickens—see them staring in awe at the dead girl, like a child fallen down a well.

"Go!" says Mercier's wife to the children, but as with the adults, they are held helpless. To see what? Arthur's coffin of rounded red mahogany is dulled and water softened in places but remarkably unspoiled. Not so Vitalie's. After one quarter of a century, the soft white pine has collapsed, turned to mush like wet newspaper, revealing what? Two empty eye holes. Face gone, washed clean away, like blood in rain. An icelike mist has formed over the last rags of her white dress. Gone, all of her. All but her imperishable red hair, still burning like a flame.

"I thought so," someone said, an echo in the old woman said, and right then the Widow Rimbaud knows: she knows exactly what needs to be done. Going back to the gig, the old ghost takes out the old white tablecloth, hard starched and much ironed, which a voice of cherished whisper had advised her to take today. Then, back by the hole, thunderstruck, she collapses, *whump*, on her bottom, like a baby. Actually surprised. When, before anyone can stop her, she swings her old legs down into the hole, into the rushing, cave-smelling darkness. Holding up her arms.

"*Down.* You heard me, *down.*"

"But, Madame," reasoned the gravedigger, "there is no room for two—"

"No, only I. Only her mother. *Down*, do you hear me?"

And patting Arthur's coffin—*Hold on, you*—she feels it hot in her hand, Vitalie's hair, her actual hair, red and still warm. And what else? Ribs. Vertebrae. Eaten-out bones. Tiny pebbles of fingers, like pearls on a string. Now, however, the widow is absolutely calm, for this is a woman's work, putting such disorder to right. *Lay the table.* Lay it down, cleanly. Lay it down, resolutely, like the old family silver. Nothing asunder. Put the bones each to each, the knives, the forks, the spoons. *Lay it straight.* Lay it all, all of her, into this small wooden box, not even a chest, which they swing down to her, as if it were any help. Then, when this is done, she takes out the scissors, which just that morning this same vesperslike voice had advised her, *Slip these into your pocket.*

Snip. See how it cuts, like fresh flowers, her beautiful hair. See how it fits in her hand, then how it feels, deep in her pocket, safe with her keys and paring knife—hers, still hers.

She reaches up exhausted. Why, God? Can't I just stay? *Please*, with my Vitalie? Let them cover me, with dirt, clods, and shovelfuls, useless old woman. When, stumbling, she falls against it, hard. Hard like an elbow, it pokes her. So she pokes it back—*him*, Arthur's coffin.

And she thinks, Mahogany. Arthur, of course, *he* got the mahogany, while his poor sister, she got the soft pine, to collapse on her, like a failed cake. And above, in the light, in a circle of faces, blinded, here are all these *hands*, these *strangers*, these horrid wriggling *fingers* grabbing at her. And scarcely do they haul her up than look! Of course. They forget the old lady. Instead, they are throwing down ropes. Ropes to take *him* out first, the great Arthur! Before even his poor sister!

"Did you not hear me?" she cries. Before thirty witnesses, like a devil, it leaps from her throat. "Are you deaf in your ears? I said her first—*her*, not him."

Good, so she said it. Good. Then she looks down at him, helpless as a mouse squashed under her two black shoes.

"Wait for heaven, Arthur Rimbaud—big shot, you! This time you will wait and like it, boy, just as I have waited on you."

Book One

Godlike Birds

THE CARAVAN TOWN OF HARAR
IN ABYSSINIA, NOW ETHIOPIA, 1891

1 ♪ The Bastard's Last Day

Every morning at dawn they emerge from the desert, black women with earthen red jugs, tall, thirsty jugs atop their heads, their hard-calloused bare black feet squeaking as they pound down the long, broken road, through the floury red dust.

See them in the pulverizing sun. Wrapped in shawls of white cotton, two long and tremulous forms start up the mountain, their tall jugs making them look like giants in the distance. Miles they will walk up this mountain, then miles back through the volcanic desert, and all for one jug emptied upon arrival by begging children and fiery, wooly-haired men in raw cotton tunics carrying long black spears and heavy daggers—white-eyed warriors who snatch and gulp their fill.

But today it is not just the water that brings the women out of the desert. It is the news, the gossip, which is juicy, like a burst mango, especially on this, the Bastard's last day. *If* it is his last day, that is.

On this point there is much debate, competing rumors, the biggest being that the Spice Woman, the very girl the Bastard dishonored, will at last confront him. Avenge herself. Humiliate him in some way. No one wants to miss *that*, the humiliation of the *frangi*, the foreigner.

"Look at the sun," says the taller of the two, a quick, sharp girl, pretty, with a wide gap between her front teeth. She slaps a vicious fly. "Come on. If we don't hurry, he will slip away."

Then at the next pass, a third joins, then a fourth, then a fifth, this one carrying a basket piled high with juicy dates—dates with pits they spit, *pthu*, when they speak about him.

"This is the day," insists the date woman, bossy and a big talker but often right about such matters. "A woman from the caravan told me. Five men pulling twelve camels—*twelve.*" Her eyes grow wide with irritation. "Don't you understand? The Bastard needs four camels *just for his gold.*"

"Just once," says the youngest, staring at the sky, "just once I want to see his face. Frangi devil."

"No," squeals the oldest, a very beautiful woman, a real looker. Scared of the devils and jinns, she wears on her chest an ornate silver cylinder containing a message written by the sheik himself, abjuring any who might cast doubt upon her virtue with the evil eye. "I will not look! Never, at those eyes of his—of that *blue.* But please, if an evil urge makes me look, promise! Seize me hard by the hair!"

Then everything changes. With just a few feet more of elevation, suddenly all is green and cool, jungle palms, date and banana trees and, on the ground, a small clan of the long-faced gelada baboons, several with babies clinging to their backs. Then, round the next bend, a bad omen. Hunkered atop a white-boned tree, four enormous vultures can be seen, slouching black heaps with absurdly tiny heads—white, like centipedes. Then the young woman squeals, ducks as they hear:

"*Pheeeeeeeeeee—*"

The great shadow swoops. Seizing the jug upon her head, she looks up, to see him silhouetted against the sun. Amazing, the creature is almost the size of a man, an angel with two pumping swells of wing. And higher, circling in the clouds, wings cutting like scimitars through the blue sky, dozens more of these magnificent birds can be seen—the great kites of Harar, godlike birds, rulers of all the sky, the kings!

Beware, butcher. Turn even for one second and the swooping, spade-tailed kite with his hand-sized claws, he will snatch your meat, then perch nearby mocking you, tearing it with claw and beak. And way up there, high on the bluff, there is where the kites live, on the walls of what looks like a great mud ship; there it is beached on the great massif from which one can see for a hundred miles. This is the ancient mud-walled city of Harar, a place of some 12,000 souls, thousands of goats, and innumerable dogs. And now, as the women see, it is a city suddenly blocked. No reason. What reason? The gate is blocked, as always, by the sheer arbitrariness of life in this part of the world.

As the sentries push people back, it's chaos, what with the market-day crowds bumping and buzzing and shouting. Men with goats slung over their shoulders. Bawling camels piled impossibly high with firewood and bananas and hempen bags. Donkey carts with wobbling wooden wheels tall as doors. And people bringing strange birds and boys holding dik-diks, tasty antelopes the size of rabbits, their long legs bound like sticks with leather thongs. And blocking them, at the head of the great gate, in their old white uniforms stand the impassive Egyptians—now mercenaries, their cohorts driven out some years before by the vengeance of the great Menelik, Menelik the Merciless, the capturing king. Holdover former occupiers from the north, the Egyptians stand with their rusted rifles and purple fezzes tightly wound in white cloths to combat the sun. Going *You* and *You*. Or *Not you*, if they do not like your looks—out.

"Look at this mess!" The date woman spits. "*Late.* I told you."

The other shades her eyes. "And today it is the day? Are you sure?"

"Silly girl. Was sure ever sure?"

But five minutes later, pushing through this river of people and animals, mud and husks and rinds, they arrive at the Feres Magala, one of the town's two squares, and there at the well must be fifty women, all waiting to catch a glimpse of the Bastard, otherwise known as our luckless hero, Arthur Rimbaud. Alas, Rimbaud is hastily concluding his self-exile in this African Elba. Hiding behind those arched green shutters. Treed!

"Yes, it is true!" shouts the date woman, holding her wares over the crowd. "Today he goes, the Bastard! Look, dates, fresh dates!"

"But no, you are wrong," dismisses her rival, another date seller. "They say tomorrow he goes—*pthu*. Away, the thief."

"But how?" asks the youngest, pressing her shawl against her face, poor girl, as if to ward off some dreaded contagion. "But how can he go when his leg is so fat and sick? He cannot ride."

"Ride!" sneers another. "With his money he will buy a golden leg! Two! The devil, *he* will find a way."

Out is the way, and hastily, too. For even now, upturned on sweaty backs or balanced atop heads, the last dregs of A. Rimbaud Ltd. are being rapidly disgorged into the street: desks, crates, hempen bags, tusks—yours, at a fraction of their wholesale cost.

Two stories above this scene, the besieged proprietor peers out—well back from the peeling, rickety louvers, his face striped with bars of sun and shade. Ah, but not back far enough. For just then the rising sun illuminates his silhouette—exposed! With that an ululating cry can be heard. It is the chorusing, cicadalike cry of fifty female tongues clucking.

"Ayyyyeeeeeeeeeeeeeeeeeeeeeeeeeeeeeeeeeeeeee!"

*U*nfortunately, our hero has lost the element of surprise. For although it is not the actual day of his departure, it is the last full day of his tenure at this torrid, misruled school. And a downcast day it is, too.

How sad to be misunderstood, when for years, in his missionary way, he has tried to be good. Not *great*, he would hasten to add, but merely good—good enough, living a modest, human-scale existence that might be characterized, if not by faith, exactly, then by its very simplicity and decency. Good works. Even charity. Well, of a kind . . . if he could manage even *that*, hang it.

And indeed, until only very recently in these parts was there any stain on his otherwise faultless reputation for actually *good* goods, for fair dealing and sure delivery within days or weeks, as opposed to months. A. Rimbaud, known as far as Cairo and Nairobi as a steady man. A handshake man. A man who honored his word, paid his debts, didn't whine, and ran a tight ship—rare in this land of fugitive oddballs and crooks. But look. Even now as a woman, keening *Ayeeeeeeee* and suffering some kind of spasm, is gesturing horribly at him.

The crutch groans. As he turns away, it spins like a peg on the rough wooden floor, his one crutch and his one good foot—the left. It's his right leg that is now the problem, specifically the knee, now swollen to enormous size. *Merde . . . les varices!* Varicose veins! This continues to be his stubborn diagnosis, and even now, incredibly, he remains wedded to the idea against considerable medical and commonsense evidence to the contrary. Why, even as recently as a week ago, obstinately he had marched on the bad leg. Stamped on it. Rode with it until it was numb. Varicose veins: this remained his steely reply when people presumed to inquire or insisted on staring.

And when at last, to relieve the swelling, he was forced to tear open the knee of his trousers—well, fine. Indeed, the knee was purple, but a commanding man, a deliberate man, he does not change his answer. Never, even as he dispatched his poor mother to scour Charleville, their town, and even Paris if necessary to find a special sock. A medical, elastic stocking he had seen in some months-old newspaper. Just the thing to compress the veins. Pressure. For him, this is always the answer: pressure.

Alas, when said sock arrived ten weeks later in a mildewed package mauled beyond recognition, the sock did not work, hang it! In fact, just as his mother had predicted, the sock only worsened the condition. And then last week came the final blow—a crutch.

It was the leg that had started this nonsense with the women. Arrogant *frangi*! This was not just bad fortune. To them, it was God's retribution for his having chucked the girl out three months before. Because the girl could not give him a child, not even a girl child, let alone a male child, the *frangi*, the foreigner, he had thrown her out, but see then how Allah punished him! As anyone could tell you in Harar, the backed-up man poisons, the poisons from his bad seed, they had seeped down his leg. Allah, who sees all, Allah the Just had turned his leg to stone, his business had failed, the girl had triumphed, and every day now female justice waits outside his window, praise be to Him—*al-hamdu lil-lah!*

Oh, it's bad, quite bad, and he knows it. But it's not just the leg, it's his whole life, even the state of his room. Papers strewn. Drawers hanging out. Bags half packed. It's life with the stuffing pulled out—evicted. For yes, admittedly, he had done—

Or rather, it had so happened—

Fine then, he had let happen a rather stupid thing. A rash thing. An obstinate thing. And, perhaps most unforgivably for his European colleagues, a rash and *unnecessary* thing, ejecting the girl. "Good heavens, man," as one English bloke had put it. "What *are* you thinking? Have you a positive wish to die?"

The girl also had a family, and a large one, so throw in "impolitic," too. And yet, having found the girl, this flower sprung in the mud of the bazaar—well, for once in his life, Rimbaud had done the brave and honest thing and followed his heart. And yes, it was regrettable, but certainly he had made copious amends to the girl and her family. Hecatombs of amends—God! People had no idea what he had paid to her people—for months—in his vain efforts to hush it all up. And all too characteristically he had thought, I can fix this. Set her up fresh—in Egypt, perhaps. Find some wealthy man. *Une belle situation.* A governess or mistress position, perhaps. *I'll fix it.*

Pack of dogs! Bandits! And after all his generosity to the town, too.

Anonymous, most of it. Oh, they didn't know the half of it, ignorant savages. The leper colony, for example. Had he not donated bandages, then even frocks to his friend Father Lambert and the little children in the school adjacent to the quarantined "hot" compound? Quite beautiful healthy children, too, even as their parents, earless, noseless, fingerless, boiled in their own skins. The children! Among whom he would sit, as if among wild monkeys, when he was feeling low. Voices raised in song—remember? On his birthday? How they had sung to him so beautifully!

But it wasn't just the orphans to whom he had been so kind. Thanks to him, ten, twenty, probably thirty men had been inoculated—alive merely because they worked for him. And the food! Piles of food he had given away during the famines, why, openly in the streets, stopping the wildfire of hunger before mobs sacked his store, or worse. Could they, could any of them, appreciate his generosity, his sacrifice?

No more. Tomorrow, after long years of comings and goings in the region, he will leave it, all of it, the reputation he wants and manly competence as he knows it, and all in the hope that his mother and Roche, even France—that this time it will be good, or at least better than it was before. For a man with the pride of Lucifer, it is a point of particular pride that he himself has organized his rescue, himself and his gold, kilos of the gold protected by a dozen gunmen, wild Yemenis and Somalis, mostly, bound to him through a local chief whom he had long supplied. Ruthless, efficient men. Blooded horsemen personally armed by Rimbaud himself—five of them with the Remington lever-action repeater rifles so prized—he loves to point out—by the American cowboys. Rimbaud was proud indeed that he could procure such weapons. And tomorrow at dawn they will come for him, a dozen men with guns and spears and bandoliers of ammunition. A trotting armory, each man carrying, athwart his hip, the long Danakil dagger, a heavy, J-shaped rip of steel that curves like a sideways smile. Reaper men. And reliable men. Or so he hopes, carrying all his gold.

Before dawn, they will be off, with him leading the caravan. And not walking or on horseback but carried—carried on a stretcher. This will be his ordeal, broiling in the trackless desert under the unending sun. Twelve days later, ten if they are very lucky, they will arrive in Zelia by the cobalt blue sea. Then away he will go—away on the first steamer smoking back to France. Away from these vulturous women keening, "Ayyyyyeeeeeeeeeeeeeeeeeeeeeeeee!"

2 ꝯ What the Night Said to the Night

But it isn't just the women at their well who have their eye on him. Later that night, awaking from a bad dream, Rimbaud realizes that, once again, his mother is right about him. Right about the leg, right about his needing to marry, and right about his crawling back home—hatefully right about everything.

In this dream, he is four or five. It's a winter night, freezing cold, and they are in the barn at Roche—the birthing pen. The lantern smokes. His breath smokes, and before his five-year-old legs, fat as a rain barrel, lies a dying cow, Marie. Her calf is stuck, *something's* stuck, and he is frantic, crying, "*Maman*, get up, she'll kick you." But, lying on her side in the straw, rolling up her sleeve, his *maman* is all concentration, peering up Marie's black bum.

A witch. The boy has heard it so whispered. People in the town say so and, as for Paul, the hired hand, he knows so. "The cow's as good as dead," he says. "The calf, too." "Enough," says his mother, slicking her arm with the cow's own butter. "Now hold up the lantern."

Then up the blubbery black lips she slides her fingers. Black pie, it sucks and spurts. The dead cow shudders to life and, like that, his mother is gobbled up, sunk to the shoulder, when, *splat*, out they come—*born together*, his mother and the slick, wet calf, jumbled in thick, wet snakes of umbilical rope. They're both upside down. The calf's neck twists around. Brown and wet, he's like warm clay, smoking he's so new, and the boy's ears are clanging, and he is shouting, "Is it is it is it?" Alive, he means. "Of course it's alive," says his mother, stirring a piece of sharp straw in the calf's nostrils, an old farmer trick, to itch her to life. The calf snorts, twitches. Look, the nostrils are smoking. Then Paul hoists the lantern. "Lord, the calf has five legs!"

And after that, in gigs and wagons, from miles around, people come to gawk at Cinq the cow. It's a sign, that fifth leg. God's finger, thinks the boy. Pointing at *them*, the Rimbauds. Warning all against the witch.

*A*nd look at him now, still drenched with this dream of a five-legged cow, a boy still floating in the blocked and unknowing soul of a now bitter man. Fine freckles and lines mark his face. His thick boyish hair is gray blond, close-cropped like that of a soldier or convict, and below the gray blue eyes and sandy lashes there is the chevron mustache, a Muslim touch, like the fez and his fluency in Arabic, Amharic, and a host of local dialects. How old is he at thirty-seven? Younger than he knows and older than he can possibly be, living in a place where the years are doubled, like prison sentences.

Truly, to see him lying here in the moonlight, it is hard to know how old this man is. Whatever happened? Who was he once, before too many things happened? We are looking at the face of a man who, having survived himself, now finds himself bobbing in the middle of the desert, the lone survivor, clutching his body like a life preserver.

And yet, even faced with life's worst, there is in him a wildly optimistic side, times when he will think to himself, But who knows? There are medical miracles, salt cures, and even operations, if it comes to that. And perhaps if you're courageous, if you don't panic and you tough it out, you may return to Abyssinia. Perhaps even better than before. For really, who knows?

All through the downslide of these past few weeks, such optimism has been his mantra, this sunny voice telling him, Who knows, who knows? Look, you can only do so much. Perhaps you will return to Harar, possibly with new investors—bankrolled. Then there is La Société Géographique, which, in its February 1884 bulletin, has published his account of a harrowing three-week trip into the interior region called the Ogadine. True, it was only 150 kilometers, but you didn't need to go far to find yourself surrounded by hard-muscled, bushy-haired men whose life's ambition was to spear, then castrate a godless white affront such as yourself. Anyhow, his report upon which he had pinned such hopes, it had gone mostly unnoticed, but it was a start, he thought, the point being he had reinvented himself as Arthur Rimbaud, *explorer, ethnographer, scientist.*

And quite possibly he *will*, he *might*, he *could* return with this new French wife his mother has been dangling in her letters. All picked out, she claims. Young? Old? Pretty? Not so fast: of course, his parsimonious maman withholds even the most rudimentary details of said maid, even as he, mad with curiosity, holds his breath for months, to spite her by not asking. Desire. Desire withheld. This is their little game, mother and son. One of them, anyway.

Nonetheless, Rimbaud can picture this woman, a sensible, handsome, and *presentable* woman, bustled in her *embonpoint*, with lyrelike hair carefully arranged with combs and tucked up under a smart hat. A solidly French (but not stupid) woman, with whom he will have a son. Father a son, rather. Fatherhood. As a fatherless boy, at this stage of his life, he finds the idea of fatherhood deeply appealing, he who once had dreamed of being a child of the sun, running down a foaming, exploding beach. A world so new it was forever being born, like eternity.

And the world he will return to after fifteen years away? Unrecognizable. The Eiffel Tower, the buildings of the Exposition Universelle de Paris of two years before, all this is new, just as Paris now has a model sewer system in which, for a modest fare, well-to-do, big-hatted ladies with a taste for the stygian—indeed, ladies holding parasols—can glide through the gloom in lantern-hung boats.

Yes indeed, in an explosion of steel and steam, electric lights and dynamos, the modern industrial world was booming, and all built by the very men he had once spat upon: businessmen and bankers, men of science, engineers, and riveters—men of steam, like Georges-Eugène Haussmann, architect of modern Paris, or Charles de Freycinet, creator of the first state-owned rail network. These "types," once dismissed by him as the slaves of bygone orders, twenty years later, he now holds these men in abstract awe—men hot to pan the Yukon, conquer the North Pole, or, like Ferdinand de Lesseps, dig the Panama Canal. And so, even in an Africa backwater like Abyssinia, Rimbaud maintains a keen interest in amateur engineering manuals on such odd and diverse topics as metallurgy, the stringing of suspension bridges, and the manufacture of tiny precision toys—tumbling clowns and monkeys clapping cymbals and such. But will his bullheaded and unimaginative mother procure for his edification said self-bettering books? Could the old witch not see?

MOTHER JUDGMENT. Books to buy *where*, to do *what*? Has the heat driven you crazy? What do they even *make* in that place?
PETITIONER SON. Why am I still waiting for the aforementioned volumes? And two months without a word from you.
MOTHER JUDGMENT. (*Silence.*)
SON *blinks*. Three months have passed without a word from you. I am still here, with the idea that I will remain here for another three months. It's very unpleasant, but this will nonetheless end by ending. I do hope, however, that I soon shall see these books, especially the one on suspension bridges.
MOTHER ON HIGH. Bridges in the desert—built by whom? By you who never so much as lifted a hammer?

But here's a question: Where would one even *start* in a thousand-year-old civilization in which antiquity slumbers like the Sphinx? With what conceivable workforce or industrial capacity? Here, in a hut as hot as an oven, you will find half-naked zombie men drenched in sweat and soot—low-caste men of a scavenger tribe, expert makers of knives, axes, and scythes. Dazed by the narcotic *khats* they chew, tiny green leaves mashed and wadded in one cheek, one man works the wheezing ox-hide bellows, two more wield the great spark-splattering mallets, and a fourth, the tong man, then plucks from the fire a pulsing, livid heart of iron ready to be shaped. But honestly, tintinnabulating toys? Does Rimbaud fancy these men are thrifty Swiss in disguise?

What can he be thinking, then, this missionary of modernity? Or writing, for that matter. For here we come to another issue that cannot be ignored in his strange late letters. Namely, the even more perplexing matter of writing *style*, or rather the utter absence of style, indeed a regression to his earliest schoolboy days in which, like other children under the rod, he numbingly memorized, then recited in schoolboy sing-song, all the rivers and streams of France. Consider a representative passage to his mother and sister:

> Dear friends,
> I arrived at this country after twenty days on horseback through the Somali desert. Harar is a city colonized by the Egyptians and dependent on their government. The garrison is made up of many thousands of men. Our agency and our storehouses are here. The saleable products of the country are coffee, ivory, skins, etc. The country is at an elevation, but the land is cultivatable. The climate is cool but not unhealthy.

Contrast this with:

> *It has been found again!*
> *What has?—Eternity.*
> *It is the sea gone off*
> *With the sun.*

> *Sentinel soul,*
> *Let us whisper the confession*
> *Of the night so void*
> *And of the day on fire.*

Or this incantation:

> *O seasons, O castles*
> *What soul is without flaws?*

> *I have made the magic study*
> *Of happiness which no man evades*

> *A salute to it each time*
> *The Gallic cock sings*

Ah! I will have no more desires:
It has taken charge of my life.

Which again raises this disquieting question of language and style. Namely, how a poet prodigy of almost unfathomable abilities could willfully *forget* how to write. How could such a man disable a style and unlearn ageless rhythms—stubbornly *resist*, as one might food and water, words and their phantom secrets, indeed the modern secrets of language that he had been the first to discover, in his teens?

How, in short, could a poet of genius systematically erase his own life—*unwrite* it? How? Why? To what conceivable end?

3 ⨎ The Rimbaud Luck

The lanterns are two golden balls in the darkness. "Come *on*," says the one.

In black rubber boots, down the hill they trudge at 4:00 a.m., two dumpling-skirted, lumpy-sweatered women hauling steaming buckets to the barn where the beamy, big-eyed ladies are now loudly stamping and mooing, Feed me milk me feed me.

"Well," says the mother in the darkness, as if a malicious voice has just whispered it. "I now know that Arthur's knee is worse than he has let on. Much worse."

"Mother," says Isabelle, his one surviving sister, a thirty-year-old girl-woman still half asleep, "how can you presume to *know* this?"

"Because, daughter, I had a dream."

Setting down the bucket, Mme. Rimbaud turns up the lantern wick, licking and smoking. "Hold up the lantern—up." Turns the latch, then pushes light into the piss-perspiring beast heat. Cats, skinny barn cats, leaping, mewing, and twirling round her ankles—*things needing things.* *Dehors!* "Out!" Then, bumping Isabelle as if she were a cow: "In with you, *in*." Claps the door, then continues: "Of the four of you, Arthur always kicked the hardest . . . as an infant. Are you listening to me? He kicked me last night." Isabelle is now staring at her in bafflement. "In my sleep," insists the mother, "he *kicked* me."

"You mean, as a *baby* Arthur kicked you?"

"I mean, I felt a kick. Last night. How do I know if he was a baby? But then I knew—I knew it's bad."

"But, Mother, you always think the worst. You jinx it."

"Jinx what? It *is* jinxed. Good lord, your brother doesn't need me to jinx his life."

At this, Isabelle plops the rag into the hot, soapy water. Rubs her nose on her woolen sleeve, wipes down the udder teats, drops her stool, then starts wringing. *Sploosh, sploosh, sploosh.*

"Ignore me." The mother stands there, burning. "Go on with your pretending. You'll see I'm right."

Sploosh sploosh.

"And, you *hate* that I am always right. And I hate always having to *be* right."

Grabbing the next cow by the tail—by the balls, as it were—Madame hand-jacks her, bucking and stumbling, into the stall: seize the tail and, rest assured, Bossy will follow. Wrings out the rag, then starts wiping. "You'll see. Or rather, two months from now you will—as usual. Monsieur Michaud!"—this is the hired man, another itinerant tippler and oddball—"Get in here! You and your two friends. And not too close to the lantern, lest you blow us up, all the alcohol on your breath."

And not merely is the old pest probably right, thinks Isabelle, but she is *wrong-right.* Mme. Rimbaud always sides with the worst, and at the pessimist's betting window, almost invariably, she is handsomely repaid, Arthur's leg being a case in point. For the past two months, they've been skirmishing over the leg and what it portends, especially now that Arthur's problematic return seems all the more probable. For after all, as an enterprise run by two women, their little life has worked well enough. "Quite well," Mme. Rimbaud will chirp when Isabelle gets too down at the mouth. Down, that is, about being stuck, lonely, unmarried. Meaning—to her mother's way of thinking—falling into all her boo-hooing female feeble-headedness.

Which is all to say that Roche, this five-hectare Amazonian caliphate, is a female-run enterprise. Meaning that Roche runs, despite the usual vagaries of weather and pests, moderately, consistently, and on its own—without men, since the Michauds of the world, bottle-sucking itinerant worms that they are, obviously do not count. Nevertheless, this impending sense of *Arthur*, of his return, this weighs heavily on Mme. Rimbaud, who, in her son's absence, has even further mythologized (if such were possible) his stupendous ill effects on ordinary life.

Ignore her bluff, then. Her anxiety grows by the day.

Well, if such worries chafe Mme. Rimbaud at 4:00 a.m., evening is worse. Evening, that flabby time of the day, as the old woman calls it.

"Shoo! Out, cat."

Clawing the rug, Minet—their one, outnumbered tom—flees for his life. The old woman looks around. At the clock in its idleness. At that fly bouncing off the pane—*whack*.

"Honestly, I preferred him when he was poor."

No antecedent. None is necessary.

"Mother," sighs the daughter, "in three lifetimes, Arthur could never earn enough money to satisfy you. Even if he *had* become a barrister. This was your fantasy, not his."

Money, another topic, for never are they idle. Even now as supper simmers, mother and daughter are absorbed in yet another little money-maker: needlepoint. Pillows, doilies, fancy dress panels. Even framed whimsies: *Let Peace Reign Through Our Little Abode.*

"Sewn, they think, by ill-paid village simpletons just blind with happiness," says the old woman. Her voice, never raised, sounds like the coughs of a small, asthmatic dog.

And yet, the deep concentration of needlepoint, the slow, shallow breathing is, in its way, calming. "Because, of course"—another stitch—"he always puts himself on the wrong side of luck. As if"—another stitch—"at this point"—she coughs a dry cough—"he must prove the obvious."

"Which is?"

"Failure. What else?"

The needle stops; Isabelle drops her head.

"Maman," she says, marshaling what little stubbornness she has left, "Arthur is not a failure. He has a business. Property, too."

"*Business.* Do we see him in the *Congo*, running diamond mines? Of course not. No, he sells hides and ostrich feathers for floozies. Low-profit trash. *Mon Dieu*, did the boy learn nothing from me?"

*M*oments later, in the barren dining room, beneath the portrait of Jesus with his hound's eyes, they take their meager supper. Leek and potato soup, a piece of Rocroi, a soft, creamy cheese covered in fine cinders and buttered on yesterday's almost stale bread. There they will sit at a long, rectangular, otherwise empty table with rattling tallow-soaked boards at which Isabelle occupies the same place—and indeed the same, still wobbling chair—at which she has sat since the age of two listening to her mother's soliloquies. As for the three remaining chairs—those of Arthur, Frédéric, and Vitalie—these relics hang in the barn, tilted high in the rafters, flying away like three witches.

Once more, Madame rings the tureen with a dull spoon.

"Daughter!"

Clumsy steps down the stairs: Isabelle steps, losing steps, retracing steps. Again, the mother trumpets at the ceiling.

"Good heavens, can't you ever just *leave* a room? Daughter, you are like a burr, always sticking to things."

Whump, Isabelle hits the bottom stair: young-pretty, old-pretty, man-hungry, her hair pinned up with combs, feathery strands falling in semidisarray. Silence is served. Bowls are stirred, but little is taken. It is their nightly contest of feminine virtue, that is, over who can consume the least, pitting Mme. Rimbaud's flagellating self-denial against Isabelle's purposeful-seeming vacuousness, periods, as now, in which Isabelle will dutifully sit, rabbitlike, chin tucked into her neck. Madame stirs, then restirs her watery soup. Holds her spoon almost pastorally in midair. Narrows her eyes—her final pronouncement on the subject of Arthur.

"Hear me now. Because here is how it is with your brother and his knee. God has given your brother a cross, *un travail*. But, being Arthur Rimbaud, naturally, he denies it—no. It is varicose veins! It is a bruise. It is anything but what it so obviously is. But will he yield before God? Will he yield in his arrogance?"

Isabelle's chair honks back. "Meaning what? That Arthur deserves the leg? So you can be miserably right again?"

Insulted, the old woman rises suddenly, her old knees cracking like two broomsticks. But no sooner has she taken the bowls and turned her back than Isabelle snitches a piece of cheese—openly. The mother jerks around; she always takes the bait.

"I saw that! Then *eat*. Openly, not sneakily. *Eat*."

"Eat what?" Pure provocation. Isabelle is like a cat with a mouse in her jaws, the tail still switching.

"I—saw—you—" Snatching up the remaining plates, the old woman shuffles around. They are in a diorama. It is the reprise of a very old play, and we are now hearing something she might have said fifteen or twenty years ago—to a child. "Go on then, you and your brother! Eat it all up! All of it, like the pigs! Root, root, root."

*T*hen, at 8:30 p.m., it is Compline, prayer time in this nunnery of two. On her knees and elbows, Mme. Rimbaud kneels over the creaky iron bed, in the room with the listing washstand, the one chair, and the battered breviary now open to Psalm 91:

> *He shall say to the Lord,*
> *"You are my refuge and my stronghold,*
> *my God in whom I put my trust."*

> *He shall deliver you from the snare of the hunter*
> *and from the deadly pestilence.*

Vivid shadows mass around her, and as she prays, with one hand she pinches her eye sockets, wallowing down on swollen, watery knees. Awe and pain. Crowd it out. Pray for pain, like rain, since it is bound to come. Like the Prodigal Son, Arthur will return. Or worse, her other son, Frédéric, the estranged, he too will return. Fat sot. Years ago she had turned him out. Nonetheless, she heard the periodic reports—knocking girls up, lying drunk in the road. Or once, most grievously, selling newspapers in Charleville—*newspapers*, can you imagine? *Mon Dieu!* Any day now, she expects to see Frédéric carted home, found months after the fact like Mme. Moreau's son, another drunk lost in the snow; who, come spring, once found, had to be scooped up with muck shovels and hayforks. *And this is* my *fault, Lord? I birthed him and I raised him—is that not enough?*

Snuffs the lamp, smacks the pillow. But then, with a final bounce, like an indigestion, she remembers it, another bee in her bonnet.

A newspaper article. She'd seen it in her solicitor's office. Just that morning, in fact. This was after Mass, when, to further punish Arthur in absentia, Madame had amended—yet again—her much-revised will. With which, even from the hereafter, she would pull the strings, plying Isabelle with drips and drabs of money, while Arthur—as a moral precaution—would find himself written out. Heh, locked out entirely.

Anyhow, it annoyed her, coming upon this article concerning this high-hat Russian count, this blowhard *writer*, whatever his name was, with his long white beard and big carbuncled red nose. To whom it seemed idiot peasants and Jews from the city would flock—Jews from all around the *world*—begging the so-called count, this charlatan, to tell them the secret of life. Can you imagine? For days and weeks at a time, they camp on his lawn like locusts, these softheads, denuding his apple trees and picking his pole beans bare. But finally, glory be! The door opens and here he is with his red snout, white beard, and big Cossack boots. And on their knees, how they grovel before the old jackass.

"Please, Count. Please tell us the secret of life."

Secret—another *male* raising his little finger, serving up his horse apples as if they were Sunday dumplings. Heh, thinks the old woman, counting her black sheep. Send these dunderheads to me—I'll tell them the secret. A woman's secret, too. Pick a rock. Pick up a good heavy one, then lug it between your legs for sixty-odd years. Secret!

Zzzzzzzzzzzzzz.

4 ⚘ Dogs

The dogs of Harar, the incessant dogs. Every night, the town dogs battle the hyenas for the butcher's slops and the beggar whom no one will bury, and tonight, Rimbaud's last night, it's terrible, packs of dogs insanely baying and barking and scrapping until they are covered with bloody slobber. No one calls them. No one owns them. And so it escalates, the snarling and barking, until the shriek that sends his heart exploding through his chest.

Never before in Abyssinia, not even growing up on a farm, had he realized that animals can scream, not like this. The victim, just below his window, is one of the larger dogs, but he is nothing once the hyena bitch sinks her teeth into his windpipe. Fanged apes. To Rimbaud, the hyenas are almost mythological, terrible raging sphinxes. Half creatures, with big heads and powerful chests. And yet absurdly propelled by puny, withered legs—chicken legs, almost.

Beware the hyena's stare. Yellowy eyes. Hypnotic, never veering, locked on her quarry. And never snarling or growling like a dog but rather emitting panting, fretting, seemingly frightened yips. Give up, mutt. The dog stupid enough to lunge for her, even the largest, has no chance, and the mad thing is the dogs always lose, always, night after night, hyena killing dog, dog killing dog, until once more it stops. And then, candle lapping the walls, in her nightgown—with that seamlessness of dreams—his mother shuffles into his room. Pokes him—up.

Arthur, Arthur, why aren't you up! You have an examination.

In his boyhood and teenage years, she was forever rousting him out of bed for endless rounds of study terminated by examinations lasting, some of them, for four and five hours. Indeed, by the age of fourteen, the boy felt like a great waddling foie gras goose—not with a succulent liver but rather with force-fed mental muscle. Ramming the funnel down his throat, the masters filled his young gullet with grain, brain grain, and, to be sure, for a time the boy exulted in the attention, the power to dazzle, the prizes, the whispering girls, and the approving mothers pointing at him, this model boy—why, the smartest boy in the county, they said, if not the smartest boy in all of France! All this was his due, and each May Mme. Rimbaud would gloat to see his name, *their* name, printed in the local rags: Arthur Rimbaud, *her* Arthur, inseparable from her. Rimbaud on the *tableau d'honneur*. Arthur Rimbaud. Winner of all the laurels.

Most memorable, every May, were those ordeals of mental single combat—the national poetry contest, the Concours général. Locked alone in a classroom, in his blue trousers, black coat, and the stringy, sagging tie then in fashion—in this cage the boy was given nothing but some sheets of foolscap and a pencil with which he wrote, to the clock, over many hours, for many preening masters, overweeningly long poems. Show-offy poems. And make no mistake: these masters were immensely proud of *their* boy, poor, tireless wretch. God help him, to be *hers*, this woman always waving her arms when she came to the school. Doing, as the masters put it, her dreaded *da-di-da*, as if she were some insane conductor. Bah! she exclaimed, dismissing them. *Chiens savants*, clever, performing dogs.

Long, intricate, and metrically complex, these exercises took as their models a range of classical Latin poetic forms: dactylic hexameter, followed, perhaps, by elegiac couplets and hendecasyllables. Long beat, short beat, spondaic leaps—well, whatever the case, these classic trotters were then arbitrarily applied to unimaginative or simply torpid topics not of the boy's choosing: In Praise of Justice. Or, The Shadow of Dido on the Ruins of Carthage. Or, still more rousingly, The Ashes of Themistocles Returned to Athens. On your mark and get set, messieurs, for the clock is ticking. *Go.*

And off he went, face flat to the table, and no tapping, peter pulling, or shilly-shallying—*pensez-vous!* The boy was a mad machine. Shoulder bones bunched, cowlick erect, fidgeting and cracking his knuckles, the boy wrote these poetic parlor tricks almost metronomically, yet with such verve that word of his prowess reached even the dusty rococo-encrusted, bust-presiding offices of the highest educational authorities of Paris. Who duly dispatched two bearded, black-suited, black-top-hatted worthies to palpate the lad's lobes. Learned men, Gobineau's disciples, the two men were steeped in the new but promising science of phrenology, a way to determine character as revealed in the facial-cranial-racial structures.

Indeed, at none other than the Faculté de médecine de Paris—in the medical amphitheater—these same two worthies had presented before a crowd of two hundred in their top hats and waistcoats. Or rather, two hundred and four, if one counted the four male cadavers lying naked on blood-guttered marble slabs. Gaslight reflectors illuminated the scene. Marbleized white flesh. Wide-open faces unreacting to the fly that landed upon the cheek of the middle man, then, inching, proceeded to explore the recesses of his nose. *Voyez . . .* see here, gentlemen, cried the moderator, here we have a common laborer—a simpleton—along with a learned professor, a vicious murderer, and a Jew. A little game, then, doctors! *Alors*, guess who, eh, guess who.

"This is what we will be looking at," said the taller of the two men, unfurling before Mme. Rimbaud's eyes a sheet on which she saw depicted a head dissected into the cranial zodiac. Specifically, the twenty-seven mental organs forming the worm bucket of human attributes otherwise known as *character*.

"Cuts of beef," said she, unimpressed. Again, she flapped her palm. "No nonsense now, Monsieur, twenty francs. In my hand."

"But please, Madame, in the cause of science. For the pride of France."

"Come, come," said the hand. "Do you think me a fool, Monsieur? I have four at home, and no man to feed us. Pay up."

Greedy peasant—they paid her. Whereupon they turned to the boy's cranium, pounded like a fresh scaloppini from his poetical exertions. As for the subject of these inquiries, the two doctors did not engage *him* with their chimerical depiction of the brain. Nevertheless, they thought it peculiar, if not impertinent, that so clever a boy did not inquire and in fact evinced no interest whatsoever, the little snot. Well, really, this taunting knuckle cracker! This desk humper and peter puller with his supercilious smirk!

"Monsieur Rimbaud," intoned the taller and dourer of the two, "follow, please, my two fingers."

The man's beard was tallow slick and otterlike, and so, in his utter boredom, the boy had named him the Otter, then decided the other was the Hedgehog, this for his bristly puffball of a beard. In fact, lying under the Hedgehog's prognathous jaw, this hirsute *cud*, the boy could see copious crumbs and even yellow speckles from that morning's egg yolk.

"Please, Doctor, the calipers."

Shaped like a giant C, these were measuring instruments fitted with spindly tines and queer springs, which they then fitted over the lad's mental antlers. And still not a howl, as they peered into the phantasmagoria of his mental sensorium.

"Here, here," said the Otter, plastering down, like flypapers, the greasy flaps of his now exercised hair. "*Attendez*, Monsieur Rimbaud."

Whereupon he struck a metallic tuning fork, then moved it—furiously humming like a wasp—before the boy's blank eyes, searching for some reaction, *any* reaction. Still nothing. Whereupon the Hedgehog—first asking the little know-it-all to recite, in Greek, two hundred lines of Homer—clapped his hands over the boy's suspiciously small ears, *deviant ears*, then bade him recite, this time in Latin, two hundred lines of Virgil. *The Aeneid*, book 1.

"Louder, please," said the Hedgehog, as the boy gargled and the Otter followed word for word, with his trot—

> *Aeolus haec contra: "Tuus, O regina, quid optes*
> *explorare labor; mihi iussa capessere fas est.*
> *Tu mihi, quodcumque hoc regni, tu sceptra Iovemque*
> *concilias, tu das epulis accumbere divom,*
> *nimborumque facis tempestatumque potentem."*

Perfect to the syllable, the little rat! Then the trouble started.

"That's enough," said the mother, jingling her twenty pieces of silver. "Come now. You have had your fun."

"Patience, Madame," said he, standing well back. "We have scarcely begun."

"I would like," said the boy, "some water."

"Later," shushed the Hedgehog. At this he got down to eye level with him, as one might with an obstinate schnauzer.

"A question, Monsieur Rimbaud. I know, I think, what *we* think. But what do *you* think about yourself? Of a boy such as yourself. Such a bright boy. What? I wonder."

The boy looked as if he had tasted spoilt milk. "Of myself, Monsieur? And who would that be? I am quite sure that *I* think nothing."

"Nothing?" said the Otter, looking at his colleague. "Can such be possible? And are you not greatly pleased with your *triumph* here today? That men such as ourselves, medical men, scientists, learned men from the Academy, should be examining your cranial apparatus? At all this fuss over your—your *mental faculties?*"

"Water," insisted the boy. "I *asked* for water."

"No water," insisted the Otter. "Your brain will blot it up."

"Like a sponge," agreed the Hedgehog. "Next, your hands."

As if they were stinking fish, the Hedgehog flipped them over, whiffed. Unmistakable, that gluey odor—loathsome. It was the web-fingered swamp smell of Onan and his solitary crimes. And, with those outsized hands of his, his eel was bound to be disgustingly large. Pink. Crooked, too, no doubt—another subject of study, one worthy of Euclid, the hypotenuse of cranium to crank. But then, rank boy, he yanked back his sticky digits.

"When I get my glass of water."

"Well," mused the Otter, to his bristly partner. "*Now* he is not so bored with us."

Attention, Messieurs: now the mother bear was getting agitated. As warned, they saw the dreaded *da-di-da*, the windmilling arms, the compressed lips.

"Arthur," she thundered, "*Big Brain*, were you not listening? They said it will cause your brain to swell."

"Mother," he replied haughtily, "has *your* head swelled—ever—with a drink of water?"

"Offer it up!" she said, for these knifelike flashes of intelligence frightened her. "Imagine how thirsty our Lord was as he hung on the Cross!"

"Ah," replied the boy, rolling his eyes, "then that explains it."

"Explains?" prompted the Otter, grabbing for this morsel. "Explains what?"

Down his nose the prize boy peered at them. "In church, Messieurs. Surely, you have noticed how our poor Lord's head slumps there on the Cross. Did he drink too much water, do you think? Or do you suppose, Messieurs"—he paused with just the trace of a smirk—"do you suppose our poor Lord was *drunk?*"

"Madame!" cried the Otter.

"Young sir!" chided the Hedgehog

"Blasphemer!" howled the mother, not to be outdone. "Oh, you'll taste some slaps once we leave! *Un! Deux! Trois!* A Holy Trinity! Enough, Messieurs. Now do you see? Do you see what I, a woman alone, must contend with?"

"But, Madame, in the interest of science—"

"As the esteemed mother of such a—"

Bigwigs. She knew at once what they wanted.

"Good heavens, Messieurs. Can you be asking to feel . . . *my* brain?"

"Twenty," bid the Otter.

"Thirty! And you'll be *vite-vite* about it, too." Muttering, she stuffed her needlepoint into a bag. "But mind you, Messieurs, be careful, very careful of my large bumps."

"Bumps, Madame?" At this they shivered like wet dogs.

Picture it, they thought. Years from now, in the Musée de la Société phrénologique de Paris, in the Halls of Madness, in cloudy, piss-colored specimen jars, there they would bob, like prehistoric eggs. Two brains. Mother and son. Peasant and genius, opposite sides of the same moon.

"Easy, Madame," said the Otter, raising the great calipers.

But at this, she sprang. Snagged her nestling by the collar—*up*. Then, with a smirk, left them high and dry. Left money on the table, too—a first. Moments later, as promised, three sharp reports are heard:

"God the Son!"

"God the Father!"

"God the Holy Ghost!"

Slap! Slap! Slap!

*R*emarkable thing, though. The boy was not the usual mathematical or musical prodigy, say, like the seven-year-old, periwigged Mozart dressed in blue satin and white knee britches, mesmerizing kings and queens as his tiny fingers swept up and down the keys of his little pianoforte. Rather, he was that rarest of rarities and oddest of oddities—a prodigy of letters.

And by sixteen—and then writing his own poems—Arthur Rimbaud was not merely dazzling or surprising, say, like young Thomas Chatterton, dead at seventeen, a century before this time. By then—not that anyone then knew it, of course—Arthur Rimbaud had anticipated, and exceeded, Dada and Surrealism, had checkmated and rewritten fifty or sixty years of future poetry, had barged headlong into the twentieth century, and then with the recklessness and bravado practiced, in France at least, only by painter provocateurs like Honoré Daumier or Paul Gauguin.

Go on. Stand them all up. Name one. Anyone. What other nineteenth-century writer managed to break through to the twentieth?

Poe—a first dark industrial explosion, an inventor of forms, the detective story for one, but in diction thoroughly nineteenth century. Baudelaire—a dazzler and an outlier dancing on the razor's edge of beauty and perversion, yet stylistically still in the classical mode. Mallarmé—a lord of sonoric discipline and a boundary stretcher but still a flowery, rather precious nineteenth-century effusive. Wilde—very close, at least in humor, and a great master of prose, but in poetry (save for "Ballad of Reading Gaol"), a hothouse, late Romantic when the parade had long passed. As for the titanic, hairy-chested Whitman, that great liberator, hankering, gross, mystical, nude, however magnificently the bard sprawls and swims, his long, powerful lines still teem with the prolixity and Yankee gimcrackery of that age.

And Emily Dickinson? Ah, but she was her own century.

Not so Rimbaud. Indeed, by his teens, at his height, the boy had rid himself of the florid, bowdlerizing earnestness of his time, with its pieties and fripperies and oddities of punctuation. In fact, with one shrug, he pretty much had freed himself from the prevailing notion of poetry, which, however artfully, was finally written in the language of common sense. Meaning, at least on a basic level, that pretty much anybody could read and understand it, just as anybody could see what typically was all too evident. True, there were exceptions to the boy's harsh judgments—precious few, like Albert Mérat and Paul Verlaine. But otherwise, what was the *point*? the kid wondered. Where was the power and mystery? Who would ever want to be *that* kind of poet? An obvious poet. Really, a butler poet with white gloves holding a silver tray for the reader.

Never! Being a wild child, an immortal, he was more than ready to die for the cause. Which, being a kid, was to *revolutionize love and transform life*. In this great cause, he was elliptical and irrational. Dissonant. Obscurantic. Crazy. Throw in scatological, too. And so he was alone. Out of his mind *with* his mind. The Pied Piper had outrun even the rats.

Still more unsettling, the lad was a peasant savant, a hick, why, a *Belgian*, almost. Indeed, as Baudelaire had warned, "The over-egoed and over-arted Belgians are so civilized / They are sometimes syphilised."

And, worse, born to this bullheaded plough woman of no particular education. Odder still, there was the case of Arthur's brother, Frédéric, a virtual twin. Who, until almost the age of sixteen, the mother had dressed like a doll, just as she had Arthur—her two doily boys. Indeed the next year, when the Hedgehog and Otter begged to examine poor Frédéric's noggin, the mother summarily dismissed the idea—as preposterous, ridiculous.

"That one?" she said of her second son. "Don't waste your time. There is a muck fork in that boy's future."

*O*ur Arthur, then, was not only a bona fide miracle but *her* miracle, about whom she was—early on, at least—extraordinarily, if secretly, vain: that this boy of hers could be so brilliant; that of nothing she could produce something—amazing, even if it was of the testicular male subspecies. Pride, then. This was Mme. Rimbaud's sin of choice. And as a realist, she recognized it and suffered terribly because of it, and then in a way our age will never comprehend.

Pride was her weakness. And pride was precisely what she prayed against and confessed to, even as she hotly blew on it like a coal, into full and dangerous effulgence. Others knew of her outsized pride. Around Charleville her pride was legendary, second only to her ability to sense, and pounce upon, distress.

When trouble made its rounds, over the hill the unfortunate soon would see Mme. Rimbaud's black buggy. Before the gendarme and *le croque-mort*—the undertaker—before even the worm, she was the early bird.

A woman had to be alert, she said. To drunks being carted home. To public notices. To gendarmes at the door, to distressed crops, women weeping at the pawnshop, and the like. Obviously, unlike the males, she couldn't get her news at the various "troughs," the tavern and cafés.

And make no mistake: in her way, Mme. Rimbaud could be charming when she wanted to. Very, when money was involved, and especially with the desperate or blithely unsuspecting. The Rimbaud children would hear, "The Rivières are having trouble." Or still more vaguely, "There is trouble up the road—don't speak of it." Crossing herself. Actually shivering, lest she contract the human disease she most dreaded—failure.

And yet: she was a midwife of failure, Mme. Rimbaud. Made house calls, too. At the first whiff of bad news, she would tie her black bonnet into a big bow, then climb into her black gig. Spokes spinning, away she went, first to the *boulangerie* to pick up the *pain de campagne*—that resilient country loaf nested so fetchingly in a napkined basket in which the unsuspecting would find a pot of fresh butter and her pungent black cherry jam.

Odd thing, though. Cut loose from her children, Mme. Rimbaud was a woman set free on these strange excursions. Indeed, when the prize presented itself, she could be playful, shameless, even getting down on her knees to hypnotize a rooster.

Hush, children. Cluck-clucking, she flattens old Red in the dirt, sweetly jibbering the chickenish of sexy hen talk. Now observe: again and again she draws, before Red's crossed eyes, a line in the dirt. Line after line after line, until even her young audience grows sleepy. When—

"Voilà!"

Red rises, his comb a spastic asterisk. Sputters, crows, flaps, and quakes—this as his harem, pantaloons bouncing, dives beneath the chicken house. Hypnotizing Red, Mme. Rimbaud almost hypnotizes herself. Look at her, laughing with a gaggle of children. However briefly, some hidden school-mistress self appears; she experiences actual mirth, even pleasure, to the point that she must wipe her eyes. But of course the Rimbaud children never see this side of their mother, ever.

Once this bit of tomfoolery is over, it's back to business. She returns to her defeated neighbor crouched in the doorway, elbows squeezed between his knees. "Monsieur, save what you can, while you can," she says helpfully. "This will be your last chance."

When the rot is on the wheat and the pox is on the herd, who can argue with this? He can't. And even then, walking through house and barn, pointing at things, no sooner does she name her price than her captives, almost hypnotized, silently carry them to her gig. Then away, black horses! Away from this contagious house! Spit on a sou. Pull out a hair. Toss it over your left shoulder, snap the reins, and *never* look back.

And so, driving away in her overburdened gig, she would be clucking, thinking what a pity that "pauvre Arthur" in Africa did not have *her* as his partner—someone smart and tough. Heh. She'd make them pay up! Even the fat black king!

But now to have to *wait* upon Arthur's return from Africa—to be cast as the powerless old woman, this is beyond Christian; it is superhuman, unbearable. And with each week, towering and funneling up, her anger only grows. Indeed, the only thing greater is her dread at his impending return, blackening the skies like the locust clouds over Pharaoh's Egypt.

5 ∮ Old History

Worse, it all feels so familiar, bailing him out again. It takes Mme. Rimbaud back to the old days, his poet days, twenty years before, when for months at a time, perhaps forever—perhaps dead this time—he would run away to Paris. Back to the arms of Paul Verlaine, whose teenage wife, saddled with child and social humiliation, began to write to Mme. Rimbaud. Heart-wrenching letters. Scandalous letters, horrors beyond her comprehension. And yet, inevitably, six months or a year later, something would blow up and, like a homing pigeon, back the kid would come to Roche, always back, and then as blindly and arbitrarily as he had left. Often this would mean walking clear from Paris, some two hundred kilometers, traipsing from village to village and farm to farm with no money, no blanket, no kit. Nothing but his pencil and penknife and a soggy wad of paper upon which, toward sundown, a hunched-over boy rocking and murmuring and blowing into his hand wrote:

> *The Wolf Howled*
> *The wolf howled under the leaves*
> *And spit out the prettiest feathers*
> *Of his meal of fowl:*
> *Like him I consume myself.*
>
> *Lettuce and fruit*
> *Wait only to be picked;*

But the spider in the hedge
Eats only violets.

Let me sleep! Let me boil
On the altars of Solomon.
The froth runs down over the rust,
And mingles with the Kedron.

Well, one may say that poetry is pure thinking, or pure feeling, or memories recollected in tranquillity. But this was not merely thinking, feeling, or memory, much less tranquillity. It was, if anything, the search for invisibility, pure oblivion, as he hurled himself back to the blind fear of home.

Dogs barking. Moon in streams. For days he would barge headlong down deserted roads, resolutely *not* thinking, a will and a walker, a bum and a stalker, with his big, rough hands, burr-studded coat, and rumpled hat. Raiding fruit trees. Sucking eggs and sleeping in barns—running, walking, jerking off when necessary. *Keep going don't sleep don't stop.* Never stopping until at last his boots reached the roiling, silvery weeds of the river Meuse, dark-braiding, propulsive river, his home river, gleaming like a blade under the moon. The rocks were treacherously slippery and the water, especially in spring, was too fast and deep. Frantically, like a dog on scent, he turned left, then right, then clambered up the bank to the humped stone bridge, where for some time he could be seen, standing in the middle, peering down at the muscular black water, water unending sweeping beneath him, pure blind will, like a sheet of liquid iron.

Then, on the other side, dropping down the culvert, he fell into waist-high wheat, whirring burrs that scraped his coat, first wheat, then hoof-pocked, boot-sucking bottomland, until at last he saw the slate roof of the white house shining in the distance. Roche: wide, well-tended lanes of rye and hay and oats for which he, lord of no account, had never once lifted a finger.

He always came in past midnight, and each time was the same. The kitchen door was unlocked, and no sooner did he lift the latch than a raging, cored-out hunger drove him to the larder, there to wolf down half a ham, stale bread, raw eggs, even her preserves, a whole jar, pawed out as if by a starved bear. When, suddenly, he would wake up sickened, panicked like an overheated child who had spent the day playing, only to realize he had a *body*.

Not that *la vieille rombière* was fooled, *ever*, with her freak ears. At the sound of the floorboards creaking upstairs, groaning with the sodden weight of his ingratitude, one ear would perk up. It was almost reassuring. Exactly like the kid's father, years ago, when he would stumble home drunk.

*T*he next morning, however, the prodigal was masterful. Near noon, when he tumbled down the stairs, already the tension was such that he'd never left. Arrogant lout. Filling the doorway, he was larger than she remembered, the protuberant planes of his broad blond face now misshapen, as if his bones had outgrown his own skin. And the toll on him. Knuckles cut up. Bruises on his face. Clothes a shambles. Standing back, she realized that she was now frightened of him, much as he, too, was afraid—afraid she might try to strike him, in which case he'd have to break her stupid neck.

"*Bien*," she said with a sarcastic tremor, "we are back."

Icily, awaiting the onslaught, "That's right, Mother, I'm back."

"Well, I'm not supporting you. *No*."

"God." In a stagy voice he narrated his saga. "For days he walks home. To *her*. And yet when she first lays eyes on him, his own mother, what does she do but *threaten* him. God."

"You! Don't you dare turn your back to me, Arthur Rimbaud! Why did you return? Why? Don't touch that. What? Can I expect the gendarme this time?" Like barks, her questions followed him through the house, "So your pig friend, he threw you out? Eh?"

"I threw *myself* out."

"*Et voilà!*" How she adored being right. "Heh, even he didn't want you! And with that big brain of yours, what then did you think? That you would roll unannounced into *my* home? Your big brain, it told you that all this is *open* to you? Of course. Please, come in with your muddy boots. Please, put up your feet. Eat everything. Do nothing. Watch your mother slave for you, eh?"

Maybe he wanted this inquisition. Needed it. Perhaps in a sense he returned home to feel again, to be slapped awake. The chair honked back. Look. He was a giant, invulnerable; her words, her vituperation, her primitive fear, they slid right off him, like ice off a slate roof. No matter. Clear to his lair at the top of the house, she dogged him, while in the room below, his two sisters huddled in fear, hearing:

"What? You who refuses to work! You, with no prospects! Who just shows up here with your open jaws, uninvited!"

Slam.

Then she was slapping his door, beating it like a man's chest, her voice magnified by the narrow stairway. Barking, "How dare you? Do you know what Madame Verlaine writes to me, the awful things? Are you *insane*? I ask myself. *Possessed*? Do you know what she tells me while you cavort around Paris, you and that devil, stealing the food from her poor child's mouth! Do you know what the Church says about such—*arrangements*? That you are now abominable in God's eyes."

Vicious little prick. Suddenly, he snatched the door open, so she almost fell in. Then stood over her. "Go on, bloody *scream*, you old axe—you're good at that. And what about you? Do you think that you did not drive my father away? That he was not revolted at the sight of you?"

"Me? Your father abandoned *you*! All of you, with your endless squalling and needing! And you with the devil in his flesh! The *devil*, do you hear me?"

But this was too powerful, too close. As might have been predicted, the old woman reversed course. Fell to her knees, seized his fingers, hot tears running down her neck, begging, "Pray with me, *please*. Do you not see what I am doing for you, my child? That I would get down on my knees before you? Before God? Do you not see?"

"Get up!" He starts to drag her, then drops her; it is all he can do not to slug her, clinging to his legs, "Jesus—there's your man! A bloody corpse."

At this, again she flips, ripping and scratching at him. "Condemned before God! Does this mean nothing to you? Do you care how your little sister cries, always thinking you are dead? Do you care about the shame you heap down upon us? That the whole town laughs at you— laughs! The great genius. Just like his father, another big talker. And doing what in Paris? Used *comme un chiffon*, by an older man, *un chiffon!*"

Or maybe he returned to see how far he had fallen, that he might fall further, faster, more heedlessly. Damned was the plan. The plan was, there was no plan. Publication—but what on earth would that have proved? Or the university—the trough. The law? Even more ridiculous. In his new order, all laws would be abolished. A job? Never. He was a poet. Let the world pay.

Still, to be fair, he was then all of eighteen, a hormone-mad former *collégien* who, half the time, would give his poems away. Away like cooties, lest these hallucinations perish with him during these frightening periods when his cycloning brain would not desist and sleep refused to come.

Had he merely been consistently sullen and hateful, this would have been one thing for his poor mother, but of course he had no such coherence. Witness his sisters, both famished for him, starved for any male presence, as in their room he played the hero, the long-lost brother and confidant. Listen to them, thought Mme. Rimbaud, *laughing and having fun.* Never! She did not approve of males, even siblings, being in the rooms of young ladies. To hear their laughter. His casual male duplicity. That behind their doors he could act almost normal, putting on the Arthur Theater, as she called it. How the girls shrieked as he played the part of the train conductor flipping his lid at this kid, this ticket jumper rummaging through his pockets . . . *Ticket, my ticket, wait, wait! I know I have it.* Then, grabbing his own belt, theatrically, he hurls himself off the train, rolls across the floor, then comes to rest by their puckered, wide-eyed dolls, before whom he is just a kid laughing hysterically, his big red hands flopping. And from the other side of the room, his two sisters, the canaries in this air shaft, they stare at him in wonder—at his male power to shrug it off and leave without a second thought. To *leave.* Imagine that!

6 𝄢 Pilgrims

This was 1872, Rimbaud's eighteenth year, two years into his siege of the Muse. It was then that the first blow fell, at breakfast one morning when Vitalie coughed into her napkin, then shrieked. Blood, it was covered with a bright mist of blood, and when Mme. Rimbaud examined it, although she said nothing, she saw everything. It was Veronica's veil, perfect in every detail, the bloody visage of Christ who died on Calvary, the hair, the lips, and cored-out eyes of suffering. Hope did not blind her. She had no doubt what was coming.

There were of course mountain sanitariums and other places for consumptives, well-known places, good places, and certainly Mme. Rimbaud had the means to send her baby to such a place. But to avail herself of the usual recourses, this would have presumed that Mme. Rimbaud herself had the usual power to leave—that she was able to seek the help of other mortals, to change direction, even to hope.

Pas question. Home was the best cure. Open windows, cold air, camphor rubs, mustard plasters, and of course long bouts of prayer. This was the way, God's way, even as the girl, hacking and wheezing, began to expel leechlike spots, then bubbly white spots of lung foam, small caterpillars at which she would placidly stare, as if then they might move.

Vitalie knew, of course: the dead-to-be always know. Her body was in insurrection and she was leaving for heaven, and with an odd thrill she knew, devout girl that she was, that her mother knew that she knew. No secrets now. Why, everybody in Charleville knew. Pathetic, horrifying, to see Mme. Rimbaud firing one doctor, then another, helpless before the inevitable. And Arthur? As a male, naturally, he was absent for this part, though Mme. Rimbaud wrote to him her usual long, prayerfully disconnected letters. She wrote to him repeatedly, but at this point the two so-called roommates were in London, self-exiled and successively evicted, such that almost nothing reached him, not even through the normally reliable school chum channels.

But then late one night while praying, Mme. Rimbaud had a vision. It was a vision of Chartres, of a family pilgrimage to the great cathedral, a place of miracles built during the feverish outpouring of Mary worship that swept France in the late twelfth century.

The passion in those days, the fear. Death had ears and sickness had wings, and yet, miracle of miracles, in an ornate golden box the town of Chartres had—and don't ask how—Mary's tunic, her actual tunic seen by the actual eyes of Christ. And so from all across Europe, pilgrims and cripples and the blind and the dying, they all came to bask in its holy radiance. A wooden cathedral was built around it. The cathedral burned down, then a second, and when the tunic didn't perish in either fire, its survival was declared a miracle. And so on that blessed site, over fifty years amid ever-rising tides of darkness and evil, stone upon stone, the great cathedral rose, until it could be seen like a great Ark itself, beached on those vast level plains of hay and barley and oats. Fortunate thing, too, for the devils were so thick, the witches were so crafty, and sickness was so rampant that the poor, fleeing this plague, actually took to living in the church, they and their animals, all taking shelter in Mary's vast stone barn. In similar fashion, some six hundred years later, the Rimbaud women also sought shelter in the great cathedral of Chartres.

And so on the train two days later, after passing through Paris, when Mme. Rimbaud and her two daughters saw the great spires rising over the fields and trees, truly, as they gazed upon that massif of time-begrimed stone, for the first time in months Mme. Rimbaud felt unburdened, certain, even vindicated. Later, entering the church, the three women anointed themselves with holy water, then humbly entered the towering nave, frankly frightened at first even to look up, as if they might see the face of God.

Vast-echoing Goliath. Smelling of snuffed tapers and old hopes, the great cathedral was a hollowed-out man-made cave of light, a veritable mountain of gray limestone laboriously sawed into pieces, then reassembled into arches and domes and tall shields of stained glass, intricate jewels of red and clear and of a blue found, in all the world, only here. *Hail Mary, full of grace, the Lord is with thee, blessed art thou amongst women, and blessed is the fruit of thy womb, Jesus.*

Long dresses gliding over the massive, foot-polished stones, through forests of columns, the three Rimbaud women thrilled to feel so small, to be *specks*! To add their voices to this ceaseless, surflike echolalia of voices—lives flying up to God!

No longer were the Rimbaud women oddball hermits, not now. By trains and omnibuses, by wagons and on foot, pilgrims by the dozens—whole legions of the faithful, rich and poor alike—kept arriving, and in every nook, there were confessions, and in the side chapels, there were Masses for the dead, and everywhere it seemed there were votive candles to light, holy flames of blue and red, touched to life with slender tapers. Look, there were saints' statues to kiss and, they heard, remnants of the Holy Cross. Imagine, *tiny splinters of the actual Cross!* But happiest of all, for Mme. Rimbaud, there was Mary's tunic, which had protected the Virgin, she was convinced, from the prowling hands of her husband, Joseph. Who, even if he was the good simpleton carpenter they claimed, was nonetheless a man. So it seemed to Mme. Rimbaud.

Still, she could go only so long distracting herself with such thoughts, numbing herself with these prayers that God would not answer, waiting in vain for the soft, warm rain of fresh belief. Any belief that could defy a word like *consumption*. Ach, these lying doctors, these useless priests.

Belief, failed belief, this was what crushed Mme. Rimbaud—belief, betrayal, and now her anger, that after all her offices and prayers and good works, that even so, her baby would be taken from her, just as her son, once her hope, was surely bound for hell. Failure then. She was an utter failure, she knew this now. Failure was her prayer. She was a failure as a mother, a failure as a wife, and a failure as a woman. *I am a failure, a failure, a failure.* But lo, as she shuddered and wept into her folded hands, down it fell finally, a single feather of mercy, twirling down from the stars, whitely down a million miles from the kingdom of heaven. And when she actually looked *up*, for the first time in months, she felt hopeful, even forgiven, light, almost happy, as she stuffed money into all the sick and poor boxes. And so one after another, as to a bath, she and the girls, they all went to confession. But once inside the confessional the size of a coffin, once shut up in that airless abattoir of sin, stinking with sweat and fear—*zip*, the black screen opened before Mme. Rimbaud's frozen eyes. Exposed, she shrank in fear, desperate to ask the priest, this candlelit silhouette, the terrible question that now weighed on her.

"Father, I made my confession yesterday. I talked about my poor daughter who is sick—don't ask, please. But you see today—*today*, Father, I come to you about my son, my youngest son, because perhaps *he's* the problem. I mean, if he's the reason this awful thing has happened to my daughter." She paused a moment, licking her lips. "I know this sounds crazy, Father . . . but I came to ask . . . well, how would one *know* if one's own child is demonically possessed?"

The shadow flickered; she could almost see his eyes, two somber ovals, like bloody tears, in the darkness. "Madame," replied the priest, "you mean, then, that your son spits, fights, raves, curses God?"

Garlic—she could smell him, his breath, his armpits, his maleness. "Father, he fights *me*. And he hates God, hates him. Yes, even at fifteen he refused to go with us to church. It was then that he started writing on the walls, the village walls. Writing *things*, Father, vile things, even on the walls of the church, slanders against God. And now, Father, he runs away to Paris, living . . . with a *man*. Openly, do you hear me? An older man—in unspeakable sin, if you can understand me."

The darkness ruminated. "And where is his father?"

"Oh, his father, he is away, away with the army in Africa." Although a hysteric and a chronic exaggerator, Mme. Rimbaud was not a liar. And yet an irresistible fancy bloomed in her mind. "Because you see, Capitaine Rimbaud, my good husband, defending our colonies against the Mussulmans, against fanatics—well, at such distance he is powerless to help us. Oh, he tries. He sends us letters, money. It wounds him to his heart. But he is a patriot, Father, so he is away, always away. In Africa, as I say. Algeria, I think. Someplace like that."

Would the priest not catch her in this awful lie? For after all, closeted with God, as he was, wouldn't the priest just . . . *know?* Finally, after a long pause, the priest said carefully, "Yes, children do terrible things, ridiculous things. But possession is exceedingly rare. Rather, Madame, I think you need to pray with me today. *Persévérez dans la foi,* this is what you need, my child. More faith is what is needed here."

"*La foi?*" She hissed through the jewel-like perforations of the screen. She was outraged! The presumption, that he could be so deaf and so disparaging of her sex—a woman starved and he tells her, in effect, to *eat faith.* "But, Father, I have broken my *knees* for God; I have given Him my last *heave.* How can you tell me this, that I, of all people—that *I* need faith! Yes, and a pair of angel's wings, too! Father whatever-your-name-is, come now, do you think that a woman would ever just *sit* in there, as you do now? That a woman would just *sit* there on her little throne and tell a *mother* such utter nonsense? You who have never been a parent! You, on your high horse! Why, a woman would make a better priest *any* day."

Here they were at Saturday vespers, and within two minutes, God's own emissary was rapping on the confessional, his mouth hard against the screen, hissing, "Madame, mind your tongue. And listen to you, speaking heresy, suggesting that women should be priests, while here you bitterly complain of your son's heresy. And in Chartres, Madame! Of all places! To pick a fight with *me?* Ah well, Madame whatever-your-name-is, I think the bad apple does not fall far from the tree, eh? *Ehhhh?*"

She slapped the confessional. The maternal rebel ran outside, Eve expelled without Adam into the evening light, out into the courtyard. There she was, in the strange shadows of the dragonlike flying buttresses, looking at her almost murderous hands, then at the barn swallows twittering, sweeping the skies for mosquitoes—mere birds! *Les hirondelles sont hautes*—the swallows are so high—good weather, never better . . . such small, such stupid things. The ants and beetles beneath her feet, even that dog loping down the drive, all *living* when here her own flesh was dying, dying! Then she heard footsteps. It was Vitalie, doomed and now right behind her, skinny as a stray.

"Maman, are you all right?"

"Leave me, please." And looking up, she said audibly to God, to the Deaf One in the sky, arrogant *man*, "Do you see? Do you see this? Must my children chase me? Must everyone ask of me *everything*?"

"Maman," cried the girl, frightened. "Maman, what is the matter?"

But her mother charged off, weeping. And damned beyond even anger, Mme. Rimbaud was what she never was—beaten and now ashamed.

*B*ut then that night, in all the annals of faith, truly, an amazing thing occurred. In those days, there were no hotels, so they slept in a lady's house, a very nice lady and, one might have thought, the last decent woman left in all the world. This was Mme. Isambert, an elderly widow of noble mien serving in the rectory. Here clearly was a woman who had suffered—as on the Cross—the seasick pounding of the marital bed, the drunken, often disappearing husband, and the ungrateful children. And so, late into the night, in hushed whispers, Mme. Isambert talked to Mme. Rimbaud, as women do, about this death of which she had spoken to no one except the priest. The good lady listened, and to Mme. Rimbaud's amazement, she actually heard herself talking, openly talking, woman to woman, even about her deepest shame—her youngest son.

"I fear I have raised the devil. Do you think I exaggerate? We live in shame. Even in Paris he is infamous, living like a wild animal. Worse." Grief, she muzzled it like a sneeze, pinching her lips.

"But Madame Rimbaud," whispered Mme. Isambert, "you cannot let him sap all your energy, your peace—not now. Madame, God's arms are but weeks away from holding your daughter. You can't help your son now—no. All your energy, your womanly self-control, your love, all this must go to your daughter. To her, and her only."

Ravaging day! In the snake pit of Charleville, it would have been inconceivable for Mme. Rimbaud to quietly receive or accept such sensible advice, to hear the gentle voice of reason, leading her like a horse from the burning barn of her life. Mme. Isambert asked her, "Do you remember the story of the daughter of Jairus? The daughter whom Jesus raised from the dead? Just so in unblemished white garments he will raise your own daughter. Do not give up. As for your troubled son, he is but what? Twenty? Twenty-one? Yes, he may seem to have no heart, a dead heart. Yes, he is selfish—as all boys are at that age. And yes, you must be realistic, of course, but you also must be hopeful and of good cheer—he cannot remain so forever, and time is on your side. Not until thirty are men truly lost."

Lost! Was over never over? she thought, swollen-eyed. Was enough never enough? And just as his job was to foul up, it was hers to clean up after him. Perfect, she thought, they were complete.

7 ♭ Abandon Ship

"Monsieur, wake up, the men are here for you! Everybody! Do you not hear me? *Crowds.*"

Downstairs, a door slams. Then Rimbaud hears the slap of sandals, swift, light feet coming up the stairs. And here he is, a young black man in white robes—blinding in the early sun. In the red sun, even the twizzly filaments of his young beard ignite. It is his servant, Djami, late, when he is virtually never late. So begins Rimbaud's final day in Harar. Behind the sun, behind schedule—behind. Rimbaud shoots up.

"Good God, it is half past six! What are you up to? Why are you so late?"

"My child, Monsieur. He is sick. Fever—very sick."

"Sick," repeats Rimbaud, for it is obvious that Djami, who never lies, is lying. And here it comes, what they have been arguing over, bitterly, for the past two days.

"Monsieur," says Djami, leaning down, "today no good. No good today. No go. Too dangerous. The *frangi*, he will be killed. This is what they whisper, Monsieur. This is what the people say."

"Nonsense, there is no bad or good or better day. Now, up. Help me up."

"But, Monsieur," says Djami, gesticulating, "don't you hear? Crowds, I tell you. The camel men and gunmen. All arguing, because they can smell the money. Bad day, bad day. I swear to you, before this day is over, somebody will be shot."

"Djami, listen to me," says Rimbaud in that ever-calm, hypnotizing, implicitly threatening way that, unfortunately, the white traveler soon picks up in such places. "Have you loaded Desta? *Inside* the warehouse? As I instructed? Out of sight? Did you?"

Sure-footed Desta. Right now she is the richest camel in East Africa, saddled with the bulk of Rimbaud's gold hoard: primitively cast gold bars, Maria Theresa doubloons, and small tapering ingots crudely struck, like glowing nails.

"And *you* loaded her," hectors Rimbaud, "you alone?" Tone, here it is all in the tone. Here a man survives through tone, which is to say, in an endless play, he *acts*.

"Yes," says Djami, emphasis added. "*As I told you.* Only me, *as you said.*"

Rimbaud has trained Djami to issue quick, precise reports, and the young man is now multilingual, whip smart, albeit with strange translational notes. And now, to Rimbaud's infinite pride, Djami at twenty is a man, married, with a beautiful wife and a son of almost one year. And to those who will wonder (thinking perhaps of Lord Byron's lewd romps with dark pony-haired boys in Albania and Greece), without being naïve, the answer is no. Oh, in Rimbaud's early, strangely public sexual life, when as part of his poetic program to reach the Unknown he was undergoing a "rational derangement of all the senses," yes, of course. This is not to say he would never again do such a thing—of course he could, why not? But here? Never, and the reason is as much a fundamental shift in Rimbaud's psyche as it is purely a matter of survival. In Abyssinia, if one were discovered, there could be howling mobs, even stoning in the heat of the moment. But perhaps more to the point, sexually he is a chameleon, an opportunist, and this is not the time nor the place. Different man, different situation.

Djami hauls him up by the shoulders.

"I *am* up." Shoving down his arms. "Easy. God."

An orphan, Djami—his mother dead in childbirth, his father of some fever, and his siblings scattered fish in a general sea of catastrophe. Six years ago, when Rimbaud found him, Djami had been a street urchin running with a pack of boys, dusty-haired "nothing boys" one step removed from the equally ownerless dogs. But this boy, Rimbaud saw, this one was different: impertinent, as all street boys are, but genuinely observant, almost prescient, with a rare zeal for detail. Devoted and, better yet, discreet. Trustworthy, too. Like a barnacle, the boy attached himself to Rimbaud, and he was quick to read once Rimbaud taught him, and then with a pleasure and a degree of patience that surprised him in a street boy. Caught right on, just as he did when Rimbaud trained him to load camels and read ledgers, to use mental arithmetic and value goods— above all, to ferret out the truth in this land of grinning, stalling liars. Moreover, in a land where the whole idea was to drag things out— negotiations, payments, and, above all, leaving—Rimbaud had taught his protégé to get to the bloody *point.*

"No," insists Rimbaud, hobbling, as Djami nudges the brass chamber pot into place. "Later. Later, do you hear me? I need to bloody *leave.*"

"No," insists Djami, waving his supple index finger as they do. "Do you want the people to see you in this way? On your last day? Do you?"

God watched. This is how Rimbaud thinks of the native men, as moral creatures and especially when it comes to their natural functions. Hot shame. The way the dark men will summarily lift their robes, then squat, without a thought, to urinate in the streets. Beneath the all-seeing gaze of Allah, the Muslim men are forever purifying themselves, horrified to dribble so much as a drop on their faultless robes. Any stain. Squatting, they will take little flecks of mud or rock like burning coals and daub these chalky fragments on their members, blot it up, even a drip, while floating above, like a vast and milky eye in the rising wind, Allah, the all-seeing, Allah hovers like those great-winged birds the kites. And so five times a day they pray. Why, once under threat of attack, Rimbaud's Abyssinian party dropped their guns and readied their prayer carpets. "Do you want to pray or die?" asked Rimbaud. The men stared at the *frangi* in incomprehension. Pray, but of course.

Dribble tinkles brass. "Lovely," mumbles Rimbaud, as hot droplets spatter his bare toes and Djami's, too. "What a memory, huh?"

"No shame, Monsieur, never with me."

Rimbaud half grins. "Allah won't mind today? You're sure?"

This coaxes a smile from Djami. "Not today. *Rabbina yusahhil*, May the Lord make things easy."

Yet the truth is, Djami is furiously angry, shamed and humiliated at Rimbaud's iron refusal to take him with the caravan. Angry that this man, like a father to him, should leave him "soiled like a woman."

"Soiled," his exact word, and it carries a history.

Six months before, Rimbaud had done essentially the same to the young Harari woman who—to his way of thinking, anyhow—had gotten him into this mess. Woman, concubine, intended wife, the girl, named Tigist, is now seventeen, perhaps eighteen as best they can calculate such things here—in any case, far too old to marry. Besides, Tigist's most precious commodity as a young woman, her virginity, this has been stolen by him. Even as he tossed her away.

Beautiful, too. The Spice Woman, this Tigist, she is *the* girl—truly, a flower sprung in the mud. And if you are a man, you can bet she knows that *you* know how beautiful she is. For from all across Africa, from thousands of miles away, men come to Harar to see such girls as Tigist.

Of girls like Tigist songs are written. Around braziers—sparks whisking up into the night—the laughing caravan men, rolling on their haunches, mold their hands to suggest her volumes and movements, the gripping, man-stripping wriggle, when the Harari girl climbs you, oh boy, like a monkey on a tree.

Blended from Arabs and Negroes, and Turks, French, Italians, English, and Greeks, these Harari girls, they are born of everyone and everyplace, with smooth, tea-colored skin, thin noses, and clear, shining eyes—eyes of a pale brown, almost blue. Between, actually. The color *between*.

White teeth, too. Owing to the water, it is said: sweet, sand-washed, free-flowing water, not—according to Djami—the dirty water from the iron rocks, which gives the girls in some nearby villages, even some quite beautiful girls, the brown donkey teeth. Never in Harar.

Forearms with nut brown skin—skin drawn with spiraling henna tattoos, like fine netting, to snare the merchants and big buyers with the bags of money tied under their tunics. Such is Spice Woman's job, her spidery, charming specialty—men. Every type of man, too.

It was with this woman, girl woman, this dark-haired Harari, this Tigist, that Rimbaud made the first of many fatal, and frankly foolish, miscalculations. It began with the idea of taking the girl, any girl, into his house, and it continued with the even more fantastically stupid idea of keeping Tigist and Djami, two teens under the same roof, to quarrel endlessly over how tea was to be served and laundry pressed and who could say what to the cook. And Rimbaud was actually surprised! It was the kind of thing that made his *frangi* colleagues pound the tables, laughing until the tears ran down their cheeks—his daft and utter *surprise*. That Rimbaud!

The outcome, then, was as loud and messy as it was predictable. Yet here, when he had been warned repeatedly—by Djami, by his European comrades, and, above all, by the killing looks he got on the street—here he was, a man in his thirties, moony as a seventeen-year-old over the girl. Mad in a way.

And why now? This was the other question everyone asked. For here in a town legendary for its beautiful women, for years he had virtually never looked at women other than whores, never until that day in the market when the Spice Woman wiped cardamom on her brown wrist, blinked her pool-dark eyes, then held her beautiful, bespangled wrist out to him. Smiled and said, "Smell, yes. You smell. Smell good, yes?"

Little flirt. Except for with the town whores, he had no practice or knack with women. Feeling sick, actually frightened, what with the heat and his sweating, he feared that he smelled. Heartsick, he left, slunk off only to sneak back the next day, braving dirty looks from the girl's mother and the usual phalanx of aunts guarding their prize, staked like a goat in the bazaar.

But the real shocker came three weeks later, when Rimbaud, now filled with passion and purpose, picked up his lever-action Winchester, called Djami, then, gun draped over his shoulder, marched to the girl's house to bargain with her father. Poor Djami came along to translate. Or rather, since Rimbaud spoke the language almost perfectly, to confer on what was *really* being said, as negotiations spun into three mad nights. It was entertainment. Breaking off. Walking off. Called back— was the girl a rug to be sold? Nights of men wildly gesticulating, the dodging father, the silent brothers, the obnoxious uncles, even the neighbors and various menacing cousins who hung around outside with their daggers and long pistols and muskets. One always knew when the deal was about to crescendo. For then, fanning a brazier of red coals, a barefoot slave girl would start the dreaded coffee ceremony, sprinkling on the sharp, woody incense that sent up choking clouds of smoke— smoke that even drove out the flies as Rimbaud stood in the doorway, coughing and runny-eyed.

As Rimbaud soon divined, however, it was not the men who ran the show. No, it was the women listening in the next room, cackling and second-guessing and muzzling the girl, squeaking with disbelief as she heard her price soar higher and higher—a record! And yet in all those days, never once did Rimbaud see his intended, or any other woman, for that matter. Never in a strict Muslim house.

Finally, though, after yet another phony walkout, a deal was struck, but at appalling cost. Mortifying, really. In one fell swoop, Rimbaud had all but destabilized the local economy. Five hundred francs! A thousand, some said. Outrageous, groused the Europeans, that these people, these thieves actually thought they could get away with this. And did. And all thanks to randy Rimbaud.

But there was another reason Rimbaud had paid this premium on top of the ransom, and this was the untidy fact that he stubbornly refused to marry the girl—or not now, or not just yet. The *frangi*'s stalling, this was the true source of the upset now shared by the family, the well women, and the town. Arrogant *frangi*! Dishonoring the girl and her family, and here when he had promised. Promised upon his honor to marry her.

Later, he said. In a few months. By Ramadan certainly—soon.

*A*nd then what? They had a year together, half of it over the moon, that is, until the marriage issue became intolerable. But it wasn't merely the idea of marriage. It was the notion of permanence. Or really the presumption, the burden, of love, meaning weakness and what weakness said—any weakness—in a very dangerous place. Not to mention what Rimbaud's mother and sister would say, thinking their Arthur had married the devil and the night. Stalling, Rimbaud came up with a million reasons, but really, for the once freethinker, marriage was only the pretext for something still larger boiling up in him, until summarily and inexplicably—and then in utter rout and panic—Rimbaud told her one night: *Out.*

All lovers fight so there was no lead-up, or certainly nothing like this. All at once Rimbaud told her this, then stood there frozen, thinking he deserved it as she screamed and wailed and broke things. At which point, feigning calm as she lay immobilized and trembling with rage in bed, he gathered up her belongings. Then early the next morning, he packed her off, humiliated, with a group of armed hirelings—home with yet more money in an attempt to appease her family's wrath, with honor certain to be avenged.

Newspapers, even if they had any, couldn't have spread the news any faster. Immediately, all that more temperate minds had tried to forestall, especially in the *frangi* mercantile community, down it all poured upon the faux groom. He had the girl's family making threats and sharpening their spears against him. He had the howls of his comrades, solid businessmen—the very men who had worked so hard to gain the town's trust—all painted now as *frangi* dogs, liars, unbelievers. And of course he had the women by the well, still waiting for justice below his blighted establishment.

And so, later, when the well women heard about his sick leg, that "stinking goat" hanging off his body, at this news there was great glee, for in fact it explained everything. A jinn in the *frangi*'s house, one set loose by the girl, had poisoned the leg with all the backed-up man venom. And it was so big! Why, the leg was swollen to the size of a water udder. As for his puny middle leg, it was limp. Limp! laughed the date woman, holding up one little finger.

Smacking wash and spitting seeds, so said the women at the well.

*A*nd so the night before, in that final frenzy of packing and binding, tossing and deciding, all around the house Djami had followed Rimbaud, twisting on his crooked crutch. Look at Djami now, the insolence of him! Peering around Rimbaud, he stares into his face, as the master tries to look away:

"What is that word?" demands Djami, waving that finger as they do. "That word you use? *Expend—Ex—Expend—?*"

"Ex-pend-a-ble."

"Exactly! This is all I am to you now. Nothing. Not even!"

"Oh, good heavens. Don't be so dramatic."

"No, expendable. Oh, when you are done, for you then it is, *Go!* I have no further use for you. And this is *you*." Making his point, he slaps his hands back and forth. Washed of you—done.

Rimbaud spins around.

"*You* expendable? Good God, *I* am the one who is expendable here. Must I have you, too—my only family—tormenting me?"

"Family! Do not insult me, saying we are family! Now you lie, Rinbo! Lie to the girl, lie to her family, to me, to everyone—lie. This is what you do."

Look at Rimbaud now, red-faced and humiliated—so vain about his good name and reputation, his iron word. Shooting back, "You see my leg. You *see*. You know as well as I do that my chances out there are not good. Bad, in fact. So what am I to do? Throw your life away as well? Or have you taken a slave—beggar your wife, and leave your son an orphan? As you were? Would that not be the ultimate selfishness?"

"*That* Allah will decide, Rimbaud. Not you, not me."

Willfully his employer absorbs himself in another pile of papers. Receipts. Contracts. Keep, keep. Burn. Then, feeling more in control, softening, Rimbaud says in that lofty thespian manner required, and indeed expected, of the *frangi*, "You know, old friend, some people might say I was doing you a service."

"Service!" At this Djami blows up. "I who *stood* for you. Stood for you. Answered for you against the people. Many people. Who protected you, many times, with my *life*, and now I cannot go with you? You know how my world works, you *know*. For me to stay behind, I am a woman, dung—lower even. I have no honor. And when you leave me, I may be killed anyway, throat slit like a goat. All because of *you*. People angry with *you*. And all you must *do*, Rinbo, is what you can never do. *Ask*, that is all, *ask*."

8 ♪ Bad Day

Something breaks in Djami that last morning, before they face the mob now gathered in the square below. There can be no pretending, not now. Rimbaud will never return, and this will come to no good end. Things should be said, honest things, heartfelt things, but there is no time, thank God. And so in silence Djami straps around Rimbaud's thinning waist a corset of gold, four kilos' worth, enough to slow a bullet or endow a village—gold, more dangerous here than dynamite.

The sagging vest is like a pair of lungs with armholes; it is heavier than life, this corset of gold bars. But this weight that he feels, it is not because of what this small fortune *represents*, or even the years that it might purchase. Nor is it because of the years of suffering, penury, and odiousness that it took to amass his hoard, such as it is.

No, what stops Rimbaud cold is the terror of losing it all—of losing it at the last possible moment. Of being pulled down, like a wildebeest, and just when he is on the verge of hope.

Hope is the wound, he realizes. Of all people and at the worst possible time, he, Arthur Rimbaud, realist, scientist, cynic, is actually suffering from hope. Despite everything, he hopes.

Well, he bluffs himself, buckling on this vest of gold. No one will take it without a fight. For inside this muscular gold cuirass he stuffs a .32 revolver. Then, in his right boot, in case of capture, a two-shot derringer, once in the head for a speedy exit. While alive, however, there are other remedies. For reaching under the bed, Djami hands him a double-barrel 10-gauge shotgun, a bludgeon of Damascus steel loaded with 00 buckshot. Nine balls fat as hailstones. Nine in one blast—enough to bury a charging lion.

God, however—Allah, or Jesus of the Ascension, that heavenly swimmer doing a slow crawl in the clouds above—*He* is not impressed. These peashooters don't change the facts about Rimbaud's left leg, black and blue and bloated. Take a whiff. There's no hiding it. Hunkered down in the scorched grass, Mme. Hyena and her clan will sniff him out. *Here you are meat and to meat you will return.*

The door bursts open.

Downstairs, in their white uniforms and fezzes, three Egyptian sentries, his part-time hirelings, jump up as a fourth, hoping for a *baksheesh*, a tip, charges up the stairs. The Egyptian seizes an elbow, then attempts, fool, to relieve the erstwhile poet of his gun.

"I've got it," he barks, hanging on his one crutch.

"Heavy, you heavy," says the Egyptian, with a runny smile.

"Rot. Pay attention."

Teetering on the rafters above, pigeons peer down while below, in the early cool, rises the not entirely unpleasant stench of commerce: bare earth, dry-rotted leather, and spilled spices kneaded by hundreds of bare feet to the consistency of some yeasty kind of cheese. A. Rimbaud Ltd., what is left of it. Bags of coffee. Kegs of bullets. Elephant tusks. Ten years—all junk now. Look at it. Stinking stacks of half-cured hides. Pots and trinkets. Even a box of cheap missals. And stacked in boxes, piled almost to the ceiling, is his principal stock in trade—smuggled Remington rolling-block rifles, bought, most of them, for Menelik the king. Old and outmoded, said items (in the manifest) are castoffs from various European armories smeared with thick protective grease and wrapped in oozing brown paper, which the heat has curdled to a kind of vile-smelling molasses. Purchased at auction by his agent in France in lots of a hundred, seventy-five francs each. The poet then sells them for around two hundred and twenty francs. Why, almost a threefold markup. Assuming, of course, that one actually gets paid. Or not eaten alive by arbitrary taxes imposed by the king via minor sub-lieutenants. Well, good riddance, he thinks. Have at it, weevils.

It's like a hanging. Rimbaud can hear the crowd outside, waiting to see his face in his hour of shame. And so, sick to his stomach, with a practiced recklessness, he raises the gun, hits the door with the heel of his hand, and lurches out defiantly. And for one eternal second—silence.

Three hundred pairs of eyes, all riveted on him.

Blue black in white robes with oiled hair, the warriors are waiting, muscular twists of men bristling with spears and daggers and some with brass-tattooed muskets. Glazed eyes. Impassive lips. And in every cheek fat lumps of the narcotic *khat*s, bright, tiny, woozy-making leaves of an alarming green.

Zip. Zip zip.

Armed loiterers, these warriors—they have wives and beasts to do all the work. All that moves are their horsehair fly whips—zip—over shoulders. Zip zip, go the frog-tongued whips of these casual tribal murderers and herders of women, warriors, if you'll notice, with strips of leather hanging off their knife hilts, each commemorating an enemy killed. Raiding or waiting to be raided—fighting the rival's increase—this is the warrior's work, and night after night it continues, this eternal murder game of snatch the bacon. No killing, no honor. No honor, no woman. And until you kill and castrate an enemy, steal his stock, rape his wife, and slaughter or enslave his family—until then you are a woman, without even the honor necessary to *have* a woman. And so, wails and fires in the night. The Issa, the Itu and Galla, the Asaimara and the Aroussis, the Ogadines. We are the mighty, the many. We are everything and they are nothing. Spears in the night.

Zip. Zip zip.

Hanging on his one crutch, balancing the shotgun, Rimbaud can feel the gold vest burning his guts, molten gold, as if he has swallowed the sun. For right now, as he well knows, each warrior is wondering exactly the same thing, namely, where his gold is, and how much the *frangi* has, and which man will get it. Slaughter him in the road. Snatch out his balls like two eyes, void him, then strip him like a goat. And yet the men sit, as always, blank and glassy-eyed, hateful and dazzled before the *frangi*. *Later.* Nighttime is their time.

But day. Daytime is for beggars, and it is the beggars who now mount the attack. A starving crowd on the heels of a famine, this is an angry crowd, and when it starts, it sounds like the tearing of a sheet. Rich *frangi*. Fat-bellied *frangi*. Like rain in a puddle, they dance their triumphant crowd dance, a jostling, poisonous, hand-flipping gimme-gimme dance, shouting: "You, you, you! *Frangi!* . . . *Frangi* now. You! Now me! Me!"

By the dozens, they crowd up, stick-armed men and cricket-voiced widows—women squeezing empty breasts or holding forth wailing, runny-nosed, swollen-bellied babies. And most frightening of all, pot-bellied children with white starvation hair and hands like small shrunken gloves. Clawing at him.

"You, you, you—"

"Off!" he hollers, brandishing the shotgun, "Off of me—"

Boom!

A rifle goes off, two, then three, and here they come. Tunics blow-ing, criss-crossed with bandoliers and daggers, it's Farik's men, *his* men, Somalis, Sudanese, Arabs—jackals for hire, wild men with pistols and rifles, long spears and the heavy, curved Danakil daggers. Horses stamp-ing into the crowd, his gunmen raise the dust, a hot, worn-out, dung-laden dust that cauterizes the nostrils, like the stench of a snuffed match. *Boom!* Spears lower and swords rise. *Boom! Boom!* That second volley scatters them. When, out of the melee, like some lost Roman legion, here come his carriers, big, tall, dusty men—Oromo, big, strong men, four teams of four. This part he has planned with his usual logistical meticulousness, down to the last bullet and bag of feed for the horses.

"Go! Go now!" cries Rimbaud, raising the brute shotgun. "Double wages today. But only if we go now. *Now*, goddamnit, do you hear me?"

In this momentary lull, pushing them back, Djami grasps his hands, then lowers him onto the waiting stretcher, a length of canvas stretched between ridgepoles—adapted, in fact, from one of those seemingly insane construction manuals that the poet had inveigled his penurious mother to purchase for him. Lying on his back, level with the dusty feet of the mob, Rimbaud is now as helpless as an overturned tortoise. When—with a heave—he is launched. The porters hoist him skyward, up like a flag, sixty-two kilos of meat such that he is camel high. Eye to eye, in fact. For *look.*

Before him now, craning over the crowds, the camel's eye is goblet-sized, jet black and edged with dark, blubbery creases, like India rubber. And before the animal even hears the whip on its rump, the great eye contracts, disgorging one salty tear—one sip for the thirsty green fly that fastens on it, hot, like a spark. And *look*.

More flies. Bottle blue, black blue, green blue. Particles of life.

Then the flies are two swarms, two whirling balls. Like lungs, he thinks. Breathing, almost. Like a concertina. No, a corset, a black corset of flies, was it? Hadn't he thought this, dreamed this, written this once?

For suddenly life is taking, even for the apostate poet, a spectacularly strange turn. Seeing again. That's it—*seeing*, such as he hasn't seen in years, back to his runaway days, a dirty child raiding the treasure house that God left unlocked. Days of light and storm when, high above, clouds coiled and spoke and limbs crashed and leaves blew white—then shot away, like bats! Cold and darkness coming. Then, coldest of all, that windy, hair-raising excitement, the sudden zero of writing. Writing—*you*, my willed and willing disaster, my storm. Writing, you be my coat. My war, my faith. My only command.

Bitten-down nails. Moving lips. When he wrote—that is, when life yanked him hard by the hair—he always moved his lips, mumbling and murmuring to himself. Trees shook and shone like ice. Leaves struck his nose and electricity seized his hair, until he felt like a candle, a very blown-down candle, to the point that he forgot his own hunger as the wind commanded, *Write more.* So, opening a rusty penknife, he whittled his already whittled-down pencil stub. Then, trembling, moved it over the dirty paper, then covered it with his body as the rain splattered down, walloping hot pellets that lashed his back and ran down his nose. And camped over himself, over words like hot food, he pushed and pushed the pencil, until suddenly it stopped: literally stopped, and he dared not look or speak.

"Monsieur!" comes the voice that breaks him from this reverie. It's Djami. Shading his eyes, Djami is pointing across the street.

"Monsieur, don't you see? Look. It is Monsieur Bardey! All the *frangis*. See? They come to see you go."

9 ♪ The Poet Who Didn't Know It

A proper send-off it is, too. For across the road, Rimbaud sees a very welcome sight. In his freshly stropped boots, tweeds, and tie, it's Bardey, the so-called lord mayor of Harar. It's Bardey and the "chaps," his confreres, a dozen or more all turned out, having drunk all night to fuel themselves for Rimbaud's not-so-fond bon voyage. And all of them, to a man, are now blocked—blocked rather conveniently—by the rising headwaters of the mob. Thank God. How men dread good-byes.

"A proper send-off," Bardey had told the chaps earlier. "I mean, after ten years, the least we can do is bloody see him off."

As Rimbaud's employer, benefactor, and frequent apologist, Bardey is perfect in the role of the father-wise, merchant-diplomat savior, and not just for Rimbaud but for a whole host of castoffs from Europe and America, why even one poor fool, a cowboy soon deceased, who had arrived sporting an American Stetson hat and twin six-guns. In the case of Rimbaud, most observers would have said that Bardey was heaven-sent, his deus ex machina—when, for example, the rash Rimbaud royally pissed off the king. Or again, when he, a white man, struck a black man, the sort of thing that easily could have triggered an honor killing. But just what *has* rubbed off? What exactly has Rimbaud learned in ten long years in this country? This remains unclear.

One thing is for sure, though. Save for Cecil Rhodes with his diamonds, Alfred Bardey is the best cared-for chap in Africa: best fed, best rested, best turned out, and far and away best manicured in his Van Dyke beard and Panama hat. Bald but nobly so, with two slick curls that twirl, Disraeli-like, around his small, white ears.

Never ruffled. Never in a bad temper. Never—almost—on the losing end. Even more unnerving, while all others stomp about drenched in the heat, the fellow never seems to break a sweat. Then again, why should he, with two handsome mistresses on either end of town, not to mention an unquestioning wife very nicely set up in Mayfair. No sir, no clap for Mr. Bardey! His life is one vast tent pole, all set up for him, wherever he goes. One does not see Mr. Bardey slouching and sneaking (unlike Rimbaud) into the town's two bordellos. And equally unlike Rimbaud, Bardey takes regular annual holidays. By contrast, in his ten years here, the poet has set a world submersion record. Except for a brief trip to Cairo, never once in that time has he approached the fires of European civilization. And for several interminable years before this time, he rusticated in Crete as a troubled construction foreman, then in Aden as an ill-paid clerk. In short, serving an apprenticeship to nowhere—that is, until Bardey gave him a go.

In fact, it was Bardey who, one year ago, had heard (quite accidentally from a traveler) about Rimbaud's growing and indeed extraordinary poetical reputation, then taking shape in Paris. As Rimbaud was all too well aware, he was already something of a legend, the subject of rumor, fantasy, and ridiculous speculation, and yet far from being flattered, he found it all tremendously *irritating*. Had he *asked* to be published? Had it ever been his *aim* to be famous? Had he ever *cared* what people thought? And so when Bardey asked him about these reports, Rimbaud did not deny them. He just refused to discuss the matter. Fame. Poetry. Any of it.

"Oh please," the once-poet protested. "Every French boy *writes*. Let us not waste our time with seventeen's frothings."

"Slops," "frothings," "inanities"—Rimbaud utterly rejected his literary leftovers, even as Bardey pressed his Paris bookseller to locate all writings existent. As a lover of Coleridge, Byron, Wilde, Hopkins, Poe, Baudelaire, Mallarmé, Tennyson, and, provisionally, even the shocking and shamelessly great Whitman, Bardey nevertheless despaired, where Rimbaud was concerned, of finding any known path in. And yet, he had one word for Rimbaud's poems: *undismissable*.

Far from birds and herds and village girls,
I would drink, kneeling in some heather
Surrounded by soft woods of hazel trees,
In an afternoon fog warm and green.

What could I drink from this young Oise,
Voiceless elms, flowerless grass, cloudy sky?
What did I draw from the gourd of the colocynth
Some golden liquor, insipid, which brings on sweat.

Such, I would have been a bad inn sign.
Then the storm changed the sky, until evening.
They were black countries, lakes, poles,
Colonnades under the blue night, railway stations.

What did he drink? Why? How then did he become a sign for an inn? An inn! Before Rimbaud, poems rhymed, certainly had a certain number of syllables and stresses and caesuras and such, but essentially they were versified prose. They didn't mystify or take wild leaps, they were not obscurantic, they did not thumb their noses at the reader.

"Oh, I don't know that I understand it," lamented Bardey to the chaps, "and I would be hard pressed—save for Baudelaire—to say where on earth it came from. Much less where it fits. Which leaves me with my original word—*undismissable*. Unexplainable. Ranting and obscure in parts. Even nonsensical at points. Throw in jejune, too. Yet, through it all—and I shall say it again—powerfully, inexplicably *undismissable*."

"Ah," said one of the wits, "and what do you think dismissed Frère Jacques to this hellhole?"

"I told you," groused another. "Rumor has it he killed someone."

"Come now. People think we've *all* bloody killed someone."

"Or we're all brokenhearted. Jilted." This got a small laugh.

"All right," said the heavy one, Mercer, to Bardey. "We're thick-headed. So read the bloody thing again. Not that one with 'bad sign on the inn' or whatever the hell it was. I mean the other one. You know, the one with the ABCs."

"Very well," said Bardey, who then intoned:

A black, E white, I red, U green, O blue: vowels,
One day I will tell your latent birth:

A, black hairy corset of shining flies
Which buzz around cruel stench,

Gulfs of darkness; E, whiteness of vapors and tents—

"E!" cried one. "As in *E*-nough. If he hates his own bloody work, why's it our job to bother with it?"

"But," remonstrated Mr. Bardey, who in his mild way could get heated about such matters, "the trouble is, it is *not* nonsensical. Fantastical and willful, yes. But—"

"—Give me Tennyson," chuffed Mr. Beet, blowing smoke from a well-chewed cheroot. "*Theirs is not to make reply, theirs is not to reason why, theirs is but to do or die.* I love tub-thumping, bleedingly obvious stuff like that."

Of course it turned fractious. Exegesis—Jesus! Here Bardey found no known landmarks and indeed no compass whatsoever, or not according to the known knowns of other great poems. Which, however obscure at points, were—as Bardey reminded them again and again—poems that could be *gotten*, unpacked, and readily puzzled out.

Well, for a gadfly and puzzler like Bardey, this was torture, having in their midst a literary man who sat quite mute on the topic—quite willfully so, as if he had been taken prisoner. It was impolite, it was boorish, not to mention unwise to stiff one's employer. Indeed, it matched Rimbaud's equally stubborn refusal to play chess, cribbage, poker, charades—games of any kind. Still, Mr. Bardey tried.

"You know, Rimbaud," he ventured one day, "I've always said that poems are like oysters to be winched open and drunk for their liquor. So different from novels, I think. Novels are more brute force. More excavatory. Well, don't you think?" With some impatience he waited, then added heatedly, "Well, might you at least bloody agree with *that*?"

"Bardey"—and Rimbaud sighed one of his long sighs, as if the world would then bore and frustrate him out of existence—"as I have told you, *I* do not *think*. Yes, I *wrote* them, I suppose, but so what? I cannot help them now. They are like children, or rather, estranged children, and I think that is quite enough. Today I do not write poetry. Nor do I read poetry. Or novels. Any of that creative nonsense. And, if you will kindly indulge me, I do not discuss poetry, something, incidentally, that I almost never did." The poet sat with his thoughts, then allowed, "In any case, I don't think any artist can rightfully *explain* what he did. And anyhow—well, so what?"

"But, Rimbaud," begged Bardey, "at least be so good as to talk to me about *past* poetry, *other* poets, or poetry in general. I've no one here with whom I can discuss such matters. Oh, when I took you on, I knew, of course, that you are well educated and even classically trained, much as you have sought to disguise it. But I had no idea you were literary, or thoroughly literary, or not to such a degree." Winching open an oyster, indeed. Again Bardey waited—to no avail—then exploded, "Oh, come on now! It's as if some famous singer arrived here, then refused to sing."

Rimbaud just sat there.

"Very well, then," thundered Bardey. "But answer me this. Why, in your 'Vowels'—so why should the letter *U* be green? Why not black? Or blue? Or red?"

"What!" said Rimbaud indignantly, in mock alarm. "Do you mean to tell me that *U* is *not* green?"

*A*nd famous, too, said Bardey. Well, growing fame. This brought howls of disbelief from Rimbaud's colleagues. Famous? This mercantile monk yanking recalcitrant camels and counting rank hides? Famous? This tightwad sweating every sou?

And hardheaded? God! Even before this discovery, Bardey had repeatedly come to Rimbaud's rescue—why, even as recently as last week, when, as a mercy, Bardey had bought him out. Good terms, too. Scrupulous to a fault, Bardey. Extraordinary man, really. And only now, as Rimbaud glimpsed Bardey across the street waving to him—only now in his tardy way did he see it!

"Ah, me," said Bardey almost fondly as he waved, "I mean, gentlemen, how very fortunate we are, unlike our departing friend, to have no definable *talent*. No defining passion. No real vocation in life." For such an indefatigably cheerful man, Bardey loved twilights.

Let's see. Besides Digby, there is Tucker, the erstwhile telegrapher. There is Buckey, whose fiancée fobbed him off. And Duchamp and Ancelli, the Italian, most amusing chap. He and his brother Marcello— Marcello the Unlucky—who had been stabbed and later shot, then poisoned unsuccessfully by a disgruntled servant. Eleven in all. And, with the exception of Bardey, they all showed too clearly what results when bachelor oddballs are left, by the fairer sex, to roam unshorn, unwashed, and sartorially unsupervised.

"Well, gents," said Tucker, unlimbering himself to squirt the wall. "I shall say this for our poet. He could step in shit. In *that*, none was his equal."

"God, could he! The girl! Or Menelik, ready to boil him in oil!"

This was Menelik the warrior king, a sort of modernizing Yahweh buying Gatling guns and steam trains while smiting villages and armies with the rifles Rimbaud smuggled and finagled for him—despite rather pro forma European efforts to eradicate slavery and pacify the place. How naïve, thought Rimbaud. Pick your chaos. Someone had to establish order here, and it might as well be Menelik. For a born cynic, Rimbaud was nothing if not swaddled in naïve hope.

"Well," said Mercer, who, rumor had it, was about to be cashiered, "my personal favorite was when Rimbaud publicly slapped the camel man. Never forget how Rimbaud stood there, actually *indignant*, when the mob came for him. Wronged, you know—misunderstood. As if he was upholding justice."

"There it is," intoned Bardey, nodding soberly, ever the apologist for his unfortunate protégé. "He was too mentally . . . astringent. Too . . . aesthetic. As I told him so many times, *of course* these people shilly-shally. *Of course* they pilfer, and so would you, were you in their shoes. But no! He held them to a *standard*. Had these high moral . . . *theories*. 'Come now,' I told him once, 'no need for a scalpel where a butter knife will do.'"

But before they can more fully dissect this, Digby blurts out:

"Lord, look who's coming. It's Friar Hopeless!"

"Late to the dance, as usual."

"Shoeless."

"Still clueless."

It's a white man in his thirties. Pulling on his shirt and stamping into his shoes, he is being followed by an imposing, exasperated woman pulling by the wrists two distraught children. White children. Almost unheard of here.

"*Daddy*," cries the girl, "Daddy, wait for Mummy!"

"Come *on*," trumpets the man. Dropping his knapsack, the man ties one boot, leaves the other untied, then starts off again, bellowing, "Mr. Rimbaud! Monsieur *Rimbaud*!"

Forget it. Rimbaud can't hear him. Blocked by the crowd, Rimbaud is still oblivious to this family of four chasing after him. As for Bardey and the chaps, Digby raises an invisible glass.

"Gentlemen, a toast!"

"Here, here!"

"To the *poet*! Who didn't *know it*!"

10 ♪ Old Maid

Mme. Rimbaud meantime is hardly alone in chafing at the prospect of Arthur's impending return. With every passing day, Isabelle feels a similar anxiety tinged with resentment that she should be stuck with her mother in this mooing, feeding, forever-needing *manure* factory near the Belgian border. And not just stuck but hopelessly unmarried when here her female contemporaries have long moved on.

It is an old and humiliating story, and yet in Isabelle there burns the hope, albeit languishing, that if she is freed from the queen's clutches—freed to live somewhere, perhaps to work in town—that some good man, even a considerably older one, will find her. This remains Isabelle Rimbaud's survivor's creed. *I will be found.*

And yet this trap in which she finds herself, it is not just her mother's doing. In Isabelle's mind, her undoing is very much Arthur's doing as well.

For after all, if Arthur returns, he will return with money and then, having money, likely he will marry. As any man can, especially if he has money. But will he marry and leave? Guiltily, Isabelle worries about this, for if he leaves she will be trapped at Roche as before. What most upsets her, though, is that her mother, the traitor, claims to have a wife all picked out for Arthur. A wife! Like a suit of clothes. It's all set, Mme. Rimbaud claims, even as she refuses to divulge the name of the lucky lady.

"But, Maman," says Isabelle, doing her best to sound calm and reasonable, even as inwardly she trembles with rage, "why won't you tell me her name?"

"Don't worry," snaps the mother, who now hears herself being called a liar, "I have someone. All picked out, too. Don't you worry on that account—oh, I have the girl. *If* indeed that is what he wants—never mind the leg." The mother nods. "And *that*, daughter, is all you need to know."

"Girl, you say?"

"Woman. A *wo*man. And none of your tricks! You heard me. I refuse to discuss it."

"But Maman, honestly, who on earth would I tell? The cows?"

"Does the priest share the secrets of your confession? Does the doctor tell the town your troubles? Eh?"

At this, the mother looks immensely vindicated, the poaching cat padding off with a mouse. As for Isabelle, now spinning around, her eyes blurt up, Why? Why not me? Because I'm an old maid?

There in the hallway, by the front door, hangs a dull, time-spotted old mirror. Round like a face and hung with old hats, it seems to Isabelle like a little old lady friend, a wise, sweet old lady veined with age and slowly losing her silver, bit by bit, like sand sifting through an hourglass. And so, every morning before Mass, once Isabelle shucks her heavy India rubber boots and cleans herself up—in those precious seconds before the mother's hammerlike heels hit the stairs—Isabelle consults her lady friend, the mirror. Who now is asking Isabelle what she feels—really feels—since the day before, and the day before that.

Well? thinks Isabelle, plucking a chicken feather from her hair and flicking it. *Pfffth.*

You are too skinny, observes Mme. Mirror. Granted, a bit plain, but certainly pert and pretty enough. There are men out there for you.

So why not me? Why won't Mother help me find a man?

Don't be foolish. Why ever would she? Only a fool would lose her only daughter to marriage. Especially an old woman with a farm to run!

Finding her a man. Rationally, Isabelle knows this is an absurd expectation. Clearly, matchmaking is the last thing her mother would have the guile, the patience, or the female connections to contrive—never mind the motivation. Still, if she *tried*, thinks Isabelle—well, her mother could make her daughter's desires known to the right gentleman. For example, to M. Dumont, the telegrapher, a widower with four children. Or even to the town recorder of deeds, the wordless, never-married M. Chaumas, who walks as if on two erasers, gliding between the shelves.

Mme. Mirror stares back at her. Then try Sunday.

Sunday? Even if Isabelle *wants* to go to town, to stroll and, frankly, troll the bandstand (where the mustached *soldats* patrol, hands stuffed in their brass belt buckles), well, how is she to broach the question with Maman? How?

Mother, I think I'll go see the band this Sunday.

Sunday, Mother, I might just go for a visit in town.

Mother, on Sunday, I might just take myself into town.

"And, pray, to do what?" sneers her mother, blinking, when finally she hears this floozy nonsense. "To see what, *strutting* around amongst those stupid idiot peacock men and the town sluts?"

"I do not *strut* around."

"Wantonness and unhappiness on parade. Good heavens, daughter, you've seen the show. You've seen all there is to see." Isabelle stands there transfixed, remembering this last conversation when—

Rap, rap, rap!

Isabelle jumps. It's M. Lucas, the hired man, with his listing walk and hairy, dangling hands, those sex flippers. Another itinerant oddball. Turning, she sees his teeth, long and crooked, like old fence pickets. "Tell Madame the gig is hitched!"

Clump, clump, clump.

Down the stairs tromp her mother's blocky black shoes with the waxed black laces like two whippy mustaches. In the sun, her muslin dress is black and sheeny—blinding, like sun on water. As for the bonnet, that sermon against vanity trailing two black ribbons, it is dented and twenty years out of style. And shaped like a coal bucket. Let them stare. Keeps the fools away.

"Enough mooning," snaps the old woman. Mme. Rimbaud twists the bonnet ribbons in a fat funeral bow around her overburdened cheeks. "Now come *on.*"

"*Me?* Maman, I'm waiting on *you.*"

"Let's go. And where is your hat? Or your missal? Or gloves! Good heavens, you are like a sticky burr—never can I get you out of the house."

"Gloves," remembers Isabelle, now running down the hall. "Gloves, gloves . . ."

It's true. No matter how hard she tries, Isabelle is forever forgetting something, and that something, misplaced ever so momentarily, is precisely the chestnut that her mother seizes on so triumphantly, thereby ruining everything and explaining everything, beginning with the most obvious fact, that, just as she is always right, Isabelle is always behind, and usually wrong at that. And so as fast as Isabelle collects her things, checks her things, *double-checks* her things, then runs outside, late, late, late, it's déjà vu. It has a kind of music box quality to it. A dream quality. Countess, her mother's mare of spotted silver, Countess is already trotting and the black gig's big-spoked wheels are whirling like two hoops, crunching down the long drive. Is Isabelle even there?

Ahead lies the warm, green middle distance, where the morning mist is burning off the fields. Crows take off, caw-cawing. Ducking grasshoppers, Mme. Rimbaud snaps the reins, now aimed like two long pistols down the road. Then what happens? Isabelle forgets. Anger has gaps. As with her gloves, Isabelle forgets, blanks, loses time, until suddenly here they are again, just like yesterday and the day before that, *whoa*, at the old stone church, mossy green at the piers and, above, almost black with age. The two women venture into the cool, aged darkness. Hastily dipping their fingers in holy water, they cross themselves, then head up the aisle, past the various contagious old people, who always seem to croak on the first day of spring or summer—anytime the weather turns. Except for Isabelle, they're almost all old, *old* old, sagging, tremor-kneed men at that point in life when they don't even glance at two skirts, one with a good bum—quite good—sweeping up the worn gray stones. At the usual pew, the old woman bumps her in. Like a cow, thinks Isabelle. In you go. In to be milked of heavenly feelings. *Moo.*

Disaster, Isabelle often thinks. Her mother almost seems to pray for it, to summon and expect it, like a dreaded rain. Look at her. Fingers pinching her eyes, the old woman is slumped in agony, kneeling at the bleeding feet of Jesus, blood trickling down his toes. Ugh. To pray to a dead body—*who said that?* Bizarre, to hang on a wall some poor tortured corpse—*don't think that.* Makes her flesh crawl, to have all these feelings, these *thoughts.* So, self-conscious, Isabelle ducks, covers her eyes, leaving open, in the crevasse between her fingers, a weep hole to spy on the men, any old man, floating in the misty morning brine in this lifeboat for the faithful. In which Isabelle isn't so much praying as conjugating:

I could marry.
I might marry.
Someday I will marry.
I never will be married.
I need a man to marry me.
Some man should marry me.

"Good heavens," says the mother later, as they clop through town, "must you stare at every last one of these male weevils?"

It's like dousing a cat with water.

"What are you even talking about?" the daughter sputters. "Who are you to presume? How do you know what my eyes see?"

"Good grief, don't start your crying. Look if you must—have your pick. But let me assure you, daughter, each one is a grief in borrowed trousers."

11 ✌ Magic Carpet

Flying above the crowd, meanwhile, jarred and jostled and bounced, Rimbaud is getting a final earful from Djami. Running beneath him, his upturned beard like an axe, Djami is chopping away at Rimbaud's resolve.

"And who will care for you? These here? Murderers? Buggerers of goats?"

The crowds, the shooting pain, the blinding white distance ahead— as he holds the poles of his aerial gurney, Rimbaud's voice is almost staccato.

"*My family.* As I've told you. My family will care for me."

Wrong answer. Prying Djami has seen the mother's terse letters. Even with his rudimentary French, the orphan can read between the lines.

"Rinbo," he says—order is slipping, he who almost never calls him 'Rinbo,' as the townspeople do—"Rinbo, you are wrong. *Wrong.* When does she speak of home to you? When? Why does she not want her son home with her? Why? Why does your sister never write to you? Why, why, why? Because she cannot write?"

But Rimbaud is still stuck at the sister. "Because my mother writes."

"Writes what? Hospital, hospital. Money, money. Cold, like the snow. Don't make your long faces at me. Who will roast for you your goat in France like you like? Who will rub your sick leg? No one!"

"*They* will. And you, Djami, for the last time, you will stay here. Why won't you understand? I am concerned about *you.*"

"Concern! Now you make me laugh, Rinbo. *Liability.* Your word. This is all I am to you, liability. How you think."

Rimbaud sits up, stung.

"As you wish! Farik! *Farik!* Must I have you tied up? It is time—now go. Go—"

Djami stops dead.

"No, *you* go, Rinbo." Djami smacks his camel stick. "Go to your *frangi* peoples, cold peoples living in their houses of snow. Go home, fool. *Go!*"

12 🎼 Spice Woman

But even this is not the end of it—not yet.

Spent, Rimbaud flops down in his do-it-yourself stretcher, holding the sides, seasick. But barely has he steadied himself than, near the Erer Gate—the gate aimed like a great siege gun, east toward the sea—feeling a twinge, he bolts up and sees her, waiting for him. Seething. His Tigist.

Of course, Rimbaud has been expecting her—dreading-hoping, sick for one last glimpse. Of those impossibly large, dark Abyssinian eyes, like spiders. Of her beautiful, brown translucent lips, like pillows. Before him, her beauty stands like fear itself.

As for those would-be Lotharios across the street, the chaps all night banging drunken songs on the battered, untuned piano covered with cig-arette burns, they can see too clearly that God is a comedian. Poetic jus-tice that Rimbaud should see Tigist with her spoiled, surly eyes, the boiling eyes that the old women daub with kohl paste—that she should turn up, one last slap, even as Djami breaks away.

Tigist, Tigist Tigist. Funny, even that morning as he was, uh, wiping himself off, having conjured with lust the girl he had thrown out, even then he recalled how in the early days she had thrilled to hear her name on her *frangi*'s lips.

"Say it," she said, used to say, her sly tongue poised against the roof of her mouth. "Tigist." Glottal. "Say it, Rinbo. *Tigist.*"

They played the same game when she fed him—hand-fed him, rather, his spicy goat, a kind of goulash simmered in spiced, clarified butter and the red chili–laden berbere sauce. *Hot.* Hot sauce. Hot bits. All to be picked up in small pinches with the thin, spongy ingera bread, which replaced so ingeniously, he thought, napkins and utensils. The girl loved to hear her name on his *frangi* lips. "Say it. Tigist, *Tigist.*" Then, in this game of eating, would urge him "Eat, eat," sopping up the good sauce with further bits of ingera, this in an operation that could easily last the better part of one hour, until the girl was jammy for him, rubbing herself and smiling that pout-face capable of sending boys her age scurrying like monkeys into the trees. Tigist called the shots. She knew the love secret. Love was food, and food was love, and the secret, at first, was little bits. Little bits of ingera. Little, to make it last. Fatten him up. And so, in her insane girl-love, in her first love, offering him this catnip, she hand-fed him, just as later she hand-screwed him, pulling back her knees, aching to be wide for his manhood, hissing, "Tigist. Say it, Rinbo. *Thiiiii-gist.*" Like a thistle on the tongue.

"Look," said she, on top later, bouncing on his bone, "I am a horse rider!"

Breathlessly watching in utter disbelief, he was, he saw, actually screwing her. Beauty itself. *Him*, an old man of thirty-five, rocking and thrusting, saying in a kind of sweet, willed death, "Tigist . . . Tigist . . . Tigist . . . Tigist."

Love drunk, sex mad, the girl was those first months, almost frighteningly adoring, a great dark wave of *girl* rising over him, dominating him. But then, alas, there came Tigist's insane, angry days, tearing through his things, imagining he was still frequenting the whorehouses, looking at other girls. But no, she wasn't insane exactly, just at that knife's-edge female age between thirteen and eighteen. Pure turmoil, tearing through his papers, then demanding, once more, that he read his mother's letters to her.

"Read them to me. None of your tricks. *Really* read them." Then: "Hah! She thinks you have a girl! You tell her, yes! *Tell* her, Rinbo! You promised to marry *me*, not these ugly, cold *frangi* girls."

Then she switched subjects. Keep him off balance. The girl was cunning.

"What is wrong with your sister? Stupid, I think. I think your mother milks her like a goat."

He looked at her in horror. "Enough. There is nothing wrong with her."

"No children! How old is she? Really." *Really*: this was her power word, dripping with whatever she wanted to drizzle over it. *Really. Really.*

"Twenty-five." He stopped. "Thirty. I don't know."

Squealing, Tigist fell back, kicking her feet at the ceiling, she was laughing so hard. "An old goat! That's what your sister is! And your mother, old cow, ha, she *milks* her."

*T*oo much. Finally, it was just too much for him. Too much noise. Too much arguing. Too much rutting and spewing. And too much of what he found so unfamiliar and even scary—happiness. Even the possibility of happiness.

And it was confusing. In his poet days at sixteen and seventeen, he had been the top man with a poet a full decade his senior, a grown man whom he could make cry like a girl. Here, bitch. Jutting, the boy clutched the man's balding head to his groin. He rammed him from behind, slapped him, and stole his money, then, worst of all, refused to talk to him, sometimes for days at a time. Youth was a special skin, and cruelty, alchemy, especially if you had been sent to earth to change life and revolutionize love. As a boy, however, he had been beautiful, even angelic, in a way problematic to achieving these ambitions. Hence his need to render himself unkempt and obnoxious—ugly and disturbing, dissonant. And so men feared him. Of course they feared him. Such is the fascination of the scorpion. Its sting can be fatal but it cannot sting itself.

Alone now, Rimbaud almost never thought about the past or who he really was, but then that was half the problem with the girl. She raised too many expectations, too many of those answerless life questions that he had so brilliantly ducked for a million years. Notions like *love, forever, tomorrow,* and Tigist's now desperate issue of *when.* When will you marry me? When, when, when, to the point he would fly the coop. Grab his rifle, slam the door, then head off, ready to explode.

"But, Monsieur," Djami would cry, running down the street after him, "Monsieur, you cannot go alone! They will hurt you, these people. Are you crazy?"

"Go!" he ordered, driving Djami away like a dog. So off he went, out through the north-facing gate into the land beyond the walls. Down the road, any road. Up the mountain, any mountain. God damn them all.

By then, he fled almost daily in long, punishing, knee-jarring marches. Anything to exhaust himself. Anything to quell his jabbering brain in this great race of acquisition, in which his every sou and second, his every *move,* counted and was counted. It was not mere greed propelling this relentless self-scrutiny. It was, rather, the unfolding of the destiny in which once again he, the changeling, would be another, just as, as a poet, he had declared, *I is another.* Rebaptized, he would be that new man, *le capitaliste* dynamiting mountains, diverting rivers, and charting new seas. Anything but that useless, impoverished wretch the *poet.*

And he was not a cripple, not then. He was ruddy and hard and heedless, his lever-action, shell-shucking .44-40 Winchester carelessly swung over his shoulder, one round in the chamber and four behind it, asking no man's permission. When he was feeling out of control, he liked that feeling.

Alone up here and angry with her—swallowed in this hostile vastness—he felt like a water strider, the so-called Jesus bug, walking on water, clinging to the barest membrane of human tolerance and good will. And he liked this, too, the peering-down-the-gun-barrel thrill of it, alone out here, beyond help.

Come. Come kill me. Come on. Why not? He was rich. He was alone. As for this smooth-sliding Winchester, it was priceless to the skinny men. To the skinny, wooly-haired men, the man who could take his balls and this gun, he would be a man of whom songs would be sung around the fire. And so the wooly men shadowed and dogged him, this unbeliever, this white *offense*. Spears in hand, in robes of raw white cotton, they stood like grim angels, watching this man now taunting them. And all because his woman had shamed him, because they both had failed. Or rather, because in a wave of sudden disgust and fear, once again *he* had failed in bed.

On one such day, after another failure in bed, he came upon a herd of young camels. Juveniles. Sapling-legged colts, more than two dozen in number—dodging and dust raising, playing—they were joyously running in tight formation, khaki-colored camels covering, like a wind, the khaki-colored hills.

Look, look, said his soaring soul, to see them undulating, flocking like windblown birds, then launching off again en masse. For as ugly and ungainly as the grown camel is, in this world there is almost nothing more lithe or supple or joyous than a colt camel first stretching his long, knobby legs, flying with his camel flock.

When, suddenly, the camels slowed, then snorted at him, *E-yaahh*. So he stopped. So they stopped, crying, *E-yaahh. E-yaahh. E-yaahh.* Spooked, they spoke to *It*, him lying in the bush, smoochy-lipped camels, with those queer stalks for eyes. And then, as suddenly, they forgot about him and Rimbaud saw why.

For down the draw were eruptions, glowing red wounds— water-gorged buds so red and turgid it was almost obscene. It was spring, and the cactus was in bloom. Red, juicy cactus flowers burning in thickets of baize green.

These were great spiny cactuses, masses upon masses protecting equally massive termite mounds, turd-brown, cement-hard cathedrals of regurgitated mud, some fifteen feet high. But none of these obstacles dissuaded the camels, nothing could, as the blooming fruit burst in their maws, oozy and syrupy. It drove the bees mad. The flies, too, but the camels were in no way discouraged, pushing into sticker thickets that would have shredded a man.

The pain. It made him want to eat one of these squishy, juicy red eruptions bristling with steel needles. *The pain.* Try it, said his mind, for now the camels were frenzied, bleeding from their mouths and flanks, their thorn-studded ears flipping spastically. Yet inoculated, it seemed to him. Protected by the vast pleasure that somehow canceled out the pain of all those stabs and prickles. He closed his eyes, half praying, *Please, God, please, be silent.*

But no, he could not, *would* not: never could he just *be*. Be grateful. Be happy. Be in love. It made him feel trapped, stuck. Such that, rearing back, he raised the gun and, almost stupefied, fired it, at the sun, scattering the camels. Anger, a towering, overpowering anger. Up it rose like a pillar in the sky.

Boom!

Again, the sharp punch of the rifle, that sweet, ear-clapping shock as up it streaked, higher, hotter, angrier than the sun. Again, he cocked the demon thing. *T-zing*, the spent shell flew out and the next round rammed home. And dazedly taking aim, once again the gun hammered back, only to return the echoing roar of answerless answers, off the equally answerless rocks.

His eyes clenched; his heart stopped; the sky shattered and down it plummeted, an avalanche of showering, soul-shattering ruin. Ineluctably connected. Magnetically attracted. To him, to him, to him . . .

*S*o as usual, he delayed and dithered, bottled up, then shut down, thinking of nothing, absolutely nothing, for days on end.

Tigist, meanwhile, became increasingly suffocating, at times hysterical, screeching and tearing at his now utter passivity, as he dodged and demurred. Or rather, as he endeavored to explain, again, in his very learned fashion, the ways of the inexplicable.

Or rather, to explain himself *out* of love.

Or rather, to revise. To couch sorrow in a less sorrowful and correspondingly *brighter* context. Forget it. Screaming, Tigist threw open the shutters, hurled out clothes, then raved to all of the town. So began the saga of the now blighted establishment of A. Rimbaud, Trader.

And so for some downhill months again Tigist's period would come and, true to the purity laws, she would withdraw. Sweet freedom! Holy peace! In fact, in mood and precise indistinctness, it was reminiscent of those late prose fables he had written at the tender age of twenty or so. Prose poems. Poem tales. Really, a music box of magic words that, when you cranked it, played naïve songs of circuses and gruesome monsters and happy children. Of disconnected things connected with a kind of mad logic, by the magic spit of dreams.

So many children there were in these old poems!—*O Childhood days—wasn't the body a treasure to spend?—wasn't love the peril or strength of the Psyche?*... Children laughing, children running; a troupe of child actors and children at dawn, waving their arms at the sky, thrilled to be alive, *freed*, in the first air and rainbows after the Flood, which had wiped clean away the old, dead world of ogreish parents and their pious falsities. Here, confounding and confabulating, were new fables, tales of many things, including love:

> *A Prince was tired of merely spending his time perfecting convention-ally generous impulses. He could foretell amazing revolutions of love, and suspected his wives of being able to give him more than their complacency, enhanced with ideals and wealth. He wanted to see truth and the time of full desire and satisfaction. He wanted this, even if it was a misuse of piety. At least he possessed a large reserve of human power.*

> *All the wives who had known him were murdered. What slaughter in the garden of beauty! They blessed him when the sword came down. He did not order any new wives. The wives reappeared.*

So ran the fugitive phantasmagoria of the now old prince's thinking. Now, many years later, having fallen into the well of love—and with no recourse to magic swords—the prince was trying to think of an honorable way, of *any* way, out. When, with great prescience, matched by his equally great experience in such matters, much like writing, Arthur Rimbaud, trader, simply forgot. Quite simply, he . . . forgot.

13 🎼 Amnesia Anesthesia

That was it, forgot. It wasn't a conscious or a cruel thing; it was a kind of thing, a mercy, really, to forget. A powerfully powerless male kind of thing, forgetting until one morning when at last he told her—*out*.

As in *OUT.*

Arrogant man. Did he think he could just rid himself of her by saying biblically, three times, *I divorce thee, I divorce thee, I divorce thee?* Explaining didn't work. Coaxing didn't coax. And when she again became hysterical, grabbed for the knife, and threatened to cut her throat, well, that settled the matter. Proved his whole point—the girl had to go. With money and all amenities, obviously—but go. Out. So spoke the prophet who once foretold the time when the endless servitude of woman would be broken.

*A*h, but his canny mother five thousand miles away—who somehow had her suspicions about all this—for some time, like a soup, Mme. Rimbaud had been stirring her son with specious claims about having "someone in mind" for him. Honestly now, Mme. Rimbaud casting herself as *l'entremetteuse*—the go-between—the doyenne of New Romance! She knew her son was distractible, and on this point she was correct. For her ridiculous offer, this bluff, produced in Rimbaud even more fantasy and drift and ambivalence, especially when the French-learning Tigist found the letter and exploded. At Ice Woman, as she called her prospective mother-in-law. At her and his stupid, silent sister, barren *cow*!

"You lie with me now," the girl ordered, spreading her tasty yam for him. "Come! Yes, you come, and I will make you hard. Stupid Ice Woman. Ugly woman. Now be a man. Be hard for me. What is wrong with you? Look at you hanging like a dead chicken. Do you want people to talk? To call me barren? *Give me child.*"

But now as he is being carried out of town on this great gurney, this seems so long ago. Ages ago. And who am I now to you, a cripple—*who*, he thinks in shame.

Fool!

Waving her horsehair flyswatter, Tigist, with those spidery dark pools of eyes, Tigist just fans him away like bad smoke—*go*. Then she, too, turns away, while he, lying on his back, transported as through the afterlife, passes under the great gate, then down the sun-pounded road, down the great Harar massif, past staring wooly-haired men holding tall spears. Vacant-eyed men. It was they who owned the night, and they who would be watching, intensely, as Rimbaud's party pushed east toward the sea.

14 ‡ Sticky Burrs

Gone! Free! But alas, not quite. For behind the column there remains that very discombobulated man now running and ballyhooing, his family struggling behind him as he rushes to catch the camel-clod train. It is, in fact, the very same man at whom the chaps had their big laugh. The same gent who, on Tuesday last, Bardey had sacked in his office.

"Hallo! *Halloooooo!* Monsieur Rimbaud! Monsieur, will you kindly hold up?"

And so it stops, this vast mammalian centipede, the camels looking at the horses and the horses at the men, at this *man* now bellowing and sprinting.

Fortunately for him, he has help, this queer pilgrim. For after him, walking smartly but with considerably more dignity, comes a stoutly handsome, resolute woman in a dun-colored dress and prim hat, carrying—wisely, against the piercing sun—a battered black umbrella. And after her, scuffing and scowling comes a grumpy, unwilling girl of perhaps ten, pulling an equally unenthusiastic boy of eight or so.

Children, Rimbaud thinks, white children, strangest of all creatures wearing crudely woven straw hats that resemble enormous mushrooms. Their shoes are broken, entirely inadequate. And after them here rumbles their belongings, or what remains of them. Piled in a creaky cart with wheels the size of barn doors, their evicted life groans along, drawn by a dog-sized donkey led, in turn, by an even tinier manservant, an ancient, bent-over, turbaned man with a long switch. Obviously, all they can afford.

"Thank you, thank you, thank you, sir," cries the young Englishman.

Having succeeded in stopping this exodus, he changes step. Look at him striding up, pouring sweat, but now more smartly, as if buoyed by a pumping military band. He is a slim man but strongly built, strung like a bow. About him there is something bumptiously martial, palpably religious, and distinctly ridiculous. For here he comes, thanking one and all. Why, all but thanking the camels and Rimbaud's scowling band of killers, with their spears and daggers and repeater rifles.

"Thank you! Lovely day. Fan-*tas*-tic. And thank *you*, sir . . ."

His teeth flash. Strong teeth. Two rows of grimacing desperation as he peers up at Rimbaud, already seasick on this rocking trampoline. "*Mr.* Rimbaud, sir," he says, swatting his lifeless slouch hat. "Fergus MacDonald! Mr. Bardey sent us, if you will recall, sir. Hem, a little tagalong to Zeila? Surely you remember, sir." Then, to seal the deal, he proffers a wide, flat hand. Incredible, thinks Rimbaud. As if MacDonald's pulling *him* into the lifeboat.

"Do you not remember?" he continues, still more desperate, trying to break Rimbaud's cold stare. "Mr. Bardey, his grace, kind soul, he was so *very* kind as to ask you on my behalf. On *our* behalf, rather." Pointing behind him. "There, you see my wife, Adelaide. And there are our two children, Lolly and Ralph. Do you not see, sir? The, um, *extremity* of our situation?"

Rimbaud is still looking at these four—no, five—liabilities, counting the old wretch with the donkey cart.

"Easy, sturdy children, too," he adds. "Oh, have no care there, sir.

All able. All ready. And I know Mr. Bardey," he labors, "he will appreciate your munificence on our behalf, what with the poor children, you know. Especially since we are, shall I say, at this unfortunate time, well, rather low on *resources*. But what with your sterling reputation, sir, and your many acts of kindness, well, I know that *you* worry about the children—I can see that. But sir, if I may say so, without you it might be *weeks* otherwise. Without your generosity, I mean to say. Upon receipt of which I will bless you, sir. And pray for you. Depend on it, sir. Fergus MacDonald, servant of the Lord, shall forever be in your debt. And Mr. Bardey's."

MacDonald is thirty, perhaps. His face is sunburned and wind scraped, and as he pulls off his hat, his balding forehead is shockingly white, embossed with a livid red crease from the rotting sweatband of his hat. He is wearing a white boiled shirt, now dirty. His suspenders are frayed and sagging, his brown trousers are dusty and his pull-on boots have thoroughly stretched-out elastics—hardly the equipage for a long desert trek. But to Rimbaud, the thing most amazing—shocking, in fact—is that, even in his desperation, the man seems *happy*, serenely so.

And yet, for one who despises helplessness—who finds it horrifying, as his mother does—Rimbaud experiences the man as queasy-making. Embarrassing, as the bearers lower Rimbaud to the ground. Swatting his hat, Mr. MacDonald is like a dog on his back, banjoing his hind leg that you might further scratch his belly.

"Bless you, sir. Do you imagine? Do you think?"

It is then that Rimbaud recalls the fatal promise he made—stupidly, in the haste of leaving, on that same day in which Bardey had saved *him* by buying him out. Such that Rimbaud feels, for him, a very strange urge, the tug of gratitude.

"How shall I put this, Rimbaud?" the ever-tactful Bardey had explained, laboring to convey Mr. MacDonald's bizarre saga. "We want him—off the boat. Oh, the chap tried, good heavens he tried. Early on, I counseled him. Strongly, I *advised* him. And then for a while, and I mean a very little while, I even held out some dim hope for him. Or rather, hope based more on the strength of his wife. Poor woman. As you'll see, a *fine* woman. Commanding, even. Can't see why she stays with him. And so," he sighed at last, "it did not work out. Utter disaster. A menace, actually. And all, you understand, in his exceedingly nice way. Too nice."

At this Bardey's face reddened. "Well, we can't have some, well, *nitwit* killing our profits. And all because of God, of course. In this self-deluded friar's mind, he thinks God frowns on too much profit. And so we have a man, in my employ, virtually giving things away—by the handful." He sighed again. "His grateful flock, they looted his wagon. Burned his Bibles. Stole his boots. Lord, you should have seen him. Half naked. Job emerging from the desert."

"And?"

"Well," ker-hemmed Bardey, "it is most unfortunate—criminal, really—but he brought his whole family with him. Young children, too. *Here.* Can you imagine? And what I cannot understand, well, that the wife seems quite able, really."

Bankrolled on the fumes of a modest, now vanished inheritance, Fergus MacDonald was, irredeemably, Fergus the Failed, Friar Fergie, etc. "Well," Bardey concluded, "finally I sacked him, of course. And this, mind you, after conferring with the local clergy. Who, to a man, agreed most heartily that the lad was 'done,' as they say."

Pity Mrs. MacDonald; pity the children, too. For their father could neither convert nor barter. Nor did he drink, or smoke, or curse, or carry a gun. Or believe in quinine and inoculations. And worst, he was so frighteningly *sincere.* This is what made him so very dangerous in an already dangerous place. But before Rimbaud can send him packing, here's the wife, an attractive woman, in fact the first European woman he has seen in several years. The children, though, are another matter. Scowling, they are none too happy to see their father pleading with some sunburned cripple lying in the road.

It must be fever, thinks Rimbaud. Propped up now, shotgun across his lap, weirdly famished, Rimbaud is looking at the children, then at Mrs. MacDonald, at her thick blond hair coiled and pinned beneath a once primly stylish but now chipped straw hat. And yet to him she feels strangely elegant—elegant in a bypassed way—in her long gray dress and starched white shirt, draped in a white shawl of native cotton. But what especially recommends her are her sturdy boots, man's boots, much worn. Such competence—but with *him*, poor thing! Indeed, it spurs in Rimbaud an old nursery rhyme from his days in England: "Peter, Peter, pumpkin eater had a wife and couldn't keep her . . ."

"But, Mr. Rimbaud," pleads MacDonald, "we've no place to go. And as for the children, sir, don't you worry. Little soldiers, these two. Five months here. Hard months. Believe me, sir, they know the ways here."

"And you'll have a trained nurse," adds Mrs. MacDonald, invisibly but decisively taking over. "Monsieur Rimbaud, you should know that I have worked in a hospital, and you, sir, need attention. The children will be fine, and if you will kindly notice, over there, sir," she pointed, "over there you can see our cart. We have the food and necessary water. *I've* seen to that . . ."

Nursed, though. The idea of being *nursed* strongly appeals to him in his present state. *Touched by* a woman's cool hand. And there is something about her—her plump arms, her competence. Fine, he consents.

"Up now. Let's go," he tells his grumbling litter bearers. "On your feet."

So, with a jog, up he goes, our difficult hero. High as an elephant, as behind him, compressing and expanding, here comes the smelly train, an accordion of men and beasts, oozing and undulating at a funereal creep through the slow-slithering heat. The lad, though, Ralph, already he has his doubts about their ailing host. In the boy's mind, clearly *he's* the liability.

"But, Daddy," he hisses, pulling at his father's hand. "Well, *really*, Daddy, look at him. How bad is he?"

"Mind your tongue. He is *Mr. Rimbaud* to you."

"Well, I feel sick," frumps Lolly. "Daddy, what, walking *ten days*? Daddy, I want to ride in the cart."

"Come on, Lolly," he moans. "You can see the poor old beast. Now, please. No more dawdling."

"And *think*, children," chimes in Mrs. MacDonald, her contralto voice rising like the road. "Now you must think," she says, "now we *all* must think of how lovely it shall be once we reach the sea. Imagine that, bathing your toes in sloshing warm seawater. And sand, my dears. Not this sand, but *beach* sand squishing between your toes." And then with the proffered sweet came the firm push, "Now *walk*."

Book Two

Monsters Together

I AM CHOSEN, I AM DAMNED.

— PAUL VERLAINE

15 ❦ A Whiff of Immortality

Let us leave them for now in the desert. Fame beckons! Paris awaits!

For on news of Rimbaud's encroaching fame, the Paris papers and *revues* were all in a lather, unable to find the great poet, lost of all places in the wastes of blackest Africa. Which left only one option: to find instead the man who had made known to the world what otherwise might have been Rimbaud's lost and willfully *un*published writings.

By then, however, our peerless guide was no mere mortal. For in Paris only two years before this time—in none other than the neoclassical, gilt-encrusted Olympian hall of the Académie française—he had been called to join the company of such immortals as Montesquieu, Boileau, and Fénelon.

But just who was there to advance our poet's case when he came before literature's hanging docket? Almost no one, for he had behind him no powerful patrons, or salon, or school. He'd abandoned all that, burned his bridges, too. He did, though, have several critics— young but influential men who passionately cited his unique tonal ability to create music of rain and mist. Of gnawing regret and fugitive suffering, and—one suspected—of a suffering that was both deserved and entirely self-inflicted. In short, the music and angst of our modern fallen state:

Falling Tears

Soft rain falling on the town.
—Arthur Rimbaud

Falling tears in my heart,
Falling rain on the town
Why this long ache,
A knife in my heart?

Oh, soft sound of rain
On the ground and roof!
For hearts full of ennui
The song of the rain!

Tearfall without reason
In my sickened heart.
Really, no treason?
This grief has no reason.

By far the worst pain
Is not to understand
Why without love or hate
My heart has such pain

In a time when most poems were still earnestly literal and pictur-
esque and "about" things—and written in a profusely fussy antique
style—here was a poet modern in his vertigo and anomie, modern in
tone, and modern, indeed, before anyone precisely knew what modern
was. To more hidebound sorts, all this was new and raw, if not *wrong*.
For certainly, the poet did not insist on being a "poet," say, like
Wordsworth standing exalted in his cape on a windswept crag overlooking the moors. His words could have been set to music. They drummed
like rain and pulled against reason; they ached like real pain in the dark,
almost dumb way of deep sadness. His true themes, then, were loss and

murk, guilt and dread and, yes, moments of unalloyed joy and pleasure, even lust, so much like our own. It was—what? More mortal. More destructive and confused and conflicted. More *something*. But new, that was the thing—new.

This man, our guide—shameless, penniless, and a convicted criminal—was, by most norms, the last one whom any sensible person would have picked for the role of "Prince of Poets." Indeed, once so named, our hero was plucked from the gutters, washed, flea-dipped, and shorn. Then, in a set of borrowed tails, our Lazarus was stuffed in a horse cab and off he went, bleakly sober, to a glittering dinner, where he was formally declared *Immortal*.

Oh, never mind that later that night he hocked the tails for a piece of tail—indeed, for a three-day howl in the lowest scuppers of the Left Bank. It was too much. In much the way hunting hounds are so deliriously compelled to roll in dung and dead things, somehow, the poet had to throw the pack off his scent.

And what a howl it was, to see this new-minted Caesar carried on all fours by four whores, laureled, lewd, and pink. And by the way, just to set the record straight, it is historically inaccurate that on the third night of these escapades, it was Toulouse-Lautrec—*alone*—who rode the bard's hairy back, waving the moist brassiere of a nursing mother—a "milker," as they say, for those who relish that sort of kink. For in fact, there were *two* little people bucking on the poet's back. The second, a she, was none other than that celebrated dwarf Mouée-Mouée, an intimate of Tom Thumb's and *une fille aux pieds*, so-called, with her almost prehensile, penis-plying feet. Succulent perfection, with just a hint of crud in the petal-like moons of her toenails. *Whiff!* Ah, this put hot spunk into our poet's pen! Sweet inspiration!

> *I want to get away into your thighs and cheeks,*
> *You whores, the one true god's only true priestesses,*
> *Whether you're long sworn in, green beauties or antiques:*
> *O to live in your clefts and cleavages*

. . . .

Your feet, so squeezed and sniffed and kissed and licked from soles
To toes, each toe mouth-organed, and then the ankles too,
With their slow veins that snake in coils toward their holes,
Lovelier than saints', or heroes' feet, and what they do.

It was, in short, a grand time to be a Brahmin bum and this bum in particular. Indeed, for the gendarmes of Paris, there was now a standing edict from none other than the prefect of the Paris police, who decreed that, no matter how outrageous and objectionable his behavior, on no account was the Immortal to be pestered, detained, or arrested. Or only as a last resort for his shambolic royal protection.

And, indeed, at this time he did live quite royally, rent-free, in various Paris hospitals—a man quite normally healthy, you understand, or healthy enough. Here, often, he received noble guests, for example, the lofty and increasingly portly Oscar Wilde. Now *there* was a visit.

It was a pilgrimage, Wilde's homage to visit this societal Judas goat. To Wilde, Paul Verlaine was a Socrates of sorts, seducing the youth and otherwise yanking down the breeches of a hypocritical and disordered order blind to the perfect love of men and boys so sacred to the ancient Greeks. Wilde, in any case, was a man who knew how to make a scene. See him in his baggy dark evening suit–cum–lounge pajamas. Flanked by two haughty boys and advanced by a throng of doctors and nurses, down the hall he barged, the great Irish wit, a large, fleshy-shouldered man with a vast horse face and shock of dark Irish hair, and all the while switching from demotic French to English to French again. And all, you understand, in a rush of perfectly parsed, faultlessly modulated utterances.

"*Cher maître!*" he cried, "my avatar!" So he began, much the same as he had greeted the American god Walt Whitman in Brooklyn, yet another invert Dionysian—truly, *a new man*, this white-bearded Moses aiming his staff down the long American road. Flush from the literary success of *The Picture of Dorian Gray,* Wilde offered the great sodomite many charming gifts: green absinthe, pastel, licorice-scented cigarettes, and a wonderfully odiferous brick of black opiated hashish—that and two dozen alabaster roses, presented with a bow in his white-gloved hand. And, being a gentleman, Wilde did not particularly mind, and in fact quite understood, when the Immortal no sooner received these gifts than he tapped him for a few francs that, fairly needless to say, he had no intention whatsoever of repaying. As Rimbaud had taught him in his nasty urchin days, let the world pay, all these lesser poets, men of affairs, and sucker patrons. The world is our billfold!

This is not to suggest that our poet was lazy—true, unemployable, yet in his way quite diligent, a hustler, in fact. Why, every day by midafternoon (and, naturally, after an eye opener or two), he was, no matter how ravaged from the previous evening's escapades, at full moral attention, ready to receive God's weak signals: even if utter crap, he always put down *something*. Of these scribblings, the raunchiest he sold to a fetishist who framed them among other unmentionables in his ducal dungeons. Never fear, though. No fool, our poet kept fair copies later published under his notorious Black Fowl imprint, charming numbers kept under the counter with sundry rubber novelties and photographs in the French style. Articles that, once purchased, were wrapped in slick brown butcher's paper and tied with strong cord like a round of beef.

It was, in short, a wondrous time, free, openly dark, and *sportif*, such that the all-entitled few were doing things not so much vile or evil as simply unknown and indeed unimaginable to ordinary folk. In Whitehall, Jack the Ripper was hunting trollops, with Dracula soon to arrive. In Paris, meanwhile, the normally correct hommes d'affaires who brought the poet's porno wares, these same doughy-faced, mustached men could be seen—rapt—in the front row of the Moulin Rouge, so close they could feel the hormonal heat and smell the *actually sweaty aroma* of twenty flouncing girls with no underwear, *none whatsoever*, under hot, buttery lights. Bouncing bowler hats! Rat-a-tat! Inches from their pop eyes, skirt-raising, muff-flashing bawds were swinging their legs such that the pater familias could see clear up the Champs-Elysées to the Arc de Triomphe—why clear to their very orchids, some of them, as they did the cancan! *Meeee-yow!*

And so, like a crazy hurdy-gurdy, it was starting that pagan cult of self and self-consciousness and rules to be violated, all because there still *were* rules—all this was starting up. Starting up, too, because extreme fame was technologically possible. Roaring, in fact, the rotogravure and steam-driven rotary presses, all propelling starlets and scandals, cads and low-road royalty, low life and the hot life, with moving pictures soon on the way! And our boy, goat that he was, eating on both sides of the fence, why, he was one of the earliest pioneers of public debauchery, a lover of long-mustached Paris sewer men, butcher boys, parlor maids, and even the stray clochard when he was especially hard up. Indeed, putting aside his poetics, in terms of degradation and derangement, truly it could be said that our Immortal, like de Sade and Byron and Baudelaire before him, was among the very first to set it off.

That is, once the great ur-punk Arthur Rimbaud had first set *him* off. Flick! Rimbaud was that match.

*F*or see how far the Immortal had traveled, or fallen rather.

Twenty-odd years before this time, the outlaw was a son-in-law, poor thing. And trying so hard, Verlaine was, in his droopy tie, top hat, and briskly shined shoes. Here was a nice, if tippling, young man lavishly supported by his in-laws, with a love-bedazzled young wife barely past puberty. He even had a job of sorts.

Of course being a poet, it was the usual ceremonial dumb poet job, some scrivener sinecure in which one could arrive late, then return from lunch respectably drunk. It was a living, but barely, laboriously copying some mind-numbing legal document with a scraping goose quill. Copy a bit, blow on some drying dust, then snooze half the afternoon on a green and greasy desk blotter. It was 1866, and with no other choice, he was rigidly, officiously correct and entirely bourgeois—still ages away from the incorrigible antics of his later years. It was indeed a narrowly circumscribed and straitjacketed time, tight-collared, gloved, bonneted, girdled, top hatted, and hoop skirted, although well medicated with the various opiated restoratives then available, especially for the female set. For these reasons, it was an age prone to hysteria, palsies, and female catatonia, not to mention the saintly "invalid mother" who, unable to take it anymore, blew out the candle of life and took to bed. For the husband, on the other hand, there was always alcohol, mistresses, and, for those on a budget, aging prostitutes. And so the men, wife beaters, sots, and boulevardiers, with ready means of escape, clubs and mistresses and bistros and such—the men were just fine. Tip-top. Never better.

It was, then, a world utterly tied off. And, in the Immortal's case, ready to blow. For who was he then? God knows. A mamma's boy trying, against nature, to be good, he was living on the first floor of a small manse in Montmartre with his adoring bourgeois princess and, living over them, controlling them, his overbearing father-in-law and still more formidable mother-in-law. Zeus and Hera, he called them.

But he was a professional, our boy. He had made his debut. He got on. Why, he even had a modest poetical reputation of sorts. Two salons welcomed him with a small retinue of devoted, able enough, but otherwise forgotten versifiers who did their bit. In fact, he was then one of a school, the Parnassians—anti-Romantics, reacting against all those *feelings*, especially when they were the *English* feelings: Coleridge and Shelley, Keats and Byron, stormy giants who for decades had stolen the show while taking the stuffing out of the next generation—especially in France. And so under the banner of art for art's sake, the Parnassians wrote deliberately smaller poems. Gems. Artfully wrought, classically correct, airless, and rigorously *unfelt* poems like the following stanza, taken from the Immortal's first slender volume, *Poèmes saturniens*, AD 1866:

Pushing the narrow sagging gate aside,
I walked into the little garden-bower
Which the sun, that morning, softly glorified,
Bespangling with wet sparks the smallest flower.

Or this from another sonnet:

I suffer, suffer fiercely: the first groan
of the first man driven out of Eden
is an eclogue by contrast with my own!

And the small cares you have are like the play
Of swallows, my dear, in the lovely heaven
Of afternoon, on a warm September day.

Paul Verlaine, arise then! A lapdog no longer, wasting your life, crocheting such metrical doilies.

Tell us, then, how your Hansel, Arthur Rimbaud, fooled the old Witch with a knucklebone, then ran away, a demon angel with his soul on fire. Sing to us of unquenchable angers—of literature as a blood sport, a criminal enterprise, and war by other means. Sing, heartbroken even now, of the teenage Pied Piper who wrecked your marriage, destroyed your reputation, spent the better part of your inheritance, then led you, a grown man, into the whirlwind, beyond which lay the portals of immortality.

Sing, great shade, of the monsters together.

16 ♪ Heaven-Sent Turd

Patience. Before Rimbaud meets Verlaine, we first must better understand what will propel the little freeloader to Paris, to ride roughshod over Verlaine and terrorize its frankly timid poet population. How could a mere child incite such uproar, setting salon teacups rattling? And this from a kid who, only months before at the Collège de Charleville, had been model-meek and compliant—eerily so.

Back, then, to 1870. Back to the time when Rimbaud is fifteen and a half, just before war breaks out. Back to that cold, drafty house with the mansard roof, where the floorboards creak and churn—like the boy's bowels—beneath the crushing weight of Mme. Rimbaud's near-constant agitation.

Bam bam bam. Down the stairs.

Bam bam bam. Up again.

Again and again—and a night prowler she was, too.

God! The boy would think, nervously biting his thumb while hunched over Cicero's *De divinatione*, doesn't the old witch ever get tired?

Never. For hearing something, anything, with her freak ears, once again she's bellowing up the stairs:

"Arthur, are you hard at it?"

Observe the boy now in the relatively sunny *before*—before things explode—when his life is as normal, relatively speaking, as it ever will be. Perfect eyes. Perfect hearing. Perfect skin. Hair still cut, nails clean: studious, well dressed, polite. Perhaps most amazing under the circumstances is that fact that behind those angelic blue eyes burns a soul remarkably intact, million-leaved like a great oak lifting its branches, aroused, in the evening wind. And yet, to some, this large-ness of soul, this *whatever it is*, is intimidating, and even threatening. Leaving his mother with just one way to control him: keep him employed.

"Arthur, I said hard at it. Hammer and tongs!"

Look at him running to the landing. Blond, pale, and sturdy, he is a psyche awaiting further instructions. Heart beating, he hollers down the narrow, crooked stairs built by the drunken hands of his maternal grand-father, a collector of beef fat and intestines, offals then laboriously boiled to produce nitrates for the manufacture of the munitions used to cut down, by the hundreds, the mutinous masses who rose up in 1848. *Je m'y mets*, he hollers—I'm at it. And so, historically speaking, the Cuifs, say what you will, are profiteer guardians of the public order, solid, crafty, and taxpaying—even while drunk, in the case of Mme. Rimbaud's father, whose ear holes could have housed a family of warblers. Cuif *père* had never failed to profit from any investment. Nor would his daughter—not with this kid into whom she had sunk tutors, suits, and books. Why, into whom she had sunk everything, even as she felt him slipping. Yelling again:

"I don't hear anything up there!"

"Hear *what*," he says, "the sound of me *thinking*? Calm down, I'm working."

"None of your cheek, boy! Don't make me come up there."

Worse is the increasingly hidden and unknown nature of his "work." Which for her, of course, is not work at all. And so Mme. Rimbaud has many choice names for her son.

Big shot!

Genius boy.

Prince Milksop!

The Spoiled Prince.

Never mind that studying is his job. At any time on any given day, if only to wake him up—or because a cow has miscarried, or because her piles are throbbing, or because she's had more bad dreams, or just because—here she comes, rumbling up the narrow attic stairs, *bam bam bam*. When *BAM*, every time, he jumps as the door batters back. Jumps, you see, because he has to wait. Because if he turns and peers around, even in the slightest, she will accuse him of dawdling and daydreaming while here *they* toiled, and all so he, Genius Boy, could think his great thoughts and sit on his royal fanny! And so, to wake him up, she'd give him a shove or whack. Wake up. Grow up, mooch, and never forget: you're going to make us a pile of money someday.

Worse, she had two lumps: the genius-idiot to study, and the idiot-idiot—this would be Arthur's brother, Frédéric—to be the genius-idiot's whipping boy. Frankly, to do what, to her mind, Frédéric was born for, to muck and haul and chop. Why, Frédéric's *maman* even had a shining vision for her elder son—that of a Paris sewer man in gum boots, rain hat, and oilskins. Picture him, in his small boat, a gondolier poling through Hades of *merde*, using a specially developed shovel-cum-paddle, *un rabot*, both to propel himself and to unclog the converging headwaters of the city's stupendous waste streams. This subterranean Seine, it needed men with long soup-strainer mustaches and strong stomachs, indomitable men who could break the blockages caused by logs, murder victims, parasols, butcher slops, and so forth. And don't overlook the wine corks of Paris, thousands and thousands of corks that, once cleansed of that in which they had been stewed, could be cut down for perfume bottles, then sold to the unsuspecting—yet more revenue! A pension, too! And, of course, steady money for her in her old age. Such were her maternal dreams for Frédéric.

Never mind that Frédéric, but a year older, is of normal, if not above normal, intelligence. Because Frédéric is not Arthur-grade, he is, for her, *l'ours de la famille*—the family bear. Whose labors allow Genius Boy hours of study undisturbed in his Olympian aerie.

Alas, like his long-departed papa, Frédéric is also a drunk-in-training, subject to frightening violent fits. Blackouts, too. Meaning that Frédéric must be kept busy, always, while Arthur studies and the Rimbaud sisters, "the two mice," mostly hide in their room, whispering with the sound of crackling paper. As one might expect, except for supper, minor chores, and prayers, the girls are never seen, just as they never question, sass, or rock the boat. In short, each child has a favored mode of *egress* against the mother's near-constant *ingress*. A way to magically disappear.

But what of Madame, now gripped with the terrifying night sweats of menopause? Clammy blankets. Fevered dreams. Rape, pursuit. Thick, gruesome cocks held in much-aggrieved fists . . . and that *smell*.

Then there is her fear of the all too real, as that morning years ago when her father no sooner pulled out than he spat, *"Merde!"* And, looking down, she thought, I'm bleeding to death! "See, Papa," she cried, "see what you did! God has seen and now I'm going to die!" "Stupid bitch," he replied, "you've started your monthly." Squatting, he wiped himself on the bloody sheet. "Now clean it up!"

Such is Madame's mental proscenium circa 1870. Two teenage males. Males in rut, making horrid sounds and leaving these *stains*. For which—beyond confession, Communion, and abstinence—there is but one remedy: hard work. Work like good lye soap. Work is the way. It is

The Farm Way, and The Farm Way is The Hard Way. And so, to show them, every spring, up from the depths of the barn she would emerge with a swarming basket and a bucket brimming with water. Time for that dreaded annual chore, which, being as there were no real men present, naturally fell to her. And so on her watery knees—as her daughters wailed—one by one, hard by the elbow, she plunged them into the cold, clear water. Spring: time to drown the barn's gush of kittens, some scarcely the size of mice.

*A*nd so it begins again. Every day *again*.

Again, the boy is up in his attic roost, reading for a lark the puerile Caesar's *Gallic Wars*, possibly the dullest, most megalomaniacal book ever conceived. *Veni, vidi, vici*, I came, I saw, I conquered. Yet another French humiliation: horn-helmeted wild men crushed under the massed shields of Caesar's legions. Corpses piled in smoking heaps. Vultures feasting. Golden armbands raised to the sky—*Hail Caesar!* When again, downstairs, the Caesarina can be heard bellowing.

"Arthur! Working?"

"Working!"

"No tricks!"

"Working! Working!" He smacks the book. *Goddamn!*

Then deep from the bowels of the house, he hears:

"No, Frédéric, you will do it. *You*, I said! Arthur is at his work."

"But it's *always* my turn."

"Because I *said* it is your turn! Now out with you! Out!"

Then, *bam bam bam*. It's Frédéric, shoving him in the back.

"*Merdeux!* Leaving *me* to shovel your shit! Tell her, you bastard. Stick up for me! Just once!"

"And say what? *What?*"

Bam!

Here she is, flying across the room, slapping Frédéric with both hands. Hysterical, like a bird trapped in a window, she is sputtering, raging, erratic. "Get down! Get down those stairs, you!"

And look at Frédéric, frightened of this woman whom he could crush. Stammering, "If he—if he—if he—"

"Maman—" intercedes Arthur.

"Shut your mouth!"

Without even looking, she backhands him—knocks his head back, such that he feels drenched in hot vomit, the vomit of shame. His shuddering, ear-ringing shock. Clutching his throat, in panic he thinks, *I've swallowed my Adam's apple*. But for her, this is comical, his girly histrionics. Guffawing back at him:

"You're not hurt! Lord in heaven! *Two* babies I have—"

"You'll see!" rails Frédéric, raising his fist. This is her biggest fear—*them*, turning on her like two curs.

"I'll get the chicken axe!" hollers Frédéric. "*You'll* see, you old bitch!"

"*You*," she sneers. "And I'll have *you* thrown in the asylum! In chains."

He kicks the door. "I'll cut my own throat! In the village square! With the axe!"

"—In chains! Drooling on yourself, do you hear me? *Drooling*—"

"—With a sign around my neck! Blaming *you*, you bitch!"

*A*nd so it is spring again. Blooming, blowing spring again. The crushing weight of *spring again*. O, the earth having to resurrect itself again.

Again, the thick-armed, anvil-footed ploughman.

Again, singing the same stupid plough songs.

Again, ripping open the dead ground. Crushed rye heads. Dead seasons. Bones.

And yet, for Arthur Rimbaud, from the black muck erupt pale green stitches, the first true lines of a new voice—his:

The Sun, hearth of tenderness and life,
Pours burning love over the delighted earth,
And, when one lies down in the valley, one smells
How the earth is nubile and rich in blood;

How its huge breast, raised by a soul,
Is made of love, like God, and of flesh, like woman,
And how it contains, big with sap and rays of light,
The vast swarming of all embryos!

And everything grows, And everything rises!
                                         —*O Venus, O Goddess!*

Flesh? Blood? Sap? *Embryos!* His diction is scandalous. Disgusting. At this time, no one ever would have used such runny, prurient words. Reading this, the boy feels happy and stunned—freed. But as suddenly, hearing her yelling again, he peers out the window. And look, down in the black muck, clad in leather slop apron, here is Frédéric stumbling along in his enormous wooden barn clogs, which resemble two foul potatoes. See him now, wrestling down the hill, wobbling in a wheelbarrow, a green and steaming heap of cow slops.

Or rather, Frédéric is racing behind the violently jerking handles of the now ominously wobbling honey barrow bouncing its gelatinous contents. Which—being Frédéric—upends its liquid contents, straw and manure, *rr-araugh*, as if a giant had retched.

Again, Frédéric's screams of rage.

Again, his sisters peeping out their window.

Again, Arthur lowering his quarto edition filled with obscene comments by the many valiant lads before him who died of boredom reading Caesar's *Gallic Wars*, on the subjugation of his ur-French precursors. Who, in battle, might have sounded much as Frédéric does right now:

"*Merde!* Goddamnit! God damn you, God!"

A window flies up. Rrr-augg*hhhhh*. Wrath pours down:

"Blasphemer! Get up, idiot! Blame yourself, not the Lord!"

"I'll cut my throat!!"

"I said, finish it!"

"I'll finish it, you bitch! I'll finish *myself!*"

Finish it? thinks Arthur. It's unfinishable, this tarry slop pit

Frédéric is filling at the foot of the barn. And look. Floating in the family cesspit, before his eyes, he can see his forebears, the Gauls, bellies bobbing, gazing at their twisty black toes. And staring down at his brother, Arthur can *feel* them, a line of hairy-backed idiots going back to the Middle Ages. Why, clear back to the days of consul Julius Caesar, grandmas and grandpas and aunts and uncles and half-wit cousins. Folks roaring, gamboling drunk on the feast of Saint Michel, if they were lucky. Otherwise, people half starved, snoring away the winter in snow-whomped, manure-banked, beast-packed huts. And the horror is, Arthur *feels* them. *Smells* them under the ground, coughing and slapping and picking at themselves. Peasants! And all he can think is, How? How *he* can be of *them*?

When, from the room below, Arthur hears his little sister Vitalie—all feeling—exclaim, "Poor Frédéric."

And what does *he* feel for his brother? Anything? But does one need to feel to write a poem? he wonders. And who, then, would be *doing* the feeling? He or the so-called poet? Was *not* feeling actually a *form* of feeling? he wonders. Peculiar boy. These were some of the strange questions then churning through his mind.

For the problem is—the boy's worry is—that he does not feel sufficiently.

Or rather, that he feels *in*sufficiently.

Or rather, that he does not feel *in the same place or with the same heart* as other people do—normal people.

For suddenly, he can't take Communion without wanting to spit it out—Christianity, like a bad tooth.

But these are just early symptoms. Lately, spooked, he wonders why he feels this *thing* fluttering inside him, this newly risen angel all but breaking his ribs as his mighty wings unfold.

But the trouble is, it's so unpredictable. How It—because it's an It—can be so scarily, twitchingly *present*. And as suddenly *gone*. And as terrible as his fear of It's taking over, there's the fear, once gone, that this angel-devil, this demon, this power or deceiver might never return, and what then? *Then* who would he be? A prize what? For just as this new double being, this nasty, ravenous caterpillar, is gnawing out his insides, so he also feels the buried child within him dying. He *stinks*. Everything about him stinks. And however wicked he is, what no adult will ever understand, once it was pure innocence that drove him. Joy, even.

Joy. Can an adult even imagine such an Edenic state? How in school early on, when he answered a question, unraveled a line, made a leap, how he felt such joy that he would bounce, actually bounce, as if from the baby still coiled inside him.

He wonders why he feels so abominably—cold.

That's it. So cold, so *high*, so criminally arrogant, looking down upon all creation. Peering backwards through life's telescope at these— these ants of people. Even his hands. Insect feelers that write.

Then what happens? At a word, a sound, the strum of light, flicker of leaves—as suddenly, he is God peering down on life, in all its helplessness and ridiculousness. For look: one miserable Sunday, after another boring sermon, as the boy exits the church, *there it is*.

See it, glistening in the sun, where the wagons wait and the hitched horses slumber with one rear hoof raised. Look! *Cow droppings on perfect ripe blackberries.*

Shit on fat, black blackberries!

Biting his lip, insanely he squeezes himself. It's their own private joke, him and God—the last thing any of his bowdlerizing contemporaries would ever notice, or think, much less write, in their stupid nosegay poems larded with these rarefied, artified *feelings*. About *them*, the poets, having feelings! Or, deeper still, with so many of his French contemporaries artfully *resisting* feelings.

I write because I feel
And I feel because I long
And by longing have profound thoughts.
I feel so you can share in my experience,
A poet such as myself having such majestic
Feelings on your behalf.
For I, and I alone, have ever felt such feelings.

But what is greater, then I resist all feeling, the poetic expression of it,
Pure art, because I hold it all inside.

But what about the counterargument, thinks the boy, plain nasty
*un*feeling, without all the phony, putrid, arty language? In a flash, he can
see it, a new poem entitled "First Communions," one of the first pro-
ductions of what might charitably be called his angry, bratty, scatological stage. And yet a strong, clear light shines through with an unfussy
style and a sense of reality that only a country boy would have:

Really, it's stupid, these village churches
Where fifteen ugly brats dirtying the pillars
Listen to a grotesque priest whose shoes stink
As he mouths the divine babble:
But the sun awakens, through the leaves,
The old colors of irregular stained-glass.

The stone still smells of the maternal earth.
You can see piles of those earth-clotted pebbles
In the aroused countryside which solemnly trembles,
Bearing near the heavy wheat, in the ochreous paths,
The burned trees where the plum turns blue,
Tangles of black mulberry and rosebushes covered with cow droppings.

Blasphemy! All in the voice of a young girl, a feminine alter ego
who, extending her tongue in Communion, feels an overpowering
nausea—nausea at the putrid kiss of Jesus.

And it's all written, thinks the boy, written all across the sky. Written even before it *is* written.

Look up, poets! From the ass of heaven, down it falls, a heavy
brown mass of pure feeling. *Thump.*

17 ⨍ Bad Apple

This same Arthur Rimbaud is now a brain for hire, forging, for the school's dolts—those who can pay—essays that mix Attic mastery with the most deliberately boneheaded mistakes. Which, being dolts, they copy word for word. And so the class is roaring-laughing, as, like a pistol shot, Master Delporte's supple cane smacks the miscreant's desk. Dark hair splattering, the master is now shaking Rimbaud's work for hire in the fat, freckled face of the woeful Jacques Sorel, whose ample cheeks are painted with two livid red handprints—slap, slap!

Again, the cane smacks Sorel's desk, inches from his quivering nose.

"Abominable plagiarist! Do you presume to insult my intelligence by claiming—liar!—that it was *you*, imbecile, and not *he* who wrote this?" Indeed, he is pointing his cane, that rapier of pain, at the pure puzzlement of the wrongly accused Arthur Rimbaud. *"Moi?"*

Beginning to make trouble in school, to goof off, the prize boy has now morphed into the rebel hero. A Byzantine. A brigantine. Lurid strange.

Delahaye, Gorgeon, Doinel, sometimes Lalande, like a pack of dogs, they all follow Rimbaud after school. Circumscribing vast circles around Charleville, they talk, his followers, about poems and particularly stupid, grotesque, or simply ridiculous people—and, of course, girls, although this goes nowhere; why, in Charleville, the girls are so locked up, so stuck up, that it's thrilling just to have a girl turn up her nose at you!

As they walk, sometimes the boys make up serial poems, each taking a line, then trying to top the other. Round the town they troop, one rolling-gaited, orangutanlike organism with ten feet. The so-called Poet's Circle.

"And there, in a long and lovely space."

"She forced him to see, without a trace."

"That's a stupid line!"

"Two stupid lines," cries Delahaye, the drum major. "Arthur! Give us a line."

Squinting, the kid looks like a grasshopper working up a spit. "Delahaye," he says very slowly, "I am not thinking of merely *a* line. I am thinking of a *poem*. Complete."

"Called what?" Delahaye plants his feet in the road. He is a fleshy, well-loved, well-fed boy whose prosperous family keeps a store. And, much to Arthur's chagrin, Delahaye's blue-eyed mother, so pretty and well dressed, she utterly adores her son. Imagine that.

Arthur is still squinting, pondering.

"The title of the poem?" he says. "A trifling point as yet—who knows and who cares? I told you, it's already written—"

"Listen to him," challenges Delahaye. "Then *what*, prithee, is it *about*?"

"About?" The kid stares two holes through him. "What an idiotic question. Do you think a poem is merely 'about' what it's about?"

But Delahaye, unlike the others, does not kowtow to him. "Oh, bullshit. If it is *written*, Rimbaud, then what is it *about*?"

The hands jiggle, ever the marionetteer. "Well, I suppose"—goggling for effect—"I suppose, Delahaye, that it is *about* two children. Two orphans."

"And?"

"Well, they're poor. Miserably poor, with no father—"

"Ah," cries Delahaye to the other boys. "So you see, it begins just like every Rimbaud poem, 'Once upon a miserable time . . .' "

"And their mother dies. And they're so horribly poor—"

"The nose. Watch his nose! Sure sign that he's lying—"

"And they are so poor and so shut-up, the children think the funeral wreaths are"—now he has them—"New Year's decorations!"

"New Year's decorations!" cries Doinel. "From a funeral? That's dreadful!"

"And stupid," seconds Delahaye. Who two beats later says, "Write it down."

"Not yet." The kid walks on. "I'm waiting."

"Rimbaud, you'll lose it! You'll just think of something else."

"Quite the contrary. Write it too soon and you *will* lose it."

"Then you *have* written it."

"No, but I can see all the words. The rest is mechanical. As I say, I just haven't written it down:

> —*A mother's dream is the warm blanket,*
> *The downy nest where children, huddled*
> *Like beautiful birds rocked by the branches,*
> *Sleep their sweet sleep full of white visions! . . .*
> —*And here—it is like a nest without feathers, without warmth,*
> *Where the children are cold and do not sleep and are afraid;*

Delahaye snorts. "Sure, Rimbaud. Bare like your house at Christmas. No decorations and no presents. And you insisting your poems are the expressions of a new *objective* poetry! Objective, my ass!"

18 ‡ Life in the Veal Pen

But after these interludes, back he went to the veal pen, as he thought of it. And little wonder. For even now, in the fetid depths of the barn, *le veau*, the spring veal, can he heard bleating.

No, *le veau*, superfluous male, you were not born to run and graze—to grow muscles, sprout balls, then go wild, chasing small children across the meadow. No, *le veau* was not to be red-blooded but delicately pink-fleshed—was to be kept bloodlessly anemic and weak in his reeking pen, where only a few stray splinters of light can pierce the fetid gloom. Separated from mother and herd, for five or six months—eight at most— *le veau* was a subterranean albino, a mushroom in the dark.

Le veau, however, was anything but starved, or not for milk. Pails and pails of milk he had, but not from the delicious speckled teats of his mama, whoever *she* was. Spoiled milk, watery cheese, and butter slop, all was ravenously licked up in the same pen in which his neck remained pinioned between two posts worn smooth and stuck with bits of hair and flesh. *NaaaaHH*—kicking. *NaaaaHHH*—so batty the calf licked even the bent nail in the wall until his tongue bled. Anything to feel *anything*.

But *le veau* hadn't entirely given up. The battle was on when his hole was mucked out and not least when he made his first and last transit, drooling pink foam, as three farmhands dragged him out into the sun's blinding white terror. All this the boy felt in his own veal pen, in the gabled apex of the house with its lone, ogre-eyed window, the same through which he stared for days, writing poems. Letters, too, dreaming of what *le veau* dreamt of—escape. And he was cagey.

Hearing the dreaded *bam bam bam* up the stairs, quickly Scheherazade would hide away what he was writing—*really* writing. For now his ready nib was scratching many messages. All masks. Pretending on foolscap to be seventeen when for a fact he was naïve fifteen. Pretending, above all, to be breezy and worldly-wise when he was anything but. Charm 'em. Baffle and bamboozle 'em. But be delivered! Here is part of what he wrote to Théodore de Banville, leader of the Parnassian poets and a man said to be sympathetic to the young and aspiring:

Cher Maître,

We are in the months of love; I am seventeen. The age of hope and dreams, they say—and now I have begun, a child touched by the finger of the Muse—excuse me if this is banal—to express my good beliefs, my hopes, my sensations, all those things dear to poets—and this I call the spring.

If I send you some of these verses—and this thanks to Alph. Lemerre, the good publisher—it is because I love all poets, all good Parnassians—since the poet is a Parnassian—in love with ideal beauty. It is because I esteem in you, quite simply, a descendant of Ronsard, a brother of our masters of 1830, a real romantic, a real poet.

That is why. This is foolishness, isn't it? but still?

In two years, in one year perhaps, I will be in Paris—*Anch'io*, gentlemen of the press, I will be a Parnassian! I do not know what is inside me . . .

that wants to come out. . . . I swear, cher Maître, I will always worship
the two goddesses, the Muse and Liberty.

Do not frown too much as you read these verses . . .

Then he hears the girls shrieking, "Arthur! Arthur, do something!
Frédéric has gone mad again."

The boy throws open his window. Pigeons diving. Wind exploding,
and look! It's Frédéric on the attack, waving the chicken axe as storms
of Roman arrows rain down. And, seeing their great leader, out of the
brakes and thickets, up from the hills, raising swords and blowing horns,
up rise the Gallic hordes, wild men with buttered hair and broadaxes,
thwock!

Old bitch!

Thwock! Thwock! Thwock! Thwock! Attacking the great craggy black
oak, Frédéric Rimbaud is hacking her apart, when over the fields a voice
can be heard, a voice almost singing, as if she were Demeter or the Virgin Mary:

"Frédéric Rimbaud. God sees you, Frédéric Rimbaud. Do you think
that God does not weep—weep—to see you hurting his poor old oak
tree? Frédéric Rimbaud, who would dare to raise a hand to his poor old
mother? Return to your work!"

And so it ends as it always ends. How drunkenly Frédéric stumbles
around, axe limp at his side. How, beaten, he stares at the stupefying
sun, then at her, bathed in holy victory. Wiping his face on a muddy
sleeve, Frédéric Rimbaud then slogs down into the undergloom of the
barn, where *le veau* can be heard, *Eee-yaHHHHH.*

And from this attic roost, Arthur Rimbaud, poet inviolate, utterly
removed, he watches all this happen, helplessly happen, quite *as if he had
written it.* And look, the last fraying gusts of spring snow—a sugaring
that blew so briefly over the ice-glazed puddles—all vaporized in a blast
of sun, leaving only the torn black loam and the blacker woods. Woods
where, if you were Frédéric Rimbaud, you could scream and hear
only . . . wind. Where you could raise your axe and hit only . . . trees.

Or you could count the trees, then the fence posts, as his sister

Isabelle often does, walking alone, up and down the road. Or, like Vitalie Rimbaud, you could write in your diary. Or, as in Arthur's case, you could gaze at your own reflected brilliance and waste stamps on unanswered letters—you and *le veau*, both still licking the bloody nail.

19 ⚡ Prayers Answered—It's War!

But, O Holy Day, several months later—on July 19, 1870, to be exact— the Rimbaud children are delivered. War breaks out!

Had only they known what to pray for.

For although the French emperor, Napoleon III, is indeed the nephew of the diminutive scourge who once terrorized Europe, it must be said that this sickly, opiate-addicted second-generation heir has none of his uncle's martial bearing or tactical brilliance. But Napoleon III heeds his generals, just as he points to the reflected glory of his ideas in the jingo press, parroted by the same feuilletonists and writers whom he pays to whip up the French public and give him a casus belli. In the thrall of Darwin and Wagner and Ranke, these writers concoct a whole stew of theories—perverted in the case of Darwin and magnified in the case of Wagner and Ranke—all supporting national destiny and the clash of nations. Necessitating the racial hygiene of periodic bloodlettings waged on a continental scale.

*I*t is high August, harvest season. Dry roads, long days, splendid time for marching, and so the emperor has declared war not only on Prussia but—Mme. Rimbaud is almost convinced—on her, Mme. Vitalie Rimbaud de Charleville! Only miles from the Belgian border, Roche, like Charleville, is right on the Hun invasion route to Paris. Dead center, in fact.

Les sales Boches! cries the French press. Hah!

This time, promises the French press, this time they will go through the meat grinder, these sausage snappers. And just look at them in their ridiculous spiked helmets and brown uniforms—*brown* in a continental army, well, really! No color! No horsehair flourishes! No plumery! No sartorial sense whatever.

In the lull before the first glorious battle, there is great ferment and excitement in Charleville. On the parade grounds of Mézières, Charleville's sister city, can be heard swelling bands and, far in the distance, the *whu-ump* of the French artillery tuning up. As for the kid, wading streets filled with soldiers, why, to hear him carrying on, one might think that this vast human spectacle had been undertaken entirely for his amusement. And at fifteen perhaps this is true, as Charleville's armed yokelry muscles past him, fat grocers and beery butchers of Charleville's ferocious home guard, their jowls puffed out in their itchy old woolen uniforms. Now on holiday, many are already packing picnic baskets, eager to see the Huns get a good hiding. And so the young Ezekiel can be seen fomenting in the bars, all but taking bets on his country's defeat, just as he can be found rabblerousing in the park, sneering at the laboring military band and his fool contemporaries, all racing to sign up. Not him!

"Christ, this is *France*. Are you out of your minds? You'll only get walloped!"

"You oughtn't to talk like that!" cries an old man. Garlanded with medals, he rises indignantly from the bench where he sits with two other old gentlemen. "*You*, Monsieur, you could find yourself under arrest if you continue with such seditious, cowardly talk!"

"*Ah, tu m'emmerdes, pauvre pépé.*"

"What!" cries the old hero, medals atremble, "What do you dare to say to me?" Abruptly, his rage turns to a leering smile. "Wait. I know you, you little turd. You're one of the Cuifs. Boilers of entrails! I know of your mother, too, the old horror. And you know what, boy? I think you're a *chicken*."

How can he answer this? Already a crowd is gathering, so he has to bolt, and not just out of fear of arrest. Chicken! The man has struck him where he lives, and as he melts through the throngs, the young egotist burns with shame—shame both for who he is and for being stuck with the Bouche d'Ombre, the Mouth of Darkness. A mama's boy. A chicken. That's all he is. Enlisting, at least the other kids will get away.

*N*ot that the kid is wrong about France's recklessness declaring war on the nation with continental Europe's most formidable army. Indeed, he is not daunted in the least by news of the first meaningless skirmish, when *les Boches*, outnumbered three to one, are repulsed. With trains snarled and the tracks blown up to slow their invasion, the first Prussian units are nowhere near full strength, but now Charleville, like the rest of France, knows with moral certainty that God stands with the French.

"To Berlin! To Berlin! All the way!"

And indeed at Saarbrücken, as the French generals review their forces, they are satisfied, more than satisfied, to see their crack marching infantry, their glorious horse cavalry, their frightful artillery, and a wondrous new contrivance, the lead-spitting, multi-barreled Gatling gun, hand-cranked like a meat grinder, and to much the same effect. In great excitement, these and other strategic advantages are conveyed to His Munificence, astride his magnificent high-tailed black stallion, the same upon which he had been hoisted that morning hors de combat. Alas, His Eminence is a bit under the weather. It's not just the usual constipation from the opiates to which he is addicted. It's also the camp trots running through his army, a result of the now overflowing latrines.

And so, three hours later, with what growing outrage, with what dismay do the emperor and his leaders watch the swirling, mounting confusion as yet another adjutant on another sweaty mount gallops back with yet more bad news. Then rout and panic: the Germans punch through, and His Royal Highness escapes—by a whisker—the gleaming sabers of the crack German cavalry. Worse the frightful rumors, too true, that the ignoble emperor had escaped—escaped through pure ruse, riding out under the white flag while hidden in a medical wagon.

In little more than three weeks, it all collapses, humiliation upon humiliation . . . in Wissembourg, Spicheren, Reichshoffen, and others. Until finally, in Sedan, utter collapse, followed, within hours, by the emperor's surrender and abdication—*raus.*

Kaput, then, for the emperor. But victory for the seditious young Arthur Rimbaud. One of the people, he is now a nonlaboring, capital *W* Worker—indeed, a nonrevolting revolutionary still hiding in his room and jumping each time his mother barks. Yet, without knowing it, under this relentless pressure, the boy is turning coal to diamond. All with two of the most powerful forces known: rage and humiliation.

20 Monster Boy

But back to the days just before France's defeat. Days when, feeling herself losing control, Mme. Rimbaud is wearing out the floors. Rape! Ruin! *Men* . . . Hun men in hobnailed boots would soon be stomping her glorious fields of rye. The Huns are close, too. One can hear the field guns, the howitzers, and great siege mortars:

Whu-ump. Whu-ump-ump.

"Get inside! Stay inside!"

For here in the blue night sky—red blooms reverberating off the clouds—it's raining down, the promised eighty-seven trainloads of Hun retribution. The Rimbaud children, however, see a very different picture.

War! Change! Anything!

Why, in France's last crushing weeks, even the girls are thrilled, ready to flee like horses from a burning stable. As for the chief saboteur, the unlikely Frédéric Rimbaud, he is now known as the Viper. At supper, brazenly swilling beer from a take-home bucket, he is openly defiant, the swine, upending the beer bucket, braying like a bullfrog, then wiping his unshaven chin with the back of his hand. And when the mother attempts, finally, to slap sense into him, this time he seizes her hand, bends it back, then grins as she drops to her knees in pain. "Viper! Hateful sinner!" she sobs, then rages out. For even as she drives her sons away, here, paradoxically, is her greatest terror: being left. Knowing this on some level, later that same night, drunk, the Viper steals money, then takes off. So what if the ship of France is going down? The next morning, following in his father's footsteps—and then, so drunk he can scarcely stand or sign his name—the Viper enlists.

*W*huuuuu-ump. Whuu-ump-ump-ump.

The next night, as Arthur watched from his room, the red flashes of the siege guns could be seen in the rain-swollen thunderheads, a death system rolling over the eastern rump of France. Was he scared or thrilled? Truly was there any difference? Well, his stiff peter, *it* sure knew how it felt as it rose, his big asparagus, then thickened in his coaxing hand. Thus began his stropping strophe, his bed going *ump-ump-ump-ump-ump* as his head sang the Angelus, *Marie, Marie—Marie with the big-big-big-tits*. But once done, once the rocking subsided, in that twinkling after-daze, he thought, Tonight's the night.

To Paris, that's where he'd go, he who had never been more than twenty kilometers from Roche. To Paris, where there were street barricades and pretty girls and poets wearing red kerchiefs—poets with guns! But how? He was just what his mother said he was, a born titsucker. Why even stupid, spineless Frédéric, even *he* had the courage to leave.

"Look at the sky!" howled his sisters in their room directly beneath his. "Maman, don't you see? We need to go!"

"And do what?" she cried. "Hand Roche over to the Huns?"

"But we'll be blown up!"

"Pipe down. Have you no faith in the Lord?"

"But, Maman, look—look at all the wagons. Everybody's getting out of here."

"Timid people! Faithless! They're not even close, *sales Boches*."

Then he heard Vitalie hissing up the stairs, "Arthur, *Arthur*—"

Hissing, because of course their mother did not want him ruining them, influencing them, doing you don't want to know what. So finally, screwing up his mangled courage, the boy snuck down and found the two girls rolled in a ball on the bed, so scared even their hair was snarled together. So he freed their hair. Then he got their brush and did the forbidden: sat on their bed, beside their packed valise and the dolls all dressed to go. Sitting down, he did what he'd seen only the girls or his mother do: brush hair, girl hair, in long, soft strokes. "It's all right," he whispered, happy for once to be a brother and not his mother's dog. "Ha!" he bluffed. Snuggling down with them in their little blanket, he felt cozy, normal for once, a real brother. "Who's afraid of the Huns?" he said. "Maman will attack them with her rug beater! They'll run for their lives!"

But of course, even these innocent whispers pierced her nightcap, and so there came the dreaded broom handle, pounding the ceiling. What sickened him, though, was how he bounded back up the stairs, *you tit-sucker, you baby.* Throwing himself on his bed, he was now defenseless, crushed between his two brains. There was the spasmodically happy, powerfully instinctive, but too easily quashed child brain. And, for better or worse, there was his adult brain, steely and critical, cutting and cynical. Just as the Germans were crushing France, so his adult brain now pounced upon his cowardice, his puerile and pathetic dependency. And, between these two, hammer and anvil, came a poetry so often distanced from the facts of his life or personal feelings, that is, beyond mockery and rage. Had ever a fifteen-year-old been less prone to "poor me" or personal heartache? All was objective—outer. All was observed—mimicked. There was no mask, or need for one, no conscience, no baggage. None of these things that only blind adults. In fact, only one thing still stuck to him—her.

*L*ying there, in the womb of himself, the kid was sobbing—imprisoned like the Count of Monte Cristo.

A freak, he thought, that's who you are, a helpless, stupid freak. Like the Monster Boy, he thought suddenly. This was the carnival freak he'd seen earlier that summer at a circus sideshow. Piss-smelling straw, the licking torches, wild-looking gypsies banging drums—it was a scene irresistible to men and boys. No females allowed.

Come! Dare! See the Monster Boy! challenged the man in the bowler hat strutting the boards, beneath the licking torches. For here, high above him, flapping in the wind, heraldlike, were lurid, crudely drawn canvas backdrops. Towering images old as the Middle Ages, picturing—around the Monster Boy—the Worm Man, the Human Bat, and a geek who bit the heads off live chickens.

"*Alors, alors*, I warn you, gentlemen, this show is not for the weak of heart!"

The drums picked up the beat. Swilling from a bottle, the barker blew real fire, and the wind picked up, causing the great placard-sized canvases to inflate in horror like flabby cheeks. So the boy did it, bought a ticket, then entered the torch-lit darkness, where, squinting, he saw this skinny apparition, chained to the floor. Stooped, the size of a small ape. *Quelle farce!* cried the man behind him, a heckler demanding his money back. *A fake?* thought the boy. *As mangled as the poor kid was?*

Deflated dark angel. Disfigured as he was, it was hard to imagine he'd ever been born or been a child or had a mother. Curled long nails. Flayed nose. Hideous curled-up lips. And worst of all, the flapping gills cut deep into his neck—gills! And his acute, trembling terror—this seemed real. With his jagged hair and his teeth filed to points, he hissed and spat to keep people away, and just as freely the audience, men and soldiers, gibbered and raged back at him. "*Connard,*" asshole! cried one—and out it shot, a long, brown whip of chewing tobacco that snagged the kid, then ran down his face to loud guffaws. Acid. The Monster Boy shrieked and jerked at the chain. Howls of laughter. Another shower of stinging nuts.

Connard! Connard!

Nobody stopped it. The barker laughed, too, laughed even as he sold them the nuts bulleting across the room. But look, thought the kid. The bloody iron collar around the kid's neck, it was paint, not blood; it was just red paint. Fake, absolutely it was fake, and yet even as the muscleman threw out the heckler, the man yelled back that the Monster Boy was just a *comprachico*, just a child mutilated, *purposely* mutilated. "Mutilated?" asked the kid, as the muscleman hauled the heckler up by the belt. "But who did that?"

Was he stupid? "By his parents, of course," said the heckler. "They mutilated him, then sold him like a pig."

Sold! At this word, the kid burned with rage and embarrassment, to think of parents mutilating their own child. Selling him to be exhibited along with the pickled cock of Alphonse le Géant. Probably off a stallion, before which the woman with the quivering breasts now moaned and shimmied. A freak show, he thought. Why, this was the biggest veal pen going. Grab a torch! Set fire to the place, burn it down. But then what? What would Monster Boy do in life? Trapped between childhood and adulthood, the Monster Boy was now so lost, so terrorized, that all he was, *was* the role.

Well, innocence wasn't going to save anybody—not that night. Realizing this, the boy shot up, bolted through the crowd, then dove into the greasy summer darkness—late, desperately late. Running down the road, he could think only of escape, that when it got really bad, he'd run away, then if *that* got bad, he'd run away from *that*, and then from the *that* of *that*—until here's Roche. When right in front of the house, flat on his back, to trip over, here's Frédéric. Dead drunk. Right where his friends dumped him as a joke, grass and bits of vomit on his lips. But then, as he tries to haul Frédéric up—blackout. Down he goes with a rabbit chop to the neck.

"Leave him." On his back, dazed, he sees her peering down at him in her billowing nightgown, her long gray hair blowing free and scentless for no man.

"Leave it," she says. "Drink with the devil, lie with the devil."

"Maman, stop! *Stop it.*" He takes his brother by the arm. "Frédéric, *up*—"

"*Inside.* Leave it."

"*It*? Are you crazy? That's your *son*."

"*That* is no son of mine. Now *in*! In before I brain you again."

He didn't argue. To his everlasting rage and shame, he let her, and he saved no one that night. Not the Monster Boy or Frédéric, lying in the cold dew among the slugs and crickets.

21 ⸲ The Sleeper

The Monster Boy: It was he whom Rimbaud remembered that glorious night as the German guns played their lullaby of *whuu-ump ump-ump*. For that was the night, late in the war, when he, Arthur Rimbaud, *Poet*, finally broke out! Like war!

Conveniently forgetting his sisters, he crept down the stairs, then down the darkened hall, past the room where the ogress slumbered. The kitchen door was unlocked, so leave it open, he thought—wide open. Let the Huns pry open her cold thighs.

Two thin franc notes. No blanket, no food, no coat. In fact, besides the two hands stuffed in his pockets, the only thing the kid had was one fat wad of paper, two stubby pencils, and the little penknife he used to whittle them to points. No matter. In ecstasy he splashed through the bouncing, slapping rye, diving into what he came to call *free freedom*, thinking, This will be forever. Yet even then his more adult brain, the heckler, snarled back, You dope, you know you'll only come crawling back.

River flashing. Water rushing. Cold moonlit stones as he crossed it, swamping through cold black, knee-high depths. Then, heading for the guns, the excitement, after some three or four kilometers, look, over the hill—long, throbbing flames. Big guns with explosions so loud and low his ears popped. Wonderful! He whooped. He swung his arms. It was like dancing in the rain. And through the fog, farther on, here it was, the real show, boy: soldiers hunched over long-bayoneted rifles, rows of tents and campfires winking far into the distance. But God, the stink! Probably a thousand men, he guessed. It wasn't an army, it was a beast, shucking fields and ripping down forests. And dumping its crap. Stinking crap piles. Crap everywhere.

When, stumbling down the embankment, he jumped back, his heart blurting into his neck. It was *a boy*, a sprawled, twisted, open-mouthed, upside-down boy soldier under his upside-down rifle. Two angry black stains on his blue coat. Gray clouded-over eyes. *Hoo*, the kid snorted. Drew in sharply his loosening guts—farted. Then, not knowing what better to do, he pulled out, like bandages, his sweaty-soggy wad of writing paper, white and blowing in the wind.

When, *whump*, he lost his footing, then slid down the muddy embankment as the poem flooded up into his eyes. That's sick, he thought, you can't just *write* about this kid lying here dead. But then through this same dialectic, with new practicality, he stood up, legs spraddled, harvesting the kid's pockets. Nasty buzzard. Especially since the kid was French. Sharply, he pulled the corpse up by the lapels, then patted the boy down, lard cold. Then, as he dropped him, he felt the empty lungs expiring, that and the twisted, frightening way the agate-eyed boy turned away, almost shrugged, as if now he just wanted to stay dead.

Crap. Two franc notes, a broken clay pipe, and a little rosary that hadn't exactly served him. But wait, he found a plug of cheap tobacco, sniffed it, then stuffed it in his back pocket. But finally, after he'd taken everything, a voice told him he had to do *something* for the poor son of a bitch. So, with a shudder, he closed forever the clouded-over eyes.

"Night, brother."

And although the very next day he would be caught ticketless on the Paris-bound train—beaten freely by the conductor, then the gendarmes—despite the black eye and cut-up mouth, he didn't return home empty-handed. Clear as newspaper dispatch and cold beyond pity, here's the record—mostly true, save for the improved scenery and night turned to day:

The Sleeper in the Valley

It is a green hollow where the river sings
Madly catching on the grasses

Silver rags; where the sun shines from the proud mountain:
It is a small valley which bubbles over with rays.

A young soldier, his mouth open, his head bare,
And the nape of his neck bathing in the cool blue watercress,
Sleeps; he is stretched out on the grass, under clouds,
Pale on his green bed where the light rains down.

His feet in the gladiolas, he sleeps. Smiling as
A sick child would smile, he is taking a nap:
Nature, cradle him warmly: he is cold.

Odors do not make his nostrils quiver.
He sleeps in the sun, his hand on his breast,
Quieted. There are two red holes in his right side.

22 𝄞 Destroy

"*Dehors, bon sang*—out! When will you get out? I'll not support a lazy, nasty, drunken brute!"

Witness Mme. Rimbaud, mezzo-soprano, on the stairs, singing—to the upper boxes of heaven—her heir-banishing "Marseillaise."

How quickly times change. Fully one year has passed, and for the kid, as with any other adolescent, it has been a year of rapid costume changes, of renounced ideas and dizzyingly brief phases. Yet one thing has not changed: despite a string of three- and four-day breakouts, his sixteen-year-old teeth still retain their death lock on the Original Tit.

But it wasn't merely Mme. Rimbaud upon whom the little brute had spat. Now, in Charleville, people began to see scrawled on the village walls—in infernally backward letters, as if written by the devil— *MERDE A DIEU.* Shit be to God. And so *les Carolopolitains*, as the denizens of Charleville were called (and even as they experienced that buttery French form of schadenfreude at the widow's rude comeuppance), now they, too, wanted the little prick gone.

There was also the matter of his deranged appearance. Hair: greasy, long, and stringy. Manners: nasty to nonexistent. Clothes: stinky sheeny. Add to that the now unrecognizable bowler hat, the floor-dragging coat (swiped), and (swiped too) the clay pipe—*le brûle-gueule*, the mouth burner—that he smoked upside down, dribbling ashes. A loiterer, a vandal and teller of lewd tales. A mooch and a swiper of drinks. So *les Carolopolitains* now saw their fallen star.

And yet he was not merely a disgrace; he was a *willed* disgrace. For even as he demolished the old effigy of Prince Perfect, by the week, if not the day, he was molting, forgetting, shedding, disowning, even while remembering, as it were, new forms. Reckless expression and irrationality. Obscenity. Obscurantism. The scatological. Really, childishness combating the stupefying effects of what might be called *adultishness*.

And yet, very importantly, he was deciding, with guillotinelike swiftness, what he hated or merely found boring, and all while realizing the very things he would not do, or be, or give the reading public—as if he much cared about *that*.

Particularly nauseating to him was the overly artistic, the idolization and trivialization of "art"—of art as "pursuit," or a "calling," or, still worse, a "profession." In fact, in his rants about contemporaries—the fossils, the academicians, the dead, and the imbeciles—he rankled at the mere technicians, the same who, as he put it, insisted on zoological principles when he wanted a five-winged bird. Meaning that, almost by the month, he would renounce everything, reverse course, then lash himself to another mast, bound for some new destination.

But what of his contemporaries? As counter-Romantics, the Parnassians fled emotion, or at least genuinely *emotional* emotion of the base and vulgar variety experienced by ordinary humans. Sculptors of the word, they were all about form. As for subject matter and imagery, they thrilled to the bygone glories of antiquity—heraldic horses and mythological beasts and gazeless statues of chiseled alabaster. Here, to make it more concrete, examples are warranted. Accurate examples. And so, in an effort to elevate *sense* over some perhaps contrived metrical structure, the following poem excerpts—all taken from Rimbaud's immediate contemporaries—are rendered in *prose*. Take this passage, for example, from the work of their putative leader, Théodore de Banville, the same to whom the boy had sent his first self-conscious appeal the year before:

> *Sculptor, seek with care, while awaiting inspiration, a flawless marble with which to make a lovely vase; seek for long hours its form and engrave in it no mysterious loves nor divine combats. No Heracles victorious over the monster of Nemea, nor birth of Cypris on the scented sea . . .*

There was the equally rococo José-Maria de Heredia, who wrote with great flourish about the queenly Ariadne and Bacchus, the god of the grape, bringing vast orgy in his wake:

> *. . . And the kingly monster, flexing its broad loins, beneath that beloved burden paws at the sandy arena, and, brushed by the hand that trails the reins at random, roars with love as it bites the flowers of its bit.*

> *Letting her hair cascade down the arching flank, amber clusters amid the black grapes, the Bride does not hear the muted bellow . . .*

There was also Théophile Gautier, tapping his magic wand before rendering in webs of purest spun sugar:

> *Symphony in white major*
> *Curving the lines of their white necks in tales of the North we see swan-maidens swimming on the old Rhine, singing near the bank.*

> *Or, hanging on some branch the plumage that clothes them, they display their glossy skin, whiter than the snow of their down.*

Among these women there is one who comes down to us sometimes, as white as the moonlight on the glaciers in the cold skies . . .

There were others, of course. "For us, a sorrowful generation consumed by visions and insulted by his angelic sloth," Rimbaud wrote, "Musset is fourteen times worse! O the tedious tales and proverbs."

Indeed, for our teenage apprentice, his contemporaries—with two conspicuous exceptions—fell into three categories: the dead, the imbeciles, and the merely innocent—let us not pause overmuch.

Paul Verlaine, though, was a real poet, he declared. But Baudelaire, he said, was the first seer, the *king* of poets, a real god. Consider this from Baudelaire's "Consecration," a poem that—quite aside from its vitriolic power and clarity—spoke of feelings the boy could not fail to notice:

When by an edict of the sovereign powers
the Poet enters this indifferent world,
his mother, spurred to blasphemy by shame,
clenches her fists at a condoling God:

"Why not have given me a brood of snakes
rather than make me rear this laughing-stock?
I curse the paltry pleasures of the night
on which my womb conceived my punishment!

Since I am chosen out of all my sex
to bring this scandal to my bed and board,
and since I cannot toss the stunted freak,
as if he were a love-letter, into the fire,

at least I can transfer Your hate to him,
the instrument of all Your wickedness,
and so torment this miserable tree
that not one of its blighted buds will grow!"

Or this from Baudelaire's "Lethe":

Sullen, lazy beast! creep close
until you lie upon my heart;
I want to fill my trembling hands
with your impenetrable mane,

to sooth my headache in the reek
of you that permeates your skirts
and relish, like decaying flowers,
the redolence of my late love.

In drowsiness sweet as death itself
let my insistent kisses cloud
the gleaming copper of your skin.
I want to sleep—not live, but sleep . . .

The boy's harsh judgments made him no less harsh with his own work. "Burn it," he ordered his old friend Delahaye, shoving at him another mass of papers. And Delahaye promised. But, like many a designated burner, Delahaye lied and dithered and kept it safe. And although, on some level, Rimbaud knew this, he had achieved his primary objective. He had gotten it out of him, and away from him, like a tapeworm pulled from his guts. So much for the Muse.

But then, out of all this negativity, came something positive, a revelation that no poet or artist of his time ever had had, or could have had. A transformation of this magnitude required tremendous pressure and fracture, bad blood, bad history. In short, a role for which the kid was perfect.

First, he had the screwup advantage. Having left the *collège* with no baccalaureate, not only had he failed spectacularly but he had done what no local child had ever done—willfully turned himself into a lewd public menace. No interest in bathing. No job. No girl. And yet, despite his outward rebellion, as the boy knew too well, he was stuck, awaiting further orders for a mission that remained unclear.

Looking for clues toward his great project, he had ransacked the school library and stolen every book he could stuff down his trousers. And yet, as we've seen, he found little to love, and almost nothing to teach him—other, of course, than what he parodied and stole from lesser poets with neither acknowledgment nor apology. As the young vandal wrote around this time, "Newcomers are free to condemn their ancestors. We are at home and we have the time."

It was then that he experienced the first shocks of this revolutionary project. It came one day when he actually *saw* himself, like a face in a pool—saw the child self, now grown, that all his life he had harbored. Of course many a child harbors—at least for a while—an imaginary friend. But upon taking up residence, Rimbaud's double had remained hidden in him, much as the boy Rimbaud had once hidden in his father's military tunic, a fortress of blue and gold braid that smelled of sweat and the tropics. That is, until his mother found it and burnt it. Threw it, evil thing, on a pile of straw, smoking and stinking like horsehair as she turned it with a pitchfork.

Hiding, then, was the only solution. At school, during the morning roll call, when the boy said "present," he was in fact absent—his double did the prize boy's grind work. And so until now, without fully realizing or acknowledging it, he was two: the one who wrote it and the one who then *un*wrote it, refuted it, then gave it away, another bastard left on a church stoop.

It was then, in his doubleness, that the first great revelation hit him: *Je est un autre.* I is someone else.

I is someone else? In 1871, this was gibberish. Fractured grammar. Crazy talk. Other than the denizens of asylums, people, like blocks of stone, were whole beings with names and jobs and addresses, not separate compartments and selves—why, selves wasn't even a concept. And so, like Athena bursting from the head of Zeus, his manifesto was born in a revolutionary letter, written in one frenzied night, then sent to the two people who might appreciate it, his pal Demeny and Georges Izambard, his former teacher, who found a fat letter in his morning post. What was the man to make of this? It was Rimbaud's now famous letter of the *voyant*—the seer. Seeing, in this case, far into the next century, how art would be waged, art as war, war as art. It began, familiarly enough, with a round of insult:

Cher Monsieur!

You are a teacher again. You have told me we owe a duty to Society. You belong to the teaching body: you move along in the right track. I also follow the principle: cynically I am having myself *kept*. . . .

In reality, all you see in your principle is subjective poetry: your obstinacy in reaching the university trough—excuse me—proves this. But you will always end up a self-satisfied man who has done nothing because he wanted to do nothing. Not to mention that your subjective poetry will always be horribly insipid. . . .

Now, I am degrading myself as much as possible. Why? I want to be a poet, and I am working to make myself a *seer*: you will not understand this, and I don't know how to explain it to you. It is a question of reaching the unknown by the derangement of *all the senses*. The sufferings are enormous, but one has to be strong, one has to be born a poet, and I know I am a poet. . . .

For *I* is someone else. If brass wakes up a trumpet, it is not its fault. This is obvious to me: I am present at this birth of my thought: I watch it and listen to it: I draw a stroke of the bow: the symphony makes it stir in the depths, or comes onto the stage in a leap. . . .

The first study of the man who wants to be a poet is the knowledge of himself, complete. He looks for his soul, inspects it, tests it, learns it. As soon as he knows it, he must cultivate it! It seems simple: in every mind a natural development takes place.

It was mad, of course. Why, at one point the boy said the poet soul must be made "monstrous," then added: "Imagine a man implanting and cultivating warts on his face." Warts! thought Izambard. Well, there was only one thing to do with such nonsense and that was to do what any sensible person would have done under the circumstances. Izambard put the letter in a box, then promptly forgot all about it.

23 ⸙ Two Poles

But, other than colossal laziness, there was another reason Mme. Rimbaud couldn't get this poltergeist out of her house. For late that summer, as the war was winding down, after yet another failed breakout, the kid returned with two uncharacteristically autobiographical poems. Two poles, one describing something wonderful and the other something horrible. Two facts as different as heaven and hell.

First, the happy poem, the happiest, most beatific and unselfconscious poem that he had ever written or would write.

In fact, had the other poem not happened—or rather, had the tragedy behind the poem not happened—well, who knows, the boy's writings might have pointed toward a life of projective joy. Or at least a degree of serenity before the facts of who he actually was.

Green—green was what invaded him that day when he came upon a green inn called the Green Cabaret. All green. Green the willows and the grape arbor, green the gables. Green the walls, the chairs, the tables— green everything, a green as green as his hunger as he stared through the green window. But greenest of all was the buxom young serving maid dressed all in green in a dirndl with green flounces. Who then bent down to serve a man—slyly down, sweeping him with bosom, braids, and ribbons. When, *wham*, dinner was served.

At the Cabaret-Vert

For a week my boots had been torn
By the pebbles on the roads. I was getting into Charleroi.
—At the Carbaret-Vert: I asked for bread
And butter, and for ham that would be half chilled.

Happy, I stretched out my legs under the green
Table. I looked at the very naïve subjects
Of the wallpaper.—And it was lovely,
When a girl with huge tits and lively eyes

—She's not one to be afraid of a kiss!—
Laughing, brought me a plate of bread and butter,
Warm ham, in a colored plate,

White and rosy ham flavored with a clove
Of garlic—and filled my enormous mug with its foam
Which a late ray of sun turned gold.

It was God's gift—a beam of green, unalloyed joy. Such joy that, two days later, even half starved and mosquito bitten, the kid woke again into that wondrous state when God moved in him like a river and shook the trees. It was a feeling of overflowing, a command to attend and *shut up.* All followed by a sunny day that made him feel like a dizzy, giddy child, not so much running as falling forward.

War? In this touched state, even with war still on, there was no fear. Like the air in the air and the wind that moved the trees, nothing touched him but everything went through him—even the artillery shells going *whu-ump* miles away. As for the nearer ones, they tore like sheets and exploded with a palpable pressure on the eye—that close, *and it was wonderful,* roaring over the next hill like the distant crash of the sea.

And France, with a crumbling and humiliated army, France was merely counting the days to defeat. But why should this concern him, a poet? The poet was a soldier. Poetry was war and war was poetry, and that morning, through shattered forests, free from his mother and God-cloaked in invincibility, he found the war so irresistible and now so close that he couldn't even mind the shells shuddering down, which shook his knees, *whu-ump, whu-ump.* And in the air—smoke. Smoke snared in the branches, and not just the burnt-match smell of gunpowder. Here was pungent cook smoke carrying the good greasy stench of sausages, sizzling army sausages—hot chow! Well, why not, thought the boy, maybe some softhearted cook would take pity on him, a poor, starving kid . . . a *war orphan*. Hey, that might work. And seeing soldiers, French soldiers, his brothers in arms, why, the uncatechized masses now ready to revolt and be free, well, naturally the boy walked right over.

When, suddenly, he is surrounded by boots, muddy boots on a muddy road. And above those boots, *in a way he knew ages before*, he saw hard, angry faces. Unshaven faces. Faces that, with a show of teeth, suddenly all have the same idea.

"We're going to make it hard on you, kid."

And one soldier pushed him forward, while another pushed him back, while the third, like a vile frog, squirted a long, brown tongue of tobacco spit. Amazing, in his shock, the kid watched it snag his sleeve as, with a yelp, the first wolf dragged him down.

By the neck. Smashed his face down in the mud—*kill me?* Bucked him up and spat twice in his hand—*but how?* For it all seemed incredible—*I'm not German.* Soldiers wearing blue, not brown—*soldiers from my own country.* Soldiers hauling down his ripped trousers—*me, a French citizen!* And look, here in his pocket, he had two more poems, beauties—sacred words. Words given to him, *whispered to him*, by God.

When, abracadabra, in a spray of gibberish, *it was not him.*

It was not him whom they were splitting like a chicken, *ittth itth itth*, first one, then two, then three, then a sloppy fourth. For suddenly, shattering and showering down, it was instead *a poem—a picture in the sky.* A million twittering dreams. A hammock of balls slapping his chin—wondering how a man's face could be so red with legs so white? Blood was red? Choked to death? *Why?* There was no pain. *The children all sang.* There was no suffering. *The sky is white.* Outcry—but why? *Pay attention. God is teaching you something.*

Squashed on the ground, he could hear his breath going *ithh iitthh ittthh.* And look, right there beside him, *in this little land*, crawling between the shuffling boots, was this *poor little guy*, this *black beetle* bumbling along, *come on, fella*—missed by a boot—*try, try*—missed again—then *goo*, dead, and God watched that, too. *And the children singing and jumping rope over the rainbow? Over the cold snowflakes trailing down? And, closing their eyes, the children held out their tongues and waited—*

When, with a suck of wind, out it came, God's own member, as slick as spit and as fractured as the stars. With this as recompense.

The Stolen Heart

My sad heart slobbers at the poop,
My heart covered with tobacco spit:
They spew streams of soup at it,
My sad heart drools at the poop:
Under the jeering of the soldiers
Who break out laughing
My sad heart drools at the poop,
My sad heart covered with tobacco spit!

Ithyphallic and soldierish,
Their jeerings have depraved it!
On the rudder you see frescoes
Ithyphallic and soldierish,
O abracadabratic waves,
Take my heart, let it be washed!
Ithyphallic and soldierish,
Their jeerings have depraved it.

When they have used up their quid,
How will I act, O stolen heart?
There will be Bacchic hiccups,
When they have used up their quid:
I will have stomach retchings,
If my heart is degraded:
When they have used up their quid
How will I act, O stolen heart?

24 ⚘ Land Captain

"Careful," cries Rimbaud—but they are not careful. "Slow"—but the native porters do not slow down, not when they themselves are in a semi-trance of pounding, slipping, bone-crushing agony. The MacDonalds and their two children? God knows—behind, evaporated, vanished in the dust—as down he swoops, down the brick red wash in his banging hell toboggan.

Pain. Pain is the beat and pain is the way. Now he is all pain, borne by black feet caked with white dust, feet hammering down vast, slithering, dried-up riverbeds that, in an instant, without warning, could become a raging, muddy, man-devouring torrent. And all from a mere smudge in the sky a few miles away.

The contingency and *fact* of such realities—the moral burden of being responsible for this party, the children especially, in his precarious state—all this makes Rimbaud increasingly angry. Furiously angry, and angry above all at the scarily agreeable Mr. MacDonald, whose religious scruples, apparently, do not permit him to carry a gun—notions that, when they come to Rimbaud's attention, send him into a near paroxysm of fury at the man's fecklessness. But, for the first two days, Rimbaud mostly manages to quash these feelings, and then for just one reason: namely, his strange esteem for Mrs. MacDonald. If, indeed, *esteem* is quite the word.

It shocks even him, feral creature, that he should now be so desperate for the woman's approval. At a look, a word, a touch, with virtually any contact whatsoever from her, he can feel a wave of dizziness and hunger sweep up his neck and scalp, and merely because she has brought him a cup of tea—*tea*. It is not sexual, exactly, and yet how it thrills him as quietly but forcefully she invades his person, even as she subtly undermines his command.

"Drink it," she said, leaning down and handing him the warm metal cup that first night, as the sky darkened and cooled—cooled quite precipitously—even as the day's torrential heat welled up, almost buoy-antly, from the ground. "I shall require you to eat something, too, Mr. Rimbaud," she continued as, over him, he felt the pressure of her bosom and handsome, plump shoulders. "And," she added briskly, as he sat there dazed, like a boy being read to, "once we better know each other—tomorrow, perhaps—I trust you will permit me to examine that leg."

At this he nearly spat out his tea.

"*Tomorrow*," she repeated, her smile peeping out beneath her very dusty straw hat, tied, or twirled rather, Abyssinian style, with a once-white scarf. Playfully she added, "When we *know* each other better." Then, smiling down upon him, with a plump maternal hand, she felt his forehead, which—quite beyond his inflated temperature—flushed some-where between dream and desperation.

In turn, this queasy, now problematic need for her warmth and sym-pathy and approval, this further stokes Rimbaud's almost irrational anger at Mr. MacDonald, anger and incomprehension that so fine and sensible a woman could marry, much less remain with, such a man, much less accompany him on such an ill-advised journey. Then again, Rimbaud does not ask himself what her role might have been in this debacle. Clearly she wears the trousers.

Hour after hour, as he thumps along, these thoughts absorb him, even as they defeat him, for in his mind the MacDonalds are like a puz-zle that will not fit together, precisely because they *are* together. But the children, too, tug at him, give him strange looks—weird-man-cripple looks—particularly the boy, whatshisname. Right—Ralph. Splendid boy. That someday son who, in Rimbaud's mind, would be a self-willed, self-possessed little fellow sailing a toy boat, just as he and Frédéric had as boys on the river Meuse. Swift dreams, bright sun, green depths. Look down on the bottom, trout shadows, silver shadows among the swift, brilliant stones. Split-second dreams. Yes, indeed, a sturdy boy. A wor-thy boy, that whatshisname—Ralph. Never sulky. Never cries or bawls or asks to be carried, like his sister, now unfortunately old enough to know she is being tortured on a trek that seemingly will never end. But my God, thinks the adult Rimbaud the outlier, like a lion lying in the grass, to have such a bumbler for a father. *He* would not be such a father. *Never.*

Too late to marry?

But with a mechanical leg? *But surely with science the legs are better now.*

And what about that fiancée his mother has for him? *Possibly.*

But what would become of Tigist? *A spinster? Send for her? Marry her?*

You need a girl with good parents, his mother had told him. *But good breasts?*

And how would he *do* it, a cripple? *She would do it for me? Over me? In a chair?*

Yet, in contrast to these swirling ruminations as the bearers bag him along like a trophy carcass, well, good grief, thinks Rimbaud, how indefatigable and cheerful, how strangely powerful, MacDonald is, carrying his children across a muddy brown stream or combing the girl's snarled hair. Astonishing, the whispering, half-singing care he will expend, just attending to their poor blistered feet. Just that. Feet.

But how on earth can she stay with him?

Because he is a steady man? A goodly man?

A better man than I?

*S*till, beyond the merely irrational, beyond drift and daydream, once Rimbaud snaps into it as the caravan leader, he does have some quite legitimate problems with how MacDonald conducts himself, and these problems begin early—in fact, within the first two hours. It starts when Rimbaud happens to look back only to see their tiny, ancient driver, on the descent, no less, whipping the tiny donkey tied to the ridiculous tumbrel with the door-sized wheels. Poor beast. Squalling and stumbling on loose stones, the little donkey is ready to go over the mountain even as the old fool beats him.

That's it. Rimbaud's arm goes up, precipitating a slow-motion collapse as, like a broken accordion, as men and animals compress, then come to a standstill, with every eye—beast or man—on *him*. And here is his precise predicament as the caravan leader.

In a world in which, for the *frangi*, everything counts and is counted, the very fact that he would *stop*, stop now in an already extraordinary situation—and, worse, after a late start—this counts as a strike against him. Nevertheless, Rimbaud risks it. He calls for his litter to be set down. Then, as subtly as he can, calls over MacDonald. Who, with no idea what is the matter, much less that *he* is the matter, blithely springs over. It's terrible. Time is hemorrhaging. Yet here Rimbaud is—a man lying on a *gurney*, for Christ's sake—calling their man unfit.

"I'm sorry," says Rimbaud, trying to tamp down his rage, "but in three days either your man will be dead or a complete liability—him and his donkey. Now send him back, quickly. We are behind as it is."

"But, sir," responds Mr. MacDonald in his lackadaisical way. Worse, he then squats down like a peer, adding, "Kassa is very sturdy and experienced. And he depends on us."

"Mr. MacDonald," says Rimbaud with a cold stare, "please understand me. This matter is now settled. And," he sighs, "when he goes, half your things must go as well."

"But, sir," protests MacDonald, now mopping his face with a dirty handkerchief, "the man needs my employ. And Mr. Rimbaud, as for our equipage, sir, well, it includes many sacred articles, religious articles—"

"*Sir*," says Rimbaud ruthlessly, now like a stranger to all the world, "*get* in the lifeboat and do not tell the captain where or how to row. Or start swimming, sir."

"Fergus!" cries Mrs. MacDonald, lest he inquire again. "You heard him. *Up*. Let us now make our choices and go."

*F*ool, thinks Rimbaud, still smarting over MacDonald's idiocy.

Failed fool thinking that in a land of unwritten rules—inflexible rules—being *nice* would carry him through.

Putrid fool with his primitive, ballyhooing idea of Jesus, chasing his burning bush.

But beneath it all, Rimbaud is disgusted with himself. That back in Harar, what with Djami and Tigist and the beggars—that in a low moment, stupidly, he had taken on the MacDonalds and their children. That now, when all he had was his reputation, that his reputation might be destroyed—him and everyone in his party if the skinny men get the upper hand. Proof forever of the Rimbaud luck.

So it had been two years ago with one of his colleagues—Leonetti, an Italian. Wiped out, him and all his party, including his wife. Thirty-two in all, and not forty kilometers from where they now stand. Even spookier, Rimbaud, all prepared to go, had to stay back at the last minute—problems with the king. Then five days later came the terrible news. With a heavily armed search party, Rimbaud left the next day.

Coming on the scene, he thought what a mercy shipwrecks were, how clean, their horrors swallowed by the sea. Not so here. Days later, here they were, stinking, once-living men in almost archaeological attitudes, the only life spared being those of the camels and horses. Things that actually had value.

Taking out his brass telescope, he saw them to the east, not a quarter of a kilometer away, the skinny men, the defiant, lion-haired men. Through this narrow, wavering aperture, he could see them—white teeth. Mocking them. Laughing and cavorting, under the proscenium of red rock, they were like ancient actors in the bloody final act of some Greek tragedy.

*A*nd yet by the third day, whatever his failings, MacDonald is not the goat. By then, amid the heat and the tension and the slow progress, Rimbaud feels the party's frustrations directed at just one man—him. Angry at him for slipping. Angry at the burden he represents. Angry at the potential disaster if he dies. And angry most of all—after all their agonies—at the pittance they will receive should he survive.

But of all the aggrieved, none are angrier than the sixteen porters now laboring to carry him, four teams of four, angry at the leg and the dead weight of him, forever sliding and complaining. Mutinous bastards. Too bad he can speak their language. Hence his state of suspense, as he thinks, They're going to kill me? When are they going to kill me?

Well, why not? Here there is no force in law, no hope of quarter or rescue, and yet for the first days, for almost no reason he can discern, the leader mystique holds, but barely. Then on day three, a big rain falls. It's a long, dark plume. It's an inverted mountain in the sky, a floating waterfall rent with white flashes and lightning cracks, torrential in its energy. Driving rain. Hot, then cold rain, it sizzles in the mud, coming down so hard that one almost has to spit to see. No shelter, not even a tree, and in the deluge the porters drop him hard—purposely so in the rain-boiling mud, a spewing gargling sewer where he remains for five hours, freezing and virtually unprotected under a goatskin—a rag, an insult. And so, when the sky clears, as the beasts are collected, Rimbaud sends the MacDonalds on ahead—well ahead with three gunmen. Tells them to stay there, too. Then at gunpoint, by the throat several of them, the mutineers are brought up.

"Drop me in the mud!" he says, in a low, slow, emphatic growl. "Do you think you can do that and get away with it? *Do you?* Do you want to see what I am now prepared to do? Dabir!" he calls, to the leader of the killer clan, "bring it out! The *kit*. Show these bastards what we have for mutineers."

And so Dabir, with the cleaverlike dagger strapped to his side, Dabir withdraws from his saddlebags the coiled-up bullwhip of braided leather, the notched stakes, and the rawhide straps to bind the wrists and ankles—straps, swears Rimbaud, with which he will stretch them like raw goatskins, with lashes arbitrary in number and entirely at his whim.

"At even a *whiff* of insolence," he thunders. "Even so slight as the wings of a fly." He has not lost his frightening flare for drama.

"But who then will carry you?" So asks Abdullahi, their leader—a smart mouth.

"*You* will carry me, Abdullahi—even bloody. Gaze into my eyes. Do you doubt me? Perhaps . . ." He trails off. "But," he says, pointing to his mercenaries, "do not doubt *them*. Especially when I pay them. *Double*, if you try me again. Double to peel you like a banana—you and you and you, if you even so much as *displease* me."

Anger, it is like a locomotive, roaring and unstoppable—pain's antidote. But however horrible, however unsound, Rimbaud's hideous little show is effective as, with new obedience, the now sobered porters carry him off, slowly bouncing like a carcass. But then like a lost god—gazing up at the swallowing sky—Rimbaud stares down at himself, stares as through a microscope at his ruthlessness, horrified at what he was utterly prepared to do.

Still, addled or not, Rimbaud knows one thing: that if he lets up for a second, one night in a blaze of knives and muzzle flashes he and the MacDonalds will wind up like Leonetti and his wife. Twisted wrecks in the cinder road.

"*B*ut, Monsieur Rimbaud," protests MacDonald on the fourth day. Which, even among bad days, is a very bad day indeed, much of it spent clambering over prehistoric boulders. "But, Monsieur," he says, all teeth and squint, "under the circumstance, sir, we've made very good progress, have we not? I mean the poor children, sir, well, as you can see, Monsieur—"

"*Sir* or *Monsieur*," spits back Rimbaud. "Pick one!"

Rimbaud then calls down to the bearers.

"*No!* Do not set me down. This will not take long—"

"—But, sir—"

"—*Out* with it."

"Monsieur—"

"Did you not hear me? *Sir* or *Monsieur*."

"But, sir—Monsieur," stumbles MacDonald, flustered. "What with the rocks, they've had their little legs run off—the children. Suffer the little children, sir."

"Oh, good God," groans Rimbaud, "suffer *you*, MacDonald."

"Well, I expect so," he replies, attempting, for the children's sake, to turn this public beating into a moment of levity. "But, Monsieur, please. *Were* you one, once? A child? I mean, *can* you not see their faces?" Rimbaud gives a chop of the arm.

"Down," he barks as if to an elephant. "Set me down." Then, fastening on MacDonald, he thunders, "what, then, do *you* propose? That we go plod along until we run out of water? Or stay right here in a spot we can't defend? Is that *your* idea, you kind, decent man?"

"Oh, God!" cries Mrs. MacDonald in exasperation. "Oh, do let us all *go* on. And *get on*. Without all this head butting from you two *tortoises*."

"Mummy," cries the girl, joining her, "Mummy, make him stop." She glares at Rimbaud. "Like to see *you* walk!"

"Children, hush!" cries Mr. MacDonald.

"Oh, *you* hush!" snaps Mrs. MacDonald. "Yes, Mr. MacDonald, you are correct. The children are indeed knackered. In view of which, they are, I believe, entitled to have their feelings. Eh, *Mr.* Rimbaud?" Then she lets him have it. "*You*, you posh *poet*, you. You, up there. Reclining— you, sir, on your precious poet's *pinnacle*."

Clubbed. With the dreaded word *poet* she flattens him.

"But, please," says Rimbaud, still desperate for her approval, "but, Madame. I—I wish we could all drink lemonade in the shade. I do. But . . ."

25 ♪ Shame

And bad as that day is, that night is worse, the moonlit desert glistening, almost phosphorescent, like the tropical night sea. Nighttime, the worst time. For if the skinny men can see you, rest assured, once darkness falls they are coming to kill you.

Termite mounds ten feet high. Ravines. Glowing reefs of grass and bush. Swirling with light and dark, the ground is indefensible for the defender and almost hallucinatory in its vastness, cloaking like a second skin the night-crawling, diabolically patient skinny men. Of these, worst of all are the scorned young males—the Immortals, as Rimbaud thinks of them, boys of fifteen or sixteen, vicious as fire ants and hungry for their first kill so the older warriors will stop hazing them. But most of all so they can finally lie with a woman. Get laid. Be a man.

Against this reality, weapons are deployed, animals unloaded, circles laid, and fires started. Let the fire roar, as Rimbaud's gunmen fan out on snorting, reluctant horses—ten of the twelve, four with long spears to prod the bushes and run down intruders, this as the rest of the pack closes in, with repeater rifles and muskets and curved daggers.

Hy-eet. Gouging their mounts' ribs, off they trot, Rimbaud's hunter-killers. Chewing coffee beans, they are jumpy tonight, eyes on fire after several days with barely any sleep. As for supper, they eat it riding, eat it raw, knifing raw strips off an antelope shot that day, its hind quarters flipped like two saddle bags on the steaming rump of Shaheed's horse. *Hy-eet.*

*F*urze burning and sparks flying, roaring up heaven's flue. No one really sleeps or eats; other than MacDonald, flipping the pages of his Bible, no one really does anything as one anxious hour passes, then two, then three. When all jump at a distant shot—this followed, endless seconds later, by a final capping shot *so you know.* Then, after another agonizingly long pause, they hear another wild tattoo of shots, one, two, then three and more, roaring into the night.

Breaking open the breech, Rimbaud rechecks his brute-bored double barrel. Sets down his pistol, the lever-action Winchester, too, then lays out fat shotgun shells—ten in neat rows of two. Fast loads if they burst out of the bushes. Blood is squeaking in his ear, heart blood, his eyes dizzy, inhaling, as it were, the whorling, ever-widening darkness. And MacDonald, sitting by his wife with his Bible, his two children squeezed between his knees? Still unarmed. Even now, when any minute they could be attacked and overwhelmed.

Horses and men emerge from the darkness.

"Rinbo!" says the hunt's leader, Dabir. Eyes blazing, he grins as two horsemen emerge from the darkness, holding, between them, a drape of human meat. "See," he says proudly, "see what tried us."

Like cats with limp prey, they drop the bloody corpse. Fifteen or sixteen, perhaps, still limp and oozing. Eye gone and jaw shot off, flap and bone.

"God!" cries Mrs. MacDonald, "Up, up, children." Shielding the children's eyes, the MacDonalds disappear behind a tent. No matter. Furze is thrown on the fire, sparks belching—revealing men with their blood up, excitedly settling pistols and daggers and thrusting into the darkness the still warm barrels of dull-gleaming rifles, pointing where they had been, pointing where they had shot. Apparently the first attacker, badly wounded, had crawled off—to die, Dabir assures his employer. Truly. Big blood trail. Black clots. White foam. Lung foam— done. About death, the many species of death, the gunmen are as specific as Eskimos might be enumerating the many varieties of snow. As for Rimbaud, trapped in *his* world with his frightened guests—well, he is mortified. Socially embarrassed. All the more when he knows there can be no putting off this business, the children notwithstanding. For here, dead at his feet, is a bill now due. Same for the one that crawled off and the three more that ran away. For such success there must be shillings. *Shiny* shillings. *Shiny-new,* hence worth more. *English,* the best. Not the thalers used to pay the haulers and camel drivers, not for fine horse warriors such as these. No, no, *the English.* This is what they want.

Thus the bartering starts, as Dabir's men, like the solid workmen they are, gab and point at the corpse quite as if he were a gazelle.

Beau-ti-ful!

This is a word they like, Shaheed now motioning how *beau-ti-ful* that first blast that took the legs out from under him—shot from a horse, a running shot, too. Rimbaud nods. Yes, yes, he knows well the lethal .45-70. A beauty. A knock-down weapon, with its slow, heavy slug. *Don't be distracted.* Sit up, Rimbaud, he thinks. *Fuck the children. He* is now the judge and the captain, and if he is not—if at this moment he is anything less than riveted and commanding—well, then they're all cooked. *Frangi* children. White children. Here they are nothing—needless mouths to feed.

Meanwhile, he can see Mrs. MacDonald behind the tent, then behind the camels, cloaking the children and whispering. But finally she has had it. Tromping over:

"Mr. Rimbaud. Fully one-quarter of an hour has passed for this horror. Sir! I mean, *really.* Will they now *eat* him, too?"

But then, before he can even react, she, a woman, does the unthinkable. Directly, she confronts Dabir. And worse, before his men:

"Sir!"—pointing behind her—"Sir, these are *children.* Now, please, sir, take that poor dead child away and bury him. Do so, I beg of you. Or I will."

"Missis!" cries Rimbaud, so flummoxed that he forgets her name. "Missis, *sit down.* Dabir, please, the fault is all mine. Mine, and I am sorry. Big baksheesh for this, believe me. See here."

"*Twenty-five!*" snaps Dabir, pointing at the woman. "And be happy I don't kill the white meat."

And so the sagging corpse is dragged off and dumped and the men fan out again, nine, while three sleep. Later, nearing dawn, more shots are heard—two, then ten or more. Eyeing Rimbaud with fury, Mrs. MacDonald piles the fire higher. Then, wrapped in her blanket, fairly twitching, she erupts:

"And you *paid* them. And for what, sir? Shooting a boy? A child?"

"Child!" he says. "Do you think, Madame, that that so-called *child* was not coming to kill you? You and your children?"

"Pieces of silver!" she retorts, for she is a Londoner, stubborn and knowing and sure. "For a boy! Really, sir, how barbaric. How *pathetic.* How long have you been out here to have so thoroughly lost your moorings? You, sir, a *poet.*"

"*This is the system.*"

What is happening to me? he thinks. Why does he feel on the verge of tears, frantic that she will think ill of him, that she will abandon him to all there is now—to pain and more pain. "And here you come as my guest," he continues, raising his voice, "of whom I have asked not a farthing. *You* with your Bibles—yes, you, MacDonald. Do you know how it is out here? Do you? Do you think that your Jesus will magically protect you? Do not look to your wife, sir. Look at me—*me*—you who will not pick up a gun. You, sir. *Here*, sir, you are a menace. Do you hear me? A *menace*."

Strange thing, though. At this final vomit of bile and vileness, Rimbaud stops; his whole brain seizes up, as there he sits, emptied. Staring into the hot, pulsing heart of the fire, it's the hypnosis of sorrow he feels. Blank minutes. No words.

Meekly he hopes that now it is over, that maybe they didn't mind; that, being English, they will pretend, cover it over, and let an ugly moment simply pass. The fire crackles. Twigs combust and crumble, fall to dust, as he sits there locked in the stupor of observing, to his horror, the sad spectacle of himself being himself—his inescapable self. When MacDonald clears his throat. Looks up, not sad, not angry, not beaten or even particularly put out, but merely present. In the firelight, MacDonald's eyes shine gold. And then, much to Rimbaud's surprise, Mr. MacDonald does respond to his complaints. He does indeed.

"You ask me what *I* think, sir," he begins. "Well, I know, sir, what *you* think of me. And Mr. Bardey and the others, too, no doubt. Oh, I know. I made a hash of it, and that is true. *I know.* Believe me. I have been sacked and I made a terrible mistake coming here. All very true. But then what? Here I am. And here, sir, are you, and here it is. And so, sir, since I am powerless to change it, well, all I can do is accept it, my black mark, my failure, like a sin upon my soul. Yes, it happened. Indeed it did, and I did it. I don't blame my wife. Stupid or not, or rash, or blind, yes, I have dug myself a hole, a very deep hole, and yes, before my wife and children I will continue, as well as I can, to make my amends. Amends, sir. It's all I can do, just as you, sir, all you can do now is go home, home to France, and hope. Hope, sir. Hope for the best."

The fire burns. The children lie dead asleep and the wife says nothing, as Rimbaud sits there, seized up. Crushed as if by a boa constrictor in this straitjacket of gold. But it is not yet over. Mr. MacDonald has not said his full piece, and it comes with detectable heat.

"But, Mr. Rimbaud," he says, "if you really ask me, well, if you could accept such from me—if your pride was not to get the better of you, well, at this time, I think that I would pray with you, sir. Not because I'm proud or better than you—obviously not. But rather, sir, to help you at a very, very hard time in which you saw fit to help us, stranded as we were without funds or employ in a foreign country. So we pray. But praying, well, I know *that* won't sit with you. Not now. Not yet. *Someday*, perhaps. I certainly hope so. But since it won't work now, well, all I can do is to beg your pardon most kindly and sleep. Sleep, sir. Sleep and hope tomorrow is a better day."

Hot shame. At this Rimbaud's face feels burning hot. Words rise but fail to emerge, and his tongue is fat and twisted, blocking his throat. Not that, inside, he doesn't rail and struggle against the jaws that now have him by the leg. Shaken, he tells himself that with MacDonald it is all evasion and nonsense and dereliction; that this man is guilty of—well, really, desertion under fire, as it were, cowardice under a different name. Shaken and now trapped, trapped in his own life, Rimbaud tells himself many, many things. He tells himself that they, the MacDonalds, not knowing the country or its customs, that people such as they would never in a lifetime, ever, understand. The terms. The conditions. The way in one instant it could all turn on you. Blow up. Go to hell. How everything could seem just fine—until suddenly it was not.

He tells himself that he only has to hold on, to *go* on, to get home to France, home to his family, where life will be better, or at least not here, or not like this. And yet the more Rimbaud tries to dismiss it and explain and delay it, the more it flies back on him, hot as whiplashes, blinding waves of shame. Shame at his cruelty. Shame at his abuse. Shame at attacking MacDonald, a man unafraid who merely refused to fight. Shame at the sham of his life. Shame at that last searing glimpse of Tigist. Shame—blind shame—that he dismissed Djami, probably the one person he ever really loved in this rotten place, Djami, his son!

"I"—in humiliation, then in almost vomiting relief, he says it finally—"I need—"

"I know," she says quietly. "*Mr.* MacDonald, will you kindly assist Mr. Rimbaud as he endeavors to demonstrate he has a bladder, if not a heart?"

26 ⸸ Toward a Heretic Poetics

Stink, stank, stuck. The kid was *stuck.* Stuck at home, stuck in Charleville—stuck. As he wrote to his friend Paul Demeny:

> Situation of the accused: for more than a year I gave up ordinary living for what you know. Closed up without respite in this unmentionable Ardennes country, seeing not a single man, engaged in an infamous, inept, obstinate, mysterious work, answering questions and coarse evil aspostrophes by silence, appearing worthy in my extralegal position, I provoked at the end frightful resolutions of a mother as inflexible as seventy-three administrations with steel helmets.
>
> She tried to force me to perpetual work, in Charleville (Ardennes)! Take the job on such and such a day, she said, or get out.—I refused that life, without giving my reasons: it would have been pitiful. Up until now I have been able to avoid these terms.

And yet—however incomplete and slapdash—he was discovering raw beginnings of a heretic poetics. Of a brilliant, albeit half-baked, or at least not *fully* baked, *philosophy.* Indeed, an incomplete and magic-infused *manifesto* of sorts, a loud complaint that he would nail, even if it killed him, on poetry's rugged door.

Beginning with a warning from the Boy Jesus to *poets* especially—to any and all *fakirs* and art mongers out there. For any who wouldn't die in the pursuit, in hell if need be, and gratefully. As he wrote in that same letter:

Therefore, the poet is truly the thief of fire.

He is responsible for humanity, even for the *animals*; he will have to have his inventions smelt, felt, and heard; if what he brings back from *down there* has form, he gives form; if it is formless, he gives formlessness. A language must be found. Moreover, every word being an idea, the time of a universal language will come!

And more on the march toward universal progress:

This language will be of the soul for the soul, containing everything, smells, sounds, colors, thought holding on to thought and pulling. The poet would define the amount of the unknown awakening in his time in the universal soul: he would give more—than the formulation of his thought, than the annotation of *his march toward Progress*! Enormity becoming normal, absorbed by all, he would really be *a multiplier of progress*!

And more still, on an issue that virtually no one thought about at the time—woman:

When the endless servitude of woman is broken, when she lives for and by herself, man—heretofore abominable—having given her her release, she too will be a poet! Woman will find some of the unknown! Will her world of ideas differ from ours?—She will find strange, unfathomable, repulsive, delicious things; we will take them, we will understand them.

He was still sixteen, after all. He was not methodical, nor could he be at that age, and in Charleville, certainly, there was no one to advise him; there was no known path and, in a way, almost no point. At the same time, however, the kid was cagey—anything but unmindful of how to get his, get yours, and get on his way. And, to be sure, in his often clueless and unerringly self-sabotaging way, he did at this point very much *want* to get on. But how?

Be a worker? But doing what? Be a journalist? But how then would he write, *really* write? Write poems for the now aroused workers? Workers arise! But, being workers, would they, could they, understand?

> Pack of bitches in heat, eating poultices,
> The cry from the house of gold calls you. Steal!
> Eat! See the night of joy with its deep spasms
> Coming down the street. O sad drinkers,
> Drink! . . .

And what about the sundry compromises and disguises required by such pathetic forms of bourgeois subterfuge. Wear a suit? Wash face? Get up early? On this question at last he wrote his young and equally clueless friend, Paul Demeny, this in the hope that Demeny might find him some semiagreeable form of employment. But please, he added, not too taxing. Another worthy theory: workless work.

*I*t all went nowhere, of course. But then in the midst of his luckless isolation and scheming and pipe dreaming, the kid meets in the tavern a ponderous local personality named Charles Auguste Bretagne. A sort of taproom ruminant.

Bretagne, a big brain in a guppy bowl. Bretagne, poet of sorts, sucking on his meerschaum pipe. Indeed, a barroom braggart and know-it-all so competitive that he would bet on which of two flies inching up a wall would be the first to reach the top. And this while he played two hands of whist, with a two-hour disquisition on Zoroastrianism thrown in.

But give the man his due: This Bretagne is a genuine polymath, albeit without direction or degree, working by day as a clerk in a local sugar refinery. Bretagne is, in addition, two-seat fat, with swollen knees and a ragged Mephistophelian beard. See the smoke creeping up his beard—yellowy brown with nicotine—even as his rheumy eyes grope this tasty young morsel he has heard so much about.

Ah, but the kid is no longer so green. On the contrary, our lad has done his homework and he is now on the hunt. For this Bretagne, settling in on his fat elbows and quoting the great quoters, he is, the boy has been told, "*un type louche*," then a witty code term, known only to the cognoscenti, for *homosexual*. In short, a mark. Throw some darts, the kid figured, have a few pints, and let him pay. Then bum a few francs off him, never to be repaid, and give the old bird a thrill out back by the outhouse. Grim work to be sure, to stand tall and hard, hearing the grim *whop, whop, whop* as the old buzzard—even as he sucks away—desperately tries to inflate (through accordionlike rolls of fat) his pitifully small tool.

Anyhow, the point is, this Bretagne, gurgling away on his pipe—well, he knows certain people and some poets in particular. In fact, he says he knows a certain poet in Paris. One Paul Verlaine. Who, ho ho, is *too much a poet*, if you catch my drift—and drifting hand.

And so with a semigroveling, brilliantly calculating, and deftly suggestive letter—and enclosing some beautifully copied-out and this time actually *good* poems—some weeks later Rimbaud receives and, with trembling hands, reads Verlaine's gushing reply: *"You are a discovery. . . . You must come forthwith to Paris . . . to stay as my guest . . . as our guest, in my home with my charming wife . . . please, that I might toast and introduce you to all of literary Paris."*

As for this Bretagne, now that the lad had gotten what he wanted? *Ecch!* Get lost!

*I*n her frosty way, Mme. Rimbaud, meanwhile, is ecstatic about the boy's stroke of good fortune. Gladly, she pays his third-class ticket. Indeed, in a gesture of unparalleled generosity, the Vampire coughs up another hundred francs—to *stay* in Paris.

Shockingly, the boy cleans up for his big moment, and he cleans up well in the new clothes that Mme. Skinflint has bought for him. Highwater pants, stingy tie. New bowler hat—then known as *le chapeau melon*—even a haircut and clean nails. Baby-faced and "cherubesque," he is both a chicken hawk's dream and a Trojan horse: a cuddly-cute, sixteen-looking-thirteen menace.

And even as he makes ready, Verlaine—à la P. T. Barnum—is hyping the lad all over Paris. The Ardennais Annunciation! Poetry's Prince! The Uncrowned King!

*O*h, and one more thing the lad's packing: a hundred-line, just-written yawp the likes of which poetry has never seen, "Le Bateau Ivre." "The Drunken Boat."

"The Drunken Boat" is a blast as from the Jules Verne moon gun, a flat-out brawling masterpiece rocketing clear to the twentieth century. In fact, the most blindingly new and strange poem the kid has yet conceived—him or anyone else at that time. And all written at incredible speed. Essentially in just two days' time.

No clowning this time. Slick as a new puppy, the kid's got his train ticket and his grievances and a very big chip on his shoulder. And this time he is packing the goods.

27 ♪ Early Service

"Please," said Rimbaud as gently as he could to Mr. MacDonald the next morning in the early red cool, the very pleasant cool, before the heat. His guest was then on his knees. Stabbing the ground with an iron tent stake, he was endeavoring to bury the boy, now half covered with a fraying coffee burlap.

After the eruptions and ugly accusations of the night before, the furies had fled—leaving what? Dawn red sky and redder earth, a whisper of breeze. Rimbaud felt both shame and boyish anticipation. Something was poised to happen—something immense, even a baffled form of hope. Still, there was the reality of MacDonald digging and the dead boy now returned to innocence, or at least to human scale. How small the boy was in daylight. No terror, just dead. Thin black legs and two human feet.

"Honestly, better just to leave him," continued Rimbaud. "This is what he would want. As a warrior. For us to bury him, this will only antagonize them."

Lowered by two of the porters, Rimbaud settled himself on the ground, then painfully wrested himself up, supported like a very resolute crab on three of his four appendages. Down: a new sort of normal. At a gesture from him, the porters withdrew. That left three of them, Mac-Donald, Rimbaud, and the dead boy. Eye to eye with him, Rimbaud noticed in particular his fat black feet. Permanently white on the bottom from pounding the road. Cracked and much enlarged with calluses that had grown like coral over his heels and toes, immune to stone or thorn.

Otherwise, it was morning, all the party knackered, aching, stiff, and dirty. Camel hooves, horse hooves, human feet. Pollen puffs of yellowish dust in the sun as sullen, sleepless men loaded beasts and cinched ropes, the camels groaning, *eer-oowww*. As for Mr. MacDonald, thus warned he did not quibble this time; he seemed, in fact, relieved, for the grave was unsatisfactory, hard-crusted sand, like cement. Pebbly, Rimbaud noted. Pebbly with black bits, and white bits of what looked like crushed seashells, at the bottom of the world, below even the sea. Everywhere now his eyes moved; his sight sniffed at everything, moments and particulars, whoofing up life like an anteater's snout. MacDonald's Bible. Black cover. Leather, worn like an old harness. Red-edged pages. Sunburned MacDonald, who, even at this hour, had already sweated through his appalling shirt.

"If you say so," said MacDonald, with a breath. Momentarily he paused. Wiped his brow with dirty hand and dirtier sleeve.

"They—" began Rimbaud, and he, too, sighed. The effort involved. He felt like he was budging stone, a very large mental stone covering an old mental crypt. *Enough.* He wanted to be freed, manumitted—to any fate whatsoever. Anything but this. And they were getting closer to their objective, four, five days away; he could smell it almost—the ripe, the rushing ever-vastness of the sea. Far clouds, towering clouds over foamy blue slicks. He was desperate, he was relieved; he was on pins, pent up, then thrilled—fit to burst, like a schoolboy aching to be released for the holidays. And yet even his pain, this cannonball-like dread he dragged, even this was now dulled by the anesthesia of a still greater pain.

Corked. That was the word for how he felt, he thought, *corked.* Commanded to *shut up*—to listen and await further instructions. What? To be told what? Lord, what would you have me do? Who do you want me to be? Who?

"There is," Rimbaud continued after some unaccounted-for seconds of this zooming state, "no way to put it right. They will take it as a disrespect. If we bury him. Or pray over him."

Rimbaud gestured toward the uncooperative distance—being vast. "Those beehivelike formations of rock that you see—the *waidellas*, surely you have seen them." Clearly, Mr. MacDonald had not. "Well, there he shall be buried. Tombs," he emphasized. "Always on some elevation. Up on—"

When he jumped! They both did—at a rifle blast.

And look: in a plume of shot and smoke, not thirty feet away, a horse fell. On buckling forelegs, the colossus crumpled. Collapsed in a pile of hooves, neck, and trunk, as in a sweep of robes, squinting from the acrid smoke, the shooter lowered the rifle, stepped away, then reloaded, not even bothering to look at this heap he had made, or the pressured blood spurting from the small hole below the horse's quivering ear. A used-up horse was all. Finish him off. First chore of a long day.

Thirsty sand. How quickly the blood clabbered. Black pudding. Flies feeding. In seconds, the red black puddle was thick with flies, iridescent and dancing. Innocent, Rimbaud looked around as if at some imagined and very sympathetic audience. Didn't they yet see the point? After too many pounding days and nights, as expected, the horse was done, even as his replacement was being bridled and saddled. This was the bush. Quick. Efficient.

*B*ut the matter still was not finished—no.

For well in sight of this before-breakfast debacle—even as the poor beast subsided—here, across the camp, stood the two children with Mrs. MacDonald beside them, newly stupefied. Ready again to erupt. As for the children, after days on the road, they, at least, were remarkably unsurprised.

These people! fumed Rimbaud, now trapped. Doing their slaughtering in the camp! And here when he had specifically *told* the man— twice—not to do it in the camp. Do it a distance away, he told him. As was his controlling practice in this part of the world, he then asked the stolid killer to *repeat* his instructions. What did I just say? Repeat it. Look me in the eyes. Tell me exactly what you are going to do.

The host faced his two agog guests.

"The horse could not continue," he offered almost urbanely. Then, more haplessly, pointing at the shooter, "He was told, specifically told, not to do it *here*. Not now."

It was, one supposed, *an* answer. Mrs. MacDonald stood thick in shock. "Fresh meat," he offered. He gestured toward the malign hills. "Feeding the whole village, Madam." Again, he paused, that gratitude might take effect, applause perhaps. "Instead of coming at us."

"Quite." Briskly, Mrs. MacDonald drew in a breath. "Right."

It was, in short, the horridly ordinary beginning of another dreadful day.

*T*hey saw buzzards flying, shiny wings tilting in the strong desert currents.

They saw a walking stone—a giant tortoise. Toad in a shell. Yellow eyes. Grinning, the boy straddled him, giddy-up! Then was told, Come along.

They saw dik-diks, rabbit-sized antelopes. Darling creatures—duly shot for supper.

They saw on a hill, in a rare, large tree with horizontal vegetation, what looked like two ragged black sacks—two witches. No, *shiftas*, their supine guide explained. Highwaymen. Examples, hung until they fell like rotten apples.

They saw—and Rimbaud made it a point to point out to Mr. MacDonald—those grave formations the *waidellas*, which he had been so kind to mention, flat rocks piled not very high on a low hill. Mesas, almost. Slits skimming the distance, like eyes. Indeed, the skinny men, the watching men, unafraid, they stood on the same low hills, easy shots against the sky. Daring the *frangis*. Men hard as fire sticks carrying long, gut-stirring spears. Spears that wobbled ever so slightly as the men moved.

Later, they saw the night, the undersea, the gloom, when all changed and advantage shifted. *Look*, human, as an animal looks into the night when he winds the predator. Open wide your mouth and nostrils. Let the darkness fill your throat like water. Sieve and taste the oyster taste of darkness, salty and brined with fear.

Listen. Really listen.

Lions letting out roars. Hyenas yipping. Obstreperous frogs both deep and shrill. Shadows weaving shadows, in moonlit shoals—admit finally your utter irrelevance and superfluousness, for you are bait. Feed the fire. Stare at the flames. Check and recheck the guns—hope.

And the feud was on. Here was a relay race of tribes, warriors whose abomination of one another was second only to their sacred duty to kill the *frangi*, that godless affront. Every night now shots were heard. Rimbaud's hired killers, meanwhile, tried in their awkward way to quell fraying *frangi* nerves—to show, for lack of a better word, some etiquette. Two more kills were brought, not into camp but to the edge of camp—just visible, as proof. Praise the cat who drops the mouse. Coyly dribble more coins. Done.

Then, on the ninth night, six went out to patrol. One heard something, then rode off to look when, up from the deeps, like a shark, suddenly a shadow arose. Became a man who drove his spear clear through his leg—mortally gored the horse, too—as with his spear another hooked him through the back and unhorsed him. Rimbaud's other killers heard his cries as the two skinners went to work, took from between his legs their slickly warm prize, then happily left the job screaming and deliberately unfinished. And so, as was customary and agreed—promised in fact—there was another muffled shot, a mercy truly, when his comrades found him.

Returning, the leader looked at Rimbaud with a mixture of rage and shame; the others looked not at all, briefly eating and drinking before they inserted more cartridges in bandoliers, checked guns, then rode out again to exact their revenge. As for the dead man, this would be costly, Rimbaud knew, with much wrangling. Truly, when a *frangi* was involved, what normally just happened, what fell like a crumb before God's feet, suddenly it soared in tragedy, became cosmic in its consequences and hence in price. The price! Beau-ti-ful was the price.

Otherwise, no one spoke of the man—ever. It was, what was. Back there. Vanished into the whirlwind, *inshallah.* Who could count upon his next breath or second? For here there was only here, only now, and now there was only *on.* Onward. On under Allah's wing, on to the end.

*T*hey were, Rimbaud estimated, now two-thirds of the way, perhaps more. Close enough that, in his mind, almost gravitationally, like an undertow, he could almost hear the roar. Could feel the fabulous pull of the sloshing, the propulsive, the shiningly endless gray blue sea—the Gulf of Aden, then the Red Sea, then the cobalt blue Mediterranean and the quay of Marseille. Of France itself and what his mother and Isabelle would say, and then, as in a play, what he would say, and how rich and resonant it would be. A compact of implicit forgiveness all guided by the evident fact that people change. Have to. Change, as the play of life itself changes. Act, then. Stand over there. Walk differently. Smile. *Try this.*

Yes, in life it was very good to have a play, with distinct parts and well-defined words. A script—that way everyone would know what to say, and how to behave, and so how to act. And instinctively, in this much-revised play, Rimbaud knew he had to prepare, to learn his lines and *act* so as not to *react.* Or rather, not to *over*react, sparking, as he feared, some kind of fracas. Yes, this time it would be different at home, he thought, as different as he, as she, as they were different. Really, a different family. Fifteen years different.

*A*s for Mrs. MacDonald, even after her host's sort-of epiphany—and even with his awkward feints at a sort-of pre-probationary holiness—still she was cool to him. Cool if not cold, even as she brusquely cared for him, but only as a duty, much as a lady with an overabundance of cats might reluctantly feed some knee-slinking stray. His stomach had shrunk to nothing but his soul's hunger was alarming, voracious. When she brought him something, anything, he would look at her, openly like a flower, as if by looks or silence, by his evident suffering or sorrow, she might revise her now bludgeoned opinion of him. *Right.*

He, it, *that*, was a walking amnesia. Vanquished thinking. *Confess*, said a voice, *Confess to God.*

*F*or his confession would be epic; why, it might spark a world epidemic. Once loosed, it would never stop, and then—as if out of a dream—he looked at Mr. MacDonald, the father packhorse, first carrying the girl, then herding the boy. Omnipresent, like his love. Attempting, however absurdly under the circumstances, to be of good cheer. Offering his wife his arm, he helped her across a field of giant boulders. A pack animal— a mule. God's fool. Lord, thought Rimbaud, just look at the sheer brute *health* of the man, the force! Before him Rimbaud now felt near-boundless wonder, such as can only be seen through the eyes of failure.

But what about *his* family, the Rimbauds, waiting on the rock of Roche?

Fervently, Rimbaud tried; he tried to imagine, to patiently recon-struct, his sister Isabelle as a woman with lines on her face, settled bones, drooping chin. He tried to imagine his mother now old and changed— old age changed people, did it not? Mellowed them. Exclamation points became question marks. Bodies shrank and turned to shrugs. Why, some few of the old, he had noticed, once shedding the sheer labor of life (and true, after loud complaints), mercifully, they forgot who they had been and whom they had harmed—it gave one hope, these late-charming, suddenly mild antiquarians. Fists became hands, and vituperation, once the anger has been boiled out of it, really, it was a form of fear. Good heavens, all these angry, bitter old people, what on earth had they been so exercised about all these years? God knows, but he had—changed, that is. New life, new identity. Trader, linguist, ethnographer, explorer: this was what he was really bringing home to his mother. Like a boy clutching a pulsing, just-caught frog, he was bringing home a new heart. Presenting, or rather *re*presenting, himself. Look, Maman, I am a man now; I'm a success, not a mooch. I have money, too—pots of it. Home would do it. At home he would change in a way impossible in Abyssinia. Calm down. Settle down. Worry less.

And the leg? So be it. Off. Weasel it off. Chew it off if need be. Anything to be sprung and forgiven—anything to be freed from the jaws of this trap. Lose a leg, gain a soul. But who, then? Who will he be?

So Rimbaud ruminated as he bounced and rolled, holding himself against the canvas until his forearms were rubbed raw. So he dreamed as thoughts rolled by, caroming on like swells of sea. See him now, a sunburned body carried on eight thin black legs. Carried such that, from a distance, this vast organism that had formed around him resembled a great bumbling millipede scuttling across the floor of a dried-up sea. To the sea, he thinks, the blue sea. When a curious phrase presents itself: *The sea as in pictures.*

Picture, sea, he thinks. Da-dum.

Sea as in pictures. Hadn't he written something like that? Dreamt something like that once? But this memory lasts but a moment, before he thinks, *Oh, rot . . .*

28 ♪ The Blank Page

But when would he arrive, this mysterious prodigy about whom Verlaine has alerted literary Paris and now bestirred his young wife and new in-laws? Only God knew.

Discussing this very matter, Verlaine, his wife, Mathilde, and his mother-in-law, Mme. Mauté de Fleurville—petty nobility, actually—were taking tea in the salon of the Mautés' home on the rue Nicolet, a narrow but imposing street in Montmartre lined with tall, stone-faced manses, thoroughly snooty residences with pince-nez-like windows and long, dismissive stairs that no tradesman would have dared to climb.

Mathilde, his bride of thirteen months, was seventeen and almost eight months pregnant, a bubbly, buxom, now plump girl—a beauty, really—with dark hair, dark eyes, clear fair skin and a love for her husband still so young and fresh that it verged on adoration. Her mother, Mme. Mauté, to whom she bore a strong resemblance, was herself a darkly handsome but now maternally imposing woman, perched on a high-backed gilt chair with bowed legs and a royal blue coverlet. Mme. Mauté very much liked this chair, and she liked especially where it stood at the head of the room, rather like a portrait with a fireplace of ornately carved marble to her left, a grand piano to her right, and, behind her, visible through a bay of mullioned windows, a walled garden with pea gravel paths—paths such as one saw at Versailles, noted the Madame, thrilled at her creation.

Her throne room, Verlaine called it, and with evident feeling now that he was Mme. Mauté's unhappy subject. This demotion in Verlaine's status as a husband—this steep descent—had begun two months before. It was then, owing to reverses—tavern debts, a ridiculous altercation, a poem not yet realized, *and even the tides of history*—but principally on account of his being fired—that the twenty-five-year-old Verlaine and his adolescent bride were forced to give up their Paris flat and move back home. Mathilde had some money from her grandmother's estate—let him stay home, she said, liberated from the work he hated and now freed to write.

That is, when he was not twiddling, said Mme. Mauté—hours twiddling and hours more at the cafés he frequented, before returning home late and weaving drunk. Beyond the irregular hours and chaotic lifestyle, however, her wayward son-in-law had *presumed*, said Mme. Mauté. Indeed! To invite this Rimbaud to stay in their home, quite as if it were *his* home. And still more unforgivably, so late in her daughter's pregnancy!

"And he is days late," protested Mme. Mauté, who, like her husband, now knew a little something about idler *artistes* and their shenanigans. "Your young friend from the village"—hayseed, she means—"he cannot wire you of his plans?"

"This happens," replied Verlaine carefully, if dismissively, as he stirred the cup of tea the maid had just now handed him. This, to be clear, was not the frowsy Brahmin bard-bum of 1891, dividing his time between the brothels, absinthe dens, and the various charity hospitals. No, this was the slender, young, socially ambitious, exceedingly bourgeois, and—when sober—nimbly charming Verlaine of 1871. And, thanks to his wife, who picked the fabrics and hired the tailor, the sartorially correct and even dapper Verlaine in his stovepipe trousers, proper frock coat, and earnest tie. The face, it is true, remained problematic. Pug ugly, to be frank, the moonlike forehead, pasty white skin and patchy red beard like some hirsute form of creeper. And, as if God hadn't already singled him out, the batlike snout with a habit of cultivating alarming red carbuncles.

Remarkably, though, Mathilde insisted she no longer noticed this unfortunate aspect of her husband. Indeed, she even saw some advantage in it. This, as she privately admitted to her mother (and with the greatest unease, lest her mother think her vain), was her considered belief: that a man of such unfortunate looks would feel so very lucky to have a woman such as herself—and so sure that he would never again enjoy such good fortune—that he would never stray. An interesting theory, to say the least.

Attentively, Mathilde's husband (for she now saw him as *hers*) stirred his tea in slow curlicues, with a fluid, faraway air perfected in the finest literary salons of Paris, a sure sign that he was either bored or irritated or both. For sure enough, much as a sedentary cat will switch its tail when ready to swat, an irritability had swept over him . . . impudent old trollop, sitting on her pile of money and simple self-regard! Coldly, Verlaine regarded his mother-in-law:

"Well, Mother"—here he paused to indicate his weariness with her tedious inquiries—"he is a *poet*, not a rail conductor on some *schedule*."

"Ah," said Mme. Mauté overpleasantly as she returned the favor, "then is he, too, unemployed?"

"Maman!" protested Mathilde. "Paul, stay here, please—sit."

But, eyes burning, her sensitive husband was already up. "*If* you will excuse me—Mother."

"But *of course* I shall excuse you," purred the queen cat. "Just as people all your life have indulged and excused you—your dear mother particularly."

Note his rage—his very pure rage—as he exited through the room, for he was two and he was twinned, two poles always divided and always at disequilibrium. But when Verlaine was angry—and worse, when he was both angry and drunk—these two sides of him would converge, and hard, like the blade of an axe.

*B*ut how could Verlaine's relations with his in-laws have come to such an unfortunate impasse, and so rapidly? And how when, during Mathilde and his courtship and leading up to their marriage, he had written poems so high-flown, idealized, and chivalrous that at times they verged on the ridiculous, seducing him himself even as he seduced Mathilde—a girl so naïve that, for some time, she believed the ardor of his kiss might impregnate her!

Nor was Verlaine a fool. By then he knew too well that he needed the chastity belt of marriage to protect himself against his various . . . inclinations. Strange, indeed, how even a dog of a man, in a dog-whistle way, will suddenly feel his ears prick up and think, Marry. Absent yourself from the green bitch Absinthe—abstain. Whore no more. Give up, as if for some interminable Lent, the knee trembler with a sailor or some blacksmith's apprentice with pythonlike biceps, before whom Verlaine would kneel in Holy Communion, his agile wrist whisk-whisking the young man, bringing him fully engorged, into his grateful mouth. Good God, he thought in that too brief moment of post-suck *tristesse*. You're a poet and a husband. Have some dignity. *Finis!*

He had, after all, a budding poetic reputation. Why, as a Parnassian, he swam with a school known for classic order, for flawless craft and carefully balanced emotions—*embody that aesthetic.* He was invited, increasingly, to the best salons—*stay sober, keep it up.* He was a superb technician, and it was the springtime of bourgeoisiedom—*let them experience Art.* For example:

Home

Home; the snug glow of lamps;
Daydreams; a finger on the temple;
Eyes lost in loved ones' eyes
The hour of fresh-made tea; of closed books;
Sweet sensation of summer ending . . .

Then there was Verlaine's prospective father-in-law. Although not conspicuously wealthy or influential or aristocratic in the grand sense, M. Mauté de Fleurville was, notwithstanding, a noble gentleman of comfortably independent means who naturally adored, and also greatly indulged, his daughter. Nevertheless, it was only with the greatest possible reluctance—and then after months of her tears and entreaties—that he allowed her to marry this very dubious fellow whose face reminded him, he said, of a fresh truffle.

And a man of what stripe? M. Mauté didn't give a hang for poetry; he liked to stalk and shoot and mount on his trophy wall, with ironic expressions, tiny horned deer, roe deer, some scarcely larger than hares, of which he then had twelve—ah, yes, he liked to joke to visitors when he showed them his wall of horned gophers, "like the twelve apostles." As for this Verlaine, true, M. Mauté's inquiries revealed this so-called poet to be a young man of some poetic reputation and attainment. Son of a middling, now deceased army officer, he was more or less of adequate status and potential means once his mother died, but otherwise, well, really, what did this unfortunate man offer socially or professionally? Copying documents? Fetching coffee? Sorting mail? Not to mention the fact that he was almost ten years older than Mathilde.

Indeed, it seemed to M. Mauté that M. Verlaine was taking unfair advantage, writing the dewy-eyed girl these gooey *poems* . . . these faux-gallant, vaguely *obscene* poems, fixating (foot man that Verlaine was) on the foot of his beloved:

> *She stands bare-headed, eyes straight ahead; her dress*
> *Is of a length to half reveal*
> *Under the jealous folds a wicked foot's*
> *Delightful point, emerging imperceptibly . . .*

Wary that Verlaine was merely an adventurer after her money, M. Mauté insisted there would be no dowry, ever. Pure bluster. Together with Verlaine's widowed and equally overindulgent mother, the Mautés not only matched the 30,000 francs she gave the newlyweds but then set them up in a handsomely furnished apartment on the corner of the quai de la Tournelle, an address where, from the balcony, in one sweep, the lovebirds could take in the Seine and Notre Dame and Montmartre in the distance. Here, too, Verlaine had his own study with a fine view, a padded leather chair, and a sturdy desk that his adoring wife (as if leaving straw and water for an animal in captivity) had provisioned with ink, paper, expensive pens, and tobacco. *Voilà* . . . create.

So great was their passion and optimism that they married just a week after the Germans invaded in the summer of 1870—indeed, even as the Huns were trampling Mme. Rimbaud's rye and her youngest son was plotting his escape.

In Paris, however, it was not seen as a war per se. It was, rather, a summer's escapade. No one dreamed that in a mere two months the

French army would collapse, that Napoleon III would be dethroned, and that Paris—always on the verge in those years—would tumble into civil chaos. But so it did unravel after Napoleon III, the aggressor, met his final humiliating rout in Sedan, on the Belgian border. When the Huns tried their triumphal march into Paris, armed mobs, outraged at their feckless government, resisted, then rose in armed rebellion against both the Germans and the government. It was a revolt of the workers and the poor—the Communards—indeed the first revolution ever to take up the red banners of socialism. Within days, enormous barricades of paving stones, timbers, rubble, and bricks blocked the streets. Already well armed with rifles and ammunition, the home guard seized the city's cannons, even as the Germans blocked food and fuel shipments and the dithering French government plotted an all-out assault. It lasted about a month.

Given his libertine nature, Verlaine was ecstatic in those first heady days of the revolution, that is, until two toughs in red scarves commandeered him to man, or stand upon, these treacherous piles of cobbles that had been ripped up from the street. On the rue du Chemin Vert, poor Verlaine was deployed one night—driven at the point of a spike bayonet, actually—into the thick smoke and rifle flashes where the Communards were now fighting the first elements of the French army.

In Verlaine's hands was a broom handle that he had been told to brandish like a rifle in the darkness—a scarecrow, in effect. Another of his confrères, fortunately drunker than he, had been given a flag to wave triumphantly while another—slightly more convincing in the role—had a broken sword to hurl skyward, crying, *En avant . . . allez, allez!*, etc., etc.

Poor Verlaine. Trembling like a dog before a thunderstorm, he had no shame, none, as he stumbled up to the breech at the head of this gang of lollygaggers and yellow bellies. His knees buckled and quaked; at every shot he jumped. It was hopeless, hopeless. They stood him up. He sat down, *ker-thump*, with that sudden surprise of a baby. Then, amazing thing. Not two meters away, without a sound, a man collapsed.

Quite fell out of his top hat, like a marionette cut from his strings. That did it.

"I'm a *poet*," cried Verlaine, now on all fours. "Don't you understand, a *poet!*"

Ah, the adhesiveness of these sniveling cowards! Like ticks! Like leeches! The poet was a fetal ball even as the commander, a butcher, whacked him hard about the breeches with the broad of his sword—to no avail.

The terror of that one night—this was more than enough for the salon revolutionary. And so, to the Communards, he pled work, just as he told his employer, with great brio, that duty called, that he had to man the barricades. When this knavery was discovered—and all too readily, as he should have known—he was jailed for some days, leaving his pregnant wife and her parents to scrape for such siege viands as were then available: stinking horsemeat, jugged cat, leg of dog.

For Mme. Mauté, however, the final straw was when Verlaine sent his pregnant wife out to scavenge food with her father—out into the red sky of the burning city, past looters and corpses.

"I would go," he protested. "Of course, I would. But do you want me sent to the barricades to be shot—an expectant father? You at least have a *chance*. I, if I go, I have *no* chance. None."

"*You!*" sneered Mme. Mauté when two hours had passed without their return. "Sending a pregnant girl and an old man out to find *your* food! Are you a man or a worm?"

"Oh, very well!" he said, for the maids had fled. "If you will kindly calm down, Maman, I shall uncork the wine and even set the table."

29 ♪ The Wee Ones

Perhaps it was the insurrection, the civil chaos, the jangled nerves that set loose the gremlins of drink and disorder, for shortly after order was restored, when Verlaine returned to his office post copying documents, he was sacked—sacked as he had hoped, actually, having gone missing for more than a week. Not to mention the many afternoons when, after his *déjeuner*, he had returned to work stiff and surly—drunk.

Never fear. As usual, Verlaine's mother, queen of coddlers and doyenne of denial, came to the rescue of her only living child—not counting, of course, the three children that sat in jars upon the mantel. Here, perhaps, a brief explanation is in order.

The three souls in question were Paul's two moon-headed elder brothers, Pierre and Bertrand, and his sea-horse-sized sister, Edith. Siblings, from some four to ten centimeters high, the three could be seen bobbing in a yellowy liquid of a hue somewhere between pond and pilsner. Grain alcohol, actually.

But alive. If God was alive in the bread and wine of the Holy Sacrifice, then why, thought Verlaine's mother, why not these three whom He had abandoned in their prime at twelve and fourteen weeks? Almost eleven, in the case of Edith, the youngest, and—as Paul had always suspected—her mother's favorite. The tiny trio even had a name: the Wee Ones.

He remembered once picking one up—Edith. How the jar glowed in the light. Motes of sediment swirled up from the bottom, a phantasmagoria of family history. Slowly, tiny Edith floated, bumped. Froglike fingers. Sealed-over eyes, preserved for all eternity in the ultimate elixir and *fixatif*—alcohol. So, in the 1850s, every night before bed, we would find young Paul Verlaine on his knees, praying with his mother at the family shrine.

Staring at the stain, the pain. And he, young Paul, so *lucky* said his mother, a *survivor*. Or rather, since the Wee Ones were not "dead," young Paul was a young redeemer; he was extraordinary in every way, going to school, even eating his dinner. Why, even tying his shoelaces—an exemplary boy.

Even his breathtaking unsightliness (cruel, since his parents were both quite handsome people), this too made him singular, if not an apology from God. Hence his mother's obsession with him. Licking her thumb. Plastering down the errant curl. Grooming her kitten. This level of scrutiny, already high, became well nigh unbearable once her husband, captain in the engineers, died of pneumonia, at which point, aged thirty-seven, Mme. Verlaine became a professional widow, well fixed financially and—of course with maids to do everything—now free to focus in ever more minute detail upon Paul and his three siblings.

"Mother," said the boy in irritation, "why are you always *staring* at me?"

"But, my darling, can't the cat look at the king?"

"Stop staring!"

"But I'm not staring, *mon petit*. Only admiring."

She trimmed the fat from his roast beef. Then, overidolatrous, she would snitch little pieces—*his*. Anything from his plate—or life, for that matter. His dried umbilical knot. His baby teeth that she kept like small pearls of barley in a small silken purse. Or, while her little Samson slumbered, snip a lock of hair. Until, *what*?

Boy rut.

Starting at age ten, young Paul would be caught, yet again, with his hands under the supper table, feet wrapped around the legs of his chair, *erch erch erch*.

"*Ça suffit!* Hands on the table."

"I was merely brushing the crumbs off my lap."

"*Sur la table.*"

Too true. By the age of ten Mme. Verlaine's darling had developed what then was known as *the habit*, believed to be an indication of—if not the path to—*man love*, a crime so black and foul, so unspeakable and then so unknown, that the world had yet to create a suitable name for it.

Itching himself, such that the maid found upon his napkin egregious stains not those of the cook's béarnaise.

Or at Mass, leg jiggling as he gazed heavenward in unsavory rapture.

Or whisking into the W.C.—in, then out—wiping his hands under his armpits. Six and eight times per day. To the point Mme. Verlaine feared physical injury, even seizure.

Then, by age fourteen, young Paul developed a comparable habit— he began to write. How lucky were his siblings, Mme. Verlaine sometimes thought, tiny beings floating, completely contained, preserved for all eternity against injury or evil.

Bonsoir, Pierre. Bonsoir, Bertrand. Bonsoir, Edith, ma petite.

*T*his, then, is the family backdrop to the now adult Verlaine, ousted from his place of marginal employ.

Never mind that he had no conceivable grounds upon which to protest his sacking. Mother's boy that he was, where else could he turn but to his maman? Whose great gift was the ability, where her son was concerned, to rationalize and explain away virtually anything. Even her son's drunken 2:00 a.m. invasions, shouting and spraying spittle, roughly shaking her by the hair. One of his hallucinogenic absinthe rages.

"*Emmerdeuse! Salope. Où est l'argent? Bon Dieu!* Fucking bitch! I'll have my inheritance or you'll taste my fist!"

It was, of course, entirely predictable that Verlaine would be pounding on her door the night he got the sack. Why, living as he was in an age in which there was virtually no throttle on men, it was almost natural to throttle women. Witness the great philosopher Schopenhauer, who threw his landlady, come to collect the back rent, down a long flight of stairs. *Rent!* Great truths beckoned. The great man was at work, and the ignorant old bitch was bothering him.

At that time, in the sanctity of one's own home, for a man to beat his wife—or old mother, for that matter—well, short of murder, there was little appetite to stop such unfortunate incidents, especially in so private and proprietary a place as France.

"Whore! Don't lie to me! You want another one like that?"

Under the effects of the absinthe, Verlaine was pure infantile rage with a man's arms; he was fire and wind and hurricane—ownerless as evil, unaccountable as nature. He wanted money, *needed it*, his brain *craved it*, money and liquor, much as a mauling bear craves food.

Sickening, no doubt about it. But if we peer into the depths of a man's soul, then we shall look hard at it, all of it. There will be no looking away.

*E*qually natural, the next afternoon once he had sobered up and the gremlins had fled, there came another wild swing—from rage to remorse. Weeping at his mother's door, then groveling at her feet, bawling and pounding the floor, loudly Mme. Verlaine's son blamed the Green Fairy, Bitch Wormwood, Dame Absinthe.

"I'm *hideous*! I hate myself, ha—*aaaaatte* myself and I'm *hiddd-e-ous*!"

"Paul," she cried, "you are *not* hideous. You drink too much. Impulsive, *quelquefois stupide*. Well, sometimes," she added quickly, almost superstitiously, lest she curse her own seed. At least he came to visit.

"How can I live like this!" he wailed, and at that moment his horror was pure, like flames engulfing his head. "I want to kill myself! Cut my own throat. God help me! Please, a bullet, I deserve it!"

"No!" she said, furious at this blasphemy. "Never! I forgive you! Of course, I forgive you, and now you must stop this ridiculous, this horrid talk. *Stop it!*"

Completion.

Still on his knees by her chair, her torturer was blubbering in her warm lap as she rubbed his hair, a woman now in ecstasy, as soul-bruised as she was heart-fulfilled. Grief and guilt, mother and son, rocking in that after-assault, almost postcoital, sense of completion. When—

"Mother, please," he said, lifting his head, as a seasick man might from the pitching rail of a ship. "Mother, you're so convincing. Oh, how can I dare ask this of you . . ."

"*What?*" she said, now very excited. "What is it you need from your *maman*, what? Tell me."

"Could you—would you please speak on my behalf to my boss, Monsieur Michaud? Oh, would you, Mother? *I need my job.*"

Talk to his boss! True, around her throat Mme. Verlaine was wearing a necklace of fingerprints, but this was now far in the past—*her boy needed her.* And, whatever else, it was a brilliant stroke on Verlaine's part, for once away from her little brood, Mme. Verlaine was a badger, cunning and relentless. Especially when it concerned her son's fortunes.

Nor would it be a single, forlorn appeal—no, no, this would be a full-fledged *campaign.* The next day, as a knight might pull on a mailed fist, Mme. Verlaine pulled on her long blue opera gloves; she donned her furs and her fur muffler, topped off by her opera hat with the alarming *V* of pheasant quills that made the object of her opprobrium feel like a bull's-eye in a gun sight. Then, for added power, she took up her black lorgnette, two beetling lenses on a conductor's baton, ideal either to wave around theatrically or train on the popinjay who had aroused her displeasure.

All this would have been enough, but she then ordered a special horse cab, a white bath of leather ideal for the Sunday tour of the Tuileries. She sent one of the girls to fetch—for cheap from the local funeral parlor—an obscene amount of flowers, the bigger and gaudier the better. And, for further theater and moral support, she took with her two of her staff, her truculent maid and, even more formidably, the cook, a stout, red-faced woman with arms like rolling pins always ready to make a scene.

In great alarm, she burst through the door of her boy's late employer.

"Monsieur! Monsieur Michaud! I feel so awful. I see my son has tried your patience! I was so furious when I heard, believe me. And a man of your importance."

Poor man. M. Michaud had scarcely risen from his somber desk than Mme. Verlaine had stuffed into his compact arms a bouquet the size of a small child. It was all a tragic mistake, she said. Paul was unwell, sleepless, racked—*tracassé* of late, she agreed. "But, *mon cher* Monsieur," she said, as the tears started flowing, "he did not tell you, he could not, that . . . that he was particularly upset that day over the death of his treasured aunt Héloïse."

When this excuse failed, the maternal thespian then invoked art and the glory of France! The shame, the public odium, when it was found that the law practice of M. Michaud had wrongly dismissed the future of French literature. But when this, too, fell on deaf ears, the badgeress had no choice. Summarily, she collapsed and her two shrill accomplices swarmed in, even as M. Michaud's clients watched aghast.

Ah, but when Mme. Verlaine awoke, note the pathos, the charm, not to mention her need for a solicitor to manage her not inconsiderable affairs—above all, her woozily obdurate refusal to *leave*. Until, incredibly enough, M. Michaud had agreed to come to dinner—a lavish dinner for twelve, she promised. Next Thursday at eight. There, she promised, he would meet the true Paul Verlaine, the devoted son, the husband and father soon to be. And the man now resolved, she assured him, to reform his life.

A man of his word, M. Michaud did indeed come to dinner the following Thursday—naturally, in evening attire, accompanied by his stoutly regal wife in long bustled gown and furs. All was as Mme. Verlaine had promised. They were twelve—fifteen, counting the Wee Ones hidden under the black coverlets of crepe and organdy. (Eccentric, yes, the Madame, but not mad.)

Here, the honored guest and his wife met Mme. Verlaine's treasured daughter-in-law, Mathilde Mauté de Fleurville, pregnant, lovely—so sympathetic, poor girl. As for Paul, he was overdue, said Mathilde. Alas, he was sequestered with his publisher, going over the proofs of a new book of verse—utter rubbish, of course, but for the first hour it worked. Finally, Madame tinkled an absurdly tiny bell—this always brought a smile after the *apéritif*.

The table, the candles, all was glittering, and for the escargot she had the most exquisite silver clasps, said M. Michaud, amazing contrivances with steel springs to hold them, and so nicely, as, with a tiny two-prong fork, he teased them out. And the aroma of these escargots, these tidy hermaphrodites of the garden, the first of spring, with mahogany shells in which the former inhabitants, now black nubs, swam in a pungent stew of clarified butter and finely minced garlic! Dusted with *fines herbes—sublime!*

When *wham*.

The door battered back and in stumbled M. Michaud's late employee, looking himself, in his witless inebriation, not unlike an escargot.

"But, Monsieur Michaud!" cried Mme. Verlaine as he bundled his plump wife, bustle bouncing, down the coiling stairs. "*Madame*, I appeal to you! You are a mother—please! My Paul is just terribly upset! He lost his *job*, after all . . ."

*T*ruly, Mme. Verlaine had a remarkable ability to dismiss, discount, and expunge from her memory virtually anything her son did. And since, like most men, he had married his mother, Mathilde was almost equally indulgent of him, especially in those comparatively calm months before the arrival of this storied rube from the provinces.

Thus, for Mathilde it was not so much her husband's rampant hedonism and laziness and lack of employment that concerned her. It was, rather, the world's failure to understand the trials, the tempests of a man so "singular," so "sensitive," so "artistic."

No matter that her husband produced no income. She had a plan, Mathilde Marie Mauté de Fleurville. They would give up their wonderfully situated and appointed apartment. She had some money, and with two spacious floors in their house, her parents certainly had the room. And the point, she told her mother, was not that Paul had lost his job. The point was that, for the honor of the family and to secure his place in literature, Paul effectively had no choice, condemned as he was by genius. He had to do as duty dictated—*to write*.

"And, Mother, you must realize," she let slip, "since we have been married, poor Paul, formerly so industrious, he has written not one poem. Not one."

Well, for Mme. Mauté, whose job, after all, was to be *un*industrious, she was apoplectic.

"What, then, is he *doing*? Good heavens, what is a sonnet—some piffle of fourteen lines? And for how many months has he been at it, idling and drinking, and all to write nothing? *Can this even be possible?*"

"Calm down, Mother. He will emerge from this trough. He now has a wife to help him."

"Look at you—you, too, coddling him," she said, drawing down her chin to form the neck pouch that each night before sleep she tied in a bow, such that she looked like a rabbit. "You are worse than his mother. *Revolting*, giving in to his every childish whim!"

"He is my husband, Mother. I *care* for him."

"*Coddle* him."

*A*nd so, on the eve of Rimbaud's arrival, we return to Verlaine charging down the stairs after Mme. Mauté's grievous and unfair insult about a man who had, as it were, taken a priestly vow of unemployability in the service of a higher calling. And so once downstairs, he ignored the maid. Grabbed his tatty old deerstalker cap and, with it, another rough-trade familiar—his Malaccan sword cane.

"Paul, my sweet," cried Mathilde, cradling her pendulous belly, counterbalanced by her bustle. "Come back, calm down. Mother will apologize."

The door thundered.

God damn them all, he thought. *Qu'ils aillent tous se faire foutre*, these Mautés and their fat neighbors living in their fat, soft houses on their fat featherbeds of money. And all this female babbling about *le bébé, le bébé, le bébé*. Mathilde was now so focused on the baby, and now so rotund and fearful of hurting the child, that she would not perform for him her energetic wifely duties. "*Non, Paul, je ne peux pas . . . Je crains pour l'enfant.*"

Anger, it was an erection of sorts, but to achieve its full majestic girth it had to be carefully stoked and stroked. And so at the café Verlaine calls for the one lady to whom he is always faithful, his Muse, Dame Absinthe, burning the throat like the devil's honey. Fresh as a first kiss she is, two pillowy green lips exhaling that delicious fragrance of wormwood and anisette!

But my, how the Green Fairy bites. Hallucinogenic and hypnagogic, triggering rage, she causes the jaws to seize, the eyes to water, and the mind to sweat—to see in sounds and hear in colors. Mauve skies. Swirls and swipes of color, a sensorium such that the poet can feel his famished eyes swelling in size, like two embryos.

Truly, in the pantheon of alcohol, Dame Absinthe, soon to be outlawed, is no mere *drink*—no, she is a ritual. There is the glass of pale green absinthe, a glass bulbous at the bottom and fluted at the top, like the throat of a flower. There is the ornately perforated spoon holding, over the glass, a lump of sugar. And finally a silver cruet of water—icy cold water—to slowly dribble it through the accepting sugar. Sugar, this was the accelerant of this divine fire, from which the brain, with its sodden white matter, was the organ of holy transubstantiation!

For see him now, almost level with the table, Lavoisier in his laboratory. Absinthe, the aperitif one sips alone, carefully nursing one's rage. Before his eyes, the sugar water blooms. Turns pale yellow when it enters the Green Fairy, suggesting, to his somnambulant eyes, fresh spunk, a homunculus, or perhaps a worm. Meee-oowww. Forecast of the prowl to come!

And two hours later—presto! Maleficent are his eyes. Fresh from the third dive of the evening, Verlaine swings wide down the balustrade, holding forth, like a bowsprit, the elegant sword cane. Nasty piece of work! Observe, first, the natty brass head, a studded, lead-filled bijou heavy as a hammer. But then, with a twist—*tszing!* The pièce de résistance. A gleaming rapier of spring steel.

En garde, tarts and tartlettes! Hawk-faced whores! Old trollops with scalloped arseholes, pouty purses, and baggy ankles. Hah! Thighs bowed wide like overstuffed chairs, eager to receive his saluting wood. *Aaah! La chasse aux fesses*—let the cunt hunt begin!

30 ⅋ Not So Distant Glimmerings

In the desert the next day Rimbaud's English guests, the MacDonalds, caught one last, unfortunate glimpse of their now seriously fraying host.

For there on the red desert, shimmering in the distance, the party saw what looked to be white pieces of wood—wood, or birds, perhaps—white with black bits, likely residues of volcanic charring. But *white?* Rimbaud sat up.

"Down," Rimbaud told the porters suddenly. "Put me down."

Heat slithered, viscous and shimmering, as he squinted into the blazing white distance, looking first one way, then the other, confused. Now his heart was beating. Disoriented, Rimbaud took out his brass telescope. Extended it with a clap, only to see larger, more confusing white blobs, smeary in the ascending heat.

Sprawled on his gurney, he unfolded his map, now dog-eared, like ancient scripture. He laid it out in the sand. Here much of the land lay unexplored, and what had been charted had, for obvious reasons, been drawn hastily—hazy recollection, rumor, dream. *Damnit. Damnit.* He took out his brass compass. Laid it across the map, oriented it. Then with something between fear and stupefaction, he gazed at the steel blue needle trembling irritably, like a fly, as it spun and dithered.

It's not you, it's the dratted map.

Settle down. Keep going.

So he changed his mind. With some relief, he concluded, rather, that he was *wrong* about being wrong. He waved the column on. But then, within a short distance, once again, he was bothered by these white blobs. *What is bright white in the desert?* It made him squint until his eyes watered. Made no sense.

But thirty minutes later, just as a mirage will sizzle and vanish, suddenly the column was ambushed. Surrounded, in fact. For there on the ground lay the answer to what is white in the desert. It was a long, sun-bleached bone, too long to be an animal bone. Dragged and animal-scoured, it was a human femur lying in what, to his horror, now revealed itself as a field of bones. Indeed, the very bones that he had so assiduously sought to avoid—the remains of Ambos.

Ambos, pillar of fire. Three years before, with almost Old Testament fury, it had been obliterated by the king Menelik in his continuing campaign to conquer and subjugate the country—to rid it of its barbarism, ignorance, and defiance of him. In the land of the skinny, the fat man is king, and the long-bearded Menelik was a bullying whale of a man, cunning and relentless and not to be resisted. When the local potentates balked, Menelik did not interminably negotiate in the old ways. Abyssinia *would* be made modern, he promised them. He, the great Menelik, would found cities and lay railroads, he assured them, even if he had to run the rails over their bones.

Before them, scattered like a shipwreck, lay the scorched remains of their insubordination. White bones crushed in the hyena's bulging jaws. Skulls broken like crockery and others that lay whole, like great prehistoric eggs. And rags, some in kelplike heaps and some snared on cactus thorns and stunted trees, tatters faintly chittering in the breeze, like agitated fingers.

Errorww, the camels groaned in fear, their teeth the size of piano keys.

And so many. Only God knew how many. Too many, washed up in the storm. Before it, the scale of it, the tongue went dry. The eye gorged and the mind went dim—said it couldn't be, these rib cages still attached with leathery dark strips of skin and cartilage. This was a herd of animals, not people.

Listen, the breeze told the taller wind, evil is not a fairy tale. Evil lives. It is vast in scale. It swarms and spreads like hysteria. Explodes, then vanishes, ownerless as a shout, empty as the sky. But before it, to see it with one's own eyes, one is hypnotized. Only there is no hypnotist to break the spell, nothing to make it go away, not ever.

Gnats danced in globes, like invisible flowers.

Dazed, he heard a bone crunch, almost grumbling, under a foot not his, obviously.

Fortunately, the children were frozen. *If you don't notice nobody else will.*

And look. Just then a very interesting bird landed on a tree—yellow with a droopy blue head feather, like a comma.

Then he said, *someone said*, quite as if nothing had passed or could be seen, "We'll cross down there."

And it was not true.

In fact, as Rimbaud stirred from his shock, his mind, in a state of semidream, his then blank mind, revolted at the assertion of what was being averred by these bones spread out over half a kilometer. What so plainly was, was not so—was not and could not be. This was not life, and *this* life was not *his* life. Like a dog kicking grass, disowning what he had just now left, Rimbaud's thinking was now quite magical. *This happened to them, not me. I'm alive.*

Suddenly he felt so very tired. Emptied, in fact.

Then, with curious relief, he remembered, *It's Sunday.*

And look. There in the distance, like tomorrow, were the immense clouds. Wondrous, steamy white clouds—sea clouds.

The coast, the sea!

He wondered, with an odd kind of thrill, if they would hit the coast late tomorrow or the next day, and if he was lucky he would find a waiting ship, praise God, a ship on the blue-blue sea.

A bead of sweat rolled down his nose, briefly clung to his septum, then slid down to his upper lip. He licked it, salty as a tear, then stood there blinking, his eyes like dials. When, on the ground, all around him, he saw glinting yellowy flecks—gold.

Not gold—brass.

Brass shell casings.

Fat .45-70 cartridges sold in casks heavy as hogsheads. *Not his.* Perhaps not. Mercifully, he had his competitors—competi*tor*. Well, one, although he had heard rumors of two more in the trade.

"This way," he heard himself, his other, his better self say. "Here's the way," he said, as if what they now saw was the result of lightning, famine, unstoppable forces. Some act of God. "There's the gap," he said as if he were Moses. "There we will cross."

Mr. MacDonald was stumbling, murmuring prayers, herding and

shielding the children as best he could. Tied in her hat and veil, with her peeling red nose, Mrs. MacDonald, however, was now fully, horrifyingly awake as she fixed him in her gaze.

"Ah, Mr. Rimbaud," she said overpleasantly. "You are too modest. Are you not the author of this lovely *poem* that we now see stretched out before us?"

He reddened. Grasped the poles of his gurney. Go. Go.

"What?" mocked Mrs. MacDonald, trembling with rage. "You cannot share with us several odious lines? Oh, but we should *so* love to hear them, Mr. Rimbaud. Please, poet, a poem! A pretty poem to pass the time."

31 ♭ Lucky Bug

What eye can see itself? What eye *wants* to see itself?

He, Rimbaud, did not direct the guns. *He* did not aim them, did he?

He was a businessman. The country was ill-organized and chaotic, as Menelik himself was, now in a preposterous military uniform, now in a suit, now in tribal dress. Or, often as not, some mélange thereof— molting into eventual civilization, as it were. To be sure, the Europeans were very expert liars, but none so expert as Menelik. In return for money and assurances, Menelik gave the Europeans bluff assurances that he would stamp out slavery—of course, reverse the rivers, too. Yes, even as they grabbed Africa and pulled her wealth around their necks like some rich fur, Europe's anxious publics needed reassurance that their investment would return white and pure.

No slavery!

Done!

Nor would the savages be armed!

Done!

The railroad, the telegraph, proper hygiene—progress was coming.

Done!

Why, as a down payment on this new state of affairs, the railroad interests had given Menelik a model miniature railroad, with a baby-elephant-sized steam locomotive that puffed real steam. Upon this the king would ride round and round the palace, his caftan flying and his knees hiked to his chin. The king loved a good show. White-liveried flunkies stood at attention holding silver salvers containing sweating glasses of tea and lemonade; they put out stogies and spittoons and even crisply ironed napkins on which to wipe one's lips. Good show! Standing in the equatorial sun with their creamy suits and Panama hats, waiting for an audience, his European handlers, so called—the various envoys and vendors, engineers, representatives of the mineral interests— would clap as he rode around and around and around. But, good heavens, as thirty minutes became one hour—as once more the recreating potentate rounded the bend—some fell out, while the rest stood cursing and grimacing.

Toot, toot!

Frangi! Menelik loved to see them all sweaty and standing at attention, like hungry dogs, he said. Ha! Let the *frangi* fools stand in the sun—Rimbaud, too. For the old fox, it was a game, a negotiating tactic, like his threats and arbitrary taxes or even turning them all out—having waited the afternoon—because His Excellency was suddenly "tired." Wear them down. Change the rules. Pretend not to understand. Or erupt into one of his very favorite English words, *e-vent-u-ally.*

Peace, eventually. Everything, eventually. Sewers. Schools. Water in pipes. Feet in shoes. Rome wasn't built in a day.

"There, there, my boy," Bardey would say to Rimbaud when he returned in fury from one of these ritual hazings. Or when Rimbaud would rage in general about the laziness and mendacity of the populace— the utter indifference to progress, the casual lying, the all but undisguised thievery! The genial Bardey would intone, "Mr. Rimbaud, may I remind you that before crumpets and concertos someone first needs to drain the swamps. And here you are, lad, in your gum boots! Why, right at the elbow of History."

"Arsehole, more like it."

"Well, then, I am off to my *office*," punned Bardey, ever brightly. "Leaving you, dear boy, to your *orifice*."

*A*fter Ambos, later that same day, they saw something resembling a military patrol, then a small outpost with a flag—the first signs of civilization since leaving Harar now ten days ago.

Tomorrow, or the next day, or certainly the next, they would reach the sea. For Rimbaud, however, relief turned to anxiety, and not merely about France, his family, or impending medical unpleasantries. Without Djami, he was panicked at the idea of separating from the MacDonalds, and not merely Mrs. MacDonald. It was the idea that they should leave *him* before he left *them*. Yet another dream, for whatever else, Rimbaud's leaving days were now over.

So it was after they left the killing grounds of Ambos. A lizard could at least break off his tail—scuttle off, even half his length, to persist another day under a rock. Now even the crutch was useless. He was an inanimate object, a thing. When he called a rest halt, immediately the bearers set him down—down as if he were a crate—then left him like bad luck.

Left. Lying back, the shotgun straddling his lap, as if from the hereafter Rimbaud watched the MacDonalds. He watched in particular Mr. MacDonald caring for the children. How ably he followed their moods, distracted them, contained their fits, the girl especially, who, quite understandably, was in a bad way. Crying jags. Screaming fits. Yesterday, sleep-deprived, ant-bitten and sunburned, with itchy hair, the girl had screamed at her supine host, actually screamed at the top of her lungs, as if she were the sun, "I *hate* you." Then, in case he missed the point, she narrowed her swollen eyes and said, "*You!*"

Shocking. He dodged her eyes—a child. He filtered sand through his fingers, trying not to think, then found himself watching Mr. Mac-Donald playing "marbles" with small stones in the dirt. Anything.

Sticks. Or the grass he had twisted, several days ago, into a crude doll for the girl. *Her name began with H, didn't it?*

What if I'd had a son?

You'd have made a hash of it.

I could learn. I didn't do badly with Djami.

Asshole. You left Djami.

To protect him.

Left him.

I was a fool!

Yes, you are a fool, a bloody fool.

But look at MacDonald, thought Rimbaud, destitute in a foreign country, no money, no prospects—truly a fool for his family, a donkey. Yet when Mr. MacDonald arose, Rimbaud was still under this dizzying spell. When suddenly the girl—whose name, even the first letter, for the life of him he could not recall—*H? Or was it P?*—caught him looking.

"Stinking, horrid pig! Stop staring!"

"Don't hate me," he said. Pled. She looked away, sucking on her braid—exactly as his sister Isabelle did at that age.

"Miss," he struggled, still blank on her name, "Miss, I did all I can do." He wished he had a doll or something to give her, or even some plausible endearment. "One day you'll understand."

"No, I will not understand, you beast! Ever! *Now don't talk to me.*"

Slapped, violently slapped by a girl. It felt like the fever sweats, violent, clenching chills like a beating, as he thought, Her name. If only I knew her name.

Still, he thought he might have a chance with the boy. For after all, he had been one, once—a boy. *Ralph.* Excellent, Rimbaud—you even remembered the lad's name. And sitting in the sand, that very afternoon after Ambos, he found a bug, indeed, a very interesting and even unusual and quite curious bug.

"Ralph." Smiling as best he could, he held out his closed hand. "Here, I've something for you."

"What, a bug?" The boy scowled.

Rimbaud held it up, slowly gyrating. He smiled. Its legs were like black wires, almost mechanical. "It's a *stick* bug." Rimbaud waited. "A *walking* stick."

"So?"

"Well, they're considered lucky here, I think." He waited. "Lucky."

"Oh." A caustic pause. "A *lucky* bug."

"Ralph," he said, as if, with the name, he held the magic key. "It's for *you*."

"Oh, no, no, no. *You* keep it." The boy spun around. "You're the one needing luck."

32 ♪ Ill-Timed Visit

The next morning Verlaine, needless to say, was not home in his soft bed at 14 rue Nicolet. Nor, fortunately for him, was his father-in-law, M. Mauté de Fleurville. God no. To escape the waiting and female drama, the patriarch had fled to the country for a few days of hunting. It was shortly after nine—far too early for callers—that a dirty hand lifted the massive brass knocker and gave four resounding knocks, then a fifth. Then, injurious to the peace, even a *sixth*.

Naturally, one of the maids answered, then with swishing maid's steps hurried into the parlor where the women maintained their vigil for the absent Paul, the furious Mme. Mauté in her high-backed chair and, opposite her, on the lyrelike fainting couch, the dazed and puffy-eyed Mathilde, rubbing her enormous belly.

Mme. Mauté made a face when the maid informed her who was at the door. Or claimed to be, rather.

"Impossible. Did he not give you his card?"

"No, Madame, nothing."

Hauling up her overabundance of petticoats, then the swanlike bustle (a sure sign of the trollop, believed Mme. Rimbaud), Mme. Mauté then did the unprecedented and answered her own door—stunned. It was as the maid had said.

For here, claiming to be Arthur Rimbaud, was not the grown man they expected but rather a blond, blue-eyed schoolboy—*un potache*—wearing a bowler hat, an ill-fitting jacket, two twisted strips suggestive of a tie, and ankle-high trousers. And the socks! Rude blue socks, bright blue, such as a rube might knit. Fat red hands. Big feet. Even more objectionable to Madame's haute-Parisian ears was the boy's hopelessly Ardennais accent. No bow. Not even a tip of the hat.

"I assure you," insisted the boy, for the second time, "I am Arthur Rimbaud."

"Ah," she scoffed, "you play a trick on me, boy. Perhaps you are Monsieur Rimbaud's nephew." Mme. Mauté peered around the doorway, looking for Paul's feet under the bushes. Some drunk's idea of a joke.

"Paul, enough!" she cried. "No more tricks. Produce the real Rimbaud."

"I *am* the real Rimbaud."

Whereupon, as evidence, the boy withdrew from his back pocket a sweaty wad of paper. Slapped it to life, then unfolded it, damp and smeary. "There, do you see? My newest poem. Brand-new. 'The Drunken Boat.'"

"What kind of title is that?" she challenged. "Drunken boats! Boats do not get drunk—how old are you?"

He didn't just blush. His face bloomed in splotchy, adolescent dials of rose. In these hormonal days he embarrassed easily, particularly in the presence of women, and especially with this one of aristocratic bearing.

"Seventeen," he lied.

"Seventeen! I think fifteen, perhaps. And where is your luggage, young man? Did it fall off the hay wagon?"

"As you see," he said, with a crimson shrug, "I am wearing it."

"Look at this," she said, bustle swaying like the tail of a honeybee, "no clothes, drunken boats—"

Turning, she called back to Mathilde, who just then had emerged. "Do you see this adult child? He insists that *he* is the great Rimbaud." She hitched her hips, and to his mortification, he cringed—cringed just as he did when, in her palm, his mother held a slap with which to paint his impudent face. But clearly, this was not his mother, nor his class, nor anything even remotely within his experience.

"Very well, then, Monsieur Rimbaud, who arrives in Paris sans valise. Please," she said, motioning him inside. "I am most sorry that I mistook you. Now do please follow me into the *salon.*"

Torture. There he was, sitting upon—or rather, sinking into—a pouf-pillow chair of goose feathers and tufted satin. Worse, he faced not just the mute terror of women but two perfumed, splendidly dressed, haute bourgeois women of a class about which he had heard and railed but which he had never encountered in the flesh, let alone in their priggish, pretentious environs. Who, worse still, were not scolding him but merely making *conversation.* Worse, it was Parisian female conversation, as formally elaborate as it was, at this point in their brief acquaintance, quite deliberately inconsequential.

As for the house, this sturdy manse, never had he seen so many *things,* indeed so very many things that *these* things, breeding like rabbits, seemed to spawn yet more things. Tables with clawed feet. Armchairs dripping tassels. Gloomy paintings. Gold-encrusted clocks. Porcelain figurines. And mechanical maids who, like the figures on a cuckoo clock, appeared every time the old sorceress pulled a velvet rope. *Yes, Madame, no, Madame.* Swish, swish, swish.

Worse, behind the piano, M. Mauté had a trophy wall packed with horned heads, tiny stuffed heads, probably one dozen in number, with twiglike horns. What on earth *were* these poor things he'd shot and had stuffed? thought the boy. Dwarf deer? Runt mountain antelopes? Animal *poets*—murdered. Duly noted, thought the kid. Another bourgeois outrage that would not go unpunished.

"One lump or two, Monsieur Rimbaud?"

"What?" This was his default answer to any question. He stared at her—at the air—at the wall just to her left.

"Lumps," she prompted. "Sugar."

"Four." He'd never seen such a thing—lumps. *Of sugar?*

"Four? Are you a bee, Monsieur?"

He looked down. "Four, yes."

Plunk. Plunk. Plunk. Then, with the clawed tongs, she plucked up a fourth. Eyed him dubiously. Then, decorously, let it fall—*ploop.*

What, he thought, was she trying to embarrass him? Put him in his place? Ominously, the cup rattled. Tea slopped in the saucer and his face flushed crimson, and not merely owing to his natural clumsiness at this age. For here, *talking* to him, and not merely lecturing or yelling but conversing—*socially* conversing—here were actual women, one a young, pregnant, and therefore *sexual* woman and, worse, a *pretty* woman, scarcely older than he.

Women, girls, all that—how did this fit in with his program of derangement, systematic derangement, in his quest to be both seer and thug, *voyant et voyou*—the thief of fire? Anyhow, what girl was going to sign on for this? More to the point, how, in the midst of revolutionizing mankind, well, who had time to think about *that?* Intercourse. Menstruation. Sticky wet darkness smothering you.

Now, true, in the kid's manifesto about the *voyant*, he had prophesized about the eventual ascendancy of woman—that is, once her sad servitude had been broken, waiting on men, rearing kids, milking cows. But what did he—what *could* he—have known of actual flesh-and-blood women?

Little, obviously. The former prize boy over whom Charleville's mothers had once fawned was now a public disgrace effectively quarantined from the opposite sex. Then again, who were his models, his authorities? His two sisters, told to shun him? His mother? The odd, claret-gilled bachelors who had versed him at the *collège?*

"But where do you get your ideas?" inquired Mathilde, trying to draw him out.

He sighed. Rolled his eyes, hung his head. He wasn't saying

Madame, not even to the old one, let alone to *her*, another kid, *pregnant*, he thought, with her sloshing bosoms leaking milk.

"Ideas?" she said again, a poet's girl, he thought. But that black spider between her legs—*uch*.

"Ideas?" He scowled. "I have no ideas."

"No ideas?" she replied, giving him, she thought, a lovely opening to expound upon his ruminative process, his dreams. "What then do you have, Monsieur Rimbaud?"

"Kittens."

"Kittens?" she asked, at first thinking (owing to his unfortunate accent) that she had somehow misheard him. When, spastic—unable to stand it—he bolted up. Knocked over his cup, eggshell thin, then watched in a kind of willed dream as it shattered like an orgasm on the floor.

"Mon Dieu!" exclaimed Mme. Mauté. She looked at him in horror. "That was my mother's finest porcelain."

See him now, hunkered and picked on—wrongly accused, when it was the porcelain's fault. Or really, Mme. Mauté's fault for giving him porcelain in the first place.

"Mother," said the resourceful Mathilde quietly, as the maids converged. "Mother, I think it is time to show Monsieur Rimbaud to his room."

33 ⨎ Torn

Surprise! Returning from his troll through Paris's nocturnal rookeries, then a failed rendezvous with the kid at the Gare de l'Est, Verlaine was shocked—nay, stupefied—to be presented with this otherworldly *child*. This delicious fawn.

"*Cher maître*," said the boy, brightening, for he could kiss ass, and masterfully when it suited him. "I am so very honored to meet you."

Master, ker-humphed Mme. Mauté, still smarting over the broken teacup. And this from a brat who, for his hostess, couldn't summon a single "Madame" or "thank you."

"Why, Paul," she said to her son-in-law, now lizard-eyed and foul-smelling from his evening's stumble, "what *will* you discover next? An eight-year-old Victor Hugo?"

"Mother," he replied, "do you think that great wine comes only in old bottles?"

"Bottles," she said with a low glance at her daughter. "How very apt."

"Dear," he said to his wife, ignoring this slur, "how are you feeling?"

Abruptly, she turned, clearly near tears. Uxorious, he followed, as much for her benefit as for the boy's—that this strange boy should see his gallantry and protectiveness of the female flock, his male command.

"Monsieur Rimbaud, please," said the elder poet as he withdrew to see to his pregnant spouse, "do make yourself at home. I'll show you a bit of Paris shortly. Please, I'll only be a few minutes."

*S*o began Verlaine's struggles. Torn between two teenagers. Two antipodes.

He followed his wife into the room. Precariously, he laid her down, leaning too close, when he remembered, *perfume.* Any trace of trollop. And so, lest she sniff him out, preemptively he burst into tears. Another talent of our poet's—the ability to cry at will, much as a skunk, with a flip of the tail, cloaks its escape in malodorous fog.

"I was so *horrid*," he wept. "I know that—*I know.* But your mother . . ."

Keep talking.

No matter how groundless, hopeless, or off point, Verlaine always relied on this stratagem with women. And, it must be said, with often baffling success.

Mathilde knew, of course, about the Green Fairy and her ilk. But being of tender years and so recently wed, she could not have conceived the stamina and cunning—the sheer stupefying *imagination*—of a depravity so insatiable, so enterprising and gargantuan.

Now, granted, a mistress or favorite whore—*bien entendu*, most men of his class kept one or two, perhaps. But a bestiary? And in Verlaine's case, of course, the possibilities were doubled, if not trebled. Both sexes. All ages. All classes—the more louche the better, actually. Paris, then, was his amusement park and hunting ground, all the more when the poor fellow was not only bored and blocked but on short rations at home.

And here was the trouble: the omnivorous Verlaine, this sexual Achilles, for a man of his inclinations, he harbored one fatal flaw—he loved. Of course, he loved badly, inconstantly, hopelessly, ridiculously, recklessly, and violently—but loved. However rashly. However inconstantly. However disastrously—loved. And why? His mother, of course. As with any other man's mother, Mme. Verlaine was the Rosetta stone. It was she who told the story as far as his relations with women went. And while hardly "right" in the usual sense, all was not wrong with Verlaine in his dealings with the fairer sex. *Au contraire.*

Owing to his many years interned with his mother, Paul Verlaine knew women infinitely better than did most, if not all, of his sex, who at the time scarcely knew them at all. Such home training had made our womanizer adaptive, sporting, and *joyeux.* Moreover, in a time of rampant misogyny, remarkably, he actually liked, and often preferred, the company of women, including their loud disapproval—anything so long as he held the *attention* of women, even if it meant crossing rapiers with, say, the formidable Mme. Mauté.

The advantage was huge, and not merely in the cause of his habitual lying and cheating. Storming or sunny, accusing or rationalizing, this selfishly generous temperament equipped Verlaine with the extraordinary ability to absolve himself of everything, just as it gave him scandalous license to blame everyone and everything. Especially when the Green Fairy's flickering tongue was exploring the recesses of his ear.

What's more, as a man with the physical charms of a goat, Verlaine had learned—purely as a matter of survival—to be droll and charming. Surprising. Attentive. Even endearing in a maddening way. Another huge advantage over the usual éminence grise walled behind his newspaper. That is, if Monsieur was even home and not instead poking his mistress.

As yet another indication of his home training, at an early age Verlaine had learned how to cope with the deeper vales of the female psyche, preoccupied with the very topics that men bury or flee: grief, children, sickness, and all the rest—but loss principally. In the face of which, Verlaine had also learned, in the herding and management of women, what seemed to him the greatest lesson of all—to *distract*.

As indeed he now did so brilliantly with Mathilde, in her hormonally charged, weepy *grossesse*. Observe.

Role reversal, for example. That is, when—quite magically—*he*, Verlaine, became the one even more wronged and hurt—the "girl," that is.

Or when he was the naughty boy, the boy caught, while she, Mathilde, played the stern mother.

Or when he would merely be tiresome and irritating—*distract*.

Or violent, as he was that night not long after their wedding, when, because Mathilde didn't want to "do" a certain *something*, he grabbed her by the neck and threw her down—but so fast that all she could remember was the swashbuckling afterward of him holding her like a child, arms sprawled, overcome. And not so much because he had throttled her but because, in a way difficult to explain to anyone not inside their marriage, he had saved her. *Saved her.*

"Antics." "Spasms." "Fits." Or that catchall excuse, "artistic." Mathilde Mauté used the very words for her husband that his own mother did. Still, inside their marriage, this was not, as yet, horrifying. No, no, it was explainable. *Because she understood.* As love understood. As no one else would or could.

Moreover, as a Mauté—which was to say, as a person of taste and breeding—she had *la culture, la formation* necessary to understand a psyche so tightly wound. So delicate. Like a watch, actually.

Such were things that one might think when one was seventeen and a presumptive aristocrat ready to sanctify one's marriage with the birth of one's first child. Indeed, the child who, she was quite convinced, would solve everything. Stop the drinking and bad behavior. Seat him at his writing desk. Return the lovely man whom she had married.

Such was the hope of Mathilde Mauté Verlaine when Rimbaud traipsed into her life. Moreover, she would not be denied, for she was not without power or aspirations. Blessed with a weak man and a queen like her mother, she would reign supreme over their marriage. Despite all. Through all. By the sheer force of love she would become that shining thing, a wifely *success.*

Verlaine, meantime, had managed the incredible in those few minutes—those very few minutes—at his pregnant wife's bedside. For the fact was, through sheer force of histrionics, he had, in his pathos, utterly reversed the flow of the discussion about his habitual chaos. At issue were not his misdeeds and rampant irresponsibility—*jamais!* It was, rather, his oppression at the hands of her parents; it was, he said, like the Israelites living under the whip of Pharaoh!

Les Mauté! It was, he charged, their arrogance, their pretensions and low judgments. It was their failure to understand the pressures and doubts—the crucible—of his artistry. It was their inability to grasp—alas, even while fallow—the admittedly strange dance of his artistic "process." It was their cruel refusal to "believe" in him, to grasp his terrible sufferings and trials as an artist. Still more grievously, it was their ingratitude for, and utter blindness to, and apparent unwillingness to grovel before, the wavelike undertow of his approaching greatness.

"But, love, my love," whispered Mathilde, afraid her bat-eared mother might hear, "it's *their* house. And Paul," she added, now playing the good mother, "Paul, this is all you agreed to, *willingly*, as the cost of your freedom."

She brightened.

"But, Paul, my sweet . . . perhaps with Monsieur Rimbaud you will return to writing. But not," she said, lightly pinching his downcast chin, "not by being irresponsible, as you were last night."

"I know"—he misted up—"*I know*," he said, nodding. "I cannot allow your mother to upset me as she does. *I cannot.*" He stood up. A new man. A different man. Then frowned as if it were a chore, entertaining this impossibly young monsieur from the sticks.

"Well, I suppose I'll take him out a bit—Monsieur Rimbaud."

"But, Paul," she said as he kissed her, "*Paul.* Remember, Paul. He is still a *boy.*"

*H*e was, in fact, magnificent. And Mathilde's words had a very salutary effect, for they were not out *all* night. No, indeed, they were back well before 3:00 a.m.

It was then, hearing a small crash, that Madame's two white bichons frisés, as fluffy as two dandelions on their embroidered satin coverlet, pricked up their mandarin ears. Yapping and snarling, the two floor mops launched themselves down the stairs.

Oaths were heard—the shouts of Verlaine, one foot in the air, brandishing his sword cane, ready to crush one or both.

"Out, you two tarantulas!"

Then drunk, but not *as* drunk—why, almost gravitationally—the kid backed into a pedestal atop which stood a rare Chinese urn. Smashed like a great egg. The kid had struck again.

Gaslights fluttered up. Operatically, Madame gasped, her treasured urn now a fresco on the marble floor.

"My urn!"

"Vicious *rats!*" cried Verlaine, fending dogs. "They bit our guest!"

"I'm all right!" said the kid, bravely hobbling in feigned injury.

"But my urn is not all right!"

How welcome it was, Mme. Mauté's opprobrium. Why, in a matter of hours, the kid felt utterly at home, once more the subject of an older woman's wrath.

34 ⅔ Mercy Spurned

Another day in the desert. Two days. Three, at the maximum. If only his head would not seize up. If only his heart would not give out. If only, with his last ounce of will and courage, he did not collapse and lose his party, proving forever the jinx of the Rimbaud luck.

But the personal embarrassments of his condition! The daily inconveniences. The bleak terrors. Another night of wild shots—of galloping horses and twisted, sucking-stomached waiting. As the MacDonalds sleep, there he sits ready for his last stand, sprawled back against a camel saddle, almost trying to hear through his eyes, thumb rubbing the hammer rasps of his double gun.

And by day, unavoidably, the incidents. The daily little horrors seemingly attracted to him as to a magnet. And so it happened on the tenth day, in a driving downpour, looking for a suitable and defendable camp spot, they came upon a woman sunk to her calves in the rain-sizzling mud, flailing a big stick. Was she mad? To Rimbaud it looked at first as if she were striking the mud, or a snake perhaps. When out of the muck a head rose up, oblong with bladelike ears. It was a donkey sunk to its flanks in a pool of thick black mud, its long neck lashing as it thrashed and kicked, doomed.

In that mud hole, as well Rimbaud knew, was the woman's life savings—everything she owned. Up, get up. The mud was as thick and black as Persian tobacco, unrelenting. The stick came down. The hooves flailed, the mud jellied. When this did not work, with two hands the woman grabbed the beast's rope halter and yanked hard, again and again. The exhausted animal jerked. Spasmodically, the animal clawed and struggled, then gave out, its hooves quivering. Forget it. Death had the poor beast by the windpipe, but in her desperation, the woman couldn't see it. Hit him, help him. It was as if she were resuscitating hope.

"Help me," she cried, lifting her mud-drenched shawl. To show her predicament, she struck the animal again, then peered under her hand, through the splattering rain—so desperate she was now begging the *frangi*, "You're men! Help me! Pull my beast out!"

Pass on, thought Rimbaud. Don't start some native row or invite dangers when there are dangers enough. Soldier on. That was the rule.

Not this time, though. There were children behind him, English children. The English so humane. Rooting for the fox, lovers of dogs, born to confront the brute. Inwardly, Rimbaud laid it on them, the MacDonalds, his new resolve to be good, or at least *something*. But then something still deeper jolted him as he watched the little beast kicking and panting, muddy water spewing out its nose.

"Bring me up!" Rimbaud ordered the men carrying him.

It was extraordinary. The woman looked up at the *frangi* looming above her on his sopping dais. Speaking her language, too. It was as if God Himself had come down.

"Enough!" he cried. "Stand back. Your beast is almost dead."

"I know my animal." The woman was defiant. "Just pull him out and you'll see. He'll be fine."

"*Closer!*" Rimbaud gestured to his bearers, weaving blindly in the downpour. It was crazy. Even he knew it was crazy. They were on the edge of a village.

"Woman," he barked, "do you hear me? Now stand back! Stand aside."

"Why? Pull him out! You have men."

Ignore it, Rimbaud. The donkey would be dead soon enough. Even his men were puzzled.

"Shaheed, do as I tell you. Grab her. Pull that woman away."

That tripped it, for strange men to touch her, any woman. This was now a *deal*. Twisting and screaming in his grip, the woman fell to her knees in the muck. When through the rain, here were other women. Five, then ten, yelling at the party.

"It is her beast!"

"What do you do here, *frangi*?"

Then it was a bigger deal, as armed men appeared—spears, shields, swords. But once he was committed, the danger was almost abstract in

Rimbaud's mind. He raised the fat double gun. Yellow fire blurted through the rain. Nine fat hailstones—done.

Merde. People screaming and jabbering. Rain ran down his face as he lowered the double gun. He felt his hands trembling. *Merde, merde.* For here were more people, a crowd. *Fool.* Furiously, he broke the gun. Rammed in, awkwardly, another fat shell. Now, every gun was raised and cocked. As for the aggrieved woman, she was Electra, Iphigenia beseeching the crowd—a fury on this stage of flashes and thunder and bulleting rain.

"The *frangi* killed my animal. Now I have nothing."

Spears shook—warriors. Don't back up, thought Rimbaud. Make it big. And so he shook the gun in *their* faces. No pain now. His fear and rage were exhilarating, propulsive. Overpowering, in fact.

"*Hakim,*" he said, now exalted, to the killer closest, "step forward. Show these bastards what they're going to get."

The woman was unimpressed. She had the crowd behind her.

"Kill my beast! You pay! *Frangi,* you will pay me!"

"Here!" Trembling with rage, Rimbaud produced a fistful of coins. Thalers. Double the worth of the little brute. More than fair.

"This is not enough," she cried. "He shoots my animal, my only animal. Now I cannot feed my children."

"Nonsense!" He waved his arm. "Go home, woman! Go before people get hurt!"

"No!" cried an old man, clearly the headman, stepping to the fore. "*Frangi,* you will pay her more. The village also."

Extorters. Bloodsuckers. Here was every open palm, every bribe and mendacity he'd ever tolerated in this shithole. In contempt, he shoved more coins at her, then glared down at the old man.

"There—that's *it.*" Hell was in his hand. Death shook in the headman's face. "And I'm not paying your village, old man. Now, out! All of you. Out of my goddamn way."

Cursing, he loosed a blast. Yellow flame, screams. Now every gun was leveled and the crowd was chanting, one touch from a massacre.

Reload. He broke the smoking breech. His arms were twitching, electric. Never had he felt more alive.

"Go!" he cried to the column. "Bloody let's go. *Come on.*"

And his gamble worked. The village did not attack, not against repeating guns—they were not crazy. Chanting, the women flung mud. The men shook spears, and in the intoxication of that moment, perversely, this thrilled him. *Now* they saw what he was made of, by God. But his exhilaration was short lived. Clutching her soaked shawl around her face, Mrs. MacDonald shouted up at him:

"*Menace*, eh? Wasn't that your accusation of my husband the other night, you bloody maniac? That *he* was a menace?"

"And what would you have done?" he said with a glance at the very silent Mr. MacDonald. "Watched it? *What?*"

Mrs. MacDonald did not deign to reply. He'd snapped, bloody snapped. A near massacre, and for what? Two crooked hooves poking out of the mud and the woman screaming at them, screaming in the driving rain.

35 ♪ Left to God

And another man lost.

That same night, rising up out of the blear, blowing darkness, three avengers took him down, older, hardened warriors, their best. Two with spears mortally gored his horse while the third, wielding his dagger like an axe, half hacked his leg off. Never kill a man outright if possible. And so, even as he screamed, the two with spears held him fast, like a pig, one spear through his thigh and the other just inside his collar bone. Using the spear like a pry bar, the man who had him through the collarbone sharply drew the trunk back, then put one foot on his windpipe, choking off his hoarse scream. Opposite him, the second man held the leg, while the third, kneeling, blade in hand, swiftly went to work. Yanked down the wounded man's breeches, then seized his privates like the neck of a chicken—up that he might see, forever, his balls and the face of the warrior in whose hut they would hang. But before he could harvest his prize, horses were heard, then shots, including the shot that killed the knife man outright. The two remaining spearmen were as lucky as they were skilled. Dodging bullets, slippery as fish, they dove into the black pools of night—gone.

Fearing a trap, the rescuers knew better than to give chase. Now what? Thrashing slick with blood, the horse was down, and the wounded man was in worse shape. True, his leg could be tied off with a leather strip, then, once in camp, amputated and the stump cauterized, vein by vein, with a red-hot dagger. Tomorrow he might be tied on a horse, but what then? The cut was high; he would be no one, a woman, and likely would die anyway. Assuming, of course, they could even reach camp without being overrun.

No time to puzzle. Correct behavior in such situations had long been agreed on, and the wounded man, Audou Sakina, although drifting, readily understood their decision as they pulled him around, east to face Mecca and the blessed sun that, come morning, would shine upon his face. Indeed, Audou Sakina thanked them, then shouted to God as, with two blasts, they first finished him, then the horse. Leave nothing. Quickly, they stripped Audou Sakina of all valuables and weapons, laid his hands upon his stomach, and patted his cheek tenderly—left to God. Then, remounting, hotly they kicked ribs and off they rode, long spears pointing back over their shoulders as they launched into the night sky.

*I*n fury, Audou Sakina's two rescuers looked at Rimbaud, mutinous and surly as they rode into camp and dismounted, heavily stained with their friend's blood. It wasn't just the death of Audou Sakina that enraged them. As five then returned as four, they had lost face, surrendering one of their own to the enraged villagers—unworthy men, amateurs in their eyes. And all because of Rimbaud's sentimental stunt. Over what? A half-dead donkey?

Honestly, why they didn't kill him and seize the lot right there,

Rimbaud had no idea. Perhaps it was their blood oath to the chief whom Rimbaud had paid so handsomely and armed so magnificently. Or inertia. Or that begrudged but still almost hatefully inestimable power of the *frangi*, he who brought the rain. In any case, Rimbaud paid them. Later, with much haggling, he paid them dearly for Audou Sakina, a believer, as well as the hundreds, obviously, who depended upon the proceeds from Audou Sakina's unswerving sword and prolific gun.

36 ♪ Child of the Sun

The day before, upon fleeing the Mautés, they had had their hasty preliminaries, the elder and the putative understudy—the confessions, the whispered dreams, the lapel-grabbing excitement. And late that night, by which point Verlaine was far too drunk to heed fully Rimbaud's words (much as, the night before Christ's crucifixion, his disciples dozed during his Agony in the Garden), he failed to grasp the full implications of the kid's fanatical creed about a "rational derangement of all the senses."

Not rash—*rational*.

Not subjective—*objective*.

Not parlor-trained—*monstrous*.

Not personal—*egoless*.

Not *my* language—*une langue universelle . . . of ecstasies!*

And, above all, not *love*, that lying negation: *it did not exist*, posited Mme. Rimbaud's prodigal—yet. No, love, love in the old sense, was a lie. Love, thus, would have to be wholly reinvented, resulting in nothing less than revolution of the soul. As for language, it would be a language *of* the soul, *for* the soul, a universal language inaccessible to the mere versifiers who infested Paris. Rather, this new language would be accessible to the one, the *true* poet, *le voyant*, the visionary, the great scholar and criminal, the one accused! The one who, swallowing black poisons, produces, like a milk cow, blond quintessences.

Banished, then, the compromises of mediocrity. Cleansed, the contagions of the Church. Love reborn. Hope reborn—new faith, new zones, new skies. And on the shores of this new world, armed with new love and infused with *true* hope, he would run with limbs of gold. A child again. Reborn again into strength and beauty—Child of the Sun! Deathless as the sun and immense as the sea.

The fallen world, however, the real world, is gaslit, ill-lit—fog.

At 1:00 a.m. as they emerge from Le Voltaire, it is a shadowy stumble-world of small, stooped men, absinthe addicts most of them, in long swallowtailed coats and domed top hats. Down the center of the street, in a shallow channel, a residue of water gleams like the blood gutter on the blade of a knife. And beyond, framed in fantastical ruins, lo, the tarts! Four old trollops, the desperate fishing for the dregs from closing time. Clothed—*clothed* is the thrill in these figures of obscene fascination, whom Baudelaire, syphilitic hysteric that he was, had once referred to as "latrines." Clad head to toe in black, they resemble mortuary figures, queens in death's chess set. Like small Gibraltars, their bustles. Tatty hats and wedge toes to sniff and lick and obey, if that is your particular kink. And—*attention*—in the prim purses you can be sure they are secreting hat pins and razors, even sleeping drams for those ladies who specialize in drugging, then robbing the old rapers. They are an army. In Paris, a city of almost two million, they easily number in the thousands, these angels of ease—*they are everywhere*. Desire is fear and fear is desire, for syphilis is rampant, hideously ravaging, and incurable—*dare you*. Ask the syphilitic ghost of Baudelaire, the flaneur and dandy. Gamely tapping his cane, lured by the very horror of his own fascination, in death the great shade forever trolls the gutters in his white spats, kid gloves, and yellow top hat.

"*Pas si vite*," calls Verlaine, "not so far ahead."

Dk dk dkk, sounds Verlaine's sword stick, testing with each wobbling step the irregular loaf-sized cobbles. Zigzagging, the medieval street ever ascends, trapping, like dew in a spider's web, the violet fog.

"Monsieur Rimbaud, wait," Verlaine protests, for by then the young dog is half a block ahead—too far for Verlaine to see if the lad fancies women. Tomorrow, or in a few days in any case, the corruption will begin; he will offer to buy the lad his first piece of tail—a test, to see if or *what* he likes or, heh, if a good stiff cock might be his fancy!

When, with a loud bark, the visionary youth pitches over, vomits—O! Then, fresh from this swilling ode, he whips up again, laughing!

Cries Verlaine, stumbling to his aid, "Are you quite all right?"

The kid lurches back. Points at the moon coring through the fog.

"Don't you see?" he cries.

"What?" Crouching, Verlaine is now trying to draw a sight along the lad's wavering finger. "What?"

"Suddenly it all makes sense!"

"*What?*"

But, jerking erect, the boy just stumbles on, laughing.

*S*o much, then, for the preliminaries. The next day, in relative sobriety, over café and cassis, the two poets do that anxious, loaded thing—exchange work. And straightaway, Verlaine loses, for of course he has no new work—nothing but the prissy *La Bonne Chanson*, verses lacking only the lute and the tights. What a spot. Here was a place he no longer was, with no clue, as yet, *where* he is or wants to go.

The boy is brutal. There is no pause.

"These are too . . . *artistic*." To him the ultimate shame: the clever, the arty, the smug—traits ultimately self-regarding and thus . . . sentimental.

And frankly, what the kid was up against was what might be called French little-*r* romanticism. Or rather what might be described in its bald grandiosity as *unfeelingism*, an overreaction by the French against the gales loosed by *English* Big-*R* Romanticism in the first two or three decades of the nineteenth century: Wordsworth & Coleridge & Keats & Company.

Seventy years later, in France, in the main, things had not changed much. Safe, since it was not political and censorable, the Parnassian movement had, in those nervous times, given rise to the *ultra nouveau* and very smart-sounding but ultimately bankrupt notion of art for art's sake. Pure artifice. Roughly what Oscar Wilde championed before—bankrupt and publicly ruined in his mad love for a beautiful but worthless boy—he experienced the soul-scouring insides of Reading Gaol. So much for art for art's sake.

But what of Rimbaud? As a kid and a newly sexual being, he was forced to disguise his own disguises, the cooties of feeling, such that he had to hide or distort them—to throw them like a ventriloquist's voice or impute them to others. Other characters and alter egos. To anyone but him, whoever *he* was.

"I know you have great things in you," offers the boy at last. "Deeper things, certainly—I know this. But I am obliged to tell you: this is shit—shit. You must never again write in this way. Or really, *live* in this way. Great as he was, this was Baudelaire's chief failing, you know. He lived in too artistic a milieu—Paris. And here it turns rancid. Pure, putrid *style*. Rather like a man who loves the aroma of his own farts."

Stabbed, Verlaine feels a tremor pass through him. *Son of a bitch, he's right.*

"But, Arthur, please," he stammers, "listen to me. And I am not, I hope you know, merely pulling the rank of my age and experience. But—"

"Nonsense. Of course you are—"

"But you are but sixteen. You haven't been through this phase of life. Marriage. Love. Family."

The kid's balled fists hit the table.

"Haven't experienced *what*? Knocking up some dewy-eyed pubescent girl? Sponging off her parents? Is *that* what I am missing? Wake up, Verlaine! Why are your phony feelings important? Because *you* felt them? *Your* logs melting on the fire. *Your* love's soft arm. Is that all poetry is to you? I, I, I and me, me, me? Idiotic salons and dinner invitations? The empty mirror of fame? *What?*"

All this would have been enough, but once back from the toilet, with a swipe Rimbaud withdraws, sweaty moist from his back pocket,

that new poem at whose peculiar title Mme. Mauté had so recoiled—
"The Drunken Boat."

Insolent brat. Taking the nasty sheets, the bruised Verlaine sorely
wants to return the favor. Yet, within the first four stanzas, his ears are
ringing. The paper trembles in his fingers; his breathing stutters and his
flitting eye—his eye cannot stop looking.

At what? Experience says it is wrong. Rude. Jejune. Chaotic and violent. At points even absurd.

The Drunken Boat

As I was going down impassive Rivers,
I no longer felt myself guided by haulers!
Yelping redskins had taken them as targets,
And had nailed them naked to colored stakes.

I was indifferent to all crews,
The bearer of Flemish wheat or English cottons,
When with my haulers this uproar stopped,
The Rivers let me go where I wanted.

Into the furious lashing of the tides,
More heedless than children's brains, the other winter
I ran! And loosened peninsulas
Have not undergone a more triumphant hubbub.

The storm blessed my sea vigils.
Lighter than a cork I danced on the waves
That are called eternal rollers of victims,
Ten nights, without missing the stupid eye of the lighthouses.

Sweeter than the flesh of hard apples is to children,
The green water penetrated my hull of fir
And washed me of spots of blue wine
And vomit, scattering rudder and grappling-hook.

And his diction! he thinks. Crude, brawling words like "yelping," "stupid," "hubbub," not to mention the vile "vomit"—this, mind you, from a man who, only a week before, could be seen grappling the lard-white legs of an old strumpet, helplessly licking, like salvation itself, the darkened peach pit of her arsehole. *Vile?* Was that the word?

Then frightened—actually disoriented—Verlaine races ahead:

I have seen the low sun spotted with mystic horrors,
Lighting up, with long violet clots,
Resembling actors of very ancient dramas,
The waves rolling far off their quivering of shutters!

I have dreamed of the green light with dazzled snows,
A kiss slowly rising to the eyes of the sea,
The circulation of unknown saps,
And the yellow and blue awakening of singing phosphorous!

It was like a public beating, this dismantling. And yet much as part of him would have liked to savage the kid, Verlaine was an unfailingly honest critic. Even if he didn't yet understand, he knew what he knew. Knew physically. Knew from the heat, the shock, the pure animal strangeness. And—all honor to him—Verlaine never let jealousy cloud his opinion, nor did he shrink from admitting what he knew.

"*C'est fabuleux,*" he stammers. "I don't even know how to explain—account for it, so strange, so distressing at points. But *extraordinaire.*" Yet at this admission Verlaine trails off, spinning and swept out to sea in his own drunken boat—overwhelmed, as was the kid's intention.

*L*et us now speak of courage, intellectual and artistic courage. Another man might have been envious, competitive, might have run the other way, confronting, in a child, an order of talent and understanding that utterly dwarfed his own.

Not Verlaine. Whatever else, he was not another of these envious, bitter souls forever shortchanged by the world. No, to Verlaine poets were gladiators of a sort. Brutal entertainers. Drink, wench, die—glory or oblivion, one!

Fortunately, Verlaine's mauled pride was soothed to feel himself the discoverer, the impresario and father of this great literary child prodigy, rarer than the white tiger. For whom, Verlaine fancied, he would be as Aristotle was to Alexander the Great. Or as the moon-brained Socrates was to the boys of Athens—a corrupter of youth. Or perhaps, cackled Verlaine, an *extender* of youth, for he did detect in the lad some deliciously mixed signals!

The omnivorous Verlaine, then, was not without enterprise. If not plans, exactly, he had certain as yet ill-defined *aims* for his young bumpkin friend. And here sagely he hedged his bets, aiming high, even as he aimed low.

37 ♪ Poltergeist

But what was the kid thinking, having fallen into this honey pot at 14 rue Nicolet?

He had a room, a splendid room—a room in Paris at an enviable address, with a soft bed, an expansive desk and a large, sunny window overlooking the pea-graveled path of Madame's garden, a small miracle of arboreal geometry with aromatic thickets of rosemary, lavender, and boxwood, together with that staple of the French garden, the beloved red geranium.

Moreover, for the first time in his tramps, the boy wasn't a fugitive, sick with hunger and transfixed with the endless schemes of survival. Here, freed from the maternal grip of the Vampire, and with all of his needs taken care of, he could live like a mental prince, in what, for most mortals, would have seemed the ideal artistic environment. Yet, oddly, and without quite recognizing it, he missed the Vampire, for much as he had fought her, she had always contained him, whereas now he felt dangerously *un*contained, as if he might explode.

He jerked off. It was no better.

He opened Mme. Mauté's window, then for some time worked down long, supple spits. Agile spits, rapidly sucked in and out like a snake's tongue, this to see how *long* spit could stretch before, with a kind of sigh, it broke. Splat, on Madame's wrought-iron garden table.

Then things began to go missing. A silver cross. An expensive book. A porcelain figurine. In the material profusion of chez Mauté, these things were as grains of sand on a beach. Nevertheless, the thefts were immediately spotted by Mme. Mauté, second in vigilance only to the maids, terrified they would be sacked, branded forever as cupboard thieves.

Now, obviously the kid "did" it, yet in his own mind he didn't do it, and in a purely magical sense he hadn't. Rather, from on high, he watched another him, not him, do it. The Madame's silver necklace, for example, a cross with a shriveled Jesus upon it. It was the cross's fault. Morally, it offended him, this symbolic fetish lying openly on the table. With malice, he picked it up. He stuffed it down his pants, the cold metal tingling on the tip of his penis.

Then, lured as if by some aroma, like a fly, he took the necklace with the cross and snuck into a room the likes of which he had never seen. Amazing, these rich bastards. They even had a separate *room* for it.

For here before him, big as a woman, stood a bathtub, perched on clawed feet with a brass spigot that spurted water. And next door in the water closet—most stupendous of all—here was the toilet, the porcelain throne, famished for your ass, your piss, your shit. Obscene, he thought, fondling the long chain attached to the tank—the tank at the very top of the wall—that held the flush water. Pull it. Down it poured, a roaring, frothing maelstrom worthy of the author of "The Drunken Boat."

He waited until it was silent.

He pulled it again. Whoosh.

If only the workers knew what these assholes had in Montmartre!

I will call it the Ass Dragon.

Why, it made him sick, almost dizzy, how the Ass Dragon gobbled down its morning repast, then roared, *Moooooore.* Looking at the cross dangling from the chain, he realized the Lord Jesus was similarly intrigued. So, dangling him down, he watched the heavenly argonaut happily hip-hopping along the bottom. Then, being the Lord, His Holiness told the boy that he wanted to see the golden colors of sunset. So, squatting, still dangling his friend, the boy brought forth the golden waters:

> *And from then on I bathed on the Poem*
> *Of the Sea, infused with stars and lactescent,*
> *Devouring the green azure where, like a pale elated*
> *Piece of flotsam, a pensive drowned figure sometimes sinks . . .*

Then the kid made an offering. Two, in fact, plopping down upon the waters like bread fed to hungry ducks. Then, again with this vagueness—this impulsiveness that would cover his eyes to what he did—suddenly he pulled the chain and let the necklace go down the chute, *oremus, oremus.* For just as Church doctrine said that God the Son was always one with God the Father, so miraculously was the Asshole always one with the Poet, crudity in sublimity, ruthlessness in sympathy—impulses forever at war.

Good grief. Did the kid realize he had extinguished one hour and a quarter in this malign and useless exercise? But if not this, what? Flopping in his lap like two puppets, his big hands fought with each other. For truth be known, he could as easily have hung himself as set the house on fire. That knife's edge of sixteen, crazy sixteen.

*S*till, in the main, his malign efforts were working! To his immense delight, the hounds of 14 rue Nicolet were circling outside the unsavory confines of his bedroom, the very sty in which yellowy-crispy, all but ineradicable stains of an unmentionable origin had been discovered. *Starched*, as it were, on his bedding—indeed, the very same stains that graced the silken, much-humped arm of Madame's exquisitely upholstered chair.

"It has come to my attention," intoned the high priestess of 14 rue Nicolet, who paused to swallow, that she might quell the tremors coursing through her body. "It has come to my attention that certain *articles*"—he betrayed no emotion—"certain valuable and, some of them, *sacred* objects"—with a lifetime of empty hostility he kept staring at her—"and we *wondered*"—of course she could not say *I* wondered—"we wondered if you might know"—at which point he was thrilled, knowing that *she knew that he knew that she knew.* And, best of all, the boy could see she was trapped! Trapped because, in her crippling and self-deluding bourgeois nobility, she hadn't caught him red-handed like the vicious rat he was.

"Would—" she started, stopped, shook. "Would you behave—would you *dare* behave *at home* in this way? *Would* you?"

"Behave?" His vacancy was as utter as it was utterly aggressive. "But, Madame, behave how?"

"You"—her cheeks gorged—"I think you know how, young man." She stuffed down a sob. "Arthur Rimbaud, strange as it might seem, I *like* you. At least, I *want* to like you. Please, my dear, do not force me to send you elsewhere. For, believe me, I shall!"

I like you. I want to like you. Precisely because Mme. Mauté's admission moved him—at least in a way—well, obviously, and for that very reason, he could not *let* it move him, to be that sentimental, that dumb. Lie that it was, love was always the problem, especially when it involved females. After all, for all their enmity and confusion, in a certain sense, even he and his mother "loved" each other—much like two bubbling acids, contesting which would consume the other.

Love: as constituted, it was a base and lying metal against which he was an alchemist and sorcerer, transmuting lead into the solar splendor of gold—of love immortal. These half-digested notions of alchemy and the occult—specifically, of black magic, which he claimed to have studied in great depth—were hastily appropriated from the kaleidoscopic histories of Jules Michelet, notably his work *La Sorcière,* duly stuffed down his trousers several years back at a Charleville book stall.

The point was, he was a poet, not a scholar, and as a poet he knew precisely what he needed to know, and often not one whit *more* than he needed to know, in order to make a poem. And here, like a magnifying glass concentrating a sunbeam, he was studying the very thing he had never really had and thus would never comprehend—love, so called. The great lie that, in his mind, he had been sent to earth to wholly reinvent.

*V*erlaine, meanwhile—and naturally with the basest of intentions—was careful to cover his own unsavory tracks with his new toy. Hopped tracks, for in fact, nothing had happened—yet. Still, to throw the women off the scent, some two weeks after the boy's arrival, the elder poet cunningly raised a possibility irresistible to women: a bit of romance for the lad.

"Mother," said Verlaine one afternoon when, once again, Mme. Mauté was beside herself about the brat, "I'll tell you what *I* think Arthur needs—a girl."

"A girl?" She recoiled. "And who would be the matchmaker—you?"

Wisely, he let this pass. The hook was now set.

"Do you really think so?" asked the pregnant Mathilde, by then so desperate to deliver, and so vexed with her husband's erratic behavior, that she needed almost any diversion. Especially if it might divert the boy and return her husband. And like her mother, she harbored vague hopes, Christian hopes, of rehabilitating this lad clearly so abominably raised.

"Well," sighed her mother later, now entertaining this novel, if absurd, idea. "Perhaps—if he *bathes.* If he had—oh, I don't know—money. Meaningful prospects. Or, dare I say, a *career.*"

"Well," he stammered, nervous at the j-word, as in job.

"Well, what?" demanded the Dragoness. "Which comes first? The girl or the job?"

"The girl, the girl," he agreed—anything so long as they were diverted.

"Well, now, I'm wondering," said Mathilde, whose younger friends, after all, were still girls, but of course proper girls, not to mention Parisian. Still, this was appealing, especially if she and Paul could play the settled married couple charting the lad's fate. But the class issue—not to mention his frightful manners. Might their baker have a daughter? Or, mmmm, perhaps a shop girl somewhere?

"Well," said Verlaine, taking her hand, "a girl is precisely what he needs. As I myself did, my dear."

"Well, my dear," challenged Mathilde, giving him a close look, "once the child comes, many things will need to change."

"And," added the Dragoness, "a certain young lad will need to find other circumstances."

"Well, of course," he fibbed. "A child changes everything. Everything." However implausibly at that moment, Verlaine actually believed he could have both the child *and* the boy. "In fact, ladies," he added with some provocation, "I *welcome* that change."

*T*hen the second week of his visit, even as other lodgings were being discussed—and even as the siege in Mathilde's womb continued—a carriage rolled up. Metal reinforced boxes were unloaded. Dogs barked, the maids ran down, the front door resounded, and there he was, the master, M. Mauté, a heavyset man of martial air dressed in riding boots, a belted tweed shooting jacket, and stylish breeches that ill concealed his girth. He dropped his rifle cases to the floor. He called the women and admonished with his trigger finger the two white muff balls barking at what they now smelled. Then, as the women dutifully assembled—the maids, too—he opened, for their evident amazement, a wicker creel.

"*La récolte de la chasse.*" It was indeed the harvest of the hunt.

"*Ucch,*" said his wife, standing well back.

For inside the creel, in a bed of cool leaves, lay the dried and sightless eyes of No. 13 in his collection of dwarf deer heads. Teeth, tongue, two stubs of horn.

"Horrid!" she cried. "Get that vile, dead thing *out* of here."

For M. Mauté, this, perhaps, was the summit of these subalpine hunts: when he could horrify the weaker sex with the mortuary proof of his male prowess. But *zut*, thought M. Mauté, to come home and find that, after more than a fortnight away, his daughter still had not delivered! That he had to endure still more female *theatrics*.

Worse for Monsieur was this houseguest, this rank wheel of Camembert, of whom he had heard disquieting squibs in the several terse cables he and his wife had exchanged during his sojourn. No, Monsieur was not pleased, not at all, when Verlaine introduced his sullen, unfragrant friend. The creel! Here M. Mauté thought he would show the ill-mannered lad with whom he was dealing.

"See here," said Monsieur, raising the wicker. "See what I have brought back."

"What's *that*?" the boy asked, coolly peering in. Come on, what was this compared with birthing calves and the slaughtering knife?

"*That*," replied M. Mauté, "is a *roe* deer, *mon ami*. A nice buck, as you can see. Taken at a hundred and fifty meters." With a faint smile, he waited for this to sink in.

"But, Monsieur, it is so tiny."

The older man reddened. "Mere *size*, Monsieur, is not the point. This is the male of the species. Ghost of the mountains. Legendarily difficult to stalk."

"But a runt, correct?"

"A *large* specimen. For this species, large. Very large, I assure you." That did it.

"I *understand*," said Monsieur, leaning back on his gleaming boots, that the floorboard might creak beneath his now coiled bulk, "I understand you have been here for"—he cleared his throat—"for some days. Well, at 14 rue Nicolet, in this establishment, young Monsieur, we *bathe*. Yes, we have soap. Hot water, too."

Who was this old clown next to his dear mother, *la Bouche d'Ombre*—the Mouth of Darkness? Let him rant, thought the kid. Verlaine, however, was unnerved. Having grown up essentially fatherless, he was deeply intimidated by aggressive men.

"And," hectored on M. Mauté, "I am further given to understand that in this house, *my* house, certain valuable articles have gone *missing*."

"Father," blurted Verlaine finally, screwing up his courage, "I am quite sure that Monsieur Rimbaud, that he—"

"Allow me to finish!" thundered M. Mauté. "And further, my young Monsieur, I will assume, so long as you are here, and now that I am back . . ."

Stupid old prick, thought the kid. This will be fun.

38 ♪ Why?

For all Rimbaud's skill in evading his own mind, there was no evading Mrs. MacDonald's mind or her odd pull over him. But just what was that pull, exactly? Even in the space of many accelerated days in the desert, their relationship, such as it was, was difficult to characterize. Husband and wife? Mother and son? Caretaker and patient? Conscience and amnesia?

Ambos, pressing like a stone on his chest, had yet to be asked or answered, and so the tension between the two was building as they made their final camp, four kilometers, six at most, from Zeila, their destination on the Gulf of Aden, near the mouth of the Red Sea. Close, one knew, owing to the overabundance of flies and the beggars.

Sprawled against the chest, shotgun across his lap, Rimbaud closely monitored Mrs. MacDonald, even as she stoutly ignored him, chin drawn into her neck. Gone was the prim hair. Crusted in dust, it was now tied like so many sticks in a length of raw cotton. *How native*, he wanted to say, to get a rise out of her. But, wisely, he kept this observation to himself.

Then he must have dozed, for suddenly here she was before him—*his mother. Above him*, there she was, the Mouth of Darkness in her long skirt with two rough boots peeping out. He bolted up.

"Easy," she said. "It's only I."

It was of course Mrs. MacDonald. Returned with the children from their ablutions at the river, she was now as he first remembered her, and this made him extraordinarily happy, uncharacteristically so, to see her again in fresh white shirt, her last, and her hair composed as before, drawn up smartly with the hatpin and primly English straw hat. Appraising his clearly deteriorating condition, she regarded him.

"Look at you, cooked red. Will you never wear your hat?" Picking up the hat, she placed it on his head—pushed it down, then adjusted it, as if for a child.

"Enough."

"Drink."

"I did."

"More."

"I'm fine."

"*Drink.*"

He drank. He knew it was coming, the interrogation, the accusation—something. But then the girl, whatever her name was, was crying again. Your fault, said Mrs. MacDonald's eyes. And, once more, in a small wind—the wind such as a departing woman makes—she left him, rather upset, on his back. Put back into boy purgatory.

Several hours later, when he reawakened, he saw a blood red sky. Groggy, he sat up, then saw before him seven pairs of sandals neatly lined up in the sand—fourteen sandals and, before them, the fourteen bare feet of seven Muslim gunmen. Mud-red men in the red red sun. Prostrate men rising suddenly, then bowing east toward the jagged red mountains, smoldering in the distance like enormous scaly crocodiles. Tides of darkness, cloud tails, the first sharp stars. Abruptly, once again the seven men rose, then flattened themselves, then rose again, their hands open like cups. It was a scene he had witnessed a thousand times, but now it gored him, he of no faith or tribe. Truly, *kaffir*, an unbeliever—a nothing wandering a world of darkness and whirlwinds.

Ordinary pain, physical pain, this was to be expected, but here was a pain he had never let himself feel before—regret. Never, when he had feet. Not when he could leave, change the scene, slip the noose, the curse of being him, losing himself in the next day or the next town. Gone—beyond forgiveness. Cold—beyond clinging. Free—beyond freedom. But what now, with his leg crushed in the jaws of this trap? Who was he? What? *Lord God, Allah, wind in the sky, tell me what to do. Just tell me, make me yours.*

"Why don't you give me that now?"

It was Mrs. MacDonald, reaching for his shotgun. Surrender the gun.

"Come, come, dearie. We are now out of imminent danger. Let it go."

"No." He held it fast.

"Ah," she said blithely, "are we going to be like that?"

She took a rag and a small bowl of water—warm, greasy water from the fatty goat skins. Bad boy. Dirty boy. Washing him, the rag was rough and she was rough. Water dribbled down his neck, then, rather embarrassingly, down his trousers, as if he'd wet himself. Embarrassed. Afraid his men might see.

"Enough, you're getting me wet."

She plopped the rag in the bowl and took a steaming cup from one of the bearers—sweet tea with just-stripped camel's milk, mother's milk, buttery thick. *Drink.* So he drank. Drained it, then had another cup, delicious. Again, Mrs. MacDonald called the men, who now rather miraculously more or less did as she said—motioned—in a voice that was clipped and punctiliously polite. A small candle lantern was brought, lit. It was now just the two of them, two faces in a yellowy globe of light.

"So why?" she asked brightly, now that the tea had revived him. "Really, now you must tell me. Why, ever, did you write poems, Mr. Rimbaud? A man such as yourself."

He stared at her in disbelief.

"*Poems*, Mr. Rimbaud," she said, undeterred. "Now, now, don't be coy, Monsieur. Surely you can tell me. Purely *entre nous.*"

Entre nous, between us. This appealed to his vanity, that they should be, somehow, intimates connected. And, to his very enormous relief, Ambos was not the subject of inquiry. Mrs. MacDonald's mode was one of challenge, true. But it also was seductive, blackly jocular, almost cynical, thereby raising the conversation—in one balletic leap—to another plane. Metaphorical. Symbolical. Fantastical. Indeed, in its horror, it was almost abstract. Mrs. MacDonald simply had never met such a person, a capitalist, an arguable murderer, and a cynic, why, at this rate perhaps even a secret slave trader, in a poet's body. She was quite rapt with curiosity, as if she were inquiring of a lion why he ate meat.

"Come now, just tell me," she coaxed. "Just *me*. Why on earth did you once write poems? And then just *stop*, as you did. Honestly, Monsieur. How could you do *that* and now *this*?"

This, too, appealed to him, for in his inward way he took perverse pride in how he had reinvented his life, or lives, rather. "Well," he replied rather grandly, if evasively, "I didn't write *those* sort of poems."

"*Antecedent*, Mr. Rimbaud," she chided schoolmarmishly. "Poems of what sort?"

"Oh"—and he groaned—"those English things of fifty years ago. Gloomy thoughts, like your English drizzle. Wordsworth in the Highlands. Shelley on the beach. Coleridge dreaming his opium dreams. Oh, 'Ozymandias'—fine. Keats—sublime, I suppose. In any case, Madame, I didn't do any of *that*. It was *France*, and there was other rubbish at the time. French rubbish."

"So," she said, "what, then, *did* you write, Mr. Rimbaud?"

"No recollection—*rien*. Why does a jug pour out its water?" Briefly, he mounted a smile at this aperçu. Then he turned scolding. "Well, if it was Bardey who told you about this—any of them—well, they told you I do not discuss it. At all. *Any* of it."

"But I am told that people quite *love* your poetry," she persisted, with a tone now of flagrant flattery. "Positively revere it—well, in Paris they do. I am told that they think it, and you, a great discovery. Hugely important. Genius. Even classic, dare I say."

At this he grew agitated.

"I do not think of it—ever. What do I care *who* might like my little monsters? These things, these mere artifacts, these youthful slops, they are not *me*. *My* poems. This makes no sense to me. Rimbaud who? Not me. I do not *own* them. There is no 'author,' so called. Ridiculous. Pure egotism. Self-delusion."

"Ah," she said, bringing him up short, "and do you then renounce the money, too? You certainly seem to fancy *that*—money."

"Money," he said with a shrug, "there is no money in poetry—none. And I did not publish them. That was my good friend—of once—the poet Verlaine. Genius, a *poète de musique* but a drunk and a bum. So like a fool I let Verlaine have my scribblings. It is my fault, my weakness that I did not burn them. Burn them and be done with it, as I should have."

"Then you disown them?"

"No," he caviled, "because I never *owned* them to begin with. He, who, it, whoever—*it* merely *wrote* them, and I gave the little bastards away. There," he said firmly, "Enough—"

"Fine," she said briskly. "Another topic then—that terrible scene we passed just today in the desert? Who sold the necessary cartridges? I wonder. Who sold the guns? Hmm, Mr. Rimbaud? Any idea? Or are you, once more, not the author?"

"Yes," he sighed, "I sell guns. Cookware. Oil. Trinkets. All honorable products." He glared in the direction of her husband. "Some of us, not yet saints, we must make a living."

"Or a killing."

"Do you dare accuse me?" He hauled himself more erect. "Others, several, not just Rimbaud, sell the guns. *And* medicines with which fools poison themselves. *And* knives with which the clumsy cut themselves. I merely *sell* the guns, I do not *aim* the guns."

"Slaves?"

"Never," he glared, "never slaves, ever. Not in any transaction, and not easy when they are still traded like currency. But I refused—consistently. There I drew the line."

"How very principled of you," she trilled, still not convinced.

"Madame," and he fixed her in his eyes in that scary way he had, "it is very much a principle. Here where there is no line, one learns very quickly, believe me, that a line is needed."

"Well," she replied, smarting at his bluff male certainty. "So, guns then, Mr. Rimbaud. So like your poems. Acts of God. Accidents for which you, being you, are to be held blameless. Heavens no! *You* are not their author. You, pure as the snow. Certainly not—*you* did not force them to buy your wares. Do I not detect a theme, Mr. Rimbaud?"

Down came his arms; up came the venom.

"And who saved you and your children with all your English high-mindedness? I did. *And* my money. *And* my guns. But of course, you are Christians. Birds of the air. People of the spirit. So, let others feed you, and pay for you, and kill for you, while you do your high-minded leeching. Am I not getting *warm*, Madame? No?"

Imperiously, she rose, smoothing her dirty dress. Rose because she could, then regarded him with a cold stare, a man sitting helpless in the red dirt, in the bits.

"I thought, Mr. Rimbaud, that I might try—try—to get you to see some truth. A glimmer, perhaps. But clearly I was bound to fail. Good night."

But as she turned, he desperately grabbed the hem of her dress. Tugged it uselessly. Once, like a bellrope, then dropped it, staring into his shadow—spent.

"Wait," he said, too ashamed to look up. "I am sorry to say such dreadful things to you. Terrible things. I am very, very sorry. Now please, send your husband over. Only him. And I promise it will be a good thing. A very good thing."

39 ♪ The Nasty Fellows

"But when will you and Monsieur Rimbaud be home?" the pregnant Mathilde begged her husband, now anxious to leave as she lay red and bloated on the fainting couch, with a maid to daub each eye. Did Verlaine actually think that a few hours of solicitude would erase a week's utter dereliction? With Mathilde, perhaps, but not with the Dragoness, now at her daughter's side.

"Well?" said the Dragoness. "Will you answer your wife?"

"Not late," he said. "This is a reading." Rimbaud's Paris debut this would be. "Rarely do these things go that late. Unless, of course, there is great éclat."

"But, my darling," said Mathilde, desperate, even then, to be agreeable, "I am about to deliver. I *need* to deliver."

What had come of those lyrics he had once written, overpowering feelings of love and happiness and gratitude? *You've got a child coming*, he kept telling himself.

Paul, she would say, as they lay in bed, feel him. He's kicking? Do you feel it?

Feel something. Anything to shake this growing paralysis. And he had tried to prepare himself for the child, he had; why, manfully one morning for more than an hour he had sat at his desk, numbly endeavoring to write a poem entitled "The Child." The child, the child—what? Nil. Naught. Nothing. Haze over fog.

But mainly Paul Verlaine felt torn between his wife and Rimbaud. And this could well be the night, he reminded himself, not altogether sure whether he meant the new arrival or finally something physical with Rimbaud. He was not a cruel or unfeeling man. It was her first child; she was young and frightened and feeling abandoned—too true. But how could he leave Rimbaud, even younger than she, to brave literary Paris alone? And where was Mathilde's own father, the deserter? At his club, of course, smoking and playing cards.

"Oh, let him *go*," moaned the Dragoness to her daughter as he made ready to leave. "They're *males*, they're going to go—so *go*."

Wringing a pillow, Mathilde called out.

"Do you even *care* about this child, Paul Verlaine? *Do* you?"

It was then that Rimbaud appeared. Mme. Mauté rose in shock.

"What, you *bathed*? Ah," she said, nodding, "now I see! You bathe for these *poets*, eh, but not for we who house and feed you?"

It was true. His shoes were shined, his suit was brushed, and his twisted black tie hung down like two licorice sticks. All was prepared. In his still perfect schoolboy hand, he had carefully copied out "Le Bateau Ivre," then read it aloud—twice. *Dérangement* tomorrow. Tonight for careering.

"*Jeune homme*," said Mme. Mauté, attempting to convey a more familial note to the young feral. "Please, come here."

With queer pride she straightened the tie. Licked her thumb and, without protest from him, repaired a curl. In fact, for a split second the Dragoness reminded him of his mother, one of those rare, momentary truces when they both could drop the masks.

"Paul," cried Mathilde as they left. "Please—not late. This could be the night."

Strange sight. Seen from behind, to Mathilde, the two vaguely looked like father and son, off to church, perhaps. Inside the baby was kicking, alive. Why could her husband not feel that? Numb, Mathilde Mauté Verlaine smoothed her belly as expectant mothers do, rocking her own cradle. And without quite knowing why, she felt a deep, involuntary shudder.

Verlaine's branch of the Parnassians called themselves *les Vilains Bonshommes*, the Nasty Fellows, a nom de guerre earned by the poet-playwright François Coppée. An official in the Ministry of War by day, this Coppée had the looks and gravitas of a possum yet somehow had managed, in his tepid verses, to upset a critical nobody who called him, in print, "a nasty fellow."

Brilliant! Henceforth Verlaine's clan would be known as the Nasty Fellows. But nasty? Hardly.

Poets by night and on weekends, they were, by day, professors and bureaucrats, engravers and journalists, and one, Ernest d'Hervilly, an agent with the Ministry of Bridges and Roads. See them now assembling in the back of the Café Procope over some crusts and wine, the cheese already devoured. Orotund voices, rubicund faces, freely laughing and gesturing, they are anything but stiff and disagreeable, these men in their worn black boots, overstarched collars, and sagging dark suits with shiny elbows. Most are in their twenties and thirties, a handful in their forties, and there, in the front, bearded, silver-haired, and bald-pated, looking rather like an old priest, is the grand old man of the group, Théodore de Banville, now almost fifty. Banville, we'll recall, was the poet to whom Rimbaud had sent his mocking poems only one year before. And yet, although Banville had not forgotten his cheek and insolence, unknown to Rimbaud he had promised Verlaine, and with considerable foresight, that he would house the prodigy once, inevitably, the Mautés had had enough.

In his decency and devotion to his art, Banville expressed perfectly the best of the Nasties, or any other community, for that matter. And in Paris—whatever one did, down to the ragpickers and sewer men—community was essential. For the average inhabitant, Paris was dark and dank, not gay and glittering. For aspiring poets, from the provinces especially, it was a life of cheap rooms and no wife—impossible, too expensive. Better and cheaper, *le pinard*—plonk wine—and a prostitute every now and then. Not much.

And life was short: rare was the person who lived to forty-five, let alone to fifty, like Banville. Community mattered, but then what could Rimbaud, raised by a semi-shut-in, have known about *that*?

Who, then, was Rimbaud in this place, and who did he imagine these people would be? Just who was his public? His ideal reader? Well, other than God, of course.

Whatever posterity's harsh judgments, these Parnassians were not the silly poseurs and mediocrities the kid expected. These were able and committed craftsmen—decent men, amusing and intelligent. Most, too, were realists, relieved finally of the sad, wearying burden of kidding themselves about one day standing among the Pantheon. Failure, pain, rejection: the dawning, then resolute certainty that ceaseless effort and passion, or even talent, were not enough—that, all kidding aside, one was, after all, unexceptional. They knew the writer's lot. They did the work. They did it as best they could—was that not enough?

Of course the boy did not, could not, and *would* not know about this—any of it. Death in the abstract—easy to conjure. Eternity—even this could be imagined. But ordinary life—the ceaseless proof of living day after day after day? Of this, the wunderkind knew almost nothing, nor could he, obviously.

*T*hen again, *les Vilains Bonshommes* arrived with their own preconceptions.

All had seen—and some, like monks, had hand-copied to further distribute—the kid's now semidisinherited earlier works, such as "The Stolen Heart," "The Seekers of Lice," and "First Communions."

At these works the poets of Paris stared. Picked them up, threw them down, and debated them. And yes, freely admitted they were works of genius—*but.* Inevitably there came the "but."

But his rhymes, they are somewhat . . . *irregular.*

But his word choice is, well . . . *odd.*

But as with "The Stolen Heart," parts are . . . *irrational, crazy.*

But his subjects, although fresh, can be a trifle . . . *jejune.*

But, not *bad,* you understand. But . . .

And so that night, before his arrival, the Nasties could be heard fulminating.

"Has the Boy Christ arrived?"

"And did you read 'The Stolen Heart'?"

"Well, genius, clearly. But vile if true. And if not . . ."

Let us not forget, moreover, that it was the threadbare Nasties who had cobbled together the funds necessary to bring the bumpkin to Paris. As they saw it, he was their discovery. And so, quibbles aside, Rimbaud had no reason to fail and every possible reason to succeed.

And yet, entering upon this room of smiles and bows and open hands, the boy colored and froze. Froze because it was nothing like he imagined it would be—in fact, it was all wrong. So what, then, had he imagined? Poets ripping up their feeble efforts and breaking their pens, all clapping and bowing, waiting to anoint poetry's uncrowned king?

"Well, he is *so* excited to be here!" gushed Verlaine, talking enough for two, as the boy spurned a glass of water or wine, then bleakly stared at the floor, hands balled in his pockets. It was a mercy when Banville called the meeting to order.

"Well, then, Monsieur Rimbaud," said the worthy Banville, "we are honored to have you, and we welcome you, so young and talented. And I'm told you have brought us a poem."

"No," said the boy with nervous irritation, "the poem brought me, Monsieur."

Stupid. The second these words fled his lips he felt stupid and embarrassed, then angry—angry at these older men, these mediocrities, staring at him as if he were a freak.

"Ah," replied Banville nimbly, "then perhaps the *poem* will lead you to the podium?"

Rimbaud looked at him. *He woke up.* He had never spoken publicly before—school didn't count. He didn't know the terror and dazzlement of a room full of people all watching you, waiting for you to trip up. Nor did he know how a speaker loses all track of time, speaking into the void as people sit submerged, thinking what, *what*?

"Messieurs, my good sirs," said Verlaine nervously, rushing up to the lectern, "allow me to explain. Or rather to add, if I may, a bit of *context* to what you are about to hear. This poem you shall hear, it is new— radically new. But to many of you, it may strike you as—ah, what word shall I use? Rude? Obstreperous, as is the way with youth?"

Men were staring. The boy's cheeks were now as red as two candy sticks.

"You see," Verlaine continued, like a magician announcing his next feat, "on my first hearing of this poem, I was, I can tell you, *shocked*. Note, my friends, I do not say this for effect—no. For the simple fact was, I did not know what to say. I had to let it sink in, really over many days. I will also tell you, often I didn't properly know *who* was talking. The way things flowed. The way some of it seemed, quite deliberately, *not* to make sense." He smiled at the kid—he was just trying to prepare them. "Make sense, I mean, in the way that *I* make sense. I and most people, perhaps. But, as I say, often I did not know *who* was talking and—"

"Then stop talking, Verlaine!" cried a voice. "Let the boy *read*."

"Read! Read!"

Are they daring me? thought the kid. He was petrified, but he couldn't flee, not now. His head was on fire and his ears were ringing— he saw spots. Pulling out his pages, his hands shook. Then no sooner did he still his hands than his knees were trembling. Nonetheless, he started, his voice quavering:

The Drunken Boat

As I was going down impassive Rivers,
I no longer felt myself guided by haulers! . . .

One blew his nose. Another drilled his finger into his ear. Verlaine looked around. Closed eyes. Stone faces. Pained squints. No, he realized much too late, this was not a poem to be read aloud:

Sweeter than the flesh of hard apples is to children,
The green water penetrated my hull of fir
And washed me of spots of blue wine
And vomit, scattering rudder and grappling-hook.

"Vomit?" said someone quite audibly. "Did he just say 'vomit'? In a *poem*?"

A titter was heard. Coughs and nose blowing, ear tugging, twitches. But by then the kid was deaf, numb, a voice in a body reading:

I followed during pregnant months the swell,
Like hysterical cows, in its assault on the reefs . . .

"What?" said another. "Is it now *pregnant hysterical cows*?"

"Gentlemen," chided Banville, staring with deep concentration at his boots.

Had his audience had the text to follow, this would have been bad enough. But reading it aloud, and badly—a fiasco. And just what was this phantasmagoria that he was reading? A poem, of course, had a clear speaker or *point of view*. A poem had a more or less consistent *tone*. A poem, however fanciful, was obliged to *make sense*. But what was anyone to make of this—these violent shifts of perspective, this drunken *illogic*? But at long last—seemingly hours in a mere twenty minutes—he concluded:

> *If I want a water of Europe, it is the black*
> *Cold puddle where in the sweet-smelling twilight*
> *A squatting child full of sadness releases*
> *A boat as fragile as a May butterfly.*

> *No longer can I, bathed in your languor, O waves,*
> *Follow in the wake of the cotton boats,*
> *Nor cross through the pride of flags and flames,*
> *Nor swim under the terrible eyes of prison ships.*

He stopped. The room fell as still, then Verlaine—someone—clapped. One clap, then two, then—not knowing *what* to say—they all were clapping. *Thrilled*—anything for this ordeal to be *over*. But then, as the clapping subsided, before the kid could flee, a gentleman with a shock of dark hair, beard, and mustache—Léon Valade—asked:

"Monsieur Rimbaud, if I remember correctly, in that penultimate stanza . . . how does it go? 'A water of *Europe*'—I believe this was what you said—it then becomes a *puddle*? Presumably, a sea, then *a puddle*?" In evident alarm and vexation, Valade looked around for support and found it in the folded arms and nodding heads; nobody then made these wild leaps. "*Then*, Monsieur Rimbaud," he continued, "in two lines there is a child releasing a *boat*, then"—he sighed—"then, I guess, he is an *adult*? Do you see? I—I—I just wonder if you might explain. Since"—he smiled—"since it is so very interesting to us."

"It is not," replied the boy coldly, "my job to explain."

"But," said the elder poet, swiping his long, slick mustache, "but, Monsieur Rimbaud, surely as poets, it *is* our job to explain, to be clear."

"No," said the boy testily, "but you see, when I read *your* writings— many of you—you labor to explain. To merely be *clear*, as if a poem were, what, a *newspaper*? Read once, then used to wipe your—"

It was, in short, an incendiary debut, as the young honoree not only bit the hand, but even managed, on the way out, to pinch a hat and a pair of gloves.

40 ✲ Poison Ink

Two days later, the child was born—at home, of course—after twenty-seven and one-quarter hours of labor, a marathon in which, naturally, the men of 14 rue Nicolet had gone almost entirely missing. More-over, the child, a boy, now had a name—Georges—although for Verlaine at that moment it might as well have been named Nobody.

Being a Mauté, the scion, in a way horrifying to their hardscrabble guest, had his own infant principality comfortably separate from his parents, a place with embroidered ruffles over the ruffles and—to dis-guise the legs of his crib, which Mme. M thought unsightly—even Bo Peep pantaloons. The child also had many long, equally ruffled silken gowns, each with a starched bonnet that, once tied, make him look like an enormous squalling flower. For like his papa, baby Georges was a voracious swiller of fluids, occupying not only Mother but an equally depleted, red-faced wet nurse who had recently delivered her sixth. Suf-fice to say, amid the continuing siege, young Mathilde was not the same pliant naïf she had been ten days before, not now, saddled as she was with *three* children—baby Georges, his papa, and now this versifying urchin from the sticks.

Three a.m. Drunk again.

After another bad night, Georges was sleeping in the crook of her left arm when the door burst open and his papa—paralyzed—collapsed into bed, very nearly crushing the child. Mathilde bolted up. Georges was bawling and his father was snoring, reeking of the tavern and—good heavens!—the horse dung thickly mired on his boots.

"*Get up!*" she cried, shaking him. "Paul! You almost hurt the baby—wake *up*." Furious, she gave him the elbow. "There's a *child* in this room, do you hear me? *Your* child!"

"Shut it," he muttered. "Little shit."

"Miserable baby!" She shoved him again. "*You*, who cannot even bear to *look* at your son?" Then again—hard, in the ribs.

"*Bitch!*" He stormed up. His eyes looked like small coins. Dazedly, he whipped around. "Whore! You whore!"

"Indolent lout!" she retorted. "I, whose family *supports* you, and to do what? To guzzle and root about and write nothing! Ah, but you have *your* son now, don't you? Your rude and filthy son, Rimbaud—"

Rimbaud, this was what set him off. "Whore! Rimbaud is twenty of you."

"And leads you around by the nose! Like a fool! *You*, who won't so much as look at your own son, let alone pick him up."

"What?" he roared. "Up? Pick him up, you say?" Colicky baby Georges—normally with his nurse so Mother could sleep—he was in their room, bundled in his blanket. When, before she could even react, her husband lurched up and grabbed the infant, hypnotized with rage, swaying drunk.

"Paul, put him down!"

"Down?" he mocked. "Down, do you say?"

Beneath Verlaine's blank gaze, the squalling infant might have been a rump of beef in soggy butcher's paper. There was no hesitation. He flung the infant against the wall, then watched, in numb horror, as he hit the floor.

"*Monster!*"

Hysterical, Mathilde swept the child up, then jammed herself in the corner, the baby balled in her arms. There was no time to scream. With that frightening alacrity of drunks, Verlaine, insensible only moments before, was just inches from her face, head swaying like a snake.

"Bloody fucking bitch!" He grabbed her by the throat. "Dare you!

About"—he lost his page—*"Dare you!"* He raised his fist. "Rimbaud! Eh?
Ehhhhhh—?"

Dazed-eyed. Spittle-lipped. Lower teeth jutting. With each curse the
cords of his throat trembled, as slowly he seized her by the mouth,
twisted her lips to a beak, then uttered low as an oath, "God *damn* you,
f-f-*pharafites.*"

Double man. Double sex and double mind. Off he went, through
the door like a sleepwalker. No horror, no memory; it sloughed off him
like water. Dark, he stalked down the hall. Darker, he flowed down the
stairs. Then, darker than darkness, he plunged into night and started
swimming, bleeding like poison ink into the gaslit fog.

41 ♒ Abandoned

Trembling under the gaslights moments later, Mathilde was peering into
Georges's eyes, gently palpating his plush arms and fat little legs. No
squalling. No expression of pain. Thank God! It was all the flounces and
swaddling that had saved him, she thought. It was the rug upon which
he had landed—a miracle. *Now what?* Ring for the maids? Call for her
parents? *No, not now, not now.* Clutching his blubbery baby warmth,
she wept her way into sleep. Then later, when Georges woke her up
crying—hungry, thank God—in her nightgown, as Mathilde crept down
the hall to wake the nurse, once again in horror she thought, What now,
what?

Shame and fear. Like acid, they were burning through her. Her parents downstairs, both sound sleepers, clearly they had not heard anything, nor had the maids. If only they had heard! she thought. If only she
did not have to tell them, for how could she tell them—anyone—about a
thing so horrifying, so heartless and insane? And especially coming from
her, a newlywed? Impossible—the presumption of innocence always
resided with the husband, always, and especially in her case, owing to
her youth. People will think it is I who am crazy, she thought, for what
sane person could imagine such a thing, a man throwing his own child, a

helpless infant, against the wall, then choking and threatening his wife? People would think, What did she do—or not do—to make her husband so angry? The whispering, the rumors—no, she decided with a shudder, not even to the priest in confession, not even if she died of this secret, could she divulge a thing so shameful. And at bottom, it was her fault, she thought: *her* failure for not controlling him, for being too consumed with the baby. Too young. Too stupid to have married him. Too trapped and powerless. Too weak.

Hide, her soul told her, *quick in the closet*, in the darkness where no one could hear her. Baby Georges by then had been put down, milk-drunk, lips twitching, with his drowsy nurse, pendulous in her wet nightshirt. Creeping down the hall, Mathilde returned alone to their room, opened the closet door, then closed it behind her—pure darkness, blessed oblivion. *Let go*, said the voice, and she did, tumbling back into the hangers and crumpling clothes, into the smell of sweat and old perfume. Then, stuffing her mouth with a ready sleeve, she let loose, choking and wheezing and screaming, until, like a broken doll, she just lay there, trembling, thinking, What now? What now? *What?*

*T*here was one witness, however. Down the hall, Rimbaud heard the ruckus and he recognized his name, and although he winced at points—and of course never dreamed the full extent of it—the cold truth was, for him, these were the sounds of home. His lullaby. Soothing in a perverse way.

Night brawls. Shouting matches. And after the kid's father left, there was the late-night spectacle of a woman man-dumped and God-banished, storming through the house. Find the guilty. Find that one pin out of place that wrecked everything. Explained everything. It was the sound of a screech owl. It was cats fighting. It was shame given lungs, a woman howling in the darkness, like a dog chained to an iron stake.

On a more practical level, however, Rimbaud felt the keen satisfaction of exercising his impossibly high ideals, in this case, by rescuing a fellow poet from the lie of bourgeois domesticity: the wife and son, the stupid in-laws, and now the brat. Enough lies. It would never last. Why, just the thought of Verlaine as a father—mad. Even in the space of several weeks, Rimbaud held no illusions about Verlaine's character.

Besides, he thought, the brat had his stupid grandfather and a houseful of women to adore him: toys, clothes, nannies—so much it was ridiculous. So why get the kid's hopes up, thought Rimbaud. Honestly, he thought he was doing the kid a favor.

As for Verlaine, there was that special, spectral terror of the morning after—of knowing, for a fact, that something horrible had occurred, even as the Green Lady assured him to the contrary.

What if the police are after me?

Ridiculous. Were that true, you would be in jail.

Which proves it! The child fell.

Fell. But she picked him up and he's fine—fine.

Fell, there's the story.

And that's all you need to say.

Picture him, wrapped in a blanket in the back of a laundry while some fellow cleaned that pelt he called a suit and a bootblack scraped the ordure off his boots. He drank two pitchers of water. He wolfed down four eggs, runny eggs, with ham and black coffee. Then it was off to the Turkish bath. There for an hour, he boiled himself, then doused himself in rosewater. And so at 3:00 p.m.—sharp—there he was, the *paterfamilias*, bathed and brushed, blue-eyed and trembling sober. Wobbly-kneed, he stood before the great oaken door of 14 rue Nicolet—Judgment Day.

He *knocked*, that was the giveaway. Silently, the maids let him in, coldly, then disappeared. Even Mme. Mauté had been warned away, her daughter having assured her—without specifics—that her tolerance was at an end. And so it began, when Mathilde recoiled from her husband's teary, ill-advised embrace.

"Do not dare touch me."

"But, please, I know I—"

"Just *sit*! Sit, animal. Sit with yourself. Sit with the truth and do not speak."

And what could he say when, pulling down her collar, Mathilde showed him the necklace of fingerprints around her throat? How to respond when she not only told him but showed him how he had nearly killed his son? *Who?* he almost wanted to ask with husbandly indignation, now confronted by his own hideous double, this spawn with whom he swam through chill green seas of alcohol. And, all too predictably, of course Verlaine broke down, falling to his knees, pounding the floor—the usual histrionics.

"If I had any courage, any decency, any . . . I simply would kill myself. *Kill myself.*"

"Oh, *stop* it. *Up!* Follow me."

Panic—her parents?

"No," she replied, happy to see him sweat, "the nursery."

"But he's napping."

"Come, coward. You will now apologize to your son."

Feel something, he thought, for there, on his back, stupendously alive and just waking up, was his child, *his own child.* Tiny balled fingers. Hair wet with sweat. Ruddy red eyelids. What do I feel? *What?*

"Paul," she snapped. *"Pick him up."*

Parisian fathers did not, as a rule, pick up their issue at this unsavory age—*non.* The child well might have been a kicking hare with long, sharp claws. Verlaine fumbled. Drew in his neck, lifted him unsteadily, then, in terror, looked at his wife for further instruction.

"Now," she said, "look at your son and hear me. I know too well you will beat me again—I know this. But if you *ever again* touch this child, and if my father does not first shoot you, then I swear to you, Paul Verlaine, I shall leave you. Before God I swear it. Even if I am excommunicated, I will divorce you. And after what I tell the courts, never again will you see us. *Ever.* Do you understand?"

"I know, I know." Bitterly, he wept, but Mathilde wanted none of it. One last matter remained—Rimbaud.

"Tomorrow he is out, do you hear me? *Out.*"

"I agree," he gushed. "In a few days. At most a week."

"*Paul*," she hissed, "hear me now. Not *days* or even *a* day. Tomorrow by *noon*—noon sharp—Rimbaud is gone. If not, I tell my parents every-thing."

42 ♪ Boy on the Cusp

As for Rimbaud, even before he got the boot from 14 rue Nicolet, unusual for him, he had been in a visible funk, a detail not overlooked by the perspicacious Mme. Mauté.

Much of it, she knew, was the letdown of his ill-starred debut, but was that all, she wondered. It was then that she recalled the observation that her son-in-law had made some days earlier to throw them off the trail—about Rimbaud's needing a girl. Ah-ha, thought Mme. Mauté. A girl, was *that* it?

Honestly, it was hard to know. For example, Paulette, the youngest of the three maids, was, she thought, quite pretty, albeit in a déclassé sort of way. Yet whenever Paulette entered the room, stiffly Rimbaud would leave—embarrassed, if that was quite the word. Just what *was* that word, exactly?

Indeed, Mme. Mauté became genuinely curious as to what a *suitable enough* girl might do, or better yet, the effect that *too* suitable a girl might have. For what was required, after all, was not *the* girl but merely *a* girl. A girl not only heartbreakingly pretty but hopelessly unattainable.

It was then she remembered Mme. de Robert's seventeen-year-old Natalie, who, much to her mother's dismay, was presently more focused on writing poetry than on finding a husband. *Poetess*, sniffed Mme. de Robert to Mme. Mauté. Bubbling like two doves, the two ladies were having their thrice-weekly tête-à-tête in two facing chairs of blue velveteen. Mauté blue. Indeed, it was the blue of the Mauté family coat of arms, a contrived artifact allegedly last seen when some chain-mail-wearing forebear was hunched over, helping his betters up into their stirrups to go fight the English. "Ah," said Mme. de Robert, ever alert for signs of social decline in *her* set. "*Poetess*," she continued, "this barbarism reminds me of that odious new title *actress*, with which the various tartlettes of the stage and the music halls now cloak their revolting nocturnal escapades."

They replaced their porcelain teacups on their porcelain saucers—blue, of course. Mme. de Robert, meanwhile, remained discomfited.

"But what if she becomes interested?" asked Mme. de Robert, albeit with great deference. Despite her unfortunate son-in-law, Mme. Mauté was seen as brilliant in the womanly stratagems of matchmaking.

"Ridiculous," replied Mme. Mauté. "*Un paysan du Danube?* A penniless rube. But of *course*, it will go nowhere. What does a puppet do when one drops the strings?"

*N*ever mind the machinations involved: Mme. Mauté's puffery about Rimbaud's genius, together with the two poems, two of the more innocent ("The Green Cabaret" and "The Hands of Jeanne-Marie"), that she hand-copied (much bowdlerized) for the impressionable Natalie. Suffice to say that young Natalie arrived enthralled, a lithe, dark-haired girl in braids, buttoned black shoes, and short white gloves crocheted to resemble white nets. More wounding still, unlike most very beautiful girls of means, Mme. de Robert's daughter was utterly natural, blithe, and unaffected.

"Ah, Monsieur Rimbaud," said Mme. Mauté as she swept into the garden where he was reading—loutishly, of course, sprawled on the divan in the same foul suit in which he had arrived. "I have long been meaning to introduce you to this young lady who"—she looked at him with a great smile—"who *also* writes poems. Very good poems, actually. May I present . . ."

Madame's dart was true. Rigidly he shot up. Colored and grunted, his big hands flopping. Incredibly, he said, "*Bonjour*," then—unprecedented—"very nice to meet you," whereupon, dropping his head, Rimbaud blindly fled the house. And not because he didn't find the girl attractive—quite the contrary. His paralysis and terror before her, it was all too emblematic of his sexual ambiguity and emotional incoherence—of the stumbling nakedness in life that he could cloak instead in art.

Beyond questions of art or theory, it was shame that propelled him down rue Nicolet, down the boulevard Barbès, onto the rue d'Hauteville, and eventually to the open market of the Halles, sweet with the smell of overripe fruit, then the sharp blood reek of flayed sides of beef and freshly split pork. A butcher whisk-whisking his knife. A woman brushing away flies. And almost dialectically, running through his mind:

Why can't I think of women?

Because I need a theory, a lie, to justify who I am?

Because, even if it kills me, I always must do the opposite?

Of the opposite?

Because I *do* hate women?

Or because I secretly hate liking to hate them?

Dazed, he looked up. Fully two hours had passed. He was on the Pont Neuf, suspended over the black waters of the ever-churning, seaward-surging Seine. Golden cupolas in the distance. Swift pigeons. Water and sky. Here was Paris in all its sweep: marble and iron, spires and statues and trees—hot, raw life, spinning him dizzy.

Peer down into those waters. Whirlpools of sex, boiling dark, boiling deep. Two choices, two poles. Here is childhood and here is adulthood. Here is male, and here is female. And here in the middle, staring at the roiling water, here we find an overbrilliant boy, wishing for a rope, for a rock, but most of all wishing he had a choice. Just a choice, when, really, the choice had already been made for him.

43 𝄞 *Out!*

But with the usual randomness, of course the kid did not drown himself. Instead, he returned to 14 rue Nicolet confused and humiliated—out of control. And so, summoning all his powers, the next day he got even.

"Monsieur Rimbaud! *Rimbaud!* Down here! Where is he! *Where?*"

It was glorious. It was M. Mauté downstairs, bellowing at the top of his lungs. A moment prior, as was his tedious custom, M. Mauté had been timing, to the second, the chimes of his many disparate clocks—a clearly hopeless task which, for that very reason, occupied large portions of his day.

When he saw it.

It was his trophy wall of tiny stuffed deer heads . . . *and everything was wrong.*

The twig horns. The dubious smiles. On those dozen hare-sized heads everything had been altered—everything. The glass eyes. The smiles. Even the diameter of the nostrils. It was diabolical. It must have taken hours, this outrage, hours daubing black paint with a brush of perhaps *three hairs.* Detectable but to one man, now about to have heart failure.

"Monsieur Rimbaud! Now! Get down here!"

But of course, the boy came right away. The whole household was there.

"Look at this!" cried the old man, now armed with a magnifying glass. Rimbaud looked quizzically at his host, with perfect, malevolent innocence.

"Ah, Monsieur, I came right away. Did something happen?"

"YOU KNOW WHAT HAPPENED!" Fiercely, M. Mauté looked to the women for support. "You see! Of course you see. *Here!*" he pointed. "And *here!* See? See? Do you not see what he did?"

The women looked at one another, puzzled.

"*Look!*" cried M. Mauté, now nose to nose with the third specimen from the right. "Notice the smile—almost gone. And that eye—now dull. And that nostril—ruined. As was your foul intention, Monsieur!"

"Intention?" asked the boy.

"Yooou." He bellowed. "Yoooooou—"

"But, Monsieur," inquired the boy, now going in for the kill, "I am confused. Is it this one? Or wait—is it this one here that bothers you . . . ?"

*A*nd yet, even after his three-week siege, with a new infant in the house—and now with this fiendish assault on his host—the lad was shocked. Actually shocked when Verlaine called him down to the foyer. There, by the door, stood a new valise purchased in advance for this great day, along with several shirts and undergarments. And there, atop it, was a fat envelope containing thirty francs of good riddance.

"What is this?" demanded the kid. He waved the envelope in Verlaine's face. *"What is this?"*

"Severance pay. Come now," said Verlaine good-naturedly, "you've thoroughly abused our hospitality—you've been brilliant in every way. Now come say a proper good-bye. I've booked you a room."

"Judas! Go screw yourself." The kid stormed out.

Let it be said: it did look odd, exceedingly, for a grown man with a valise to be chasing a boy clearly not his son. A horse cab clopped by. Verlaine hailed it, then directed the driver to troll beside the still cursing refugee, head down, beating down the street.

"Arthur!" he said, hanging out the window. "Come on now—in. I'll pay for your room. We'll eat, then we'll both get plastered."

"All right," he agreed. "But only if you shut up."

And so in silence, riding through old Paris, they came to a medieval, almost undersea wreck of a hotel on the faubourg Saint-Denis. Truly the end of the line. Buckling timbers, bleary windows, rotting walls plastered with peeling posters. It had about it a kind of horrifying grandeur, snaking up the riverine street.

They got the key. They climbed the creaking, listing stairs, two floors to No. 8, in which they found a cot, a grimy table thick with tallow, and a small window the hue of a stagnant pond.

"Well, well," joked Verlaine, setting down the valise. *"Comme . . . chez soi.* Home sweet home."

Boom. Dazed he lay on the floor—felled with a vicious rabbit punch.

"Asshole! Liar!" Slapping him, Rimbaud had him by the throat. "We'll see who's the bitch here!"

Double man and double boy. Slapping and kicking, rolling and wrestling, they were soon laughing, then not laughing at all, as they popped buttons and shucked shoes. White-fleshed youth. Rimbaud stood at full and erect attention. Jutting, pink and bouncing, he was not overlarge but, as only sixteen can manage, most impressively *vertical.*

No question how this was going to go. The elder poet was on his knees, and here, above him, like a young god, fingers locked on his throat, was his muse and master. Joy incarnate as Verlaine opened his bearded lips—well-versed lips that expertly covered his teeth, stroking and tonguing, gumming and humming to a tom-tom beat.

Mamma's boys together. So it began, really, as only it could have begun, their two-year rampage through Paris, London, and Brussels. Leaving just four people, all women, of course, to pick up the pieces: Mme. Rimbaud, Mme. Verlaine, and Mathilde Mauté Verlaine—dewy-eyed no more. And of course their leader and strategist, the ever resourceful Mme. Mauté.

Le scandale! Enter police and solicitors, the wronged, the fleeced, the injured. The mad race was on.

44 ♪ Off

Putting things right before he left Africa—this was Rimbaud's aim when he asked Mrs. MacDonald to kindly summon her husband.

Hearing that Rimbaud wanted to see him, Mr. MacDonald scooped up his Bible, assuming that *it was time*, that at last Rimbaud was ready to receive the spirit. How very surprised Mr. MacDonald was, then, to discover that it was he who was to receive. As Rimbaud explained, it was his intention to give Mr. MacDonald the very generous sum of two hundred and fifty pounds, funds sufficient, he calculated, not only to cover the family's passage home but to carry them until Mr. MacDonald found suitable employ.

Mr. MacDonald's eyes welled over with gratitude. For much as he glossed over it and trusted to God's providence, well, the truth was that Mr. MacDonald, now stammering and quaking, had been wracked over money and the blind way in which he had brought his family to grief. As for Rimbaud, naturally he was discomfited to be faced with such undisguised and, above all, *joyous* emotion. So, to distract the poor fellow, Mr. MacDonald's unlikely benefactor asked him what kind of employment he might seek. A parsonage, perhaps?

At this Mr. MacDonald's face colored. Forthrightly, he admitted that he was not qualified or educated nor, frankly, of the class for a position so exalted. Rather, it was his hope to become an omnibus driver, a horse-drawn omnibus such as you saw around Piccadilly and London's wider thoroughfares.

Here Mr. MacDonald brightened, for evidently he had given the matter considerable thought. His wife, on the other hand, thought the job very lowly—she wanted him to seek a civil service post, but he stubbornly disagreed; in his view driving would mean heavenly freedom. Obliged to wear a uniform with a hat and a badge, he would not have to even *think* in a worldly way of what to wear, or even much about where to go or stop, as the horses knew the route. Two blinkered Clydesdales. A rolling ministry, you might say. Holding the reins, he could pray and perhaps even *reach* certain unfortunate individuals, such as often rode the trams, young men in despair and unwed girls in a family way. Horses, he noticed, have a calming effect on people. Moreover, as the driver keeps his eyes on the road and not the passengers, people are relieved to unburden themselves on the driver. Any willing set of ears.

Indeed, it was curious, the calming, almost hypnotic effect that Mr. MacDonald had upon Rimbaud just then—the way he made him, however briefly, a better, more balanced spirit. Listening to MacDonald, Rimbaud was like a child being read a bedtime story. Not only was he less arrogant and exacting, but he was more patient and deferential, to the point that he wondered if there might be individuals, perhaps not overly *bright* individuals, around whom brilliant, difficult people might become *better* people. Rimbaud actually wondered about this in a fugitive kind of way.

Still, Rimbaud was not entirely without ulterior motives in making this extraordinary gesture. He now not only completely trusted Mr. MacDonald but had high human regard for him, no small thing. He also believed almost superstitiously that the man, even in his very confoundedness, was lucky—God lucky. In any event, as he presently explained, once they reached the sea, he needed his help, first in finding a ship bound for France, then in getting his gold properly accounted for and locked up in the ship's safe.

Mr. MacDonald then seized his opportunity:

"Mr. Rimbaud, we know each other now, don't we—a bit? So I thought—well, I *hoped*—that I might repay you, sir. By *praying* with you, sir."

Rimbaud nodded; he did not disagree that his soul—if that was quite the word—was in disrepair. Indeed for some time he sat there almost spellbound, as if something, some small but critical piece, might shift in him. But finally, wearily, he shook his head. "I am sorry." He kept shaking his head. "Someday, perhaps. But not now. Not yet . . ."

*T*he next day, at long last, they reached the sea.

Sand! Cool air! Gushing waves! Squealing, the children shucked shoes and chased the waves, blue boils cascading down, surging, foaming, and sucking at their toes.

Sea and mist—solar explosions—wind. The boy jumped in, submerged, then shot up, shaking his hair like a dog. Youth—undefeated. Under a tentlike shawl, Rimbaud took in this boundless energy, his eyes creased in the sun. Water slopped about his shockingly pale feet and ankles. Even the sun had changed. Ages were falling. Barriers were vanishing. Things, surprising things, momentous things were taking on meanings of which he did not yet know the meaning, even as he sat poised like a tongue awaiting Holy Communion.

And look at him. For the first time in days, he was not holding the shotgun, vengefully choking it like an old grievance. Soaking his bum leg in the salty, slow-slopping waves, watching the boy, Rimbaud felt himself falling back like those waves, back beyond childhood to a forgotten innocence.

Thus, almost unseen, Rimbaud began another distinct phase of his return.

*T*ime to strike the circus. The animals were sold and the caravan disbanded, the porters and camel drivers and gunmen no sooner paid than they scattered like thieves, taking with them the last vestige of his power and authority.

Mr. MacDonald, meanwhile, had handily proved his extraordinary luck, talking the very reluctant Captain Williams into giving Rimbaud a berth on the *Maidenfair*, an old hauler with rust spewing down her sides, bound the next day for Marseille. It was Mr. MacDonald who, for the better part of four hours, sat captive at the captain's cigarette-burned table watching the rotund and bearded Mr. Roy, the ship's purser, as he carefully weighed, and counted up, Rimbaud's fortune. A handsome sum, too—40,000 French francs, not to mention Rimbaud's ownership position in several trading enterprises and what his mother had squirreled away on his behalf. Amazing, actually. And yet when Mr. MacDonald presented Rimbaud with the signed chit on the ship's crude stationery—when at last his money was safe—Rimbaud, to Mr. MacDonald's surprise, was not cheered in the least. On the contrary. He was crestfallen.

"But look at all you've gained," encouraged Mr. MacDonald as Rimbaud stared at his winnings. Ten years. All on one miserable scrap of paper.

Rimbaud shook his head. "I cannot. I think only how much more I would have—thousands more had I not been cheated and stolen blind. Tens of thousands."

"But you knew that, surely," protested Mr. MacDonald. "I remember on my first day Mr. Bardey told me that losses were to be expected. Cost of doing business."

"Yes," admitted Rimbaud finally. "But still, it is a wicked place with wicked people."

"Well, I don't know about *wicked*," said Mr. MacDonald circumspectly. "Honestly, sir, you should count your good fortune. Rich, or almost rich, is still rich in my book, sir. And lucky is still lucky."

"I am not *rich*," insisted Rimbaud. "Or lucky."

*T*he next day, April 19, 1891, Rimbaud's steamer left Abyssinia, and in their gratitude the MacDonalds, all four of them, came to see him off.

Rocking in an ignominious oxcart, Rimbaud was ported to the quay, where the *Maidenfair* stood like a ruined fortress, with her rusting riveted sides, foul black smokestack, and a plough-like bow. Above, the small crew was making ready to cast off. Black smoke boiled out of the stack, and below, pistons throbbing, her laboring old steam engines could be not so much heard as felt deep in the pit of his stomach, churning like his dread. Dread of good-byes, dread of France, and now a dread of home masked by an overweening hope. Once so ruthless, the caravan leader felt a new and almost childish fear—that of being *left*. Imagine that, the deserter being deserted.

Leaning over the rail, the mate called down, "Time to make ready, sir."

When, down the narrow gangplank—too narrow for him—came two men with a man-overboard seat, a girdle of grommets and leather secured by a big iron snap. Another indignity, as they threaded his legs through the two holes, then cinched it around his crotch—snug. Like a diaper, as Rimbaud thought, *This is how it will be.*

As for Mrs. MacDonald, at that moment she, too, felt trapped. No false sentiment. Having made it abundantly clear how she felt about their host and his ostrichlike unwillingness to admit even the stupefyingly obvious—well, she was not about to engage in the humbug of exchanging addresses and the like. Any of that.

And yet, as often is the case with an almost certainly dying person, there was, between Rimbaud and his guests, the mutual and politely hushed-up pretense that no one was dying, that good-bye was not good-bye and that, in the end, surely everything would come out fine for the ex–caravan boss. Why do cats crawl off to die, huddled in the dark, deep in the cupboard or under the stairs? It is much the same with human souls. They hide. They hold off the shame that, in dying, they will be relegated to the shadows, as second-class citizens. So it is that the living and the dying so often pretend; they pretend about what, really, is an open secret, as obvious as it is finally invisible and unbridgeable.

Death notwithstanding, Mrs. MacDonald did not want to appear arrogant or ungrateful to their benefactor. Nor was she in any position to indulge in the bluff theatrics of refusal. And yet, as she told her husband (who seemed to believe that some miracle, some change of heart, had in fact occurred), Rimbaud's money was bad money, blood money—a stain. Don't be naïve, she told him. Rimbaud was merely assuaging his own guilt. Buying them off.

And so in those final seconds on the quay, at last Mrs. MacDonald sighed, then offered perhaps the one true thing she could say.

"Well, I warn you I shall find your writings."

Awkwardly, she brightened. Weakening, through force of habit, she leaned in as if she might embrace him, then thought better of it. Instead, he got a brisk pat.

"Good-bye."

"Good-bye."

"Good luck."

"Thank you."

Then at a signal from the mate above, strenuously, hand over hand, the three stevedores started pulling the rope. Grinning, the children let out gasps, as up the exile rose in his man-overboard harness, up into the sky. Home to his benighted France—to hearth and house, kith and kin. The returning exile's reverie was a brief one, however. For, looking down, Rimbaud saw the girl, *whatshername*, peering up. Nasty little brat. There she was, sniggering and exuberantly holding her nose, thrilled to be rid of him. Exit Mr. Flambo.

Book Three

The Demon of Hope

I WILL COME HOME WITH LIMBS OF IRON AND
DARK SKIN AND A FURIOUS LOOK. . . .
WOMEN TAKE CARE OF THESE FEROCIOUS INVALIDS,
BACK FROM THE TORRID COUNTRIES.
— ARTHUR RIMBAUD, *A SEASON IN HELL,* 1873

45 ❧ Weather Warning

"Isabelle!"

In her black Sunday tweeds, the old mother was calling up the stairs, waving a telegram from Africa. "Isabelle get down here! I have the most awful news."

Outside, the deliveryman could be seen, the same who had ridden on urgent status five kilometers on horseback, only to be brusquely dismissed by Madame with no tip, no thanks, no nothing. New to Madame's munificence, the messenger's oaths against the house could be heard as he stumbled back across the lawn, then dizzily grabbed the reins. Once more, Mme. Rimbaud called up the stairs:

"*Issssss*-a-belle."

Tromp, tromp—t-t-tromp. With that final bump, Mme. Rimbaud's understudy hit the landing, prematurely draped in a black shawl. Dark hair pulled tight in a black chignon, Isabelle Rimbaud stared in cold dread at her mother. "What, Maman? Is Arthur dead? *Is he?*"

"No, he is not *dead*," retorted the old woman, even as she stood on one foot, then the other. "Don't you understand, he *left*—"

"Left?"

"*Left*—Left Harar."

Now Isabelle was really confused. "But, Mother, you said you had awful news."

"Well," hemmed the old woman, now caught, "I meant that—that this means it's bad. Here, read it. From Monsieur Bardey. Arthur's employer. Oh dear, *surely* you remember his name. Here—"

A. RIMBAUD LEFT HARAR 10 MAY. MARSEILLE THEN HOME. STABLE BUT REQUIRES URGENT MEDICAL ATTENTION. EXPECT IN 21-35 DAYS. REGARDS, A. BARDEY, PROP., A. BARDEY, LTD.

Isabelle folded the telegram, then stood there, nervously smoothing the fold, trying to guess the true source of her mother's distress. Because to Isabelle, as with so many things, this seemed some kind of diabolical test. "Well," she ventured at last, "Monsieur Bardey says Arthur is stable. That's promising, don't you think?"

The mother glared.

"What, so your brother simply *arrives* here expecting to be taken care of?" Mme. Rimbaud teased her handkerchief from her sleeve, loudly blew her nose, then stuffed it back, one white puff peeping out, like the head of a doll. "I have," she sighed, "I have a *farm* to run and animals that require my attention. I have my appointments and church and tenants and bills to pay—*duties*, do you hear me? I cannot, and I will not, be lying about, waiting for your brother to waltz in here like some kind of hero."

Coldly, Isabelle drew the shawl around her. "Well, Maman, whatever else, he will not be *waltzing*."

"None of your cheek, young lady!"—by now the young lady was well on her way to middle age—"I *need* and I *deserve* from your brother a *when*."

So saying, Mme. Rimbaud veered around, wavered momentarily, as if she'd lost her place, then bore through the back door, down the lichen-veined stone steps, into the downy-bottomed apple blossoms tossing in the wind. It was a small apple orchard, ringed with cherry, peach, and pear. White-blooming, sun-glowing, mad with bees, it was a landscape in which the old woman now stood off angle, like a misplaced chess piece, black dress, black cuffs, black shoes. *Of course*, she thought to herself, of course he would return in the spring, in *her* time, when everything was bawling, bubbling, popping, and germinating. Spring, time to erupt. Time to open the hive with her swarms of moneymaking schemes! And Arthur thought *he* was clever, selling his guns to the *noirs*!

Hence Mme. Rimbaud's busy scheme to bleed the railroad for a right-of-way. Hence fifteen, then twenty more cows—then twenty-five. Hence nine, then thirteen apartments, dumps with rents to be collected and people to be evicted, a terrible business, to be sure—but lucrative. Then her neighbor, M. Viderequin, upon whose property she had long had an eye, he passed away and not two days after the funeral the old hawk had snapped up the place—fifteen hectares, meaning yet more beasts and equipment to procure, and three more dolts to supervise. And the old wife to be moved into one of the hovels. *Did it never end?*

It was her time. Now that she was old, with almost no need of sleep or even of food, Madame Rimbaud's ambition and energy were at their zenith, and the irony was, never had she had less need of money, which she would stuff in black-smoked, tallow-sealed jars—paper currency, gold coins, and deeds, even small diamonds, buried in the thick of night as tenderly as her own offspring.

You've done it, old girl! she would think, gloating as she drove her black buggy through the pillow-fluffer neighborhoods on the surpassing heights of rue La Tour. House cats! Let them sneer from their high brick manses, with their arrogant eaves and iron gates—parasites. And then with a shiver, Mme. Rimbaud would conjure that dangerous word *rich*, thinking how they would die if they knew how much *she*, a peasant, had salted away. Heh.

For as she drifted through the orchard, blowing and foaming, absurd or not, it was Mme. Rimbaud's great fear that Arthur, the copycat, having suckered the *noirs* with his guns—well, that through some cruel trick of fate, he might arrive home wealthier than she was. *Idée inconcevable!*

Oh, don't be foolish, she told herself, he can't be *that* rich. But why, then, was she plucking her fingers as if she'd just pulled them from a hot stove? Look to the east. Trees on fire. Look to the west. Locusts massing. South—ugly storms. North—fright and confusion.

Then she heard them, men's voices and a cow bawling. Trouble by the barn.

Feelers twitching, she walked around the side of the house. *Mon Dieu*, it was Paul, Pierre, and Jean, Sunday drunk and all hard at work—stud work, just the sport for three womenless meatheads with nowhere to go. For there, tied to a post, Mme. Rimbaud saw a large black-spotted cow. And, opposite, there stood the thick-necked M. Jacques, the bull, his long, thick spigot bounding at the ready.

"It is *Sunday!*" she cried, pulling up her skirt as she gamboled down the steps. "What do you think you are doing?"

Deaf to her entreaties, Paul and Pierre were waving their hands, trying to quell the throbbing, bobbing Jacques. As for the third, Jean, brave soul, he was on his knees greasing him up. *It* up, for blood-bowed and grievously nobbed on the end, it was fully the length and girth of a pump handle. Then, as if this weren't bad enough, squinting, Mme. Rimbaud descried—by a white spot the size of a small coin—that they had the *wrong* lady. *Alors*, it was not Claudette but her twin sister, Marie. No! Eighteen months to calve and milk, then four months off to "freshen up"—this was the rule. Alas, no bovine holiday for Marie.

"Idiots, you've got the wrong cow!" cried the proprietress of Roche, now stoutly marching down the hill, blowing her red nose. "Are you all blind? You have *Marie*, not Claudette! *Marie!*"

Too late. With a bound, the brute was upon her, bucking and clambering up, even as Jean, the greaser, bent it, then, with a furious wiggle, angled it in. Behold the stupendous Lord Jacques, stamping on his great hams, his great horned head craning over the hapless Marie.

"Did you not hear me?" cried Mme. Rimbaud, lifting her dress over the turd-thick mud. "*Imbéciles!* That's Marie, Marie, Mar-IE!"

"Oh, no, no, Madame," insisted Paul, mustache chuffing, "do you not see the little spot? *There*, do you see?"

"*That* is not the spot. It is not that large."

"Like a coin," said Pierre, now squinting. "It is the size of a louis."

"Good Madame," intervened the suave Jean, the greaser. "As Madame can surely see," he sniggered, "the matter is moot. *Monsieur Jacques est préoccupé.*"

"*Odious* man," said she, "what would you know of being occupied? Now out—out of my way." She seized the muck rake, then flipped it handle end, like a truncheon.

"Madame, please!" cried the men, trying to stop her, even as M. Jacques poured on the coal, *whop, whop, whop.*

But, crouching low, Roche's proprietress gave Lord J. the bum handle. Bull's-eye. M. Jacques bucked. He bellowed and stamped, but so vast was his tumescence, and so compliant was Marie, that it was quite hopeless. Mme. Rimbaud cast down the rake.

"Drunken louts!"

Oh, her swallowing *children.* Oh, her vanished *son.* This crushing *place.* And, like a ton of turgid, unyielding beef, it all fell on her. Always her.

*T*hat night Isabelle had a mortifying epiphany. It happened, as so many things happened, at supper, which tonight, cook being off, was a *cacasse à cul nu*—literally, nude ass casserole, an Ardennes specialty. Earth-tasting potatoes, quartered, shallots, lard, butter, a bit of hand-sifted flour, and a good fist of thyme, bay leaves, parsley—all this was set to simmer. And after precisely an hour, when the old woman raised the heavy iron lid, face and nostrils enveloped in a bloom of fragrant steam—behold, God's bounty. Pleasure itself, as if she were inhaling a cloud. But then as the two women were eating, the mother put her foot in it.

"Well, he has no head for business," she was saying. Meaning Arthur, of course. "Same thing when he was a writer. And of course, he failed at that, too."

Writer? Isabelle stopped cold. Was the old woman losing her marbles?

"Mother," she said carefully, "what do you mean Arthur was a writer? Are you referring to old school exercises or something?"

"Daughter." The mother rolled her eyes, delighted. "Good grief, where have you been for the past thirty years? Come now, you know Arthur is—was—a writer. Poet, whatever. I *know* you know this."

Incredible. Isabelle's eyes filled with tears. Lied to again by the entire universe.

"Know *what*, Mother? What do I know? Not one thing, and you never told me—ever! Or Vitalie. You or Arthur. So why, Mother, why did you never tell me he was a writer? To torture me? Ridicule me? Was that the idea?"

"Well," the mother evaded. "He was not a writer—or *writer*-writer. He was a poet."

"Stop it! As if this makes any difference. You lied! A sin of omission."

"Dear me," said the mother, confronted by this gush of blame, which she could only treat as a joke, "Lied how? Anyone in Charleville could have told you your brother was a writer. Poet, self-styled. Drivel, of course, but he wrote—"

"What?" broke in Isabelle, now shaking. "Then you *read* it? And never showed me?"

"Read it?" Inwardly, the mother couldn't help but smile, thrown a bone so juicy. "Good heavens, why on earth would I? Whatever he wrote, he only tore it up, or gave it away, or ran away. And then, being Arthur, after all the theatrics and getting shot—you do remember *that*, I hope—well, naturally he gave it all up. Failed before he could be called a failure. Remember that lost period? When he was robbed and beaten in Germany? Then nearly died in that blizzard in the Alps?"

"Mother," she said, fanning her nose as a sneeze. "None of your insulting stupid digs and distractions. Why on earth did you never tell me? *Me*, your own daughter—his own sister! It had to be intentional. Had to be. It feels completely malicious."

"Why?" the mother spat back. "Ask yourself why. Why are you not married? Why at your age are you still sitting here at this table why-why-whying me. Wahh, wahh, why. Another baby."

Naturally, this mauling had its intended effect. By then, Isabelle was wiping away embarrassed tears with the heel of her palm. In which case the old woman could be magnanimous.

"But you know what," said the mother, as if she'd just now found a sweet in her dress pocket, "now that I think about it, some man even told me—oh, when was that? Two months ago? Four? Well, apparently in Paris, some fancy-pants place published some of your brother's old tear buckets. And to some idiot praise, too. Well," she shrugged, "so what. What's the difference? Arthur never mentioned it."

Isabelle slapped the table.

"Good heavens, Mother, here your son is *praised*, and not only are you *not* proud, but you won't even tell me. Why? I could have been *happy* for my brother. That's right, happy for probably the one person I ever *wanted* to, or could, understand."

"Understand him!" said the old woman, hunkering down. "Come to your senses, daughter. In all his years away, did he ever send you one line? One franc? Or—perish the thought—an interesting gift from some faraway place? Listen to me." The old woman paused, visibly upset, for she was not a cruel woman, she thought. Truth was cruel. "Daughter, this is hard to say, but face the facts. Through no fault of yours, your brother has no real interest in you. Anybody, really."

"And how could he?" Isabelle sat there, wiping her eyes, shaking her head. "It was you, Mother, you who made him a foreigner in his own home. You barely allowed him to talk to us. Honestly, girls of nine and ten—his own sisters. Quarantined."

"Right!" The old woman flung down her napkin. "That's right! Boys no more belong around girls than snakes do in henhouses. You wait until you"—she stopped herself—"well, *if* ever you had children—"

Even she knew she'd gone too far. Breaking off, she patted her daughter's arm, signifying, to her, a hug. A peace offering. But Isabelle was already off, *t-tt-tromp-omp*, down the hall to her room.

46 ❧ New Vocation

Honestly, what parent ever *tries* to be a bad parent? For the sad fact is, all parents, even the worst, most hopeless, are honestly trying to do their best.

Fortunately, for the old woman, when all else failed, there was always prayer. And so she was squashed in her "stall," as she thought of it, the stall in the corner between her bed and the wall, where, kneading her forehead and working her lips, she knelt on a rug, on her mushy old knees. Then, when her old knees gave out, she crumpled, with some shame, on her now bony bottom. *Can I have no peace, Lord? I am not a bad mother.*

Her prayers and complaints, her murmurs, up they went like smoke up a flue—to what? God did not answer. Of course God did not answer, but by then, after this decades-long drought, the old woman had begun to think that His not answering was, in itself, almost a form of answer. Of course her faith was dry as sticks. Of course she felt famished and abandoned, but by then this fig leaf *was* her faith, a thing so familiar that she did not feel abandoned. In fact (and here was the oddest thing), she often felt the presence of *another* presence praying beside her. A ghostly presence.

For here beside her was another lady on her knees, another suppli-cant and not some saint or divinity—no, this august personage was, like her, another cow of faith, longing to be milked of her equally great thirst. Who, apropos of God's filibuster of silence, would say to Mme. Rimbaud, Don't stop. You mustn't stop. Never, Madame, for never has a woman outlasted God's silence as you have. This is why He loves you. Because you will never give up hope! That is why He gives you the cold shoulder on these long, terrible nights of being old and lonely and deserted. Because you, Madame, are like that cow, the Charolais, good for milk or meat or draft—a cow of purest white who can both feed and pull out stumps! Do not despair. When all others have col-lapsed, it is *you* upon whom He depends.

*T*he murmuring, the head bumping, the muffled sobs—all this Isabelle could hear as she knelt against the wall that adjoined her mother's room. But finally, mercifully, the commotion fell to snoring, then silence. With that, Isabelle lit her candle lantern. Then, slowly opening her door, a little scared, as always, she followed the glowing lantern down the hall, to the front door entrance, there to see her old friend, the blackened, time-frosted mirror. In the darkness, she studied her dazed image. There it danced before her, a little crackled, like a loose stone in a broken ring.

Double thing drizzling silver. As she pored over the mirror's surface, here the draining silver was like lace, there like skeletal leaves rotting on the surface of a frozen pond. Falling silver, failing silver, the black absorbed and the silver reflected, a wintry oblivion of whispers and secrets, as luxuriously warm as a fur coat. Leaning forward, close enough to fog her breath, Isabelle Rimbaud told her old friend the mirror:

But she never told me.

Of course she never told you. Why on earth would she?

But no one did! Or Arthur! Or people in the town! Or my girl-friends, well, at least before they all married. Do you know how stupid this makes me feel?

Never mind that, dear. You've got a horse. You've got a buggy—go.

Go where?

To Paris, even for three days. Anywhere. Go. Just to show her.

But how? I'd have to ask her for money. She has all the money.

Just take the money. You earned it.

But what if Arthur arrives and I'm not home? I'd never forgive myself.

Poor dear. Just look at you. Go.

But how? A train? And with what? Isabelle knew nothing about her mother's money, much less her own money. What money, when of her meager stipend one-quarter went to the church and half was saved but where, only her mother knew. As for the other quarter, a pittance, the old woman just gave it to the girl. Let her spend it on her sweets and fripperies—wasteful, thought the mother, but otherwise the girl became blue. "Then how much do I have?" Isabelle would demand in one of her not infrequent spells of sadness. "More than you need." "Fine, then I shall go to Paris." "And stay where?" cried the old woman. "In a hotel? With *those* sorts of women, breeding disease like pigeons? Do you know *why* in France more than five unrelated women cannot be legally domiciled together? Do you know what the police assume about such unsavory *arrangements*?"

It was a frightening world.

Why, only a few months ago, to prove that not only was Isabelle not going to Paris but would not *want* to go, Mme. Rimbaud had "bought" for her (part of a block auction) a rattling old gig and a swaybacked old mare. That shut her up, for never once had the old mare left the property, proof the girl was pure bluff. But then what in those parts did they call a spinster like her, now beyond thirty? Rabbit fricassee. A hopeless case. Never would she marry.

But this changed the following day. While her mother was out, Isabelle did it. Sneak that she was, she caught the horse with carrots. Harnessed her, then, with unaccustomed swats as the old nag bounced her head, Isabelle left to find some answers about her brother the writer. And where else but from the booksellers of Charleville. Or even Charleville's sister city, Mézières, if necessary.

On its coiled spring, the doorbell tinkled. Isabelle Rimbaud drew up her shawl as the bookseller rattled the lock. Naturally, she did not identify herself. It was frightening enough to ask a man anything, let alone to ask a stranger if he had heard of Arthur Rimbaud or had one of his works.

"Yes, of course," said the first, an old, old man with a gold watch chain that he fiddled with nervously. "He grew up here. Don't know if he amounted to much, or what became of him. But, Madame—Mademoiselle—if I may inquire, why do you ask?"

"Ah," said the second bookseller, younger, dark-haired, and scaly-skinned, after Isabelle had fled the premises of the first. "Then you heard," he said, clearly excited. "Yes, I thought he'd come to nothing, but now I hear that some of Rimbaud's poems were published. Fairly recently in Paris—to some acclaim, I understand."

"Indeed so," mused the third, his pipe popping as he hungrily lit it, then waved out the match. "And I have a copy—yes, I'm quite sure I do of . . . of"—laying hands on his stool—"*La Revue Noire*—if I can find it— I have an essay on Rimbaud by a very noted critic, Félicien Champsaur, who pronounced him the greatest French poet since Baudelaire. Oh, indeed, a strange, strange talent, he averred. And so young when he wrote—shocking. Eighteen or nineteen. A wild man, I heard, but great. Yes, Champsaur used that word, 'great,' and I can tell you he uses it only very parsimoniously, if ever. Moreover, I have heard there are young poets of some stripe—some school—who have formed, after Rimbaud, a Socratic *following*. Heaven knows, Mademoiselle. And where is this poet now? Africa, did I hear?" The bookseller disappeared behind various piles and shelves. "Wait, wait . . . I have a publication with many of his poems, *Les Poètes Maudits*." The cursed poets.

How her face burned as he put into her hands the chapbook with her brother's poems—that and the review, in which, with a slip of paper, he had carefully marked Champsaur's essay. Dazed, she paid him. Cheeks burning, pretending she didn't hear the flirting of his at-the-door question, Isabelle felt like a shoplifter, ready to explode as she burst through the door. Ears twitching, the old mare pulled her head around and looked at her. She looked at the mare. Then, with the leather traces trembling in her hands, she drove out of town, rumbling over cobbles, past the last homes, then down a long curving road lined with birches, silver birches following, like stitches, the flashing-green, clear-flowing brook.

No one was around, so she stopped. Preparing herself, she opened the book, feeling the sharp pages and incised type, the strange irregular shapes of poems—the almost human shapes. A blur of words of which, at that moment, she could read not a line.

The book, this fetish of the book, it had weight. It was a *fact*. And look: here, forever captured in time, was her brother's name, *Arthur Rimbaud Arthur Rimbaud Arthur Rimbaud Arthur Rimbaud Arthur Rimbaud*.

It was here, freed from her mother for all of two hours, and then with a rapture almost religious, that Isabelle Rimbaud burst into joyous, uncomprehending tears, swearing before God that no matter what her mother or anybody else said, she would tell the true story, the touching and surely holy story of her great brother—*their* story, once he returned home. Never would her brother have to fend for himself or beg their mother. No, she would care for him—him and only him, and for once in his life her brother the esteemed poet, he would have whatever he wanted, when he wanted it, and as he wanted it, without his mother to thwart him.

So in soft early May swore Rimbaud's younger sister and future biographer. No confusion now. Adrift in the gig in the sun, as the old horse walked circles, nibbling the sweet green grass, for the first time in ages it was clear to Isabelle Rimbaud what she would do, just as it was clear how much her mother would revile it as a blow to decency. A revolt against family secrecy. Why, a betrayal of the first order.

Tant pis. Mousy no more. With a pleasure almost obscene, Isabelle Rimbaud resolved that day to be her brother's biographer—a writer after all.

47 ♪ Empty Crèche

Pay attention, thinks Rimbaud, now floating and trying to collect himself—to reassert command.

Situation: He is in Marseille, alone in a white room in a white bed at the Hôpital de la Conception, warm, blooms of morphine and ether wearing off, and—he thinks—his mother and sister have been summoned. By telegram? But are they then in transit?

Alone, he knows that much. *Don't ask. Don't beg. Don't break down.* But they know. Everybody knows—what?

His gold. His two pistols. His pain—where?

Escape—but how?

Outside, he can see Jesus' brides, the assembled Sisters of Providence, five in number. Whispering, of course, always whispering, nuns in heavy black habits and starched white headpieces so tight they cause their cheeks to plump, like warm muffins. Shhhh, one says, pointing. Pain has long ears. He can hear them talking. Good, they say, the patient is awake and now alone with his grievous wound, now waiting to be embraced, like a newborn. *Très bien*, Monsieur Rimbaud. Behold, Jesus above, flying over all, like a great robed kite. Offer the Lord Jesus your suffering, offer it up! But, as for receiving comfort and mercy at this terrible moment, even vocation has its limits—the sisters flee.

And it is here, lying in bed with him—the beast, the same that stalked him across the desert, then watched him almost die on the airless ship, its iron bulkhead beaten like an anvil by the equatorial sun. White sun, white sheet. Before this expanse of white sheet, Rimbaud feels as he did leaving Harar that last day, when he looked across the white desert, blazing like freedom, *free freedom*, if only he could reach the warm, the blue, the amniotic sea, warm and sloshing like a good mother. Sun mother, mother sun, golden sun—red dial of sun, where did you go with your piercing eye of gold? Why did you leave my life, a puddle of molten gold vanishing into the sea's shining lips?

Am I crazy?

Don't do anything, he thinks now, paralyzed, and not entirely without logic, imagining that if he does not raise the sheet—if he lies perfectly still—*it will not be*. Then when this fails, he reverts to the stratagems of his youth, destitute on the Paris streets or on the road, free to be robbed, raped, or killed. About which he had written, *A voice clenched my frozen heart: "Weakness or strength: you are there, it is strength. You do not know where you are going, or why you are going. Go in anywhere. Answer everything. They will not kill you any more than if you were a dead body."* So he had written in *Season in Hell*, but what now? What, teller, is his tale now?

Upon finding a source of nectar, a bee returns to the hive, there to sip only as much sweet liquor as it needs to return to the source, then back to the hive—just enough and not one drop more. Like that bee, a human soul has only so much bravery and denial, only so much energy, only so much resilience and hope—just that much and not one drop more. And so like that bee, Rimbaud plummets, empty from the emptier air.

He is a child. *Where is my mother? Why have they not summoned my mother?*

He is outraged. *Robbed! I demand an explanation. Why was this not discussed?*

He is argumentative. *Intolerable! Where is the surgeon? The civil authorities?*

He is French again. *Is this not France? Am I not a French citizen with rights?*

He is wildly irrational. *Draft evader, you'll be caught and conscripted!*

Sssh. It's the nuns again, whispering, *Do it, coward. Raise the sheet.*

Now his hands, his whole body, are trembling as he strains forward, pressing the spot. Flat—*gone, it's all gone, everything.* He rips up the sheet, then stares at it. No knee and almost no thighbone. Nothing but a roast-sized stump bound in blood-brown gauze. Gauze with a bloom of bright blood in the center.

His eyes blurt; they burst like fat grapes. Lashes of rain, torrents of grief, awful to see, a man bawling and rocking in a blinding heart storm. This is not crying, it is the heart's nausea; it is the greasy, burning accumulation of twenty dry years of willful starvation pouring blindly down his face. Who is he now? His hair, peppery only a month ago, is now almost white. The man once so vigorous, so headlong and heedless, he is now a dying glutton exhausting his last fat reserves of hope. Shuddering and sucking, slurping and spitting, almost catatonic, he stares through the pounding rain as hot tears, salt tears fat as spits soak his nightshirt, then run burning down his belly, to the already evident pool between the legs. When:

"Hrrr-re," says a quavering voice. "Hhh—here."

A hand shoves a metal pan in his lap. He jumps. It's a young man not more than twenty, lanky, with blue eyes, an eruption of dark brown hair, and a patchy, stubbly beard. What's wrong with the kid? he thinks. Leaning in, the kid jerks, he trembles, his shoulders twitch.

"HEEhrre," he insists, shoving a metal pan under his chin.

"What?" Agog, still weeping, Rimbaud looks up at this impostor. "*You're* not the doctor—"

"I'm—the—the—h-or-der-ly." The young man smiles after a fashion. "M-iiiiii-chel." He grimaces, assembling the next statement, "I—I clean h-up."

"What?" At that moment, Rimbaud scarcely knows what he's saying, but the boy takes this literally, as if he is asking *what* he cleans up.

"Ev-*ev*-ever-ry—thing. I-I cl-lean it up. Before, d-durring, and-and—haf-ter." Again, he stops and smiles a twisted smile, spittle, a little, at the edge of his lip. "Seeee, I t-talk sl-looow. But I-I-I'm not sl-ooow. H-hee-re. Go on." His mouth tightens. "Vommm—it. If—if you have to."

At this time, of course, nobody really understands what afflicts this young man; it just is, and what is there to know? He's a stutterer, palsied and slow. In any case, let us not belabor Michel's stutter in prose—assume it and read pure and clean what he means to say. Note, rather, Rimbaud's shock at the young man's lack of horror or disgust. For a person in Rimbaud's state, this is immensely consoling—calming. Lying back down, he feels Michel's puffy eyes guiding him, cuing him in that almost hypnotic way young children are lured to listen to a story, calmed by the voice and trusting there is an end to the story, not good or bad but just *an* end. It is *a story.* It is the story of his missing leg, and Rimbaud's mind is so slowed, so primitive and unmoored, that he is floating in that hypnotic state of two boys conversing, oblivious to the outer world.

"So what do others do?" asks Rimbaud, still sobbing. *When people are first amputated,* he means.

"Huh? Everything. Anything. Lots still feel it—the leg. The pain. Even without the leg." Michel shakes the basin under Rimbaud's chin dripping tears. "Go on if you have to. Spit up—"

"Do you not see?" demands Rimbaud, not at all tracking this

suggestion. "Look what they left me, *look*. Who could fit a wooden leg on *that*?"

"Don't think about that—don't. Don't think. Here, let me clean you up."

"And where is my mother? Did they not summon her? Are they not all idiots?"

"Think I heard something about your sister."

"But I don't *want* my sister." He is now ranting. "I want my mother, do you hear me? *My mother*."

The tears, the mess, the misdirected rage—none of this fazes Michel in the least. He rolls the patient over on his back, helpless as a tortoise.

"Uh. Hold still." Trembling, Michel withdraws from his lips, before Rimbaud's pain-blinded eyes, a tiny, shining object. A safety pin. "Hold still so I don't stick you."

48 ⸱ Find Rimbaud

That same day, Félicien Champsaur, literary journalist from the Left Bank *Revue Noire*, was on the hunt for Rimbaud, and an erratic path it was, for first he had to secure an interview with Paul Verlaine—via Verlaine's various flunkies and messengers. And so the very au courant Champsaur, broad-shouldered and strikingly handsome, with a bracing mustache and an open book of thick, dark hair, he found himself facing—for the third time in two days—Verlaine's man. Agent, factotum, manservant, flunky, this was Champsaur's polar opposite, the odiferous and effusive Bibi-la-Purée.

Boho king that he was, Verlaine had surrounded himself with a sort of street court, of whom the chancellor was this Bibi-la-Purée. Bootblack, street barber, stool pigeon, messenger, and lackey, Bibi was a gaunt, pinched-faced man of forty or so with long hair, dirty long chuffs of mustache, and a broad-brimmed hat pinned up in front with a greasy turkey quill. As for the state of his unvarying black suit, it was breathtaking, so layered with filth that it bore the purplish, iridescent hue of a pigeon's throat. Bibi's bladelike nose was large and bent, his knees were bowed, and always in hand, like a rapier, was his battered umbrella. No stranger to the courts, Verlaine's man was, he loudly insisted, *"Bibi-la-Purée, Seigneur de Salis et autres lieux. Et rentier!"* That is, the Lord of Salis and other places. And, to correct the record, no creature of the streets but rather a man of independent means!

Imagine, then, these antipodes, Bibi and Champsaur, staring across vast chasms of ambition, grooming, and hygiene. At Bibi's insistence, here they were in one of the city's most squalid arrondissements, tussling over the master's fee and even more noxious terms. Adding to the odium, the overweening Champsaur was quite powerless in the matter.

With Champsaur having savaged, only months before, Verlaine's latest book of verse, Verlaine was using his grievance to chisel, through this ferret La-Purée, every last centime.

"As I told you, Monsieur," insisted Champsaur, parting his dark locks in irritation, "your demands are outrageous. Out of the question. No reputable publication *pays* its sources."

Bibi raised one dirty nail. "Spare me, Monsieur, your dubious professional pieties. If you want the master—quite besides my own fee as his agent—he will require, in his hand, through mine, two ten-franc notes shaking hands, if you understand me. And you will, of course, pay for supper and such liquid refreshments as are required to free his tongue."

"I'll what?"

"Including—I am not yet finished—those of the master's nurse-consort, Eugénie Krantz."

"Nurse?"

"Bodyguard, too. Oh yes, Monsieur, Mademoiselle Eugénie, she is *formidable* with the blackjack and straight razor. And, where the master is concerned, quick to take offense. Oh, and by the way," added the grimy blackmailer, "your quarterly will purchase, in addition, fifty copies of Rimbaud's new opus." The scrounger grinned. "To promote its commercial success."

"Will I now?" sneered Champsaur. "And where will the royalties for Rimbaud's efforts go, I wonder? Into Verlaine's right pocket? Or in his left?"

Bibi disregarded this insult; he knew a mark and he knew, for the Rimbaud fetishist, the value of his client's testimonial—only Verlaine had been present at the birth. In any case, as one richly unemployed, time was on Bibi's side.

Tra-la. Without another word and, of course, leaving the tab, the malodorous messenger rose from the table. Turning, he produced from a pocket tin a bent and blackened smoke, a choice bit fished earlier from the gutter. A match flicked to life under his grimy thumbnail. His whisker-tacked cheeks balled with thick smoke. Then, with all the insouciance of a skunk, the flaneur walked out, down the kinked street, past knife grinders and rag pickers pushing their stinking, broken-down carts heaped with the city's largesse. Paying the tab, Champsaur, meantime, thought to just leave. But then, with a snort of rage, he hurried down the street, red of face, before presenting, in legal tender to this skunk, his surrender.

"Are you quite sure?" mocked Bibi, fanning banknotes with a black thumb. "I can tell from the cut of your trousers, Monsieur, that you are a man of solid principle."

"*Café Procope,*" snapped Verlaine's soon-to-be interrogator. "Tomorrow, 6:00 p.m. sharp! *Produce* Verlaine—sober." Blowing out his cheeks, he corrected himself. "Well, relatively."

*V*erlaine, to be sure, had ample reason to be angry about Champsaur's recent savaging of his verse, as much for what it said about his current efforts as for what it opened up in him, sorrows and anxieties about Rimbaud that had lain buried for years.

No telling why this occurs, but as with any luridly bad review, others saw it first. *Did you see it?* All who alerted Verlaine to the review bore the same look of alarm, just as all professed not to have actually read it. Normally Verlaine tended to slough off such worries—fools write many things—but suddenly, after the tenth such inquiry, he bolted up from his table at the Café Procope and took off down the wintry street, desperate to see what the wolves had left of his literary corpse.

Bound for the booksellers on the rue de Seine, he wore, as usual for winter, in a woolly-mammoth-like heap, most of his wardrobe, this topped off with two mufflers and, just creasing his eyes, a lumpy woolen hat. Plumes of breath spouted from his nose, forming, on the frozen tines of his graying red mustache, two small tusks. Mufflers flapping, cane stabbing the ice, the poet rounded the corner, then stopped dead. For there gazing in the shop window, noses in the air, three well-appointed gentlemen were having a good snort and, *he knew*, at his expense. On the streets of the Latin Quarter and Montmartre, and indeed in most of Paris, the abominable immortal was a well-known figure, so the shock of these gentlemen can be imagined when they saw the object of their mirth rapping his cane indignantly and pressing his face into theirs.

And there it was, *in the window*, the review with his name on the cover in red, twiglike letters, curled Art Nouveau style, with bright green apples and sinisterly twisted vines. Lovely, until one noticed the worms in the apples, then the chortling title, "Horse Apples: The Late Work of Paul Verlaine."

Old Man Winter trod in, grabbed one from the stack at the front. Then with a glare at the proprietor, turned to page 10 and read:

There is no denying the greatness and musicality of the Verlaine of 1873—or the source of his inspiration, orbiting, as Verlaine was in those days, around the great Arthur Rimbaud, then at the zenith of his powers. That was, of course, before the crowning scandal—one of many—in which, amid allegedly unsavory living arrangements and other rumors, Verlaine shot and wounded Rimbaud, went to prison, found God, and (notwithstanding his late acceptance by the Académie) now continues, with stunning single-mindedness, his lifelong slide from grace. It is a siege that continues even to this day, where this habitué of the night divides his time (so we are told) between the city's charity hospitals, its various night pantries, and those dim warrens in which dazed figures imbibe chartreuse drinks.

Then came the kind of accusation that sears itself upon the author's brain:

Can it be that Verlaine now seeks redemption by publishing, without his knowledge, and perhaps without recompense, the work of the disappeared Rimbaud, last seen in the wastes of Africa? In the meantime, bereft of his muse, Verlaine writes and writes, and it must be said that rarely does he write an overtly bad or unmusical line. But, we might ask—of what? Despite promising moments and the occasionally striking line, these poems emerge like the efforts of an old dray horse, horse apples pummeling the cobbles as onward he plods.

As Verlaine closed the review, his hands were trembling; his face was hot, his ears were ringing, and now tears welled in his eyes, tears of rage and humiliation—wild grief as he flung down the review and stormed out. *Sagesse*, his latest effort, was at best a middling book—of course. Naturally, his best work was long behind him—he knew that. Why, then, did this young turd have to make invidious comparisons to Rimbaud? To call his whole artistic life, even his very impulse, into question? Did any artist deserve such treatment?

That night, wedged in the corner of a bucket house on the rue de Fourcy, Verlaine might well have been mistaken for a mortuary figure. Grief—it was the heart gripped in a winepress. Failure—asphyxiation. Death—one last gasp after the peerless skater crashes through winter's ice. And yet, at bottom, this was a deeper form of paralysis, a relapse, really. *"Mon grand péché radieux,"* Verlaine had once called Rimbaud, "my great radiant sin." Banished by love, Verlaine was doing at long last the very thing that for years he never permitted himself—truly grieving for Rimbaud and the dreams that had died in Brussels seventeen years before, when he, Verlaine, had shot his muse. Shot him to prevent him from leaving just as suddenly and willfully as he had appeared twenty-two months before.

Seventeen years earlier, not only was Rimbaud wrapped in gleaming youth and genius but he was perched upon the heartless redoubt of twenty—of course he held all the power. He was not, like his lover, a fool in a foreign country who—thanks to him—had bankrupted himself, lost his wife and child, and destroyed his career. Nor was he the grown man who had followed, almost without question, this kid now resolved to leave him in Belgium. To leave him cold without a second thought.

This was the same mesmeric kid who, little more than a year before, had promised Verlaine that their love was forever, destiny, *historic*, even. Who told Verlaine apropos his wife, Choose: either her or me. As for little Georges, screw the brat—die a bourgeois or come with me, now, to *change life.*

Ever the ditherer and compromiser, Verlaine didn't want to leave Mathilde and his child or, heaven forbid, Mathilde's money and creature comforts. Yet here he was, in Belgium, after Paris, after London, after Charleville and God knows where, a man now penniless and facing catastrophe, having followed a cyclone into the land of whirlwinds. Still more humiliatingly for Verlaine, it was Rimbaud—by default, the "realist" in this couple—who had to tell the grown man that their fugitive, hand-to-mouth existence was now pointless, ridiculous and unsustainable. Worse, said Rimbaud, it was *repetitive*, and repetition, needless to say, was death. Death, the stupid drunken rows and run-ins with the law. Death, the sleeping in barns and under bridges, the running out on rents.

"But look," said Rimbaud on that terrible night, in the five minutes it took him to stuff his things, like trash, into a dirty canvas sack. "Look," he told Verlaine, "you've got poems in your pockets, great poems beyond anything you've ever done. There it is, mate—your reputation." He smiled. "Go on now, no long face. Admit it. You got what you wanted, right?"

"Wanted!" cried Verlaine. "What is wrong with you! I *love* you. That is what I wanted, your love, your caresses, your thoughts. Can you be this stupid and unfeeling, you with your beguiling nonsense about re-inventing love? Creating an alphabet for feelings? God! What an idiot I have been! What an *arsehole*!"

"Can you possibly be this naïve?" countered the former idealist who, in those two years, had grown into a large, big-handed hooligan, as rough and crude in real life as he was peerless on the page. He had certainly inherited his mother's flare for belligerent ridicule. "Good Christ, enough of your whining. I told you at the outset this road would bring suffering."

"But you were never this *vicious*," said Verlaine.

"And you were never so clueless. So much of a baby."

For two days it had gone like this, but now, when Rimbaud finally reached for the door, swaying, drunk, Verlaine pulled out—or snagged rather, from his coat pocket—the cheap, ridiculous little pistol that he'd purchased only that morning in a pawnshop. It was an insult, a toy. But here it was, pointed at Rimbaud's chest, a little black finger, drifting from side to side.

"Oh, of course," sneered Rimbaud, "now for the real theatrics! *Connard!* Goddamnit, Verlaine, give me that limp dick. You're completely pissed!"

"Don't," said Verlaine, trembling. "Don't go out that door! And *don't* you dare laugh at me, you miserable little prick!"

"And do you think," threatened Rimbaud, taking a step forward to grab the thing, "do you think, bitch—do you actually *think* you can scare me with this?"

"Stop! Back! Stop—"

Bap. Puff of smoke, a small dog's cough—nothing. Confused, Verlaine looked at the gun, then lurched around and saw Rimbaud now white and dripping blood, fat red beads, splattering the floor. It was amazing, Arthur Rimbaud bereft of words, without comeback, sneer, or answer. When, *whump*, the kid crumpled, like a fallen child. Cheap gun, thought Verlaine, *it just went off*. Slipping on the blood, Verlaine shimmied down on his knees, weeping and shrieking, clutching Rimbaud around the neck, peering into his guttering eyes. Then, afraid he might be dead, Verlaine ran bloody and stumbling down the hallway, bellowing quite as if he were the victim, "Help! Help!"

49 ♪ Rocky Redemption

Shooting Rimbaud, his muse, the very Sun—this for Verlaine had been the first blow. The second, in jail hours later, was to learn that, with barely a squeeze from the coppers, the squealing little Judas had given him up. Told them everything. There it was, lying before him on the police sergeant's desk, signed, in Rimbaud's own hand. "Here is your guarantee," said the sergeant, triumphantly shaking this denunciation. "With this, sodomite, you will know well the inside of our jail. Your insides will know it too, eh?"

Then came the third blow—delirium tremens, teeth-gritting spasms so sudden, so violent, that Verlaine felt as if he were being clubbed about the ribs. And yet even as he was in extremis, with even greater enthusiasm the cops pressed him, demanding, in lurid detail, the legally irrelevant facts of their relationship.

Maniacs! thought Verlaine as he lay in his bunk, teeth chattering, gripping his hemorrhaging sides. By then he had confessed, wept, groveled—to no avail. For on the third day the gray police ferrets produced two telegrams, one from Mathilde and another from the Paris police—vile accusations and all quite true, unfortunately. Then an hour later came the final blow. This was the arrival of the jail doctor, Victor Vleminckx, a thick-backed, no-necked, mustached little man who got right to work, pulling gleaming, worrisome articles from his black doctor's bag.

"Strip," he said. "Everything." The doctor looked first at the coppers, then at Verlaine. "And, prisoner, do not mistake me for Hippocrates. When I examine you, you will not move or speak. Or *look* at me. *Excrement!* This is what you are to me, do you understand?"

Naked and craggy-eyed, the prisoner stood dazed on the cold concrete, bloated and lard white, covered with whorls of thick red hair.

"I said, *uncover*," ordered the doctor, when Verlaine attempted, wrongly, to conceal his privates. "Hands at your sides! *Your sides!*"

Verlaine watched—the three policemen, too—as Dr. Victor Vleminckx, bending close, took the flaccid tip of his penis, pulled it taut, then, taking out his ruler, measured it for edification of the court: precisely 9.25 centimeters. Alas, not overlarge.

"Hands at your side! Stand up!"

The doctor now had a pad out. Blew his nose. Readjusted his glasses, tiny, light-leaking lozenges. Furiously, he sketched, for some time actually, his nose whistling. Finally, reversing the pad, he presented Verlaine with the hairy, bestial-looking result.

"Prisoner, is this . . . your penis?"

Verlaine was agog.

"*I said*, is this your penis? Good. Then sign and date it, and I warn you, prisoner, do not tremble the pen for sympathy. Then, listen to me, you will pass it to the officers for *their* signatures."

"Doctor," protested the sergeant, "we cannot sign this likeness." The three cops burst into laughter. "This is far too large!"

"Enough! E-nough!"

Dr. Victor Vleminckx now had in his tiny hands some kind of long, grooved mechanical contraption, some kind of telescope or speculum, that the doctor might scowl into the foul, black recesses of the prisoner's soul. "You, Monsieur, will bend over. *Over.* Over the table—relax. *Wider.* Sergeant, note—you see, do you not, how distended it is. Red. Revolting. Do you not see? 3.4 centimeters of incessant buggery, you will attest—"

Dripping was heard. Black liquid . . .

"Ucch," said the doctor, wiping the fouled tool. "Wretched pig."

The door slammed.

Gone, all of them gone, and Verlaine was just as they had left him—sprawled on the desk, naked and defeated, smashed to bits. Wheezing and sobbing, gasping, he couldn't defend himself; at that moment, he was powerless even to dress or clean himself, and so Verlaine wept for his weakness and helplessness, anything to vomit out this demon, this darkness that stabbed him to his soul. Guttural it emerged, a deep, room-inhabiting groan of horror, a birthing sound that grew to a wail as he broke into hysterical confession, a dithyramb of frantic, heartsick collapse:

"Lord, I beat my mother! I beat my wife, I threw my own son, my own blood, against a wall! Lord, I shot my friend, my beloved. I shamed my family and my wife's family. Lord, I have failed everyone. Everyone who ever depended on me . . ."

Vanity, hope, dignity—there was none. Will—gone. Nothing was left—no, he had sunk too deep; sprawled lifeless across the desk, he was dead in the arms of the world. Flattened, fouled, and naked, wet with his own fluids, he was drowning in his pain, hard soul contractions, labor pains, expelling, like spiny demons, his guilt and self-loathing. Out it poured, sorrows and splashing black poisons, a flood, to the point that he was now panting, hysterical, and crying out for God. Famished for God, *any* god. Crying over and over and over:

"*Seigneur, prenez pitié.* Lord, have mercy. Please—please—please God, forgive me—*forgivvvve* me. Anything so I can die. Die—die—die—die—die . . ."

When, up in a blast, a storm swept through him, a torrent of blazing, overpowering light and blessedness. Wind and star showers. Tingling crystal ecstasies. White, like sea light. Sweet, like rain. Pure, like the sun, and then with such overpowering love as could have drowned the ocean and lit, in a single radiant second, the whole universe. Words—but there were no words. Explaining—but there was no explaining. Fear—but there was no fear, or sorrow, or want, or desire. For now was the *first second of the first minute of the first morning of the first day.* And look, up there on the clothes peg, see how it hung so brightly, a whole new life and soul, a luminous second skin as white and breezy as a sheet blowing in the sun.

But what was it? God? The god of sobriety? Some trick of mental chemistry?

Say what you will. So filled, so overflowing was Verlaine that afterward he dared not, and could not, speak. Lying on his iron cot, cradled in God's gigantic arms, he was a man forgiven, new like the dawn, freed like the rain and washed clean on the greatest day in all his life—in jail.

Jail—thank God!

Dry of drink—praise be to Him!

Cold iron bars! Rules! Routine!—Hosanna in the Highest!

Here, behind bricks and bars, like so many before and after him, Verlaine found blessed refuge from the terrors of his inner chaos. And so for the next twelve months, mopping floors, meekly caring for the sick, and, of course, having a bounce in the hay or ten, he was the reformed Paul Verlaine, upon whose quivering tongue the white Host landed, as cold and alive as a snowflake on a child's tongue. *Good*, the idea of being *good*, gluttonously good, it was like hunger, like thirst. *Lord, just let me be good.* Honestly, for a bent nail, Verlaine was true, more or less. Moreover, in his overflowing, he was now a religious poet. It was ecstasy. Deep in the night, by the glow of one small candle, he could be seen, filling page after page of a small notebook with his jail cell canticles.

The Sky Above the Roof

The sky above the roof's
So blue and calm.
A branch above the roof's
Fanning the air.

The bell up there in the sky
Makes little sounds.
A bird up there in the tree
Sings its lament.

Dear God dear God life's there
Simple and quiet.

Those soft and distant sounds
Come from the town.

What have you done, you standing there
In floods of tears?
Tell me what have you done
With your young life?

*B*ut then one black day Paul Verlaine was released—condemned, even as he petitioned the warden to let him stay. Please, warden, he begged, just another year! Just a few months until I can find my footing!

Too late. They put him on a locked train with sundry other miscreants and mental cases being shipped back to France. Terrifying, to be released into the shark-filled waters of his own recognizance. Paris, certainly, was death—a plague zone. Instead, he went to the monastery in Rouen, a blessed sanctuary of near-perpetual silence, ready to enlist in God's Foreign Legion. Alas, the father superior, seeing the pox of wantonness on his face, was all too familiar with such lost souls. Sorry, Monsieur. No room at God's inn.

*F*atherhood, then! Against all advice, the poet returned to Paris.

Shaved and sober, bearing a toy boat with a white sail, the new Paul Verlaine went to Mathilde's house—she then had moved into her own home—determined to see his son. Who by now was a lad of two or three (or four?), living in what—to Verlaine's mind, at least—was still morally and legally *his* home, as he and Mathilde were not yet divorced. And so the returnee knocked and waited. Briskly, Odysseus knocked again, when above a window rattled up—Mathilde?

No, it was her hateful old maid, Claudette, shrilly calling down, like slops hurled from a chamber pot, "Please, Monsieur, are you crazy? Go away. She will not see you, never, a convicted criminal! There, Monsieur, there are your two feet. Use them! Quickly, please. *Vite, vite!*"

"Can you not see?" he cried, arms upraised, rotating Romeo-like unto the heavens. "I am a changed man. Please, I am a *devout Catholic . . . a changed man*, do you not see?"

No surrender! He was fighting for his son, for the sanctity of his marriage and all that was sacred—for *them*. Many heard his cries. Indeed, in that genteel quartier, after thirty minutes of his bellowing, maids and then their ladies, too, could be heard jeering.

"Go home, imbecile! I will have you arrested!"

No matter. Bravely Paul Verlaine chanted his case, his *love*—why, even his resolve to seek honest employment. And so, much as the stalwart Holy Roman Emperor Henry IV stood barefoot in the snow pounding on the locked Papal gates at Canossa, so the intrepid one carried on until three gendarmes arrived in a police wagon drawn by two black dray horses with massive chests.

Hurled to the lions! Handcuffed before his child! Indeed, before the now jeering neighborhood, the police padlocked the poet into a rolling cage. A circus animal. Fists balled around the bars, standing on his toes, there he was, two eyes peeping out the slit window, watching his life go away.

"Reformed," sneered the magistrate before whom the felon-poet stood the next day in handcuffs and leg irons. "Heed me, *poet*. So far as your wife and son are concerned, legally speaking, you are a dead man. *Dead*, do you hear me?"

*D*esperation is nothing if not resourceful. And so when these appeals failed, Verlaine returned to cobble at what he knew—heartbreak and failure. Another go at Rimbaud. This occurred some eighteen months after the shooting, in 1875.

Hoping it might be different this time, after long wheedling he managed to meet Rimbaud in Stuttgart, where once again Verlaine found himself standing before a locked door. An utterly different person.

Peasant. Right away Verlaine saw it. He could see Mme. Rimbaud in his face, the hard blue eyes, the boredom, the implacable way he stood, jaw muscles kneading as if he were working up a spit. As for a roll in the hay—forget it. Almost immediately, Verlaine realized his terrible mistake.

"Look," offered Verlaine hopefully, "perhaps we will both feel differently in a few months."

"Undoubtedly, *you* will," replied Rimbaud patronizingly. "You always do, eh? But as for me, I can promise you, old chum, that I will feel no different. Not now, not ever."

Verlaine teared up in anger. "But how can you *know* this? This is ridiculous, you are but what . . . twenty-one, is it? How on earth can you speak for the rest of your life? For when you are thirty? Or forty? How?"

Rimbaud stared clear through him. "Because I don't *need* to hope. I don't *need* to believe, and I no longer *need* to write. What I need, Verlaine, is to *not* write."

"Not write! So this is your new vocation? You who wrote of what the hare said speaking through the spiderweb to the rainbow? You who woke up with the summer dawn in your arms? Who wrote, I assure you, deathless things. And all this is shit to you now? Answer me! What on earth has happened to you? To deny everything and embrace—*nothing*?"

"Verlaine, you have my *Season in Hell*," Rimbaud said, referring to his adieu to art and poetry. It was a long prose poem that, amazingly for him, he actually had published—half published, rather. No one had seen it, of course. The three hundred copies were sitting in a box in the printer's warehouse, awaiting Mme. Rimbaud's payment. Never mind she had promised to pay for it when Arthur was home in a bad way— perhaps suicidal, she feared. Now that he was better—not good, but better—so let the printer whistle for his money, having set into type, as she put it, his *wahh-wahh-wahh*. *A Season in Hell*, another Rimbaud mummy. There it was, lying forgotten in a printer's warehouse under dust, dead wasps, and mouse droppings. A renunciation that begins:

Long ago, if my memory serves me, my life was a banquet where everyone's heart was generous, and where all wines flowed.

*One evening I pulled Beauty down on my knees. I found her embittered
and I cursed her.*

I took arms against justice.

*I ran away. O witches, poverty, hate—I have confided my treasure to
you! I was able to expel from my mind all human hope. On every form
of joy, in order to strangle it, I pounced stealthily like a wild animal.*

So there would be no ambiguity, Rimbaud clarified his position:

"Verlaine," he said, "as I burned my past, did I neglect to say that art
is stupid and a lie and, above all, useless? *Useless.* Did you think I was just
writing these things to create some poetic frisson? Some effect?" He
shrugged. "God knows what I wrote. *You* have my pages. I don't. And
this will surprise you, but now I wish I had not given away all my
poems. Honestly, if only I'd had the good sense to keep them! Had I
only! Then I could burn them, all my little darlings, every last lying, stupid word."

"Ah," said Verlaine, almost choking, "and you call *me* a coward. You
gave them away so others would publish you—*for* you. So you could be
innocent. Or invisible. And all the while you do what? Walk away from
your work, your dreams? What, like an animal from his own shit? Or
was it just your usual arrogance, God exiting with a shrug after the first
six days, bored with his own creation!"

"Really, Verlaine," replied the young man, with affectionate menace,
"you, of all people, calling *me* a coward. Burn them, please, every page.
God help me, but I would. And dance in the flames. Trickery. Fakery.
Vanity. That's all it ever was."

The coldness, the viciousness and God hatred, and all this from one
who, at the same time, managed to believe with Saint Paul that charity is
the key. Angry tears sprang in Verlaine's eyes, as he stammered, "I do—
I—I do not understand you."

"Too true. And never did."

Verlaine tried again. "Please, I do not *mean* to misunderstand you. I did understand you in *our* day, you know I did—well, better than most—and I want to understand you now. But patience—God, you have no patience. And life, I must tell you, especially a life spent alone, is a ferociously long time."

Who was this stranger who had taken up residence behind Rimbaud's eyes? It was like talking to a disturbance of which the disturbance was magically immune: a lion does not know it is a lion, liable to attack—it just is, and does. "Dear, dear Verlaine," said Rimbaud at last, "do forget it. Forget me. Forget us." The young man shrugged. "Look, I wish you no ill will, so enough. Have a good life, and now I bid you good night. Time to go."

How effortless it was for him with his big hooligan hands. Cooly, Rimbaud turned and left. No past, no future, no friction. Verlaine almost marveled at him, heading down the street, in his loping headstrong walk, his big, red hands flapping with careless menace.

"We'll meet again!" cried Verlaine. "Oh, yes, we *will*."

There Verlaine stood in the German air, in the German street, weeping—left again. And not even the familiar parting tap for money.

"I *do* know you," he cried. "I *love* you, Rimbaud. And we will be together again. We *will*, you'll see!"

How wrong he was.

50 ♪ The Phantom

"You know, we have another patient due to—to amputate tomorrow." So Michel, the orderly, informed Rimbaud early the next morning, the third day after his operation.

Lovely, thought the patient, another amputee. Comrade in misery. Such was now what passed for good news.

"And," added Michel, but of course with convulsive difficulty, twisting his mouth around the words, even as he cracked his long, bony wrists, "your mother and sister are coming. Today, I think I heard."

Rimbaud gripped the armrest of his wheelchair. Where were his porters, his beasts and hired rifles—his command? Good grief, what was life now? Stewed prunes?

Here on day three at the forward-thinking Hôpital de la Conception, it was time to *get up and be ambulatory.* So said his doctor, the ebullient Dr. Delpech, the same who had amputated him. Heavyset and bearded, with tiny pince-nez glasses, Dr. Delpech was an exceedingly pleasant man who rocked on his feet and made steeples with his fingers as he pronounced upon things medical. Moreover, Dr. Delpech always had for his patients a new, overly long, and not very good joke—torture when Rimbaud, like a dog awaiting his dinner, was wholly fixated on his *life.* Or rather the *point* of his life now, if indeed there was one.

"No, no, Monsieur Rimbaud," mused Dr. Delpech with a warning smile, detecting another morbid turn in the patient's thoughts, a return to the bad old habits, the old ruts. "You must not allow yourself to think in this way. Throw that thought overboard. *Throw it away.*"

Like a conductor, with a genial flick of his wrist, Dr. Delpech banished all such negative, such *habitual* thinking, to which so many were captive—especially this one, who seemed almost to be plotting against his own recovery. *Non!* The stump, bleeding, sepsis, his mother's impending visit, fears of ever walking again, death, the future—don't worry about it, advised the good doctor. Any of it.

"You'll be back on a horse," Dr. Delpech assured him. "You can get married—I believe you were talking about that as you came out of the ether. Young man, you are still young, *vigorous,* and I tell you now, you are on the right road. True, limping a bit at the moment," he added, wriggling his large nose as he did when he snuck in a witticism, "but on your way. *Do you dance?*" he asked suddenly. "No?" he asked with evident surprise. "Well, I do, Monsieur, and I will waltz at your wedding! I will! And you will, too. Did I mention that I am prescribing, especially for you, dancing lessons?"

Rimbaud stared at him in horror. The good doctor just laughed.

"There, do you see? I am pulling your leg! Dear me," said the doctor, looking for a laugh, "did I say that?"

Laugh? Just then the patient was struggling not to start weeping, to be brave and cavalier—or something. And so, woozily, Rimbaud himself ventured a bad joke:

"Well, Doctor, then I suppose I shall do the *one-foot.*"

"There you go, that's the spirit!" agreed the doctor, the *conductor,* rocking on his feet, with a flick of the wrist. "After all," he continued, "in the desert, among the tribals, did you ever give up hope? Ever?"

Rimbaud grew uncomfortable. "Well," he admitted, "I didn't give up. But *hope?* Hope was in short supply, Doctor—much like ice in drinks."

"Ha-ha," laughed the doctor. "Now *there's* the spirit! Just like that."

It was the drugs, the residual laughing gas and ether; it was the opiates that gave him constipation. For after this examination, Michel took him outside for a "spin" in the sun, pushing his wheelchair down a promontory, over the bluffs where the wind took his steely gray hair, causing him to crease his hollow, wrinkled, now rather Mongol-looking eyes. The prominent forehead, the compressed lips, the sunburn-spotted fingers ground down like brute implements. In his lap, his large hands now jiggled slightly, still on guard, as if a skinny man might burst from the red hibiscus now buzzing with enterprising French bees.

Wearing blue pajamas with one leg pinned, he could feel the sun warm upon his face, grazing his long eyelashes. Before him, in all its sweep, lay the port of Marseille and the inky Mediterranean, upon whose brilliant surface the blood-orange sun laid down a carpet of flamelets. Such sweep and beauty—such calm, such order. This in itself was eerie and alienating, a modern world now so mechanized and routinized and pacifistic. No dung. No stench. No empty, hostile stares—no open hand. For him to go from perfect chaos to consummate French order—it was too much, like plunging a red-hot iron in water. If only he could have gone to some intermediate spot, he thought, some moderately botched place where he might have been better prepared, mentally speaking, for this vast spectacle of civic passivity. Pools of flowers and cypresses pointing heavenward like green fingers. Sunday painters at their easels. Look, actual children—white children—children eating ices in wide-brimmed hats with ribbons gaily twirling in the salt sea air. And blithe pleasure seekers, dandies with canes and cravats and women in foamy white gowns under open white parasols . . . *people at leisure, spending, and merely enjoying themselves.* All this made him intensely irritable and anxious, a self-styled soldier like himself among these *civilians.*

Then he heard Michel. Good grief. Had they been conversing?

"I *said*," said Michel with some exasperation, "do you like her?"

"Her?" said Rimbaud, craning around. "Do I like *whom*?"

"Your mother."

Like her? he thought. She's my mother.

"Well," said Michel, continuing this line of inquiry, "you were gone a long time in Africa, no?" He scratched his little goatee. "A long, *long* time, huh?"

"I was working."

As always when Michel became particularly excited or exasperated, a snail trail of spittle issued down one side of his mouth. Working his lips: "But Rimbaud, to never go home? In ten whole years?"

"Of course not. Do you think I was on holiday? I was far away, *weeks* away. I had a business to run."

"But didn't the other fellows go home? And didn't you miss her?"

"Miss whom?"

"Your mother."

Rimbaud slapped the armrests. "Excuse me, *excuse* me! Face me around."

Michel stepped in front of him. "Look, I won't tell nobody."

"Tell them *what*?"

"About your mother. How you feel about her. I won't."

"Don't be ridiculous. *Take me back now.* Inside—please."

Upset, Michel turned the wheelchair around. Then started pushing, hard. Too hard. Hitting a rut, the chair gave a jolt. Fire shot down Rimbaud's leg. But when he grabbed the pain, he found himself holding only air. Empty air from the part now separated from him, the ghost.

"Owwwww! Shit, watch it!"

His bulbous knee, he could feel it, a fireball of pain, clenched in his hands. Paralyzed, he could feel every gram of it. Pure absence, pure pain.

"That's the phantom pain," said Michel. "Leg's gone, but it still pains you. Right? We call it the Phantom."

Beauty, safety, and happiness—why, thought Rimbaud, why would life show him these things, these now useless things, at the curtain? When again, without warning, Rimbaud burst into tears.

Doubled over, helplessly weeping, Rimbaud sat with his Phantom and this baffling, fervent young man who had so upset him. And all by merely asking him if he liked his mother.

51 ❦ Chilly Companions

Meantime, on a train not fifty kilometers away, Rimbaud's mother and sister were, in their separate ways, experiencing very different reactions to the hot, flagrant beauty of the French Mediterranean.

Having attained that august and self-sufficient age where she never again needed to see anything, Mme. Rimbaud, needless to say, was repelled by this lazy, olive oily, obviously *degraded* region, filled, as she saw it, with philandering Italians, siesta-ing Spaniards, whoring sailors, and similar grinning scoundrels. Adding to her pique was the crowded train that compelled her to be disagreeably close to her daughter, why, almost knee to knee. Indeed, with virtually every seat taken, mother and daughter were forced into a grouping of four seats, two seats facing forward, two facing back. Which made it complicated, for of course Mme. Rimbaud did not want to sit side by side with her daughter. Nor, heaven forbid, did she want to sit directly across from Isabelle's hunted, prowling stare. No, no, as Madame directed Isabelle with a flick of her nail, they would sit diagonally, like strangers. And so the old woman faced back, ever back, staring at the boiling smoke from the locomotive, fleeing like the past, while Isabelle faced forward, thrilled by this sunny, gigantically new cosmorama, in furious sweep, rushing toward her starving eyes. Red terracotta. Climbing vines. Running children. Blowing wash. Pleasure—she could smell it, hot and vivid, looking at *that*, then *that*, then *that*. Anything so as not to think of that frightening word *amputation*.

But this was just the start of Isabelle's life awakening. For after some hours, as the train pulled around the mountain, for the first time in her life she saw it in the distance—the *sea*, the blue, the blinking, the effervescent sea! Her gloves pressed the glass. Before the water's vast expanse, she all but bounced in her seat. *The sea, the sea, the sea!*

"Good grief, have some dignity," scolded the old woman. "Can you not contain yourself?"

Isabelle reddened. As did the two gentlemen nearby who ducked into their celluloid collars, embarrassed to see a grown woman treated like a child by the old scold. And why? For expressing happiness? For socially isolated Isabelle, this was a slap awake, seeing in their reactions not only how brittle and daft her mother could be but how, day after day, like a fool, she took it.

And Isabelle saw something else that day. As they drew closer to the hospital, Isabelle could see in her mother's eyes a terror that she had not seen in twenty years, not since the war of 1871, when in their spiked helmets the Germans had swept down, brown locusts trampling to dust the rye fields of Roche. Look at her, thought Isabelle. An old woman paralyzed—paralyzed as only the proud can be—before the skidding, brakeless train of ruin.

*R*idiculous girl!

After this cuffing, the old woman could see her daughter angling for sympathy, doing her "hurt lip," as she called it. Oh, go on with you, she thought, disturbing people with your childish antics!

But it wasn't just Isabelle, it was the whole exercise, summoned against her will to see her son. Her selfish son. In trouble, of course, for what else would bring him home! His way, it was always his way, or no way. And imagine if *I* were in trouble, thought the old women. Would he lift a finger? *Obviously not.*

So you see? Do you see what I must carry?

I do, I do.

So replied Mme. Rimbaud's lady companion, the ghostly but, to the Madame, quite corporeal lady who prayed with her so valiantly, under the worst conditions. An unfailing lady. A lady who could pray through fogs, rugged as a statue and clear as a beacon. Never tiring or despairing, she understood, this indomitable woman, the inexplicable durations of God's silences, the long seasick periods—even these fleeting glimpses of the mere *possibility* of rescue. In any case, admitted Mme. Rimbaud to her cherished companion—let us call her Mme. Shade. Well, confiding to that revered personage of sterling reputation and unfailing good sense, Mme. Rimbaud felt terribly guilty to say this, but the truth was it was quite useless, this pilgrimage to Marseille to see her son. Oh, granted, these charlatan doctors, wanting to prolong Arthur's life and run up their bills, *they* claimed to know that his life was not under threat, but *she* knew. She knew with utter certainty that her son would die. But the shame of her knowing this, his own mother. Even to her it felt traitorous, as if she were betting on the worst.

Stalwart Mme. Shade. So bleakly reassuring.

Now, now, my good Madame, you cannot be blamed for what you know. Rather, blame them, the men, for being so blind.

But dear friend, replied Mme. Rimbaud, you know how it works. Trapped with all I know and see, soon enough I know something that, believe me, I do not *want* to know. But if I tell these ignoramuses what I know—spit it out—then they, the blind, think I am being *morbid*. Negative. *Me!* When I *know*!

And so, as Mme. Rimbaud explained for the hundredth time how, when a grown-up child dies, the poor old mother, if she is unlucky enough to be kicking and still has all her marbles—well, she cleans up everything. The whole mess. Especially with these thumb-sucking males. Grown babies. Babies with *teeth*, every last one of them.

Wahh! cries the eminent doctor.

Wahh! Wahh! cries the powerful general.

Wahh! Wahh! WAHH! cries even the pope.

Dear one, Mme. Rimbaud explained to Mme. Shade, I don't care what the age—twenty, fifty, or eighty—if he's a male, either he's seeking tit or he's whining about it, greedy as a day-old calf. And of course the less milk the poor old mother has to give, the more these blabberpusses want.

A wolf's appetite, I quite agree.

Exhausting, groaned Mme. Rimbaud. And my son is now years thirsty!

Oh! My poor dear!

*L*ook at her scowling, thought Isabelle, sneering even at the sea. And then it tumbled out, an anger buried some seventeen years, clear back to Isabelle's fourteenth summer.

It was then that her mother announced, quite shockingly, that she would be journeying to London. You heard me, London, she said. Probably for three weeks, to rescue Arthur, she said—never you mind why. Then scarcely had the girls absorbed this thrilling news than their mother made a still more shocking announcement:

"Now listen to me. We cannot all afford to go, and I cannot stand all the nonsense. So, Vitalie, as the eldest, you will go. And you, Isabelle," she sighed, "you, dear, will remain at home."

Isabelle's howls were immediate.

"Stop it!" cried the mother, covering her ears. "There, do you see? Do you not see how disgracefully you are behaving? How immature you are? You only prove my point!"

"Mother," she sobbed, "I'm *fourteen* and she's only three years older. What's three years?"

"And, Mother," offered Vitalie, "this way I'll have company."

"N-n-no!" sputtered the mother, "absolutely not! I will not have the two of you around my neck! Not when I have your crazy brother to contend with."

Apparently, Verlaine was the source of this particular problem. Still tortured about his marriage (and as usual in need of funds), the lachrymose, grandiose Verlaine had decided, yet again, to return to Paris—to *duty*, wife, and son.

Jobless, without funds, and on the verge of being evicted, Arthur, meanwhile, was sending daily, ever more desperate letters pitched to excite his mother's already simmering anxieties. Feeling tough (and really wanting to brain him), Mme. Rimbaud would think, Let him sink! Let him have his full comeuppance! But then, with a chill, she would think: But what if he does something desperate—even fatal? Good heavens, Mme. Rimbaud would think, if only one knew with children that it all would turn out in the end, then one would not worry so. Trouble was, with Arthur one was never sure.

Fortunately, this once, Mme. Rimbaud was not alone, for surrounding the two poet reprobates there were four women, all now in regular correspondence with one other. This female quorum consisted of Verlaine's mother, Mme. Verlaine; the mother-in-law, Mme. Mauté; Verlaine's wife, Mathilde; and, of course, Mme. Rimbaud herself. And so, almost weekly, letters flew back and forth, filled with the latest rumors or outrage. For let us be honest here. It is immensely reassuring when demonstrably cuckoo people behave badly; why, it's as if they're supporting the whole moral order. Moreover, Mme. Rimbaud (secretly) found it quite flattering to have, as confidantes, three ladies of another class—indeed, women whose missives arrived in thick, weighty envelopes fastened with bright sealing wax, into which the sender had pressed with her initials, incised with the almost molar-like indenture of her family crest. The news, though, was always sordid. So flagrant were Rimbaud and Verlaine that in Paris myths were springing up. For example, how Verlaine's wife had seen them together at the opera, where, even over the coloratura and the orchestra, she was heard to scream:

"Look at them both, covered with blood and semen!"

Indeed, by that point even the city's most notorious voluptuaries, sodomites, and demimondaines had been outdone, utterly outclassed by the filthy, now full-grown bruiser, leading the red-bearded sot who followed him as if he were a conquering angel. For, after all, in Paris one could lead the "irregular" life, that is, so long as one took some basic precautions. A fictitious mistress, a few cheap pieties, a transparent lie and a wink—a fig leaf was more than enough. But to be odiously, crudely obvious—to cram it down society's throat, as they were—this was madness.

Of many outrages, we shall omit the merely crude, obnoxious, idiotic, sacrilegious, or scatological—all but two of the more troubling and revealing. For example, the night at a table of poets when Rimbaud proposed an experiment. "Put out your arm." So he said to Verlaine, who no sooner extended his arm than Rimbaud pulled a knife from under the table and stabbed him deeply in the wrist. The wound, though, was the least of it. What none would ever forget was how Rimbaud watched with a malignant smile, much as a boy might stick a frog, just to see it twitch. Verlaine howled. He looked at his love in rage and horror, at which point the kid just . . . *laughed.*

Not long after this, and not even particularly drunk, the young man of science repeated this vicious experiment on another apparent ectoplasm, the photographer of poets Etienne Carjat, the same who had famously photographed Baudelaire. This time, the self-styled surgeon of the soul was mobbed, punched, throttled, then dragged out into the alleyway. Yet even as they beat him bloody, Rimbaud laughed and jeered them. *Poets!* Did these pansies not understand the pain required? The willed defilement? The viciousness and sorcery involved?

Of course they didn't. And not merely for want of talent or commitment. Let's face it: beguiling as Rimbaud's myths might have been as poems or boasts, no adult in his right mind, not even Verlaine, would have been fool enough to act them out. The willfulness, recklessness, and literal-mindedness required—the sheer negativity—this called for the dope of all dopes, *l'adolescent je-m'en-foutiste,* the hooligan adolescent.

Well, if at this time Mme. Rimbaud did not know the full and lurid particulars about *le jeune Arthur,* she certainly knew the gist. And without going into the unsavory details for her two young daughters, she knew a life lesson when she saw one. And so, just before embarking for

Britain, Mme. Rimbaud told her daughters just enough, but of course not nearly enough, to pitch them into a state of boiling anxiety.

"*Now* he wants my help," cackled the mother, vindicated that all Arthur's chickens had come home to roost. "Oh yes, when his belly is empty, *then* he sees. And why? Because we, the *women*, we have cut off their money!"

"But, Mother," begged Isabelle, trying to pump her for more, "how serious is it?"

"Desperate, eh? Desperate enough that your lazy, useless brother who has never in his life lifted one finger—that now he *wants* to work!"

How serious? So serious that, late that night, after checking on the girls in bed, Mme. Rimbaud lit the oil lantern, then got her shovel. As for the girls, having only feigned sleep, they snuck to the window—aghast, to see their mother pacing. Arms outstretched, she looked as if she were doing a queer dance, veering back and forth across the lawn, when she pounced. The spot. She started shoveling, then dropped the shovel, fell to her knees. Reaching down the hole, rocking and grunting, at last she wrenched it free. A bottle. One of her tallow-smoked money bottles. Cradling it tenderly in her arms, she glanced about suspiciously, then carried it into the house.

*I*sabelle had another surprise the day before her mother and Vitalie departed for London.

As it would be their last day together for several weeks, Mme. Rimbaud told Isabelle that she wanted her, and only her, to accompany her to church. Time alone together, thought the girl. But on the way, inexplicably, Mme. Rimbaud turned the carriage into the stone courtyard of the strangely dairylike nunnery. Looking up, Isabelle counted a dozen windows, each shuttered and bolted. All that was missing was the hay and the milk-cans.

"Stay here. I'll be only a minute."

The mother got out. Righted her skirt and centered her hat. Then went down the long stone path and knocked, bold soul, on the burly oaken door. The vault of darkness opened. Were they expecting her? Two large, rosy-cheeked nuns came out, smiled, surely thrilled to feel the sun's benediction, then followed Mme. Rimbaud down the ivied path, past the gazeless eyes of the alabaster Virgin. Wait, thought Isabelle, balling her hand between her legs as the two dark figures approached. What do they want with me? In the sun, the nuns' white cowls looked, in their recesses, like enormous white calla lilies with faces squeezed inside them.

"And how are you this fine day, my child?" asked the plumper of the two, smiling, as she patted Isabelle on the shoulder. "I am Sister Geneviève, and this is Sister Thérèse. Sister, say good morning to our young friend—"

"Good morning, dear."

And like that, they had her, screeching and writhing and kicking.

"I *hate* you!" screamed the girl to her mother.

Honestly, the mother was shocked by the extremity of Isabelle's reaction.

"Stop it!" she cried. "Stop your kicking! And where else would you, a girl your age, stay? What, with some relative? The run-amuck sons? The drunken husband? Ungrateful child! I am *protecting* you."

"Protecting me? You *lied*! Lied, lied, lied!"

"There, do you see?" cried the mother, holding her palms up to the sky like the stigmata. "Do you *see* how you are behaving? This is exactly why I cannot take you!"

*V*espers and vile food. Dark, unventilated rooms partitioned into stalls, heavily saturated with the musk of cooped-up, pent-up females. And sticky hot slaps when Isabelle Rimbaud got fresh or refused to comply. The Donkey Girl. So Christ's thirty-seven brides christened their stubborn guest.

Meanwhile, as described in her dreary, long, homesick letters, Vitalie saw Paris and London and the Ostend-Dover ferry, saw for the first time, as her brother had seen, the blue, the harrowed sea. In the massiveness of London, the world's largest city, she also saw the future, well into the next century: horse carts and omnibuses and railways that arched, on crystalline bridges of cast iron, over the prismatic London smog.

On Regent Street, with utter shock, she and her mother absorbed their first black people. They ate ices and watched street acrobats. They saw Madame Tussaud's Wax Museum, Hyde Park, and the Tower of London, then proceeded on to the British Museum, where virtually every day her brother spent hours, such that his English, albeit accented, was almost perfect. Still, Vitalie had no idea her brother was a writer, or anything, really, except a very brilliant problem. She would never have dreamt he was writing poems in prose, revolutionary poems, some inspired by the dreamscapes of London:

> *Grey crystal skies. A strange pattern of bridges, some straight, some arched, others going down at oblique angles to the first, and these shapes repeating themselves in other lighted circuits of the canal, but all of them so long and light that the banks, heavy with domes, are lowered and shrunken. Some of these bridges are still covered with hovels . . .*

> *A white ray, falling from the top of the sky, blots out this comedy.*

They went to the English seaside, saw the zoos, palaces, and museums, and ate warm taffy—in short, did almost everything that a young girl could ever hope to do. And in her homesickness, Vitalie Rimbaud hated almost every minute of it. *Hated it.*

Arthur, though, was exceedingly pleasant, Vitalie reported, much kinder and more interested than usual—why, almost like a brother. He took great pleasure in showing them the sights of London, planned things, escorted them everywhere, often for hours at a time. Still more incredible, their mother was spending fantastic sums. Eating in restaurants. Riding in horse cabs. All this was impossible enough. But then came the most extraordinary expenditure of all.

On their second week, walking in Regent's Park, Arthur led them through a chestnut grove, into a wide, rolling green. And, gazing up, they saw it, a great globe taller than the trees and almost bigger than a house. Five stories high, it was a great air balloon painted with a face, a clown's face, covered with a net of heavy ropes suspending a wicker basket in which stood a portly, red-faced man dressed in a swallowtailed coat and peeling top hat. Arthur wandered over, fascinated.

Good heavens, thought Mme. Rimbaud, was Arthur interested in air balloons now? God only knew. Yet here he was, peppering the balloonist with questions.

"Arthur, tell the man," broke in his mother suddenly in French. "Arthur, tell him we wish to take a turn." The boy stared at her in shock. "*Oui, oui,*" she prodded, "go on, ask him."

"But, Maman," he replied, thinking she did not understand. "He's saying two guineas for half an hour." Quite a sum.

"Fine, then, two guineas." Mme. Rimbaud turned to her eldest daughter. "Vitalie, we'll all ride in the balloon. The three of us. Won't that be amusing?"

Amusing? Under her flat straw hat, Vitalie was as spooked by her mother's sudden agreeableness and largesse as by this balloon with the clown face—a horrid, leering *English* clown, she wrote, practically all lips.

Mme. Rimbaud had no such reservations. As Arthur and the balloonist each took an elbow, Mme. Rimbaud, heaping up her skirts, climbed into the great wicker basket. Two men began cranking the greasy black winch. Slowly, the gasbag bobbed and swayed. Ropes creaked, and up they went, up over the trees and over the fairway, bobbing and swaying in the strong currents, all three holding their hats, especially Vitalie, squinting and peering up, ribbons twirling.

"Hold on, Madame," said the balloonist, gesturing so she would understand. "There's some wind about today."

Manfully, Arthur held a rope, and his mother clutched his arm, actually *touched* him, unprecedented, as up they rose, to the point they could see clear across London, over the harbor forested with the last wooden-masted ships and a myriad of iron steamers. And look, said the mother, pointing, for if you looked hard, curving over the horizon, under the gray clouds, wasn't that the snowlike sheen of the sea? It was *not*, as Arthur endeavored to explain, rather professorially. Couldn't be, the sea was too far. No, insisted his mother, look, it was *the sea, the sea*, and her face appeared so animated, so momentarily young, that he thought how charming that *she* thought so, quite as if she were a normal person, a woman clapping her bosom, say, thrilled by some soaring song.

Look, look! Freely Mme. Rimbaud walked from side to side, and brightly, for those thirty minutes suspended over London, there existed between her and her son a kind of truce, quite as if she were another mother and he, another son.

Years later, on the train to Marseille, recalling this old story about the balloon, Isabelle looked at the old woman and thought, *Where?* Where, in God's name, was that lady now? Trapped, she thought, and this made Isabelle feel deeply sad. Cheated, that for even one glimpse of happiness, her mother had had to cross the sea, then take her wounded son up into the sky.

"Marseeeeeille!" cried the conductor. Isabelle froze; the old woman did, too. "*Marseeeeeeeeeeille! Marseeille* in fifteen minutes!"

52 𝄞 Family Reunion

"Monsieur!" In the doorway, Michel bore a look of alarm. "They're here."

"Who?"

Rimbaud knew, of course. Straightaway, Michel sat him up.

"Oww—" His missing leg, the phantom, was radiating pain, blue red in color and sizzling like a just-struck gong. Rimbaud then felt slapping motions. Michel was combing his hair.

"Enough." Rimbaud ducked. "Makes me feel like a horse."

Ignoring him, Michel finished. Handed him his kufi skullcap.

"She looks scared." He eyed Rimbaud. "Your mother does."

"I doubt that. Rarely is she scared."

"Well, she is." Again, he pushed the kufi at him.

"No, no." Rimbaud shook his head. "Mother will find this alarming—Muslim."

"Like I said. Scared."

Rimbaud, too. For him now, it wasn't just the missing leg or being crippled. It was the idea, minus the leg, of weighing less and even *being* less, and not just in weight of flesh but in life and force. *My life doesn't weigh enough.* If only, he thought, his mother could have seen his big life in Africa, beasts and men in a caravan under his command. If only Djami were with him, Djami, his son, splendid in his white robes. Or Tigist—that he could shock her, not merely with Tigist's youth and shocking beauty but with his daring even to "be" with a native woman. Then, when these wishes ran dry, the patient thought if only she could see the floridly engraved bank draft now sitting in the hospital safe. Over forty thousand francs—the proof. No more mooching. Not for him.

"Enough." Rimbaud gripped his sides. "Fetch them, please."

"And no kufi?"

"No kufi."

Yet no sooner had Michel left the room than Rimbaud changed his mind—grabbed the kufi and was endeavoring to center it when, to his embarrassment, his mother entered.

"Arthur." Mme. Rimbaud froze at the sight of this *Muslim* with the unsanitary mustache, so thin and clipped. Vile thing, it made her nose itch. "Dear God," she gasped, "it's you. It's really you." Briefly, she misted up. But then, instead of going to him, the old woman spun around. Reinforcements were needed. Veering for the door, she called down the hall, "Isabelle!"

Horsey girl. Skirt swinging, Isabelle no sooner arrived than she burst into tears, swallowing him in her hot, sticky embrace. It wasn't just her brother's safe return or the amputated leg that triggered such an abundance of emotion. At last Isabelle Rimbaud had a mission in life—him.

Away, Roche, manure pile! Meddlesome, complaining old woman—go to hell! Ever since the news of his return, and then the revelation of his literary fame, Isabelle Rimbaud had been plotting her new life as her brother's secretary, confidante, and eventual biographer. Isabelle Rimbaud, witness to genius! Nurse. Adviser. Amanuensis.

Nor was that all. What with the inevitable travel, the various fetes, awards, and ceremonies, Isabelle Rimbaud, long given up for dead as wife material, she *knew* she would meet her future husband and that he would be no village bonehead but rather, an educated man, a literary man. A good Catholic man, too. Odious as Catholicism had seemed for so many years, under her mother's almost galvanic influence, Isabelle was now quite religious, especially in her devotion to the Lord Jesus. How inspired her eventual husband would be by her example, she thought, a woman showing fealty not only to the Lord but to her brother, who was not only a great French poet, but—she was convinced—a great Christian poet and lay missionary. Truly a modern saint helping to raise up the *noirs* of Abyssinia. She even had a working title: *Arthur Rimbaud: Saint parmi les sauvages.*

Not that Isabelle's brother was aware of this—any of this—yet. But he would be soon enough, thought Isabelle. His healthy recovery and religious legacy, indeed his reintegration into polite French society, it was all in her capable hands.

*F*ools rush in, thought the old woman, aghast at Isabelle's shameless theatrics. How could she top a show like this? And why ever *would* she? added Mme. Shade. *Having* to feel. *What* to feel? she sighed to Mme. Shade. Quite as if the old mother must have a special milk gland for these fool males, disappearing only to reappear on their last gasp with all these pent-up *feelings*.

Still, she was a mother and, stupid or not, the world had its expectations. She couldn't give her son *nothing*.

"Look at you," the mother offered after some blank seconds, then thought, *Look at you what?* Then, seeing the vanished leg, the old woman felt a more familiar and comforting feeling—rage. Idiot! Dismissing it all as varicose veins!

Say something.

"Son," she said, "this is a very hard thing." Again she stopped—quite blank. Then, prompted by the inventive Mme. Shade, she fibbed, "How much you have been in my prayers."

And came forward. Patted him tentatively, once, on the shoulder, followed by one more, last, eloquent pat—all you get. But in her son's ravaged state, even this was too much.

"Moth—" he croaked, coughing up all the sand in the desert. "Mother—"

And broke down, vomiting his grief. "Come come, son," she said— some earlier, dream self said—"such antics will not do."

Antics?

Rimbaud stared at her in disbelief. Did she not realize that he was crying *for* her—that now he *could* love her? That now he *wanted* to care for her?

"Daughter," said the mother abruptly, plucking at Isabelle's sleeve. "Daughter, let us step outside until your brother is—until he is feeling better."

But this was the new Isabelle. She leapt up, red-faced.

"*You* step out, Maman. Leave—leave if you must, you're excused. But I will remain here. *With* my brother."

But then, as these things go, as Mme. Rimbaud was heading for the door, naturally the ebullient Dr. Delpech appeared with Michel. Pop eyes darting, Michel immediately sensed the tension.

"Ah, Monsieur Rimbaud," said the doctor, "your family is here." He obliged the old woman with an abbreviated bow. "Madame Rimbaud, so very—"

"—*Widow* Rimbaud," she corrected.

"Oh, dear," he replied, "I'm very sorry. Was your loss recent?"

Isabelle smirked. Even Rimbaud betrayed a smile.

"Is this pertinent?" sputtered the matriarch, now feeling preyed upon. She then seized upon Michel with his mulish expression and knobby wrists. "And who," she asked imperiously, "who are you?"

"I'm Michel, Mad—Madame—I mean, *Veu-ve* Rimbaud. *Michel.* The orderly." Then with typical solicitude, he asked her, "Are you all right?"

"All right?" she snapped. "Don't be impertinent. Of course I am all right. The question is, is my *son* all right. Well, Doctor?"

Dr. Delpech was unfazed by this attack of maternal nerves. On the contrary. The doctor thrived on such "educative moments."

"Well, Madame," he replied, "considering where your son was four days ago, I would say he is doing marvelously. Right where he should be."

"Doctor," she said, cupping one ear, "did I hear you say *marvelously*? My son has no leg and you say he is doing marvelously?" Muttering, the Widow fished her hankie from her sleeve. Blew her nose. Then, red-eyed, promptly exited the room.

*T*wo days later, they were in the sun-filled aerie, Rimbaud, Isabelle, and Michel. Opposite them Mme. Rimbaud sat knitting. For the recently disabled, it was here, in the aerie—"the circus," Rimbaud called it nervously—that simple life tasks became small feats.

Across the room, for example, a red-faced, one-armed man was practicing putting on a shirt. He knelt. Gently, with his open shirt facing him, he inserted the left arm in the left sleeve and the right stump in the right. Then, flipping the shirt like a cape, commenced to button it with one hand and even his teeth. Rimbaud found it deeply absorbing, even moving, to see the various *cripples* here overcoming such daily trials. But the idea that he might befriend someone in his situation—that he might share his struggles or help another—this was unthinkable, as if he, too, were a cripple. Nonetheless, Rimbaud was now in the center ring—a man with one leg endeavoring to manage, simultaneously, two crutches.

"Steady," said Isabelle, bracing his left arm while Michel took the right. "Go on. You can do this . . ."

But with no leg, no ballast, Rimbaud's unpracticed body was woefully off-kilter. He lurched. He twirled. Then, with the next step, he almost toppled over, before Michel and Isabelle caught him.

"God help me," he fumed. "What am I, a bloody ballerina?"

"Don't make fun of yourself," scolded Michel. "Only makes it worse."

"But my arm. It feels like it's being sawn off." Ominously, it was the right arm, on the same side as the missing leg. "Why should it be bothering me—why? Doesn't it make you wonder?"

"Arthur," scolded Isabelle, now echoing Dr. Delpech, "you're always so negative."

"Why negative? Because I accurately report how I feel?" Rimbaud turned to the old woman. "Mother, am I any better today? Any?"

She kept to her knitting. "Well, don't ask me." She brought the yarn around. "Ask Dr. Don't Worry. *He* claims you're doing splendidly."

"I know, but what do *you* think?"

"Don't," she warned, drawing in her chin, "don't ask me what I think. You do not want to know what I think."

"*What?* Tell me."

"Very well, then." Pushing up her glasses, she said flatly, "Not good." Then added in exasperation, "Well, *you asked.*"

He blurted out: "My life is over!"

And again, he was weeping, blindly, helplessly weeping, he who led caravans. It was too much for the old woman. Moments later, when he looked up, she was gone.

*B*ad as his days could be, the nights were worse. Once in bed, flat on his back, he might as well have been shackled. It was then that his past swept back over him, in particular the period in his late adolescence when he had renounced poetry—his first amputation, as it were.

Certainly it had required eerie discipline, sawing off his talent, drowning his angel. And after poetry, then what? Doing what? Living for what? Why?

Actually, it was very much like being crippled, that period when he first gave up poetry. It was not his life anymore. All the locks had been changed, the doors, too. Almost everything had to be rebuilt and relearned; unlearned, too—like French. First, he had to confuse his mother tongue, steal her primacy. And so for several years, in a quiet frenzy, he buried himself in the memorization of foreign languages: German, Italian, Spanish, Russian—anything to keep his spinning mind occupied. Certainly he had inherited his father's talents as a linguist. Except for Russian, which he found extremely difficult, he could learn almost any language. All in a matter of weeks. Merely by walking. Literally, he would tear his phrase books into chunks, then off he would go, walking for hours, gorging himself on new words and tongues. Good heavens, thought his mother, he was exactly like his father, filling whole notebooks with galactic webs of words and yet more words. Words in any language. All part of one vast universal puzzle, if only he could find the key.

The son knew little about his father, almost nothing, and yet in its utter unknowingness, the dream was all the more powerful. In Hamburg, in a horse cab, he was beaten unconscious. Then on the Adriatic, in a place of olive trees and glowing dust—magnificent dust like carbonized sun—he was felled by a bolt. Sunstroke, a rabbit punch from God. Later, a roustabout in a circus, feeding the lions stinking raw horsemeat, he almost had his arm taken off. Off because the lion could, and in those coiled eyes laced with golden wires, truly, Rimbaud saw the meaning of life in all its unfathomable meaninglessness.

And the dream took new forms, violent forms, proof of his manhood. In Greece, a foreman, he struck a man because he was lazy and mendacious. The man and the crew attacked him, beat him without mercy, then left him for dead. This was only the first of several instances in which Rimbaud made the potentially fatal mistake of striking a man in a shame-drenched, revenge-focused male culture. No matter. He was upholding principle, justice, civilization itself. And so part of him was beaten, while, as before, the other part, the one condemned to watch, walked away in disgust. Still looking for a new creed. A new world. Better men.

Lying in bed, now almost halved, the older man, the survivor, couldn't stop thinking about this lost period, wandering the world, then the Abyssinian deserts, looking for any refuge, any livelihood, anything that fit. *What now, what now, what now?* Even at this late date, he hadn't given up on the idea of marriage. Perhaps he could return to Abyssinia, find an educated Abyssinian woman, this time a Christian woman, perhaps even a beauty like Tigist. Children? Well, they could "try." Imagine that—a father. He might even attend church. Take the sacraments. Arise. So thought Lazarus, still hoping for a miracle.

As for the young Rimbaud, the Rimbaud of twenty, in those last months before Verlaine shot him, about poetry he was consumed by the three D's—doubt, dread, and disgust. He had his integrity, and he was increasingly horrified by the cynicism, the selfishness, and the rampant irresponsibility of writing, of creating these vain word creatures, these scoops of Adam dust given demonic breath—to do what? To what end? Why, when the world was no better and never would be? Paradoxically, he was at his artistic zenith, and this, too, fed his crisis, that the poems came so easily, almost unbidden, and then almost perfect, like sorcery, as if he were God.

In this he was not deluded. His arrogance, his doubleness, his duplicity—they were stupendous. Not to mention frightening, his believing, and not without evidence, that his genius verged on the supernatural. And then, of course, Verlaine shot him.

Lying in his hospital bed in Marseille, the older Rimbaud kept thinking about those terrible days just after the shooting. It was the great crisis of his life. Once the Belgian coppers were through with him, broken and bandaged he fled to Roche, and there in a four-month period, from April to August 1873, he wrote his great adieu and mea culpa to literature, *A Season in Hell*:

My health was threatened. Terror came. I used to fall into a sleep of several days, and when up, I continued the saddest dreams. I was ripe for death, and along a road of dangers my weakness led me to the edge of the world and Cimmeria, a land of darkness and whirlwinds.

A Season in Hell was his signed confession. It was not, as he saw it, a literary work per se—it was salvation itself. Incredibly for him, he wished to publish it, and still more incredibly his by-then-very-frightened mother had agreed to pay for it, at least originally. When the bill arrived, however, the old woman denied everything; she said it was too much and refused to pay, just as he in his ambivalence, in his anomie and drift, failed to hold her to her promise. And so it wound up like virtually every other poem—ditched.

*T*en days in the hospital in Marseille was all the old woman could stomach. Even as Rimbaud begged her to stay, she packed her black bag, then tied on her coal-bucket bonnet.

"I've got livestock to tend to," she insisted. "If I don't it will be dead stock."

Fortunately, by then Rimbaud was a trifle more optimistic, or at least more resigned to his condition. Unlikely as it seemed, in his desperation Rimbaud believed Dr. Delpech when he promised that if he stuck it out, in six months' time, his life would look very different. "Worlds different, if you give yourself half a chance."

At the same time, the patient felt more sanguine about seeing his mother again, but this time on her home ground. There he felt sure she would be in much better spirits, more open, more prepared to reconcile. Such was his hope three weeks later, when he and Isabelle boarded the train for the first leg of their journey to Charleville.

The trip to the train station was Rimbaud's first real introduction to this new world, really, to the world of the next century, and a fearsome place it was, lit not with gas but increasingly with electric lights that blinked and bleeped and formed actual words. Here were billboard-sized

advertisements for products he'd never heard of, things like tooth pow-
der and vanishing cream and safety razors. Never had he seen so much
gimmickry for sale. Equally alarming was the state of haberdashery and
millinery—all changed. Gone, during the day at least, was the top hat.
Men's hats were now minuscule, like gumdrops, while women's hats
had grown to extraordinary size—small Saturns of swirling chiffon and
chenille.

As for Rimbaud himself, who would have recognized him? White-
haired, with two shawls draping his shoulder, the kufi on his head, and
the Muslim mustache, the past and future of French poetry sat quite
anonymous in the last seat in the car, freezing cold even in the summer.
Isabelle couldn't do enough for him now. She fetched him water. She
plumped his pillows. Then, thinking he might be bored, later that afternoon she offered to read to him. He was a writer. Surely he would enjoy
hearing something *nouveau* and creative.

"Arthur, I'm reading a new book by Xavier de Montépin, *La
Porteuse de pain*—The Bearer of Bread. Have you heard of de Montépin?
A novel, very touching. May I read you some?"

"Read me what?" he scowled. "*Fiction?*"

"Yes, fiction—very artistic. Creative. That is what you like, is it
not?"

"No, if you will pardon me. That is not what I like."

Poor girl. Didn't she realize that, having abandoned poetry, he read
no "imaginative" work—novels, poetry, any of it. Newspapers. Techni-
cal publications. Journals of exploration. This is what he read. Things
that were *real*.

Instead, hour after hour, Arthur Rimbaud, now used to chaos, sat
there propped on his pillows, watching, as it fled by, the shocking order
of the French countryside, the well-tended fields, the prim houses and
charming little towns—frightening.

53 ♭ Interview

Around this same time, at 6:00 p.m. sharp at the Café Procope, there occurred the dreaded interview between Verlaine and Champsaur, the *journaliste* who had skewered him in *La Revue Noire*.

Still, where Champsaur was concerned, the review was hardly the sole source of Verlaine's fury. The fact was, even before the review, Verlaine had been quite jealously aware of Champsaur—painfully so, as only a vain, unsightly man can be. And especially now when the Parisian public regarded the absurdly handsome Champsaur as the model of haute masculinity, sartorial splendor, and splashy social success.

What Verlaine found particularly outrageous was that, even as Champsaur crucified other poets, he had yet to publish his own long-awaited first collection of verse, against which the poets of Paris had long been sharpening their knives. And yet, with no real attainments, and perhaps for that very reason, not only was Champsaur a rising star in the literary world, but he was lionized in the social pages of that pictorial hereafter, the rotogravure, the subject of line drawings, caricatures, and small items noting his presence at some soiree, or some droll comment. Photographs. Caricatures hung in bistros. Good heavens, a minor celebrity at the age of thirty-one!

The curious thing, though, was Verlaine's own slavish devotion to the society pages—and, it should be added, long before Champsaur's star rose over the city's sizzling electric lights. Stuffed in ash cans or lying on tram seats, the rotogravure and the society pages, these moist finds, why, they were like pornography for Verlaine, who could be seen indignantly snapping the pages, quite as if he expected to see *his* name among the royal, the beautiful, the mighty, or the merely rich. When again he would see mention of "that eligible Champsaur," "the imperially slim Champsaur," and, most irritating of all, "Champsaur the ladies' man."

Ladies' man! harumphed Verlaine, giving the pages a good shake.

On the contrary, it was he, the polyamorous Verlaine, who had at his pleasure *two* ladies and—*and*—quite openly, numerous other undisguised dalliances. *Despite* his noble poverty. *Despite* his unsightliness. Now *that*, he thought, that was the measure of the true ladies' man!

As for his public image, Verlaine had created a new persona, in fact a new *character*—indeed, in all his narcissism and utter self-consciousness, a thoroughly modern character. Really, platonically speaking, a new public *Type*. Move over, Whitman with your shirtsleeves rolled, pretending, great as you are, to be one of the "toughs"—please. Good for you, Oscar Wilde, rich man playing the velvet-collared aesthete in knee britches and slippers. No, no, Verlaine replied, his persona was that of the bum bohemian artist king—the clowning, brawling, life-mad public crazy, beyond common morality or arrest; a type who summoned, moreover, the deeper, fouler roots of the French character, the rough and the louche, the mob and the guillotine. Indeed, as Verlaine saw it, he was a new kind of man, swimming the rapids of a new era at speeds inconceivable before the mighty mechanization of celebrity.

Down, then, with high culture! Here was the low culture that he and Rimbaud had anticipated, in fact, the same that Rimbaud described years before in *A Season in Hell*:

> *I liked stupid paintings, door panels, stage sets, backdrops for acrobats, signs, popular engravings, old fashioned literature, church Latin, erotic books with bad spelling, novels of our grandmothers, fairy tales, little books from childhood, old operas, ridiculous refrains, naïve rhythms.*

True, Baudelaire loved—from afar—the gutter and his trollops but not, heaven forbid, the defiantly crude, the lovingly low, and the aggressively stupid. Low culture, then! Cheap fame. Tin-whistle songs. Sin, sensation, and erotica, all feeding the public's insatiable fascination with the lives of playboy aristocrats, heiresses, stage beauties, frauds, freaks, hustlers, flash in the pans, and retrograde royals. Then there was the annual Paris art show, always a brawl as far as who got in, followed by howling editorials about these *Impressionists*, these mad *Fauves*, replenishing the very swamps that civilization had labored so hard to drain.

It was shameful. It was wonderful. It was *Now*, this roller-coaster-like descent. And, following Rimbaud's leap, Paul Verlaine could claim some modicum of credit for the collapse.

*S*ee him now, seated at his customary table behind the diamond leaded panes of the Café Procope, in the rue de l'Ancienne Comédie in the Quartier Latin. Heaped under layers of fraying wool cured to the condition of *pelt*, nervously Verlaine awaits Champsaur—with, at his sleeve, the hot green kiss of Dame Absinthe.

A skullcap cuts, Erasmus-like, just above his sodden, squinty eyes. The beard is thin and leonine, the forehead a looming moon, the mouth a single crooked horizontal line as might have been drawn by a somber child on a rainy day. Somebody, obviously. And behold the proof.

For, exiting the loo, here comes Verlaine's woman—one of the two, actually, Mathilde having long divorced him. This woman is not, heaven forbid, "the other one," as Verlaine often refers to her. That would be the beastly Odette, a stout, red-headed harridan who beats Verlaine for money, beats him like a dog, just as he used to beat his own dear mother. Poetry at work, *mais oui*.

But the one who really hurts and touches Verlaine, this is the lady now returning to his table. Mistress Eugénie. Eugénie Krantz, his genie.

Beautiful-ugly, ugly-beautiful Eugénie, glued together like a broken vase, with the diverging nose, the off-plumb eyes, and the tattooing of scars and old stitches. Blurry Eugénie, flickering candle agitated in the breeze. The much-revised Eugénie, who holds Verlaine utterly in thrall, suspended as she is in that vale between beautiful and ugly. Such that Verlaine can never quite decide:

Beautiful?

Or not?

Ugly?

Or not?

Tart mouth, smart mouth. Plush lips whose lush fruit was broken, like fresh grapes, by the rival tarts who, back then, worked the same streets, most of them mothers, some with seven or eight children and a dying parent in one dank room—and a pimp squeezing her, too. Poor old chippies! Eugénie in those days was a seventeen-year-old upstart *pouffiasse*, a trollop with no children but rich and even royal protectors desperate for her tight pink billfold, her globelike buttocks, and goblet-like breasts. Poor old falling-apart tarts. In Eugénie's glory days, there was no competing with her man-gripping quim as she galloped yet another gasping client to the finish.

Target the mouth—that was where the black-bonneted old trulls would descend with saps and hat pins and razors, surrounding her like a flock of buzzards, this as Eugénie, hissing like a badger, punched and scratched and bit.

Now thirty-four, bosomy plump, and dark, Eugénie has been some seventeen years on the stroll, an eternity in her profession. But even now, coming down the aisle, as much by her loud scent as by her loiter-ing walk and downward-drawing stare, upon men of all ages and classes, she has the effect of a dog whistle. The delicious shamelessness of her, in the sheeny corsetlike dress, the wicked sharp collar, the bijoux of rings, not to mention the twitching, enterprising black bustle the size of a small trunk. But the hook, the bait, the saucy pudding—this comes with the high-heeled boots with the waxed laces. Laces that crisscross, like stitches, forty-six twisted hooks.

And to think: all this and more Verlaine had for free, baying as he climaxed, *Euuuuuuuuuuuuuuuuuuuu-génie.*

*A*h, but she is messy, Eugénie. Her talk is reckless, circular, oracu-lar. Words no sooner uttered than they are taken back with a Delphic glare.

"Old toad," she said, resuming where she had left off before her loo visit, "do you really think, old fool, that in this life you will do better than I? *Screw* better than I? *See* clearer than I—do you? Marry me. Then at least you will die in the arms of love and not under the reeking fat wattles of that slut." Odette, she meant.

"Or your Rimbaud," she continued, now broadly gesturing over the table. "Another who treated you like shit. Just as you like! So, groveling like a dog, you lick his hand? Obedient to what? To a boy long dead, or certainly so as an artist? Why, then, talk to this Champsaur? So you can torture yourself over what *was*?"

The old volcano roared to life.

"*Assez!* You don't know how it was! What I gave up—willingly—to follow him. *I* remember, and yes, I did give up everything. Mad? Yes. A fool? Of course. Like rape and ruin, I followed Rimbaud, I did indeed; I followed him into the fires of hell. This, I assure you, they will never know. Or that he gave me sweet, purring caresses—again, the Rimbaud *they* will never know."

"Know what, love?" said Eugénie sweetly. "Know!" She smiled, shifting an octave. "What do you recall, you whose mind is like a sieve? Really, my dear Paul, how you write anything is beyond me, for as we both know, you do not *think*. Unlike Rimbaud. Rimbaud, he *died* of thinking. Not you, *mon petit*—"

She broke off.

For here he came, the rodentlike Bibi-la-Purée, followed, in his sleek coat and faultless hat, by the hunter Champsaur, who with a distinct look of shock curtly bowed to Eugénie, then thought better of offering Verlaine his hand. Instead, Champsaur dropped his hat. Then, literary fetishist that he was, he dropped an unblemished green-cloth notebook with *R* on the cover—*R* for Rimbaud. Pure provocation.

"Quick, *cher maître*," said Champsaur, to break the tension, "the first word that comes into your mind when I say *Rimbaud*."

Verlaine grinned, surprised.

"Running. Always running."

"*Bien.*" He smiled broadly. "And the second?"

"Destroying—God destroying."

Eugénie looked up suddenly. In her hand was a sinister-looking implement, a nail file, was it? "Hear me, pretty boy," she said. "If, in any way, you hurt this man—"

"Madame—"

"—*Bitch* to you," said Eugénie, displaying . . . what? An ice pick? It was. "Go on. Just try to humiliate him again, just try."

"I—I quite understand."

Clearly unsettled, Champsaur sat down and opened the green notebook. "And now, *cher maître*, let us begin with that first word—*running.*"

*O*n the theme of running—flight, escape—Verlaine told this Champsaur many things, things then new and even revelatory, but he did omit certain details. For example, how, on one of their highly artistic forays fleeing Paris, Verlaine, drunk, of course, and under the boy's direction, had been forced to raise the necessary funds from his mother. Naturally, for such a sensitive, intimate transaction, Rimbaud waited downstairs, holding his horse, so to speak. Still, the young poet could scarcely have failed to hear the ruckus above him.

"*Où est le pognon?*" roared Mme. Verlaine's youngest son, swaying by the fireplace. "Where's the bloody money?"

Had Rimbaud ventured up those long stairs, he would have seen that his bibulous paramour held in his unsteady hand the choicest of the family vintage. Indeed, he was holding up a jar of brackish fluid, grain alcohol, in which a wee white figure could be seen slowly bobbing, back and forth. Bawling, his mother grabbed for the bottle he held so cruelly over her head.

"Paul Verlaine! Put your brother down!"

"Of course," he sneered. "When you give me the goddamned money."

"Stop it, you're drunk, you're just upset! Now put poor Pierre down—"

"Down? *Down*, did you say?"

Smash. Wee Pierre. There he lay on the floor, a lard white tadpole lying in a hairy mass of spawn and broken glass. Which, for Verlaine, after all those boyhood nights praying before these gluey relics—well, it felt so soaring! So liberating! To the point that little brother grabbed the second of the three heirloom jars. Rearing back, he smashed it against the family hearth, then, legs wobbling, pitched over, mesmerized by the starry debris. Well, goddamn. It was little Edith.

"Good!" he cried. "Good riddance, shrimp!"

"Horrid child!" cried Mme. Verlaine, now dancing hysterically. "Paul! Paul Verlaine! Look what you've done!"

"*Done?* You better cough up that money, woman. Think I'm *done?*"

In his hand, he now had his eldest brother, Bertrand, the size of a pig's knuckle, easily the most brilliant of the four—could have been a Pasteur. "Christ," said his little brother, "I need a goddamn drink!" And twisting off the lid, held forth the vile tankard—a brotherly toast!

"Money! Or down he goes! Wee Bertrand! Like an escargot!"

"*B*ut just how strong was his hold on you?" asked Champsaur.

"All but irresistible," replied Verlaine. "And his youth was certainly a large part of it. Consider. He arrives during a time, frankly, of mediocrity with a style and a vision unlike any other. He belongs to no school. He is not another *arriviste.* No compromises. No emotional entanglements or obligations to his elders. And he had no respect, no fear—none. Compare him with Baudelaire in that regard. Renegade though he was, at least in print, Baudelaire at bottom was a thoroughly craven *Christian*; in no way was he ready, as Rimbaud was, for hell and damnation."

"But why did you stay?" asked Champsaur. "I mean why, when virtually everybody else fled. Why you?"

"Because I loved him. I was not competitive; I knew from the start that I was not of his order. Nor were they, any of them, and they all knew it. That was why they hated and feared him. Well," he sighed, taking a long swallow, "among other reasons."

"And you say you were not writing?" asked Champsaur.

"That was my other shame. Rimbaud so shocked me—his work so shocked me—that for months, artistically speaking, I was dazed. Had no idea who I was. None."

"And when did that change?"

Verlaine never hesitated. "Belgium. When Rimbaud ordered me to Belgium."

"*Ordered* you?"

"Ordered me. To the front, as it were. Just as if I were a soldier. My wife, Mathilde, was sick, you see. Very sick. So with all good intentions, I went to the druggist to get my wife some medicine. But when I turn the corner, whom do I see but Rimbaud! Who says to me, 'Come on, we're leaving for Belgium.' Just like that. 'But my wife is ill,' I told him. 'I need to bring her medicine.' 'Screw your wife,' he said. 'I'm sick of hearing you whine about her. Your kid, too. Now, come on, *right now.*' 'But I don't have a ticket,' I said. 'I *am* your ticket,' he said. And, Monsieur, with just the clothes on my back, I left."

"Just like that?"

"Just like that."

"But, *cher maître,*" challenged Champsaur, "your duty to your wife! Your son."

" 'Pick,' said Rimbaud. 'Them or me.' No doubt this sounds shameful, crazy, morally destitute, and I won't deny it. But honestly, at the time it seemed a higher duty. And had I stayed, I would have missed out on my Belgium poems. My very best. Immortality itself."

"But, *cher maître,*" protested Champsaur, clearly horrified, "more important than your *wife*? Your *child*?"

No answer. That was his answer.

Verlaine then described the journey, the train to Charleville, then the wagon that took them by night, through the thick fog, to the Belgian border. Verlaine was a Parisian, a poodle—never had he even *been* in the woods, let alone at night, crossing penniless into another country. And why? For what? he thought, fuming that Rimbaud could not bed down in a nice, dry, *charming* barn—oh no, he had to pick a damp, smelly barn packed with steaming, stinking cows. Sucking eggs. Drinking from streams. Wiping themselves with leaves.

"But where are we going?" Verlaine demanded the second day, almost weeping, he was so wet and wrung out.

"*A la chasse des anges.*" Hunting for angels.

"Stop it! This is hopeless! Pointless!"

And it *was* pointless. For Rimbaud, pointlessness was the very point. But then, the third night, for Verlaine, something shifted as a thick fog descended, fog and soft rain that fell like a spider's web over his hands and shoulders. He thought of a phrase that Rimbaud had said the night before, "Soft rain falling on the town." Nothing special. No deep import when he first heard it, but now those six words were like a musical phrase, a talisman, a lure. Fog filled Verlaine's lungs. Wet shoes. Burrs speckling his trousers. Steaming wet and cold, Verlaine was so hungry and miserable—so overpoweringly lonely—that suddenly he understood what Rimbaud had meant by an "objective" poetry. For suddenly Paul Verlaine wasn't lost *in* the fog, he *was* the fog. Heart beating, he pulled out—like bandages for a wound—a soggy wad of paper and his crumbling pencil. And oddly the fog acted like an eraser, as he realized that the issue wasn't what to say but rather what *not* to say in the usual way. Extraneous words fell away, and those that remained gleamed, deeply struck like nails:

Falling Tears

Soft rain falling on the town.
—Arthur Rimbaud

Falling tears in my heart,
Falling rain on the town
Why this long ache,
A knife in my heart?

Oh, soft sound of rain
On the ground and roof!
For hearts full of ennui
The song of the rain!

Or again, the next day, when he overheard the ownerless wind intimating the soul:

Fresh, frail murmur!
Whispers and warbles
Like the sigh
Of grass disturbed . . .
Like the muffled roll
Of pebbles under moving water.

This soul lost
In sleep-filled lamentation
Surely is ours?
Mine, surely, and yours,
Softly breathing
Low anthems on a warm evening?

"Hats off!" mused Champsaur. "And the *musique!*"

"Dear, dear," chided Eugénie, "fawning now, are we?"

"The *point*," returned Verlaine, "the point is, with my Brussels poems, in these landscapes—thanks to Rimbaud—I came to that place where the artist vanishes. As he himself vanishes in his prose pieces, his *Illuminations.*"

"For which he receives no royalties," broke in Champsaur.

"Assuming Rimbaud would even *own* the work."

"Well, he might like the money."

"The *point*," said Verlaine testily, "the point is, Rimbaud wanted these poems, his prose poems, to be crazy and innocent, but most of all *innocent, innocent, innocent*—that's what he said. And invisible. Here you have no real sense of the author. No, these poems, these dreams, they are entirely anonymous. The leaps of logic. The lack of antecedents. The swirl of imagery and willfully absent transitions. But what I most marvel at is how these poems so stubbornly *resist* meaning, while always presenting new meanings. *Ice.* To me they are like white hard ice—gleaming, pure, and slippery. Here is my favorite. A modern version of Genesis—turned on its head:

After the Flood

As soon as the idea of the Flood had subsided,

A hare stopped in the clover and swinging flower bells, and said its prayer through the spider's web to the rainbow.

The precious stones were hiding, and already the flowers were beginning to look up.

The butchers' blocks rose in the dirty main street, and boats were hauled down to the sea, piled high as in pictures.

Blood flowed in Bluebeard's house, in the slaughterhouses, in the circuses, where the seal of God whitened the windows. Blood and milk flowed.

Beavers set about building. Coffee urns let out smoke in the bars.

In the large house with windows still wet, children in mourning looked at exciting pictures.

A door slammed. On the village square the child swung his arms around, and was understood by the weather vanes and the steeple cocks everywhere, under the pelting rain.

"Astonishing," said Champsaur. "And I agree. Compared with the traditional poem, there is almost nothing to grasp onto. An ice wall."

"Well, fifteen years ago, Rimbaud's poet peers, myself included, had even less of an idea how to read, react to, or even follow something like this. It broke all the rules. Prose was the least of it. They had no precedent. Even Baudelaire's wonderful prose poems—his models, I suppose—even these are really just sketches. Well described and realized, of course, but finally unmysterious. Entirely realistic. They don't achieve the level of dream and fracture. They don't pull you into another reality, as these do."

"And do you think Rimbaud is still writing?" asked Champsaur suddenly.

Verlaine never hesitated. "No, absolutely not." He shook his head vehemently. "Oh, I've read the speculation, but I assure you, Rimbaud is not writing. Not a word. I would bet money on it."

"But, *cher maître*," protested Champsaur, "how can you know this?"

"Because Rimbaud is so inflexible by nature. Hardheaded peasant. *Not* writing is now his vocation, just as writing once was."

"So you believe he will never return?"

"To France, perhaps. But to poetry, never. I would be shocked."

"Well," broke in Eugénie, with a barbed glance at the man who refused to marry her, "if Rimbaud were to return, this one would run off with him."

"Enough," said Verlaine.

"Let me further assure *you*," she insisted, "only men are this way, this stupid, this blind. This is why the male creature needs floozies like me." She looked directly at Champsaur. "Men want to be thrilled. Do you not agree, Monsieur?"

"I do so very much appreciate your time, *cher maître*," said Champsaur with a shocked glance at Eugénie, electric, as if she had invisibly goosed him. Uncomfortably, he turned more fully around to face his subject. "And here is my final question, *cher maître*. Why *did* Rimbaud stop writing—in your opinion."

Verlaine took a drink, then sighed a long sigh at a question that vexed him. "Well, one big reason, perhaps obvious, is he grew up. Think about it. When Rimbaud was a child, or still a young man, he could believe in his dreams, could pretend, could be seduced by his own make-believe. And remember, as Rimbaud saw it, and naïve as this might sound, he had not been sent to earth merely to write poems but to *change* the world—quite literally. He actually thought that, he really did, and for a while I suppose I did, too. But of course, there was no revolution of love. The world didn't change. Woman was not freed. The human heart was the same, no better, no worse. Leaving what? For him, meaningless words on a page. Words that died in his mouth. Suicide, in a way."

"Dear, dear Paul," purred Eugénie. Clearly irritated, she was like a cat flicking her tail, ready to claw. "Like most men, you always want the *romantic* answer, when a simpler one will do. Admit it. At twenty, great genius that he was, Rimbaud was simply burned out. A dead volcano. Shot his wad."

"And—and perhaps you are right," admitted Verlaine touchily. "But the fact remains, the child in him died, and when he did, Rimbaud, in his insane pride—in his rage and his shame—told me he wished he had never given his manuscripts away. Not because he wanted them, but so he could have burned them. Like heretics. Every last word." Verlaine nodded, as this sank in. "Believe me, I do not romanticize this part." Verlaine sat there like a piece of bruised fruit, damaged and he knew it. He sat there for some time as lonely people do, then said, "Rimbaud was a man crushed. Abandoned by God. Killed storming the heavenly citadel. Overly romantic?—perhaps. But this, Monsieur, is what I saw, and this is what I believe."

54 ♪ Love Conjugated

"Will you kindly bring your brother here for supper?" cried Mme. Rimbaud to the ceiling. Not *Arthur*, but *your brother*. Forever sixteen.

As one might surmise, with Arthur's homecoming the old woman's world was almost cosmically out of whack. It started with Isabelle, the *exalted* Isabelle—the "governess," her mother now called her—now that she was done with being a dairy maid, factotum, and drudge. In her place, two had to be hired, a barn man and a maid. Or rather, four people, as fast as Mme. Rimbaud dismissed them.

Owing to his infirmity, Arthur was given a large ground-floor room, which, he being Arthur, had to be painted—painted in earthen African tones, then hung, per his orders, with funereal curtains, to better block the pestilential French light. The "cave," his mother called it. His pretend Abyssinia, she told Mme. Shade, filled as it was with infernal wall hangings and other tribal savagery. Oh yes, she added, and his Abyssinian harp, another annoyance. It was with this harp that he soothed and distracted himself. Plucking one string, he would wait for as long as a minute, then pluck another, trying to coax, to pinpoint and better *portend* his changing mood.

Dooorrrowwwww.

Drummmmmmmmmmm.

Toinnnnggggggggggggggggggggggggggggggggggg.

Mon Dieu! cried the Madame to Mme. Shade. Listen to him! He's losing his mind!

Patience, advised her vaporous confidante. Savor this time. He has not much left.

Tgggghhhhhrrrrrrtttthhhhhhhhhhhh-owwww.

Then, as if Madame had not been inconvenienced enough, Isabelle said Arthur needed a larger, more suitable gig, one with more room for his legs—leg, rather. Here, remarkably, the old woman did not stint. Straightaway, she procured a sturdy carriage with a black bonnet, in which Isabelle could be seen erect at the reins, hair tied up and wearing prim new clothes for her new station: long skirt, button shoes, and a wasp-waisted blouse closed at the throat with a cameo of carved white bone on a dial of pale blue.

But who was this apparition beside her, this large hump draped— even in July—with innumerable shawls, topped off with a droopy felt hat pulled almost over his ears. Past the weeping, raging stage, Rimbaud was in the stubborn, irritable, often transfixed phase, still trying to make peace with his disability, these jaws now closing around him.

"Thank you," he said to Isabelle one morning on their daily trip to Charleville.

Isabelle stared in shock; her brother no more thanked her than her mother did. "I'm your *sister*," she protested. "This is what sisters do."

"Thank you all the same. *Thank you.*" Rimbaud sat staring at his one foot, imagining if the one foot were somehow two feet. Thinking, If only I had been nicer, kinder. If only I hadn't been me.

They were now entering Charleville. Clopping down the narrow cobbled streets, they passed the *collège*, the *boulangerie*, and the sweet-shop, then went down to the small bridge where every day Isabelle would stop the horse, that, like a small boy, Arthur might peer down into watery dark slithers where, sometimes, he would see the shadowy back of a trout pointed like a compass needle into the current. Flickers, flecks, the hypnotically waggling weeds, green hairs streaming. Here was the river of "The Drunken Boat" and "Memory," of which he remembered not a word, although he did recall, vividly, the *feeling* of writing, the buzzing heat, the shock and sometimes sweet oblivion of being absorbed in it—*it* and not himself. As he had written so thrillingly in "Genie," one of the *Illuminations* and far and away the happiest:

> *He is affection and the present moment because he has thrown open the house to the snow foam of winter and to the noises of summer, he who purified drinking water and food, who is the enchantment of fleeing places and the superhuman delight of resting places. He is affection and future, the strength and love which we, erect in rage and boredom, see pass by in the sky of storms and the flags of ecstasy. . . .*

> *He knew us all and loved us. May we, this winter night, from cape to cape, from noisy pole to the castle, from the crowd to the beach, from vision to vision, our strength and our feelings tired, hail him and see him and send him away, and under tides and on the summit of snow deserts follow his eyes, his breathing, his body, his day.*

"But what about your friend Delahaye?" asked Isabelle, returning to a frequent topic. "Or—what was his name—Fourier, Foyatier, was it? Did I not hear that name?" Her brother sat silently, as if he had the mumps. "Arthur," she said at last, "*say* something. Please let me contact them for you. *Someone.*"

"Absolutely not." He looked indignant. "Not until I get better."

"Oh, come now, can you be so vain? These are your *friends*."

"*No*, is that not clear? When I am better."

Better? she wondered. Did he believe that? *Could* he believe that? For now there were further troubles in his shoulder, his right shoulder, a shooting pain that he described as being like a needle, a knitting needle, running almost arterially down his arm and down his side. It was the arm he blamed—three attempts on the crutches and that was it. Collapsing on his bed that last time, he threw down his crutches and never again picked them up. Refused. *Am I getting sicker? Am I going to die?* Although he pretended otherwise, he knew it was a milestone in the wrong direction, indeed a realization so painful that, quite honestly, he forgot all about it.

Picture him, then, one leg pinned, sitting in his pajamas in the sepia shade of his room coaxing moanlike sounds from his Abyssinian harp, six strong strings attached to a resonator of dark stretched skin sewn with darker gut. Rimbaud plucked it, then listened. Mouth open, an almost ecstatic expression on his face, he sipped not just the sound but the *feeling*. Remarkable, really. However tentatively, Arthur Rimbaud was transmitting feelings, hungry, lonely feelings that buzzed in his mother's ear:

Derrrrr-owwwwwn.

Dwwwoooooooonnnnn.

Drrrrrrrrrrph-oowwwwwwwwww.

*T*he harp was not his only means of escape, for even in those weeks of slow decline Rimbaud was able—in balletic mental leaps—both to banish reality and put the future in bright suspension. *I will marry. Perhaps I will marry. I might marry.* So he would think as Isabelle took him once again on his daily ride, down to the park and the village green, upon which, on a gentle rise, stood the white bandstand. Magic lantern. On those summer evenings so long ago, as the band played, almost inflated with sound and light, he remembered how the white cupola would be surrounded by people. Families picnicking. Trolling soldiers and girls—Madeleine, Joséphine, Marie. Why had he fled the battlefield of ordinary life, he wondered—girls, safety, normality? Happiness, even. Why?

"Arthur," said Isabelle, "no argument this time. Let's go to the concert this Sunday. Please."

"Isabelle," and he closed his eyes, exasperated. "*No.*"

"No! With you the answer is always no." She turned provocative. "Why? Because some know you to be famous? Is that it?"

He glared. "I am *not* famous. Don't be ridiculous."

"Look at you. At any suggestion that you're famous or have a reputation, you get testy. Why? Don't just stare at me. *Why?*"

"Must I be forced to hear and talk about this," he erupted finally, "something I have long disowned? Honorably disowned!" He grew more strident. "Is this not my right?"

"But Arthur, I've never heard of a poet—*any* writer—disowning his every word. And nearly twenty years later, there are those who think your work is *good.* Brilliant. Great, in fact."

He gripped the leather seat. "Good or bad is not the point! I am Arthur Rimbaud, *merchant and explorer.* Why can you not understand this? *Accept* this?"

Isabelle couldn't stand it, her hero raising his voice at her. Turning away, she sat hunched over, hugging herself, near tears at his stubbornness and negativity.

"No, I can't accept it. It's *horrifying* to hear you talk this way, to think this way. A writer renouncing his work. Saying it's all meaningless. Stupid. Pointless. It frightens me. I've never heard of such a thing."

*B*ut Rimbaud's desires were now exceedingly clear and simple. In fact, he now had a discernable vocation. That is, if it would have him.

However tardy or unlikely, it was Rimbaud's wish to be a son to his mother. Nothing halfhearted about it. They would forge an all-new relationship—this time an adult relationship. For look, he realized one day, between them there was now plenty of money, plenty for all three of them, him, his mother, and Isabelle. Brilliant! He couldn't wait to tell his mother. She was free. Time to let go of the dairy and her myriad moneymaking schemes. *Her son was home.* Home at last to protect her.

But this late dream, it sprang from a still deeper, more unexpected impulse, and this was to have what he had never had—love. Not his mad, ruinous love with Verlaine or, worse, the revolutionize-the-world love of his poet days—his Waterloo. No, what Rimbaud wanted now was human love, family love, mother love—ordinary love, on a human scale. And just as he needed this from her, so Mme. Rimbaud could feel in him an as yet unspecified need, as palpable as it was relentless. *He needed.* It made her irritable. After five weeks, the only reason there hadn't been a blowup was because of Isabelle, always hovering, forever in the middle, trying to keep the peace. But then one morning, guiltily, Isabelle left to visit a sick school friend in the nunnery. Rimbaud was thrilled. At long last! Here was his chance to be alone with his mother.

The old hen was resourceful, however, instructing the cook to bring her son his breakfast and lunch. As for the old woman, she was in luck— she had an eviction to oversee. The usual scene, things heaped on the curb, clothes blowing down the road, women weeping—a terrible thing, tragic, they would be in her prayers. And so with the courts on her right shoulder and the gendarme on her left, clopping down the road in her gig, the old woman returned to Roche, ringing like a bell with her own righteousness. It was near four. Surely, Isabelle was home, thought Mme. Rimbaud as she pulled up, calling to her two flunkies to attend to her old dapple-gray mare, the elegant Countess. Approaching the house, stealthily, she pulled off her big straw sunhat, bent down, then listened at the front door. But when she eased the door open—too late. Arthur wheeled in. Good heavens. Freshly shaved and dressed, too. The old woman felt a chill.

"Good evening, Mother."

"Oh," she said, "you startled me. Yes, good evening." Brusquely, she turned, affecting to be busy. "Now where was I?"

"Mother, wait!" He was smiling. Had he been drinking? she

wondered. "Mother," he said energetically, "I have something very good to tell you." He waited. "Something wonderful in fact."

Wonderful? "My son," she sighed, as to a child, for sitting in his wheelchair, know it or not, he had been deeply demoted in her eyes, reduced to boy height, "please, I have had a long day and still have *things* to do. *Many* things."

"Mother," he said, blinking with surprise. She merely looked back at him, unmoved. "Mother," he said, trying to be patient, but now with perceptible heat, "please, you *always* have things to do. This is important."

She spun around. "Listen, Monsieur on Holiday, with your sister to wait on you hand and foot while she dumps the whole farm on me." She looked at him almost for permission, a casus belli, what with him mooning at her, in that man-expecting way, waiting to be fed. "Well, that's right, you've got her, don't you? You've got your little sister to grovel before you, the great poet, but oh no, that's still not enough for you, is it? Oh, no, being you, back from your big safari, you expect *two* women to wait on you, eh? Good grief, what do you suppose I *do* here all day? Fluff pillows?"

"But, Mother, . . . listen." He paused a beat, thinking, Don't antagonize her, let her settle down. "Because you see, Mother," he said more softly, "in fact, I don't *want* you to work so hard. For I was calculating"— he smiled again—"well, that with all your money and property, and now with *my* money, you needn't work so hard. Or at all." Earnestly nodding, he rolled forward in his wheelchair. "I'm back now." He hesitated. "I'm your son, and I am home now." The old woman was now staring at him, so shocked, he thought, that now he could say it. The unsayable. The unprecedented. "Mother, I know we've had our differences over the years, but I'm your son, and—and I *love* you."

Love—that was the trigger.

"*Love*," she sneered. "Oh, of course, now that you're flat on your back, here you roll in like the Savior, eh? You, who never lifted one finger! Home at last to take care of the poor simpleminded old lady. Run the old lady, run everything! Eh? Is that it?"

He was dumbfounded. "Mother, I just said I *love* you. Did I not just say that—"

She cut him off.

"You always running away—love! You who never loved me, or your sisters, or God, or anyone—*love*. Love—you who couldn't stand it here. Love—you who could never stop running, you were just so *filled* with love!"

He was dizzy, his ears were ringing. "Mother," he gasped, playing his last card, "why are you doing this to me? What did I do? Didn't you just hear me say that I want to *care* for you? Didn't I just say that? Then why are you doing this, you always talking about Saint Paul, charity? Is this Christian, what you're doing?"

"*Christian!*" she roared. That was the word. "*You* dare to talk to *me* about being Christian! What, life chops you down to size and now you find religion, eh? *Christian!* You who did *evil* things. *Vile* things— Christian! *Ruining* the good name Rimbaud . . ."

The rest was so natural it was instantaneous. Out it all spewed. Pure venom. And all from the same son who, only moments before, had declared his love.

"Hateful, money-grubbing, *wretched* old woman! Dumped by your husband—you, with your cold, dead heart. Why did I try? Why was I so blind! So *stupid*? God! So *stupid* to come home when I could have just died in the bloody road! Died the failure you always wanted me to be. Good lord, you old crown of thorns, what a *wife* you must have been! Of course I ran away. Goddamned *right* I ran away. Just like my father ran away! Just like you drove my brother away."

"*Get out!*"

In rage, she took a step forward, pressing her face into his. Oh, it felt so satisfying, so righteous, to stare down upon him, crippled and defeated. "Look at you, *down there*," she jeered, just as if she had clubbed him. Beaten him down, like a man. Flattened him with her two fists. "Take care of *me*! Helpless, useless parasite! Right now I wish I could wheel you out where you belong—out in the *road*!"

55 ⚑ Love's Paws

Of course, there was no taking back the vile things the mother and son had said to each other, and, as with most family battles, the galling thing was, most of it was true, or true enough. Words were clubs, and they were Rimbauds, stubborn as fieldstones.

"But what happened?" cried Isabelle. "What was said?" Looking at one, then the other, Isabelle knew the moment she entered the room that something awful had happened. "You two. Like snakes coiled together. What? What on earth happened?"

"What happened is what happened," said Rimbaud, staring in one direction.

"What was bound to happen," muttered the old woman, staring in the other.

At this, the old woman turned her back on both her children, then walked dazed down the hallway to her room. But when the door shut, face clenched, she seized her pillow and crawled like a dying animal into her prayer corner. Pushing her face into the stale old feathers, she started screaming at the man who had deserted her long before her son had— God.

"*You!* Why? Why did you make me, *me*? To bear *males*! *Say* something for once. Why," she wept, "why does anybody even *have* children? Why, when either they die or beat you down and suck you dry?"

Just say you're sorry, advised Mme. Shade. Cool dell, everything she was not, Mme. Shade swept over the old woman as she crouched there, heartsick and panting. He's going to die, she said. It won't be long. Do you want him to die cursed by you? Cursed for all eternity? Dear woman, kind woman, you're the mother. Go to him.

"Never," she replied to her ghostly confessor. "Let Isabelle fawn over him, blasphemer! He can contemplate the back of my head!"

*T*wo hours later, the mother was fine and everything was perfectly lovely. Having joined her son in a fit of rage, the mother was now stirring a cup of tea, not hurt at all, eager to present a picture of rosy, finely balanced calm. "Daughter," she said, almost pleasantly, "don't be surprised at what happens next. Hear me. I do not imagine your brother will be here for long. No, no. Not long."

And the wounded son? He was now submerged in his room, from which, every other minute or so, the Abyssinian harp sent out exploratory notes:

Drereeeeeeee-eeeennnnnnnnnn.

Weirrrrreeeeeeeeeeeeee.

Rooowwwwwwwwwwwwwwwww-errrrrr.

He plucked. He waited, trying to calm down, to steel his rage not so much at her as at himself. Rage that he had been such a dupe, such a fool. Shame that he had imagined, actually imagined, that the old hag could ever change. And worse, here when he was trapped! No legs to take him away—no legs!

That night, Rimbaud had a dream of which the seed was an actual memory of his time in Egypt. The year was 1878, before Abyssinia. Then twenty-four, he was living in Cairo, a labor foreman overseeing a gang of misfit nationals, Poles, Germans, Spaniards, Greeks. This particular day, however, was not a workday, but still, as always, he awoke at 4:00 a.m.—awoke to the chant of the muezzin calling the men to prayers, *Ashhadu an la ilaha illallah . . . Ashhadu anna Muhammadan rasul Allah.*

When a voice told Rimbaud: *It's time.*

No more delaying, he thought, as he picked up the condemned—a notebook. It was a baggy volume stuffed with poems, drafts, notes, ideas. Foul nest. Old poems and new poems, they had been written in fits when he had slipped from his vow to abandon poetry. No more. Today all would go to the fire. Every word.

Downstairs, the dirt streets were filled with the sound of slapping sandals as sleepy men, men by the dozens, hurried to prayers. Chameleon that he was, he routinely passed for an Egyptian, dressed in sandals, kufi, and the long shirt, the *galabiyya*. Outside the mosque, in sandals and dirty feet, he even sat like an Arab, squatting on his haunches, holding in his arms, in an almost pregnant way, the fat manuscript. One hour later the doors opened. It was then, speaking in almost perfect Arabic, that he hired two men and three camels. The sun was rising like a hammer. They could lose no time. Grinding its big teeth, his camel bawled as they hauled it down on knobby forelegs. Then, his right leg locked around the saddle, up Rimbaud rose, ten feet high. *Hut, hut, hut.* Giving the beast the stick, he followed his two guides into the red desert dawn, into the rays and mist that stretched across the eastern sky, the doomed manuscript stuffed in the saddlebags. *It's time.*

Solar deluge. Slouching and sliding, pitching and swaying, dazed in the dry, fiery wind, Rimbaud drifted he had no idea how far. Then he heard shouts. A brown hand was tapping his leg. The camel collapsed on its calloused elbows. Craning up dizzily, he saw her gazing down upon him—a rodent before her coiled haunches and clenched stone paws. *It's time.*

It was midday, almost black it was so bright, and in the distance the pyramids loomed like shark's teeth. Hermaphrodite with the crumbling nose and suspect smile. Around the triangular face was an aurora, a brilliant cogitating mist, and as Rimbaud stared, panting, she-he stared back, crouched, if not camped over her great balls, which burned unseen, inextinguishable, like two suns. But then in the dream, the Sphinx's aspect altered. It was *la Bouche d'ombre*, he realized. *La Daromphe.* It was his mother demanding:

> *Who is the Son of No One?*
> I am the Son of No One.
> *And who never fails to fail, Son of No One?*
> I do, Mother.
> *Do what?*
> I never fail to fail. I live to fail, and I am nothing.

*B*ut what actually happened that day when Rimbaud took his forbidden pages to the Great Sphinx? What happened when he took out the notebook, ripped it up, splattered it with kerosene, then dropped the match? Greasy flames licked up. Grimly, he stood back.

"No!" cried the eldest guide, an old man.

Almost certainly the man could not read. Yet there he was falling down in the sand, lest the foreigner defile paper, any paper with words written upon it. Words on paper, in Egypt this was a thing sacred, like the Koran. Or, for all the man knew, perhaps it *was* the Koran. On his knees, the guide was singeing his fingers, picking out the black bits. In horror, he looked back at Rimbaud.

"What you do? *What?*"

"Mine," he motioned. "It is mine. Let it go."

"Bad thing, bad thing. Why you do this thing?" Squinting, the old man waved away the smoke. "Very bad, like killing child."

But, squinting, Rimbaud only splattered down more pages. Dead thoughts. Lying thoughts. Burn, demons. Words, useless words carbonized beneath the unceasing gaze of the Sphinx.

56 ⸙ Poppy Tea

It's hard enough to face a death and death's fears, let alone death's demotion and defeat. Isolated and secretive, the three Rimbauds expressed these fears in different ways.

Mme. Rimbaud, of course, assumed the worst. And yet, deep down, she felt about her son the same public shame and wish for secrecy that she had during his poet days. Hence her fear of having certain things— never mind what things—"get out," inviting vulgar inquiry and further tarnishing the name Rimbaud.

As for Isabelle, having found her calling, she could not imagine her brother doing such a thing as *dying*, especially now, when they were just getting reacquainted. Why, even to think such a thing seemed to her disloyal, gloomy—unsisterly.

But, of the three, it was Rimbaud himself who was the most curious. In Harar, after all, death was the face one saw everywhere. And yet once home he could not see, or let himself see, the now obvious fact that he was dying. And quickly, too.

As for the mother, even estranged from her son, she could not fail to monitor his decline or to marvel at how her two children could be so utterly oblivious to reality.

But why don't you just tell them? said Mme. Shade.

They'll only blame me for being pessimistic. My fault. As if I had wished it.

Then call a doctor. That way *he* can tell them the truth.

And so the next day a local physician, Dr. Colin, paid a visit. A humble, agreeable country doctor of fifty, Dr. Colin had heavy-lidded eyes and a well-tended paunch that strained the buttons of his fraying vest, from which he fished a clam-sized silver pocket watch. Popping the protective silver cover, he looked at the dial, took the patient's pulse, then did some obligatory prodding and *ahhhing* and such. Theater, purely. It was obvious the man was dying. But as Isabelle hovered and looked on, the question was, Did they know? Could they *not* know?

"And what does your mother think?" asked the doctor. Odd, he thought, that Veuve Rimbaud was not present.

Isabelle blinked. "My brother, you should know, is entirely in *my* care. Not my mother's. Mine."

"Well, then, if I may inquire, Mademoiselle," said Dr. Colin, now thoroughly mystified. "Well, what do *you* think?"

She blinked. "About what?"

"Well . . . about your brother's condition."

"What do you mean?"

"I mean, my dear, quite simply, how do you think he is doing?"

"He has pain, he needs something for pain." She sat there very blank and straight. What was he getting at?

Hopeless. Dr. Colin then turned to the patient.

"And you, Monsieur Rimbaud, have you been walking on your crutches?"

"No." Rimbaud betrayed a look of irritation. "Quite unnecessary."

"Unnecessary, Monsieur?"

"I have a new wooden leg waiting for me in Marseille. I won't need crutches."

"Ah," said the doctor agreeably. Why even go into it? The fellow wasn't his patient, and he didn't need the old woman complaining. Or suing him. And so with a smile, as he left, mild Dr. Colin offered a do-no-harm prescription:

"Poppy tea. An old wives' remedy. Try it, Monsieur. One pinch of seeds in a cup of hot water. I promise you will feel much, much better."

Dr. Colin was quite correct about the dreamy properties of the poppy seeds steeped in boiling water. The broth was thin and bitter but when mixed with a quantity of honey, once Rimbaud gulped it down, the effects were not long in coming. Like slow rings in a pool, his eyes dilated; his face relaxed, and, to Isabelle's shock, her taciturn brother turned talkative, even loquacious.

He talked about the orphanage in Abyssinia and how the little children sang for him because he had given the orphanage money—in truth, very little money and more as a kind of political favor. But still . . .

He talked, too, about the wonderful priests there, Father Abou and the sagacious Monsignor Morélou. "Your confessors?" asked Isabelle hungrily. Not quite. These were worldly men with powerful trade and tribal connections who expected, whatever else, to see their hands greased. In Abyssinia the Lord took His cut, too.

Under the influence of the freeing poppies, Rimbaud likewise talked without exaggeration and with evident emotion about how he had saved Djami from a beggar's fate. About how much he missed him and what a fool he had been not to take him to France..He talked, too, about the terrible famines and how he had helped feed the people—true, to avoid being looted and burned out, and yet, he thought to himself, were people not saved, well, a few? Indeed, he talked about a subject that Isabelle immediately resolved to forget: Tigist, about whom he spoke at length, often extravagantly, telling of his love for the girl and his valiant attempts to keep her—that is, until her troublesome family sent armed men to take her back. Clearly, the poppies were not a truth serum.

Wonderful stories. And in the hands of his future hagiographer, they would be that much more ennobling. Proof, for example, against the liars and sensationalists claiming that her brother was debauched and an atheist, when in fact he had been a sort of mercantile missionary much beloved by the little *noir* children. Who would flock around him, children by the dozens, much as the birds did around Saint Francis of Assisi.

"And why did you stop writing?" she asked one day, when he was particularly woozy and talkative.

This woke him up. "I did not *stop* anything." His irritation was immediate. "Writing stopped me."

"Because you found it evil, yes?"

"Evil?"

"Yes, evil."

"Isabelle, dear sister. Sophistry, truly. Useless, certainly. But I would not dignify it with the word *evil*."

"Unchristian, then."

"What are you doing?" he demanded suddenly. "And what does Christianity have to do with it? Are you writing down all this nonsense?"

"For myself. For the family," she protested. But he had heard enough.

"No more poppy tea," he said the next day when she brought him a cup.

"But, Arthur, your pain."

"I'll manage. Now enough. I am talking too much."

57 ♪ Final Flight

Two weeks passed, then a third, by which point Rimbaud was like a flower blooming in reverse. His arm spavined and his hand twisted like a withered leaf. Even the tingles went numb, until one morning, with a start, he told Isabelle:

"I want to return to Marseille. Tomorrow, and no arguing."

So they left the next morning, and as the carriage was being made ready, Mme. Rimbaud, in her guilt and paralysis, announced the incredible:

"I told them to hitch up Countess"—this was her own mare, the dappled silver. So the old mother said to the cobwebs, as her son, who might have been a chair, stared with great fixity out the window, then said to the door:

"It's time to go."

"We have time," said Isabelle. "Come, come, you two. Surely you have things to say to each other."

"Everything has been said," replied the mother, fixing on a lint speck on the sideboard.

"Indeed so," said the son to the wall clock. "Time to go."

Certainly this would be the last time, in life, that mother and son would see each other. Nothing had been said, of course, but it was clear she would not be going to Marseille for the end. And yet, as the mother and son stood at that precipice, the strangest thing was how, latent in their pride and hatred, there was love of a kind, a duality trapped in time, frozen for all eternity, like two bees in a lump of amber.

"*Au revoir, mon enfant.*"

"*Au revoir, Maman.*"

"Monsieur Rimbaud," said one of the hands as they wheeled him outside. With his hat the man gestured to the clouds, darkening rather ominously. "You're sure, Monsieur?"

"Yes, I'm sure," he said irritably. Humped over in his chair, he might have been a doubled-over rug. "Isabelle, *come on.*"

Isabelle shook the reins. Recalcitrant horse. Barely had Isabelle coaxed Countess out into the road than the old beast, missing the Madame, stopped dead, her ears twitching. Isabelle shook the reins. She tried sweet, then stern. All her life she'd struggled with horses.

"Isabelle," fumed Rimbaud. "Don't tickle her. Give her some whip!"

The Voncq station was only some five kilometers away, not far, but it started to rain and blow, then thunder. There came a sharp crack. The sky went white. Spooked, the old horse reared, then backed up.

"Give her the whip," said Rimbaud.

"She's too frightened. We should wait."

"Then give *me* the whip!"

Water was pouring off the gig's black bonnet, spewing down his back. It was a ghost Rimbaud saw, that of his old self, the caravan boss, the sea captain of the desert. He took the whip in his one, not very good, arm. He whipped at the old horse—he tried and tried—but the whip end didn't crack. Rather, it danced like a fly, until he collapsed in a ball of shivering, wet exhaustion. How they got to the station he had no idea. The next thing he knew, he felt wriggling hands, *people's hands*, lifting him down. Bloody hopeless. The train was long gone.

"No!" he said, shaking, when Isabelle proposed hiring a horse ambulance to take them home. "I am *not* going back. *Ever*, do you hear me? Not even if we stay here all night."

*A*rthur, look, look," said Isabelle pointing out the train window.

The next day, nearing sunset, there it lay in the distance, under a mist of violet smoke. Paris, world metropolis, gleaming like a mass of old treasure—steeples, bridges, cupolas of gold. Not for Rimbaud, however. For him now Paris was like poetry, a thing now vacant of interest and void of memories. The dying man never even bothered to look.

*V*agabond hope. At last in Marseille, Rimbaud was reunited with young Michel, with the hollow cheeks, thin, stubbly beard, and brush of dark hair. Staring in that telltale way, on the verge of tears, Rimbaud gripped Michel's palsied hand as the young man stared back, shocked at how swiftly his patient had deteriorated. Moments later, Dr. Delpech arrived. No quips this time. Leaning down, the doctor felt Rimbaud's paralyzed side and blooming, malignant bones.

"What," asked Rimbaud, trying to be jocular, "no joke for me?"

"Oh, Monsieur Rimbaud," sighed the doctor, "the joke is on me, I'm afraid."

Stepping back, much like Dr. Colin before him, Dr. Delpech searched the patient's eyes, then the sister's. Did they not know? Was it possible? Clearly, they did not, and could not. Even now, they were waiting, as if for news of some patent cure. Some revolutionary treatment.

"Monsieur Rimbaud, Mademoiselle," ventured Dr. Delpech, "I was wrong in my diagnosis, very, very wrong, and I am most sorry to have to tell you this—"

"What?" cried Isabelle "*What?*"

Already she was weeping, arms draped around her brother's neck. As for him, the Great Criminal, the One Accused, he didn't feel frightened. He just felt angry. Embarrassed. Furious at himself for having been so desperate and stupid—so blind, swallowing the greasy elixir of hope.

"I only hope it is soon."

But this, of course, was not Rimbaud's final word on the matter. Later, when he was calmer, Isabelle wheeled him around the gravel path in his wheelchair. Otherworldly, the twisted, almost tonsorial cypresses, the pale blue air, and, beyond, the blue, blue sea. In the sun, fat bees bobbed over trumpets of pink and red hibiscus. The rubber tires crackled in the cinders, and the dying man watched how his long, maundering shadow saturated, with his own life seepage, the gravel and blades of grass. In shock. Rimbaud looked back at his sister, so healthy, so beautiful, so alive. Then said not so much in anger or envy as in utter wonderment:

"And now I shall go down under the ground, while you will walk in the sun."

58   Last Rites

With any long death, there is the long and really long version. Or, in this case, the serviceably short version, for the end was not long.

Within a few weeks, as death pressed in, Rimbaud was not only snowbound with his malady but besieged with God and priests and Isabelle. This was the even more pious Isabelle preparing her brother for heaven. In this respect, her mother had made a deep imprint.

"Arthur," she said for the hundredth time, "you cannot die out of grace! Quit being so pigheaded! You must reconcile with God, you must. Do you want to perish in hell? That thought is unbearable to me. Terrifying, for then I shall never *see* you!"

"And what has my life stood for?" he replied. "Freedom, not fear and muttering superstition. What, crawling back to God? No! For the last time, no!"

"Arthur, stop it, you're being hateful, *hateful*." Isabelle had toughened up these last weeks. "Do you want to die like this? Like *her*? Stubborn and mean and vengeful? Is this what you want?"

Entreaties went only so far, however. Two priests formed the second wave—eminent priests, too, the Canon Chaulier and Abbé Suche. Isabelle told them about her brother's wicked and colorful past, his stubbornness and fame. The priests listened with deep attention. Pastorally speaking, the poet was quite a catch.

"Let the Inquisition begin," said Rimbaud weakly when the two priests entered in their ankle-length black cassocks and white collars. This was Isabelle's cue to leave—God's dragoons had arrived. Canon Chaulier, in particular, a man of sixty, bald, with tufted gray sideburns, the canon was not one for small talk.

"Monsieur Rimbaud," he said, "you know, of course, of Pascal's wager."

The patient rolled his eyes.

"Yes, yes," hastened the canon, "of course you do, but please bear with me. To refresh your memory, Pascal says that God's existence cannot be proven through reason. Perhaps. But the smart gambler would wager that God *does* exist. For after all, if the gambler bets wrong and there is no God, well, so what? But if his bet proves correct and he stays true, he avoids hell and gains the fruits of heaven. So tell me, then. What do you have to lose by embracing God? By confessing and taking Holy Communion? What?"

"I've always disliked that argument," interjected the abbé, seeing too clearly that this particular appeal was not getting through. The abbé was a harder and more common man of peasant stock, broad-backed, with a pinched face and strong hands. "Canon, excuse me, but the idea of God and dice—well, clever certainly. But I've always found it a bit distasteful."

"A trifle old-fashioned," added Rimbaud, grateful for an ally.

But then the abbé seized the moment—got down close to the patient. "You see, Monsieur, in my way of thinking, and from how your sister describes it, it is really very simple in your case. Your life, your sins, your state of mind, if I were a betting man, I would wager that all your difficulties stem from one thing. Ah," he said, catching Rimbaud's now worried eye, "and what is that one thing, you ask? You, Monsieur, you are *arrogant*. Towering in your arrogance. Everybody sees it. Forgive me, but you *reek* of arrogance. Why, I saw it just now. The moment I laid eyes on you. And, believe me, Monsieur, not because I am so very perceptive."

Rimbaud seemed utterly shocked at this accusation. "At one time," he admitted, "once, yes, when I was very young, but not now. Not as I am today. Not really."

"At one time!" mocked the priest, now almost nose to nose. "Please, do not insult me or your own intelligence. You are arrogant, still arrogant. Filled with arrogance. Ruled and blinded by arrogance. Just look at yourself. You are being arrogant right now. And for what? You, of all people, have nothing to be arrogant about—not now. Money, earthly attainments—meaningless now. Your body—already leaving you. As for your intelligence—no longer of value, an impediment, in fact. *Leave* all that, I say. Arrogance is not strength. Arrogance is just another mask for fear, a form of it. No, your arrogance cannot help you. Face it. You are going to die imminently, and I say to you, I ask of you like a brother"— his voice fell to a whisper—"*put it down.* Your arrogance is poison. Drain the pus from your soul. Let it out. Your arrogance is a mask. Tear it off. Look at you. Here you are in God's pantry, in a room filled with good things to eat, yet here you are, in your shameful arrogance, your ridiculous pride, *starving* yourself."

It was too much. In misery, Rimbaud turned his head away. "I'm sorry," he gasped, now playing the invalid card. "I'm very—sorry. Tomorrow, perhaps. Too—too tired now. Please. Too tired . . ."

*H*e fell asleep, the dying man, then sank swiftly, fathoms and fathoms, into the bent land of dreams. Primordial dreams. Child dreams, before poetry and all the disappointments and manic departures of his life. Before childhood died and the sun, too. Before Abyssinia further blackened his heart. In his dream now he is shin level with life, a small child just opening life's bright, wide door.

Tall rye. Insects singing. Young, green rye heads swaying in the breeze. And sun, splashes of sun, sun everywhere. Age two or three, he is chasing his mother in the whiskery tall grass at the edge of the rye field. *Tricks*, she is playing tricks, and he, tiny boy, is squealing with excitement because of the grasshoppers. Scratchy, fat-bellied grasshoppers. Grasshoppers filled with gacky brown grasshopper spit—the grasshoppers now whirring before him, dozens, flying like woodchips from an axe. It is his mother who makes them fly. *Causing them*, just as she causes the water of the stream, *her* stream, to ripple and burble and *come to her.* A small boy twirling and squealing. Grasshoppers! *Catch them! Chase them!*

Whirring grasshoppers with wings of light. Grasshoppers that cling to Maman's skirt, *his* maman, because she *called them*, the grasshoppers, and Maman's skirt has folds to grab, a mother mountain that feels soft and warm on his face. Please, Mother, please, please pick me up. Up into that sweet, pure sundrop of *once*, before everybody changed and everything fell apart.

And when he awoke from this dream, feebly, he called for Isabelle, then wept and hugged her. Trembling, eyes drooling, anything but arrogant, he held his sister's hand, waiting for the immense thing about to come. And although Isabelle, in her well-meaning way, went on to fabricate many things, she did not exaggerate the sincerity of her heathen brother's deathbed conversion. In all meekness, before Canon Chaulier and Abbé Suche, Arthur Rimbaud sincerely made his confession and was given the last rites. He tried to take Communion. He tried—repeatedly—but like a boy trying to whistle could not coax out his tongue.

Was it God, then? Did God do it? Did God change his heart?

Because that next day, somehow, Arthur Rimbaud was not angry, not haughty, but just a self-surrendering human, waiting almost openmouthed for death like a baby for his first spoonful of food. Truly, he was, as they say—or so it seemed—in the hands of God, a man unencumbered and now at peace with where he was going.

In fact, the day before he died, Rimbaud dictated to Isabelle a letter to the Aphinar Line, a ship company never heard of, or not in this life. In that letter, addressed to *M. le Directeur*, Rimbaud declared that he, a poor cripple, intended to book passage to Africa, passing east over the equator into the rising sun. God knew the azimuth.

He died the next morning around ten o'clock.

Epilogue

"MY DEAR VITALIE TO MY RIGHT, AND
MY POOR ARTHUR TO MY LEFT . . ."
— MME. RIMBAUD'S BURIAL WISHES, JUNE 1, 1900

♪ Blazing Constellation

As for Widow Rimbaud, having waited a month for her news, and having a full month to plan, she was well prepared when Arthur's mahogany casket finally arrived in Charleville. Indeed, she had a whole troupe of mourners prepared. And in a display commensurate with her guilt, for the first time since their balloon ride in London, the Widow did not stint.

Through the streets of Charleville, her son was borne in a black hearse of wood and glass and polished silver, a sort of mortuary music box drawn by four coal black horses with polished silver harnesses and, over their ears, tall black festoons that caused the poor blinkered beasts, much like dogs in costume, to snort and bounce their heads. As for the mourning party, mother and daughter and Mme. Shade, they rode in a sleek black coach with squinty windows through which they could peer, or peck, as necessary, at the town's queer inhabitants. Mercifully, without the public sordidness of being seen.

Officiating, there was Abbé Gillet from Rimbaud's old *collège*, followed by a drum beater and four robed cantors. Nor was that all. For after them came a cotillion of black-robed choirboys, then a frocked beadle in a cocked hat bearing his silver-globed staff, then a bell ringer, an undertaker, and, of course, the bibulous gravedigger, presumably the same who left all those rocks, for he was already quite festive.

Oh yes, and twenty somber orphan girls clutching candles.

"*Sad*, do you hear me?" insisted the Widow when she hired them. "I want dour girls, *unstained*, no older than twelve. No stinkers or nose borers. And you will make sure they are all duly confessed and have not drunk or eaten or done anything that will preclude *all twenty* from taking Communion. All of them. And no sneaking off to the toilets . . ."

This, then, was the bell-ringing, tom-tomming retinue that marched grimly all through the town, then to the Church of Saint-Rémy, where they were met by a thunderous pipe organ and a full choir. All rosy-cheeked prepubescent boys.

In all, there were some forty-seven people, all hired—with, of course, the three mourners, the Widow and Isabelle and Mme. Shade. Only them. Naturally, the Widow had put no notice in the paper, and as there was no one to invite, this made it *clean*, thought the Widow, very clean. No boo-hooing, no snoops, and no shiftless relatives with their hands out.

Indeed, except for the two little orphan girls who wet themselves and three others who fainted from standing—well, it all went tolerably well.

*I*ronically, the day Rimbaud died his collected poems, entitled *Reliquaire*, appeared, only to be the subject of a dispute between the two editors, who then had the book withdrawn from public circulation.

Some weeks later, though, soon after the news of Rimbaud's death had swept literary Paris, the very charmed Champsaur saw to it that Verlaine's interview came out—naturally, at the very peak of the public frisson.

Actually, Champsaur's interview was for the most part an exceedingly fair and faithful record of their discussion. Not that this pleased Verlaine, but then how could it? How could it feel to recall, publicly, those days of love, glory, and abandon, only to lose everything—wife, son, reputation, inheritance? And, cruelest of all, to lose the boy who had brought him glory and damnation, both.

In the afternoon sun, strolling down the boulevard Saint-Michel, Verlaine tapped his cane, tock, tock, tock. Red beard shining, his bowler hat pulled down just over his eyes, ambling, he might have been mistaken for a burlap-covered cotton bale, the bum lord greeting his public. But, whatever else, the great man was not alone, for there at his arm was Eugénie, the very picture of a tart. Naughty plaid skirt. Saucy hat. And, of course, the gleaming, rapier-like black boots over which many a naked gentleman on his knees had spat and worked the rag to a fare-thee-well.

"I sound like a selfish monster," complained Verlaine, still ranting about Champsaur's interview. "And a fool—a patsy. Are you listening to me? It's *embarrassing.*"

"Come now." Eugénie hated it when adults played pretend. "Rimbaud led you by the nose, and like an ass you admitted it to Champsaur. I told you not to drink so much."

"But, God knows," he fumed, "look what Rimbaud *gained* from me. My tutelage. My many friends and contacts. Not to mention my money."

Eugénie stopped short.

"*Paul!* You're a bloody goddamned *Immortal*—enough of your whining. I thought what Champsaur wrote was fair. More than fair." Then, like a cat flexing her claws, her mien turned mischievous. "And I must say he *was* beautiful, that Félicien Champsaur. *Gorgeous.*"

"Now, wait a minute," said Verlaine, detecting a sybaritic flicker in her eye. In his horror at that moment, his face suggested a freshly shucked oyster. "The way he *looked* at you! Now I see! Some assignation, was it? Was that it?"

"So what if I did?" she replied. "You threw me over. These pretty boys, they love a nasty treat!"

He shook his cane at her. "Miserable, faithless whore!"

"Well," she sniffed, "unlike you, at least I bloody well get *paid* for it."

Tock. Tock. Tock. Fuming and muttering, Verlaine started again, then stopped suddenly, leaning on the cane, blinking with emotion.

"What, love?" asked Eugénie, now playing the wife. "What?"

"Rimbaud. Damn him, I still can't believe he's dead. Really dead. And the madness of him—I mean to leave it all. Art. Reputation—"

"And you—"

"So laugh at me!" He paused, shaking his head. "But . . . but I thought, fool that I was, I actually thought, we would be together, the two of us—forever. God help me, I actually *thought* so, and I still feel the same disbelief. The same grief. Leaving what—poems? Was that the whole point? Bloody *poems*?"

*T*hey walked on, man and mistress, and for five years more the carnival of Verlaine's life continued, until he, too, died—died at the age of fifty-one. Died pretty much of everything, having burnt the candle at both ends, and the middle, too.

How satisfying, though. The many great and famous men who had avoided, or carefully managed their relations with, the old pariah—if only to escape the inevitable tap for money—well, the mighty turned out in force, as death redeemed him, such that people could step back, actually in awe of the Master and his contribution. No longer was he a clown, a drunk, or a pervert. He was genius in an age that idolized genius, just as he was Paris itself.

Candles were lit in his room, where he lay in his bed in his nightshirt—cheap party candles, the only ones anyone could find in his flat. A death mask was made. Then, after the newspapers reported his death, came the crush, the famous and the lowly. Mallarmé left a bunch of violets. A photographer was dispatched from *Le Monde Illustré.* Young men drew lots to keep vigil over the body, then, alone in the middle of the night, snipped off small pieces of his hair. And amid the crowds that tramped through his small dim chambers, many remembered the flitting lemon canary. The canary that wouldn't stop singing—Eugénie's canary.

Even Verlaine would have been flabbergasted at the outpouring on the day of his burial. When the casket was taken to the Cimetière des Batignolles, a quite lengthy walk, people lined the streets and every man tipped his hat. There, behind the hearse, representing the people of the streets was Verlaine's chimney-sweep majordomo, Bibi-la-Purée; clean as a baby, too. As for Eugénie—who had to be separated, twice, from her rival, Odette—she was accompanied by a phalanx of prostitutes and courtesans. And behind them? A crowd of several thousand. Poets, writers, artists, and musicians, Verlaine's cortege brought forth a river of people cloaked in black and crepe, knots of people flowing steadily up l'avenue de Clichy, to the Batignolles cemetery.

As for the Widow Rimbaud, she lived on, quite healthily, until her death in 1907, at the then astounding age of eighty-two.

Isabelle by then had a husband, Paterne Berrichon, one of Rimbaud's first biographers, a hack, quite honestly, but nevertheless a good husband who not only made Isabelle happy but, more importantly, made good her escape from Roche. Isabelle and Berrichon, then, were present for the widow's burial—just them and the priest and two gravediggers: five in all. Such were the widow's wishes, to be laid to rest just as she had lived, essentially alone.

But here is what speaks through time in that old cemetery with its cinder paths and gray mortuary houses veined with moss. There, at the head of the knoll in the plot of the Rimbauds, although three are buried, only two headstones stand, those of seventeen-year-old Vitalie and Arthur. As for the Widow, she who prepared the bed, she lies before them, prostrate, as it were, under a milky slab of marble. Clearly, whatever she said in life, and however much she pushed her younger son away, in death she wanted him close to her. Very close.

At hand, in fact. Two subterraneans of once boiling force, here they lie, love and hatred, hope and betrayal, forever coiled like figures in some heavenly constellation. Gaze down upon them, then, and wish them ease, mother and son lying forever under the blue night sky. Together at last and, who's to say, perhaps even at peace.

A Final Note
on the Poems and Writings Quoted

There has been no monkeying with the poems and writings quoted.

All the poems and letters quoted are taken verbatim from noted English translations, most from Wallace Fowlie's *Rimbaud*. Cuts are noted with ellipses.

To be sure, Rimbaud has many fine English translators, but Professor Fowlie's 1966 classic remains my hands-down favorite.

Jim Morrison of the Doors, Rimbaud's bastard seed—the same man now buried in Père-Lachaise—was another Fowlie fan, so much so that he wrote Professor Fowlie a number of searching letters before his death at the age of twenty-seven. No doubt Bob Dylan, Patti Smith, and now younger artists have pored through the same translation, still undiminished in its power to thrill and incite, perplex and disturb.

Please, read the poems. In any language they are ageless.

Acknowledgments

Many people helped and urged me along with this project. Louis Ross and John Shill, both Washington-area psychiatrists, were my first readers four years ago, and their criticisms, then fundamental, forced me to wholly reimagine my fractured main characters—this time with the abandon they deserve.

Thanks, too, to my oldest friend, Slaton White, for his enthusiasm and keen observations. Bill Schultz brought similar energy, and my close friend Judy Watson was especially helpful in offering a woman's perspective. Others who were kind enough to read and comment were my oldest readers, Jay and Gay Lovinger, my daughters, Lily and Kate, novelist Barbara Esstman, and my close friend Peter Kilman. Thanks, too, to my wonderful colleagues at work and the leader I write for. And thanks above all to my Maxwell Perkins Prize–winning agent, Amanda ("Binky") Urban, and to her make-it-happen assistant, Alison Schwartz. It was Binky who brought me to Doubleday, pairing me with my wonderful new editor, Gerry Howard, and his very talented assistant, Hannah Wood. After thirteen years without a publisher, it is good—as Gerry puts it—to be "back around the campfire."

Special thanks also go to Mme. Joan Le Gall, retired from the University of Toronto, and her son Michel Le Gall, formerly of St. Olaf College. Fluent French speakers, they helped me address a host of cultural, linguistic, and historical issues as I completed the manuscript. The medal, though, goes to my wife, Susan Segal, a psychotherapist with a keen sense of character and the bestiary of human nature. Lucky is the author with twenty-four-hour psychiatric care!

Another lucky break as I tried to imagine the Rimbauds' dairy farm: Much of the book was written in Manns Choice, Pennsylvania, on a farm long owned by my wife's family. Thanks to Garry Wilkins, a local dairy farmer who answered my many cow questions and, at one point, even let me help "pull" (birth) a calf. I also greatly appreciate the company of my pal Rodney Ferguson, Fred Bisbing, and the other good folks up the hill at the Buffalo Rod & Gun Club.

Finally, I must acknowledge my mentor and former professor, the distinguished poetry critic Marjorie Perloff. Almost forty years ago, it was Marjorie who placed Wallace Fowlie's *Rimbaud* into my hands and even checked off her favorites. What a gift. And what a lifelong influence Marjorie has been—incalculable.

PERMISSIONS ACKNOWLEDGMENTS

Grateful acknowledgment is made to the following for permission to reprint previously published material:

Anvil Press Poetry: Excerpts from "Openers" from *Paul Verlaine: Women/Men, Femmes/Hombres* translated by Alistair Elliot. Published by Anvil Press Poetry in 2004. Reprinted by permission of Anvil Press Poetry.

David R. Godine, Publisher, Inc.: Excerpts from "Lethe" and "Consecration" from *Les Fleurs du mal* by Charles Baudelaire, translated from the French by Richard Howard, translation copyright © 1982 by Richard Howard. Reprinted by permission of David R. Godine, Publisher, Inc.

Oxford University Press: Excerpts from *Paul Verlaine: Selected Poems* translated by Martin Sorrell (1999). Reprinted by permission of Oxford University Press.

Penguin Group (UK): Excerpts from *French Poetry, 1820–1950: With Prose Translations* selected, translated, and introduced by William Rees, copyright © 1990 by William Rees. Reprinted by permission of Penguin Group (UK).

Random House, Inc.: Excerpts from *I Promise to Be Good: Letters from Arthur Rimbaud* translated and edited by Wyatt Mason, copyright © 2003 by Wyatt Mason. Reprinted by permission of Random House, Inc.

University of California Press: Excerpts from "III. After Three Years" and "VII. To a Woman" from *Selected Poems, Bilingual Edition* by Paul Verlaine, translated by C. F. MacIntyre, copyright © 1976 by C. F. MacIntyre. Reprinted by permission of the University of California Press.

University of Chicago Press: Excerpts from *Rimbaud: Complete Work, Selected Letters* translated by Wallace Fowlie, copyright © 1966, copyright renewed 1994 by Wallace Fowlie. Reprinted by permission of University of Chicago Press.